# THE DYING OF THE LIGHT

## BROTHERHOOD OF THE MOON BOOK I

### MIRRIAM NEAL

Paperback ISBN: 978-1-63760-301-7

To Lauren; my broceanus, my brotato chip, my brotorcycle, my bromato soup. Without you, this book wouldn't be here. Your soul is in this series as much as mine is, and now your art is officially on the front cover. What a ride.

# CONTENTS

Liberty is not the power of doing what we like, but the right to
do what we ought.
**John Dalberg-Acton**

# THE DYING OF THE LIGHT

# ONE

BLOOD RAINED from the black sky. The storm swelled around him, the blackening sky set on fire by the rays of a setting sun. It was not a storm caused by rain or wind; it was a storm where the lightning of exploding bombs flashed before the thunder, a chorus of hoarse, terrified screams.

The earth rattled beneath his feet as another flash of lightning blew a crater in the ground ninety yards away. More blood rained down, warm and thick, dripping in his hair, his eyes.

"Captain!"

Saizou turned, peering through the chaos of hell. The gun was slippery in his hands, and he lifted it, shouting, "Name!"

"Corporal Ayu, sir!" The young soldier ducked as something whistled over his head. Another explosion, smaller and infinitely bright, seared the air, and Soldier Ayu shouted, "I need to go home!"

Saizou ran forward, toward the boy under his command. "Get down!" Why wouldn't he get down?

The terror in Ayu's voice was louder than the spray of

gunfire. "I can't die, sir! Can't we just go home?" He stumbled closer, his steps uneven and jagged. "I promised!"

Saizou lowered his gun as the corporal pushed through the smoke, his figure sharpening as he left the haze.

His right arm was gone, the side of his face reduced to blood and meat. His remaining eye gleamed white with terror, but he did not seem to realize his own state. He did not know he was already dead.

"Please, Captain," he choked. "I promised—"

Saizou ducked as the loud, metallic spatter of gunfire sounded, closer to his left this time. He could barely make out the figures around him; they were phantoms, their screams white noise in his ears.

"Captain," said Ayu, but he could not finish his sentence. He fell to his knees, blood spewing from his mouth like dirty tap water. "Captain, please, let me wake up. Let me wake up!"

*"Wake up."*

"WAKE UP."

Saizou opened his eyes. Shadows and darkness, an erratic pattern of light glinting across the ceiling—his own pulse throbbing in his head, his wrists. His body wanted to flinch, to sit up, to throw off the thin blanket that covered him, but nothing would obey.

*I've been bound. I can't move.*

*Captured—*

Prisoner.

*Can't breathe—*

A shape took form in the shadows to his left. He could move his eyes, Saizou found, but they were not yet adjusted to the dark. He tried to speak, but his throat swelled and closed, reducing any words to a hiss of strangled breath.

"It's Shi," said a deep, bulldog voice. "I'm here."

Saizou felt pressure on his left shoulder. A hand.

Shi said, "It will be over soon. Mmm...we're on the Haizawa rail to Tokyo." He lifted his free hand, pointing toward the ceiling. "We're passing through a city. I don't know which one. Those are the lights."

His muscles began to relax. He had not even realized they were tight, but now, as they loosened like knots being untied, he felt the ache of tension sink in.

Air trickled through his lungs, a little at a time, and finally he drew a full breath.

"Do you want to sit up?" Shi had shifted his stance, and now the lights flashing across the ceiling of the train car slid across his face in shades of orange and green and white. The colors caressed his mutilated visage, highlighting the open black nasal passage and the thick, angry scars that twisted the center of his face. His mane of silver-blond hair had come undone, and his amber eyes were groggy. He looked like more like a half-awake ghoul than anything else.

Shi did not ask about Saizou's dream, and Saizou was grateful. There was no point in asking, really. Not anymore. Not after months of the same dream every night. It was always there, unavoidable, waiting to attack him the moment he closed his eyes, waiting to lock him inside himself after he opened them.

The train rocked on its tracks, and Saizou gripped the edge of the bed with both hands as Shi shifted with the movement, unflappable.

"Or," said Shi, "you could lie back down," and Saizou realized he had forgotten to answer the question.

"I'll sit." He straightened under his companion's watchful gaze. "I don't need help."

"Heh," was the grunted response.

Saizou ignored it. Instead he focused his mind on their destination. On home. He closed his eyes and settled his body into the rhythm of the train, allowing memories of his domain to flood his mind. They were dusty and faded with time, but now, after five years, he would be able to refresh those memories, to bask in their warmth again. They would stop being the past and become the present once more, and that was all he wanted. The last goal he hoped to attain.

"Well, I'm going back to bed," said Shi, breaking Saizou's reverie.

Saizou rubbed his face with both hands. *Blood. Hot. Sticky. In his eyes, in his mouth.* He opened his eyes again. No blood. He nodded toward Shi, forcing a smile. "You need it."

"Yes," said Shi. "I do. What with you talking my ears off all day about your precious domain."

The thought *you can't afford to lose those, too,* came to Saizou, but he kept it from becoming words.

His silence did not seem to matter; Shi caught the unspoken joke and said flatly, "It's too soon."

"I didn't say anything," said Saizou, allowing himself a half-grin.

"You thought it. That's enough."

Saizou stifled a yawn and slapped his left wrist with the index and middle fingers of his right hand. "Go get some sleep," he urged, shaking his head sharply a few times. Sleep might wish to claim him, but he refused to be caught.

Shi grunted. He gripped the side of the bed above Saizou's and pulled himself onto the top bunk. The bed creaked as he found a comfortable position, and Saizou pushed himself back until his spine pressed against the wall. After a moment, Shi flung his arm over the side of the bunk, signaling the fact he was already asleep.

———

*"NOW ARRIVING AT STATION SEVENTEEN, TOKYO."*
Saizou stood up, gripping the edge of the bed as the train began its rocky deceleration. He brought his hand firmly down on Shi's back two, three, four times before Shi groaned into his pillow, "I heard, *shimatta.*"

A brief smile touched the corner of Saizou's mouth. He turned away from his surly companion to the luggage department, tugging it open and removing their belongings. They each carried one standard-issue black pack with adjustable straps that allowed it to be worn in whatever way was most convenient for the wearer.

Neither bag was heavy, as neither man owned many possessions. A few articles of clothing, some food, and some miscellany specific to each of them. Everything else Saizou owned— everything he had not needed during the last five years—was waiting at his domain.

He shut his eyes, wondering what it would be like to see it again; to see the houses where his people lived, to see the dust rising from the mines in the distance with the people's working songs floating softly on a cold breeze. To see the sakura trees, taller than most, lining the drive up to his house...they would be bare now, but in spring they would bloom again, and the whole domain would be kissed with soft, pink petals and the scent of cherries.

And he would see Tsuki again.

Behind him, Shi coughed loudly, and Saizou turned to see Shi lower his fist from his mouth.

Shi said nothing as he took his bag from Saizou and unzipped it, reaching in and withdrawing the things that would set him and Saizou apart from the rest of the populace.

Shi buckled his plain black sword belt around his waist before sliding his katana scabbard through the belt, adjusting the longer sword before sliding the shorter wakizashi through.

Saizou withdrew his own pair of swords. Only samurai could legally carry a daisho—a pairing of one long sword with one shorter sword. His own weapons were slightly different from Shi's, as he preferred to carry his katana across his back on a sword sash that went around his shoulders and across his chest. His wakizashi he carried more toward his front, at his left hip. This way, if necessary, he could reach back and draw his katana with his right hand while simultaneously drawing his wakizashi with his left.

His nerves strained, tense with excitement and a natural feeling of vague unease. What if things had changed? What if his own memories of home had become brighter and more beautiful the longer he was away? What if his memories were no longer accurate, or worse, what if his domain had been ravaged by the war? What if it was no longer there?

"You would know," said Shi, zipping his bag back up and slinging it across his shoulders.

Saizou did not look at him as he adjusted the straps on his own bag and lifted it over one shoulder. "What would I know?"

Shi lifted the one other item he had removed from his bag. "It's still there. They'd have informed you otherwise." He placed the mask across his face and buckled it around the back of his head. It was an unusual mask; hardened black leather studded with silver grommets, formed to Shi's forehead and cheekbones, and it closed across the center of his face in the illusion of a nose that was not there. It left his mouth, chin, and eyes perfectly visible, but it covered his disfiguration.

A distant guilt settled in Saizou's chest, as it did every time he watched Shi put the mask on.

Shi slapped Saizou's arm as he walked to the door. "Let's go."

The hall was tight, but there were no crowds to fight. The train was unusually empty, which suited Saizou. The less people pushing, the safer he felt. The safer *everyone* was—they were safe. Shi was there, and Shi would watch his back whether Saizou wanted him to or not.

They reached the doors of their car and stood, waiting, as the train came to a complete, grinding stop. The doors hissed open, and Shi stepped out in front of Saizou, taking his time to look left and right, assessing the station.

Saizou nudged Shi between his shoulder-blades. "Hey. Move."

Shi took a few more steps forward, onto the platform. Ahead of them, behind the pillars, stretched a long neon sign flashing with the names of available stations, times, and trains. Several of the lines were dead; the lights had gone out and had not been replaced.

"There aren't many people here," said Shi, keeping his voice low.

Saizou nodded, gazing at the waiting passengers. He counted nine people, not including the two manning the service desk. He caught the eye of a young girl holding her mother's hand and stared at her.

Her eyes were wide in her round face, and she did not smile, but she lifted a tentative hand in what might almost have been a wave.

Her mother sensed the movement and glanced down, then followed her daughter's line of sight. When she saw Saizou, she smiled, but the smile froze and cracked as quickly as it had come. She tugged her daughter's hand and walked quickly to the other side of the platform, near the exit door.

Saizou glanced down at himself and wondered if he looked that frightening. He hardly thought so. He was often accused of having a face much younger than his years, even if it was now gaunt and shadowed. He shook his head, clearing his mind. It wasn't worth thinking about.

"They're looking at our swords."

Saizou nodded and said quietly, "It's as if they mistrust us on sight, but why?"

Shi shook his head once. They both knew samurai were a symbol of power, but also of trust. They protected the populace and kept the law wherever possible. Now, being eyed with such open mistrust by everyone on the platform, Saizou felt an uncomfortable whisper in his head. *Something is wrong.*

"We need to leave if we want to make Akita by tonight," said Shi, glancing once more around the platform before striding toward the exit door.

Akita.

*Home.*

The station was below street level, so they took stairs up to the street. Halfway up, a cold wind hit Saizou and he paused, allowing it to blow his hair back and wash across his face. It was filled with smells of the city—food and fuel and people. It swept over his skin, filling him with a warm, wordless thrill.

Shi drummed his fingers on the rail but harbored a faint smile. "I've never been to Tokyo," he offered, glancing up toward the top of the concrete stairs.

Saizou let out a deep breath. "Country boy."

Shi shrugged one shoulder. "I prefer less people."

Saizou began to say *I don't,* but stopped himself. That had been true, not long ago. Less than a year ago, in fact, but things had changed. He decided not to answer and instead, began walking again, passing Shi and reaching the top of the stairs.

Buildings rose around them, across the street, behind them, on every side. Saizou blinked rapidly, adjusting to the lights. They were everywhere: glittering, flashing, sliding across neon signs. The office building ahead sported a sponsored ad for a casino, featuring an actress Saizou had never heard of.

Something about the actress reminded him of Tsuki. She would be well into her twenties now, maybe engaged. He found himself hoping she wasn't, although he did not ask himself why he held that hope. What if, worse, she was no longer there? What if something had happened, an accident or...

Again he cut off his own line of thought. He wished he could call her to see how she was, but it was impossible. Landlines were a thing of the past, and the satellites were controlled exclusively by the government for their private use.

Now the only people with the means and permission to communicate by phone or internet were government officials. Supposedly, it kept enemies from communicating within national lines, but in Saizou's mind it made as much sense as the belief that banning drugs stopped their trafficking and sale.

Still, it made communication considerably more difficult, and most people had resorted to writing letters or total silence. The latter was frequently as effective as the former these days.

He had to wait. He was all right with that. It would make seeing her that much more...well, more. She was worth any wait.

"So," said Shi, squinting at the flashing red light that read DON'T WALK, "we take the bus across Tokyo, and then what? Does the bus go to Akita?"

"It did five years ago," said Saizou. The light changed to green, and they crossed the street. "It should take a few hours."

"Less time than I expected."

Saizou nodded and squinted up. The sun was not visible through the thick layer of gray clouds, but he guessed it was around nine. "We could be there by midafternoon if everything goes well."

———

THEY KEPT TO THEMSELVES, walking quickly to reach the bus stop without any detours. Even so, Saizou couldn't help but notice the increased amount of people who seemed to have no real purpose or destination, sitting on benches or on the sidewalks, hugging their knees, even sleeping as if there was nothing better to do.

War meant hard times. It meant an increase in unemployment, which meant more homeless victims, which meant more beggars. It meant closed stores and hungry people and increased prices. It was expected, but by the time they reached the bus stop, Saizou was beginning to wonder if this was really the same city.

"Nice place," was Shi's only remark as they stood at the stop.

Saizou shook his head. "War takes a toll on everything. Once the war's over, you'll see what it was like. It will make a comeback. It always does."

"That's what they said about Sakamoto Hisaishi," said Shi. "Until one day he didn't."

"A boxer and a city aren't the same thing," said Saizou, adjusting the pack strap cutting into his shoulder. "Be quiet."

Shi was silent until the bus turned the corner and slowed to a stop in front of them. The doors opened, and passengers filed out, casting cautious, startled glances at the two men. Saizou stepped back, watching as the strangers gave them an unnecessarily wide berth. It was as if Saizou had become a threat to them without his noticing.

A whistle cut the cold air.

"Shinsengumi!"

The cry went up quickly among those gathered at the bus stop. Saizou and Shi turned to watch as four law enforcement officers strode toward them, cutting a path through the small crowd. They were dressed all in black. The only color on their uniforms was the red star emblazoned over their hearts.

Saizou and Shi bowed along with the rest of the crowd, but Saizou noticed that while he and Shi moved politely from the waist, the rest of the crowd stooped lower. Like they were cowering.

He traded glances with Shi as they straightened.

One of the officers stepped forward. He held an unsheathed katana in his right hand, and he leaned it back, tapping it across his own shoulder. His motions were sloppy, unbalanced, and his eyes were bright and glassy.

Saizou stepped back. A Shinsengumi officer high on duty? Even off-duty that was a criminal offense, yet nobody seemed to question it. Not even the officers behind him.

The man's inky hair was long and unwashed, his face sharp. Saizou guessed he was in his early thirties, near Saizou's own age.

"You two. Do you know who I am?" the officer asked, looking Saizou up and down. He stepped abruptly to the side, as if he had been pushed, then straightened.

"A law officer," said Shi blandly, his gaze following the other man's unsteady steps with obvious judgment.

The man's lip curled, and he lifted the katana off his shoulder, pointing the blade at Shi. "Commander Haka. You should know who I am."

"We've been informed now," said Saizou, taking a step closer to Shi, who was eyeing the officer's blade with complete passivity. Not only was this officer high on duty, he was the *commander*? How was this allowed?

Commander Haka tilted his head back, eyeing Saizou with wide, unnaturally pale eyes. Saizou was amazed the man could stand, let alone speak. "You? What's your name?"

"Saizou Akita." Saizou bowed again, from the waist.

Haka jerked the tip of his katana toward Shi. "You?"

"Shi Matsumoto."

Commander Haka barked a giddy, three-syllable laugh. "You're wearing a mask."

"Yes."

"Why?"

"I like it."

The man on Haka's right stepped forward, his hand on the hilt of his katana. "Use respect when you speak to the commander."

"I'll use respect toward those worthy of it." Shi's tone was even but his eyes narrowed, and he had adopted a stubborn stance.

The crowd around Shi and Saizou backed up several steps, and a chill swept up Saizou's neck. The situation did not seem nearly as drastic as it was starting to feel.

Commander Haka took an impossibly long step forward and brought his sword blade to the side of Shi's neck. Shi did not flinch. Instead, his back straightened and he lifted his chin, as if daring the commander to cut him open.

"I should kill you," Commander Haka breathed, leaning forward, bringing his face within six inches of Shi's. "Should I kill you?"

"Are you asking me?" began Shi, but Saizou interrupted.

"Please forgive him, Commander." He placed his palm over his fist and bowed again, deeper than last time. "He was wrong. This won't happen again."

Commander Haka glared at Saizou over his shoulder. He swayed a little, but his blade remained steady against Shi's neck. He dropped his gaze to the daisho paired at Shi's side, and he frowned, cocking his head to one side. "What are those?" He gripped the handle of the wakizashi and pulled it from the scabbard.

Saizou felt as though he was missing a piece of a large puzzle. He could not understand the situation entirely, but he could deal with the facts—the Shinsengumi commander was high, he had a blade against Shi's throat, and he was asking personal questions.

"We are samurai, Commander," said Saizou, deciding that cooperation was the best route now. "We've been in China for several years, fighting in the Emperor's war. We only just got back."

"Oh." Commander Haka blinked at the wakizashi before sliding it back into the scabbard. "Really."

"Yes, Commander."

"Well." The officer paused, ran one finger through a strand of his long, oily hair, and shrugged. "If you have been away, I guess your ignorance isn't your fault. Only Shinsengumi officers can wear any sword longer than thirty centimeters these days." He sniffed and stepped back, away from Shi. "Get rid of your katanas. They're illegal."

Saizou took a deep breath and curled his hands into fists as he bowed again. "Yes, Commander."

Nearby, an elderly man mumbled just loud enough, "Doesn't seem right, taking weapons away from soldiers who have been fighting for us."

Commander Haka did not turn around, but his eyes and grin widened dangerously.

Saizou and Shi glanced at each other, then at the speaker. Commander Haka lifted his katana again, but after allowing it to point toward the sky for a moment, he slid it into its scabbard and turned, flicking a hand toward his fellow officers.

As the commander walked past the outspoken bystander, he lashed out with his elbow, slamming it into the man's face and sending him staggering into the street. No one moved to offer him a hand as he righted himself, then hurried across the street, away from further danger.

As the Shinsengumi walked away, Shi uncrossed his arms and said in a low voice, "That was weird. The mood here is strange."

Saizou watched Commander Haka disappear around the corner, flanked by his officers. "How did someone like that become commander?"

"You tell me," said Shi. "It's your city."

# TWO

"YOU HEARD THE COMMANDER," said the bus driver. "No blades over thirty centimeters allowed. Especially not on my bus."

"And what about guns?" Saizou asked.

The bus driver gave him a leery look. "What about them?"

Saizou scratched the back of his head. *Stay calm. He's just another citizen, he doesn't make or enforce the laws. Whatever fight you have, he is not your opponent.* "Are guns illegal, too?"

"That depends on who carries them," said the bus driver. He cleared his throat and faced the windshield before calling, "Everybody not carrying illegal weapons, get on board."

Shi turned away from the bus, his upper lip curled in disgust. "Let's go. We can find other transportation. We don't need the bus."

Numb with the unexpected hostility around them, Saizou narrowed his eyes and followed Shi away from the bus station. "I thought we left enemy ground when we left China."

"Guess not."

The wind grew in strength and dropped in temperature as

they strode down the sidewalk. Saizou lifted his chin and took in a deep breath, letting the chill wash his lungs. "If we walk, it will take two days."

Shi shrugged one shoulder. "I don't mind walking."

"I don't mind walking; I mind delaying our arrival."

"Then what do you suggest, eh? Piggybacking a flying squirrel? You go alone, then. Both of us would weigh him down. I'll catch up."

Saizou could tell that their interaction with Commander Haka was beginning to twist his companion's good-natured mood into one of surly aggression and remained silent.

Shi paused in an alley between a self-serve restaurant and a secondhand clothing store and lifted his pack over his head. When Saizou gave him a questioning look, Shi said, "I'm hungry," and unzipped the pack, withdrawing a foil-wrapped protein bar.

Saizou was not hungry yet, so he folded his arms and watched as Shi crouched and tore open the foil with his teeth.

Shi took a bite, chewed angrily, swallowed, and asked in a low voice, "What do you think you'll do about it?"

"About what?"

Shi tapped the handle of his katana. "Our illegal weapons," he said, with a wry quirk of his lips. His eyes still fumed, but the heat of his temper had worn off.

Saizou reached over his shoulder and brushed the knuckle of his index finger against the handle of his own katana. "Asking us to give them up is like asking us to strip ourselves of our rank."

"Telling," said Shi. "They didn't ask. They told us."

"I wonder if it's only the law in cities like Tokyo," Saizou mused, rubbing his thumb along his lip in thought. "Or if it's everywhere."

"If it's everywhere, the samurai are screwed," said Shi. He put the other half of his bar back into the bag and hoisted it over his shoulder again. He straightened and eyed Saizou. "Which means us."

"I know it does," said Saizou. He knew Shi's words implied more than the relinquishing of their swords. Wearing a daisho was a status symbol, something that allowed people to recognize samurai for what they were. The act of taking away a samurai's katana was equivalent to destroying the effectiveness of their position.

Such as it was.

At the moment, he had no certainty about what their position was.

Saizou squinted at the sky. Impatience sang through his veins—the encounter with the Shinsengumi had been unpleasant, but the thought of reaching Akita shone brightly enough to cover it. Commander Haka and his goons were a thing of the past, and hopefully, he would not encounter them again.

"Come on," he said to Shi. "We'll find some transportation and arrive at Akita, as planned."

"Transportation that will allow 'illegal weapons'?" Shi lifted his fingers, forming air quotes around the last two words.

"When I said *find*, I really meant *buy* our own transportation."

Shi squinted at him. "With what money, exactly?"

Saizou clapped his friend on the shoulder. "With the money in my bank account."

"Oh," said Shi dryly. "I forgot. You're independently wealthy."

"Look for a National Bank." Saizou lengthened his strides, scanning every building they passed while Shi kept an eye on the other side of the street. They came upon a National Bank branch three blocks later.

Saizou looked at the tall, glass doors. With a sigh, reluctant to relinquish his katana, he removed it from its scabbard and handed it to Shi. "Wait outside. I'll get the money."

Shi took the sword and nodded his go-ahead as Saizou turned and pushed through the doors. The building felt empty —the tellers outnumbered the clients. Saizou walked up to the first available desk.

The girl behind the desk was small and pretty, and she gave Saizou a friendly smile. "Hello, sir," she greeted him, her high voice lisping through her teeth. "How can I help you?"

"I need to make a cash withdrawal," said Saizou.

"All right, sir. How much?"

Saizou scratched the back of his neck. "Fifty thousand yen."

The girl blinked slowly but nodded and began typing on the keyboard in front of her. "Yes, sir. If you'll please just look into the retinal scanner to your right, I can get that for you."

Saizou stepped to the side and opened his eyes wide, looking into the horizontal strip of florescent light. The beam flashed blue several times and went dark again.

The teller glanced at her screen. "Saizou Akita?"

"Yes."

"One moment, please."

She stood up and disappeared through the door behind her. Saizou turned around, sweeping his gaze across the corners of the ceiling, the vaulted roof, the walls. He counted twelve security cameras and shrugged his shoulders, attempting to rid himself of the anxious feeling he could not name.

He blew out a breath and turned around as the door behind

the desk opened and the petite teller reappeared with a box under her arm. She set it on the desk and pushed it through the open slot, smiling behind the plexiglass. "Have a nice day, Mr. Akita."

It was too late for that, Saizou thought, but this should improve it at least a little. "Thanks." He forced a smile. Friendliness toward strangers came less easily now than it used to. He was constantly reminding himself not everyone was an enemy, which, in turn, made him feel suspicious and exposed. "You, too."

She smiled, exposing a wide set of crooked teeth. "Thank you."

Saizou tucked the box under his arm, near his wakizashi, and ducked out the front doors. Shi was still there, leaning against the wall and scuffing the toe of his boot across the sidewalk. He glanced up as Saizou approached and straightened, holding Saizou's katana toward him.

Saizou took the sword and slid it back into the scabbard on his back. "We have funds."

"Good," said Shi, and nodded toward the lot across the street. "I know where to spend them."

————

THE MOTORCYCLES WERE Seikobutsu 7500 models. They were not sleek—they were black beasts of titanium alloy and fiberglass, a unique design that equalized speed and endurance. They had no luggage racks, but they had wide seats with enough room to sport Saizou and Shi's packs.

The dealer accepted Saizou's 50,000 yen in exchange for two of the Seikobutsu bikes, once Saizou and Shi confirmed that they were in excellent condition.

When Saizou handed him the key, Shi only remarked, "It's better than a bus," and took it.

They roared out of the lot and down the street, with Shi following Saizou toward Akita Domain. Traffic was sparse, Saizou noticed. Not for a town, perhaps, but for the largest city in Japan, it was strangely quiet. It might as well have been three o'clock in the morning.

It began to rain an hour later—a cold, pelting torrent so strong Saizou tugged his goggles down around his neck and squinted through the storm. The rain was no more than an annoyance until they left the city and the concrete streets turned into dirt roads. The motorcycles lived up to their reputation, to Saizou's relief, and his heart seized in his chest when he saw the black hills to the left visible through miles of bare winter trees.

He slowed, put his foot out. Stopped.

Shi rolled up and stopped alongside him. "Is this it?" he asked.

Saizou nodded.

A rare grin overtook Shi's mouth. "Nice to be home?"

Saizou clenched his right hand into a fist and raised it over his head and bellowed a wordless cry into the wind. Shi rested his left hand on his thigh and grinned wider, tolerating Saizou's uncharacteristic outburst for a few seconds before racing ahead.

Dwellings began to dot either side of the street, growing closer together the nearer they were to the main house. They were small and square, practical for a mining domain. To Saizou's eyes, they were more beautiful than any work of grand architecture.

The main house came into view. It was four smooth black walls four stories high, and the long horizontal windows stretched from ground to roof, catching the sun. A shadow hung in the center of one, like an unblinking eye. The tears Saizou had attempted to repress returned and spilled over, tracking down his face and wiped away just as quickly by the wind.

Out the corner of his eye, he saw Shi glance at him, but his companion made no comment as they slowed, approaching the house. Saizou leaned back, allowing his motorcycle to idle as he eyed the house.

A strange feeling turned in his chest, the same feeling he had felt seeing Commander Haka in the city. The house was in excellent condition, but the aura was different. It was not a home in this moment—it was a building, and something about it felt military. Rigid.

The two men who stepped out of the shadows guarding the front door might have something to do with it.

Saizou and Shi parked the motorcycles where they were and dismounted. Shi drummed his fingers on the pack at his side. "Home sweet home?"

Saizou rotated his neck, shrugging his shoulders and allowing his muscles to relax from hours of riding. "Close enough."

Shi grunted as they dismounted and followed Saizou as he strode up to the front of the house.

The guard on the right stepped forward. He wore no sword, but he held a rifle in his hands. Saizou recognized it as a Ganosuke, the rifle he had favored in the war. He lifted his gaze to the man carrying the weapon.

"Announce yourselves," the man said, frowning. He was maybe twenty, Saizou guessed, but his eyes were hard. There was no novice softness about him. "Or leave."

"Saizou Akita," said Saizou. "And my travelling companion, Shi Matsumoto."

The guard lowered the gun and swallowed visibly, although his expression remained set in stone. "Akita?"

"This is my domain," said Saizou. He wanted to take a step closer, to intimidate the young man, but he held back. It was not easy. "I don't know who holds it in my absence, but their services are no longer required."

The guard hesitated, then looked at his companion and jerked his head toward the door. The second guard bowed and hurried inside, letting the door slam shut behind him.

Saizou stepped back and glanced up at the tall windows and realized what he had mistaken for a shadow was the figure of a person standing on the top floor and looking down at him. When the figure saw him watching, it stepped away from the glass and vanished.

Saizou glanced at Shi, who shrugged his shoulders, a wordless *don't look at me.*

The front door opened again, and the second guard stepped out ahead of a man Saizou had never seen before. He was tall, slender and pale-faced, with delicate features and a distinctive edge in his eyes that warned Saizou not to judge him by his appearance. His wavy, shoulder-length hair fluttered in the cold breeze, and his eyes went from Saizou to Shi and back again with lengthy deliberation before he said, "So you're Saizou Akita?"

Saizou felt an immediate dislike of the man, although he could not place why. It was not uncommon for the ruler of a province to assign a temporary overseer to a lordless domain. Biting back the sensation, he gave him a shallow bow and replied warmly, "I am."

The man breathed out through his nose and lowered his

hands to his sides. "I am Shigure Matahachi." He bowed stiffly from the waist and straightened, then eyed Shi for the second time.

"Shi Matsumoto," said Shi automatically.

Matahachi's face was tight with thinly veiled displeasure, but he stepped aside and flicked his gaze toward the doorway. "Come in."

And for the first time in five years, Saizou stepped over the threshold of his house.

# THREE

THE INTERIOR HAD UNDERGONE VERY few changes,
Saizou was pleasantly surprised to notice. He stopped in the
center of the foyer and turned in a slow circle, taking in the
white walls, the geometric glass chandelier, the floating black
staircase. To some it might seem cold and minimal, but to him it
felt uncluttered. Clean. He could think here.

He turned his attention away from his surroundings and
faced Matahachi. The other man was watching. His expression
was passive, but his eyes were not, taking in Saizou and Shi,
pulling apart the details, studying and evaluating.

Coolly, he said, "I had not heard of your expected return."

"It was sudden," said Saizou, equally polite. Matahachi's
appearance was not intimidating, with a soft voice and fluid,
dancer-like movements. Still, he gave off the air of someone
whose appearance hid more than it displayed.

"You served the full five years?"

"I did."

Matahachi glanced at Shi. "You, too, I suppose."

"Four," said Shi. "Medical discharge."

Saizou was glad Shi did not volunteer the same information about him. Saizou had served his full five years, but duty and honor would have kept him fighting in the hell of gunfire and death if not for his own medical discharge. He kept this information to himself and said to Matahachi, "I assume you've been charged with holding the domain in my absence."

Matahachi bowed his head. "I have."

"How long?"

"Four years. The Prince-Regent thought it would be better maintained with someone to oversee the upkeep personally."

*The Prince-Regent?* "I wasn't aware the Prince-Regent was interested in Akita," said Saizou stiffly.

Matahachi smiled. "Now you are. No doubt he will want to meet with you to discuss your reinstatement."

"Your Lord Akita is here," said Shi. "I don't see why a discussion is necessary."

Matahachi tilted his head. "There is always the possibility that Lord Akita's health may be placed under too much strain if the daimyo is once again placed under his management."

Shi stepped forward, but Saizou held up a hand, stopping the imminent attack. "The last time I looked, health had nothing to do with whether a Lord had control of his daimyo."

Matahachi gave Saizou another slight, insincere smile and held up a hand. "The last time you looked was five years ago. Enough things change in the blink of an eye, and you expect things to stay the same for five years?" A breathy, one-syllable laugh pressed against his lips. "It's only a formality. I wouldn't worry."

Saizou took a deep breath.

*One.*

*Two.*

*Three.*

*Four.*

*Five.*

Matahachi's soft voice broke the quiet. "Ah, I believe you know Tsuki Shimabukuru. Don't you?"

Saizou felt self-control slide out of his grasp. "What about her?" he demanded, taking a step closer to Matahachi.

The other man turned and walked to the bottom of the stair, to the intercom stationed on the wall. He pressed a finger against the second button and spoke. "Lady Tsuki, we have a guest. I require your presence."

As Matahachi turned back around Saizou strode forward and gripped a fistful of Matahachi's collar, pushing him against the wall with his arm. It was everything he could do to not crush the man's windpipe; he wanted to. He wanted to break him. "Is she upstairs?"

Matahachi nodded, squeezing his eyes shut and inhaling a strangled breath of air. When he opened his eyes again, they were even sharper than before. He gripped Saizou's wrist, pushing against it, peeling Saizou's fingers away from his collar.

Saizou lifted his left hand to strike, but another grip caught it, and Shi pulled him back, away from Matahachi.

"Calm down," Shi instructed in his ear, pinning Saizou's arm to his side with some difficulty. "He hasn't done anything yet."

"Tsuki is in his house," Saizou spat, tossing his hair from his eyes.

"It's *your house*," Shi reminded him in a hard whisper. "Assaulting the man who currently holds it for the Prince-Regent might not be the best way to get it back."

Shi's common sense slowly wiped the red, angry haze from Saizou's vision, and Saizou took a deep breath, allowing himself to calm down, to reach a place where he no longer wanted to snap Matahachi's body like a burnt match.

Matahachi pushed away from the wall with his shoulder and straightened, wearing that same almost-sweet smile that slid across Saizou's nerves like a dozen razorblades. "Here she comes."

A young woman descended the stairs and nearly took Saizou's breath away. She was more beautiful than he had imagined even in more fanciful moments; five years had changed her for the better. She wore a simple outfit of blue-black trousers and a fitted jacket, but she might as well have been wearing a ball gown dripping with diamonds for how royal she looked.

He stepped toward the bottom of the stairs, and she paused halfway down, her eyes landing on him with a mixture of surprise and something...strangely like displeasure.

"Lord Akita." Her voice was clipped as she reached the bottom of the stairs. She bowed her head and gave him a brief, formal smile. "I didn't know you were returning. Did you only just arrive?"

She was not wearing a wedding ring, Saizou noticed, but the observation did little to alleviate his sudden apprehension. The Tsuki he had grown up alongside was warm and alive, a bonfire around which people gathered as naturally as moths drew to a flame. The woman in front of him held none of that warmth. It was like looking at a portrait drawn by a different artist than the one he remembered: the same person but rendered so differently that they had little in common.

"Yes," said Shi, when Saizou did not answer. He bowed to Tsuki.

Tsuki nodded politely at him. "You are...?"

"Shi Matsumoto," said Shi, with a half-suppressed sigh.

"A friend of Lord Akita's?"

*Lord Akita.* A title and a last name. So distant coming out of her mouth. Saizou rubbed his fingers together, trying to make sense of her attitude.

"We fought together," said Shi, answering Tsuki's question. "In Liaoyang."

"Oh." For a moment, she looked almost interested, but the spark faded as quickly as it arrived. "You must be tired." Looking at Matahachi, she asked, "Have you offered them anything to eat?"

"No," said Matahachi tersely. "Not yet." He glared at Saizou and Shi, but surprisingly, he did not mention Saizou's attack. Rather he held out his hand, his eyes locked on Tsuki's face. It was obvious she noticed Matahachi's offered hand, but instead she said, "Kiba, you remember Lord Akita."

A movement out of the corner of his eye caught Saizou's attention, and he stepped back, facing the door set in the far wall and deeply unsettled that he had not even peripherally noticed the figure standing there.

He was taller than Shi but shorter than Saizou, lean, with broad shoulders and long, half-braided hair. The clothing he wore was not a uniform except for the hard shoulder on his white, open-sleeved jacket. His pants were also white, but with a thin slit up the side from ankle to knee to hip. Saizou recognized the design of the outfit to maximize movement.

The man looked young at first, but on closer inspection, Saizou guessed he was older—late thirties, maybe early forties, but with features still infused with youthful beauty: dark-brown eyes and sharp eyebrows, his lips pressed into a tight line.

He did not look pleased at Saizou's presence, but he bowed politely, his long mane sweeping over his shoulder as he straightened and said in a sharp but not unkind voice, "Lord Akita. Matsumoto-san."

"And Lord Akita, you recall my bodyguard, Kiba?" Tsuki clarified, and suddenly Saizou remembered catching scattered glimpses of the man years ago. In the days when Tsuki would coax him to run across the hills and watch the miners carting gold from the yawning open cave-mouths or when she would convince Saizou to take her into Tokyo where they would spend the day throwing coins into fountains for good luck and sampling kebabs and fried pastries from vendors lined along the streets.

The Shadow. That was the name he had called the silent figure; never in the foreground but always there. Saizou had not thought of him in years, and he was surprised to see the man still serving the same purpose. He nodded at the bodyguard, and Shi followed suit, looking the newcomer up and down before glancing pointedly at Tsuki.

Saizou knew what that glance meant, and he frowned at Shi the next time he caught his eye. Shi returned the expression with a shrug.

Matahachi walked toward Saizou and stopped three feet away. With a shrewd, unwavering gaze, he asked in pleasant tones, "It would be my honor if you and your companion would stay for dinner. You may feel free to use the fourth floor tonight. It's a long trip back to Tokyo, and I would hate to see you caught outside after dark. Even two samurai such as yourselves, skilled though you may be, could find it an unpleasant experience." Politely, he inclined his head toward each of them in turn before sweeping out of the room past Kiba.

The bodyguard drew his eyebrows together and turned his attention to Tsuki. The young woman folded her arms across her chest, pointedly avoiding Saizou's gaze.

Saizou wanted none of it. He strode forward, intending to —he didn't know. Take hold of her shoulders and plead with her to tell him why she was behaving this way? But an arm was flung across his chest, stopping him before he reached her.

He turned his head and found himself face-to-face with Kiba, whose eyes were warm with a particular glint; that look a dog had when his master was threatened.

"Don't," warned Kiba. His calm tone carried an unmistakable current of ferocity.

Tsuki finally lifted her head and stepped forward, staring levelly at Saizou across the barrier of Kiba's outstretched arm. "It's fine."

The man did not look convinced, but he stepped immediately aside. He gave Saizou a sharp side-eye as he did so.

For the first time, Tsuki's gaze softened when she looked at Saizou. "How have you been?"

How had he been?

It was the sort of question that could not be answered. Not after five years of war. *How? Bloody and beaten and in pain, that's how I've been. Depressed and exhausted, unable to sleep without nightmares that terrify me. Half the time, I don't feel like a man. I feel like an empty shell or a child who wants to curl up under a bed somewhere and never come out. I wake up and I can't move, because the dreams I have are so real my body goes into shock.*

*How have I been?*

He blinked once, wiping away the mangled mess of everything he wanted to say and everything he knew he could not. Not now. Maybe not ever.

"Fine," he said, in a voice he could barely hear past the blood rushing in his head. "You?"

She tilted her chin up with a knowing twist of her mouth. "I've also been fine."

Shi's voice interrupted the awkward moment. "Now we know everyone's fine, captain? Can I talk with you?"

"Will you give me a choice?" Saizou crossed to the other side of the foyer, where Shi grabbed his arm and pulled him even closer to the wall, as far from Tsuki and Kiba as physically possible.

His temper flared, and Saizou pulled his arm out of Shi's grasp. "What?"

"What is she even doing here? You never mentioned her living in this house."

"She never did," said Saizou, sneaking a glance at Tsuki over his shoulder. She had turned around and was facing Kiba. They seemed to be having a one-sided argument; Kiba's mouth was shut and his arms were folded while Tsuki said something in a voice too quiet to overhear.

Shi frowned thoughtfully. "Do you think she's engaged to Matahachi? Maybe a mistress?"

Saizou's hand moved of its own accord, forming a familiar fist ready to punch Shi in the face, but Shi caught it almost casually with his own hand and forced it back down.

"Cool it," he said. "You've been running hot since that woman showed her face."

"Her name is Tsuki," said Saizou, flexing his fingers. He hated that punching things had become his knee-jerk reaction. He was not a violent man; he despised acting like one.

Shi nodded calmly. "And like I said, mentioning her seems to jump-start your temper, so I'd rather not use her name if I don't have to."

Saizou took a deep breath and shrugged his shoulders,

trying to ease the tension he felt in every fiber of his being. "It isn't her name. It's..."

"She's living under your roof?" suggested Shi, searching Saizou's face. "With someone you immediately disliked, and he seems pretty happy to rub it in your face. Did I leave anything out?"

"I don't like his attitude."

"Matahachi's?"

Saizou nodded stiffly. "If I didn't know better, I'd say he has no intention of turning Akita Domain back to me."

"I'm not sure it's up to him," said Shi fairly. "He said the Prince-Regent instated him here, which means it wasn't his idea."

"Unless Matahachi put the Prince-Regent up to it," Saizou replied. He brought his hands together in front of his mouth and blew out a breath. "Which is a distinct possibility."

"There are too many possibilities to list right now, I think," Shi pointed out. "We should discern what we can over dinner. Pry questions out of Matahachi, trap him into answering what he doesn't want to answer. We might have enough pieces to put a puzzle together by the end of it."

"There's more to him than he lets on." Saizou watched the doorway Matahachi had disappeared through. "But I'm not sure whether he's a deliberate enemy or a circumstantial one."

Shi shifted his lower jaw to the side, and his eyes went to Tsuki and Kiba. "What's with the bodyguard? I don't remember you mentioning him."

"He wasn't exactly central to my life before I left," said Saizou. "He was one of those people you eventually stopped noticing, the way you stop noticing the sound of rain on the roof. He's been her bodyguard since I can remember."

"Rich parents worried about her safety?" guessed Shi.

"Yes. Her father is a bakufu governor, stationed in Tokyo. He and my father used to do business together."

"You saw her often?"

Saizou nodded. "Very often. She was like a sister to me."

"Well," said Shi after a moment, "I hope that stopped a while back, because if you look at your sister that way, I might have to rip your eyeballs out."

"I stopped thinking of her like a sister when she was eighteen," said Saizou, grimacing at the implication and half-heartedly hitting Shi's arm. "Don't think things like that."

"Mmh," Shi grunted.

"Only you could turn that into something disturbing."

"You can just stop any time, captain."

Tsuki turned around suddenly and said, with a brightness Saizou doubted was real, "It's nearing time to eat, so we should probably head into the dining room."

"I've never been in a dining room," said Shi offhandedly.

Saizou paused. He had never considered that fact—and in that moment, he suddenly realized he didn't know nearly as much about Shi as Shi knew about him. His knowledge of Shi was a list of facts: Shi had been raised in a family of poor serfs, he had been conscripted to the army five years ago where he served under Saizou, he had saved Saizou's life, and he had decided to travel with him.

Nothing.

It was nothing.

He knew nothing about his closest friend and most loyal companion, and the realization struck Saizou in the chest like a pickaxe. He turned to Shi, but Shi was already moving to follow Tsuki and Kiba through the doorway. Saizou shook his head and went after them, cursing his own blindness.

*I didn't realize I was like this. Am I so absorbed in myself I no longer see anyone around me?*

No.

He had to stop this. Now was not the time for self-reflection. This was the time for planning, for bracing. This felt like the long hours before a battle. From the moment he locked eyes with Matahachi, he knew he had another fight on his hands.

He had fought wars and crossed countries just to come back home, and nothing would stop him from taking back what was rightfully his.

The Prince-Regent should watch his back.

# FOUR

"THAT WAS UNHELPFUL."

Saizou watched as Shi dropped his pack onto the floor and removed his daisho from his belt. He said nothing. Matahachi had barely uttered a single word the entire meal, sometimes flat-out ignoring questions aimed directly at him and responding to those he did choose to acknowledge with a cool smile and some vague, three-word remark. *I doubt it. I think not. Is that so?*

It was enough to drive Saizou crazy, and on top of that, Tsuki had pointedly refused to look at him all evening. She seemed set on maintaining the illusion he was not there, although she had spoken to Shi a few times when asking him to pass food.

Tsuki's bodyguard had stood behind her chair all evening, but his attention was focused equally on the other three men at the table. His expression had been slightly too grim to be neutral, but Saizou did not know whether the man felt hostile toward them or if he simply held a dislike for anyone who wasn't Tsuki. Saizou could not recall Kiba being particularly friendly at any time—but they had never interacted beyond acknowledgment of the other's presence, and that, at least, was not much changed.

"Are you ignoring me?" Shi waved a hand in front of Saizou's face, snapping him out of his frustrated mental detour. "Not that I mind. Used to it by now."

Saizou shook his head briefly, as if ridding himself of a swarm of buzzing bees. "He's tough."

"Matahachi?"

Saizou nodded.

Shi put his hands on his hips and stared at the smooth, white wall opposite. It was so clean and shiny that it reflected everything in the room like an opaque mirror. "We should check for bugs," said Shi finally. "He's probably watching us. Even if he heard me say that, I don't care."

The room was minimalist; a bed and an asymmetrical black rug, with two tall, graceful floor lamps and a chandelier in the middle of the room. Besides that, there was a three-drawer dresser and a curved fiberglass chair.

They swept the room and met in the middle. "Nothing," said Saizou. "It's clean."

Shi glanced at the intercom and held up a finger to his lips. Saizou followed his gaze and a small grin spread over his face as Shi moved quietly toward the intercom panel. Softly, he pressed the first-floor button. He flicked the panel with three fingers in rapid succession and was met by a sharp, mechanical squeal as the intercom protested the abuse.

"Just in case?" said Saizou, still grinning.

"Of course."

"A necessary precaution."

"I agree."

Saizou shook his head and stretched, nodding toward the queen-sized bed. "Looks like we're doubling up."

"Only because you don't want to sleep on the floor," said Shi.

"If there is a bed, I'm going to sleep on it. You can suit yourself," said Saizou, setting his own pack on the floor near the dresser. "You'll notice Matahachi did not mention our katanas."

"He looked at them often enough," Shi replied. He reached up and lifted the black mask from his face, opening his mouth wide to stretch his muscles. Shi had told Saizou, a few weeks after the mask became a permanent part of his identity, that it took a certain kind of balance and precision to wear a mask right. It was a talent he'd never had before, and the mask was a new-enough accessory that the wearing of it was not yet habit.

"Kiba didn't seem bothered," Saizou remarked, shrugging off his coat and tossing it over the dresser. He unlaced his boots, took them off, and pushed them up against the wall.

"I have the feeling it would have been a different matter if we'd unsheathed them," Shi pointed out. "I'm going to shower," he added, crouching in front of his pack and withdrawing a spare change of clothes. "That bed looks clean, and I'd hate to ruin it."

"Go ahead," said Saizou tiredly, waving his hand in the direction of the bathroom door. Even his bones felt weary. His mind had turned in so many circles it was now sitting down to catch its breath. "Take a hot one. As long as you want."

"I will," said Shi. "If you fall asleep before I'm out, I'm pushing you onto the floor. The rug looks nice, anyway." He stepped through the door and shut it behind him.

Saizou heard the shower turn on, and he stood in the center of the room, wanting to sit down and fall asleep right where he was, but far too aggravated to think the sleep would last. He glanced at the intercom, at that second button... He assumed Kiba slept on the third floor, as Matahachi had assigned the fourth to his unwelcome guests. Would anyone know if he tried to contact Tsuki?

*Maybe I was wrong. Maybe I created memories happier than what I had. It has been known to happen—it isn't even uncommon, if the shrink was right. Maybe the Tsuki I remember never even existed.*

Someone knocked on the door. There was no peephole, so he could not see who stood on the other side, and Saizou frowned, anticipating another unpleasant conversation with Matahachi. He opened the door, prepared to confront him, but it was not Matahachi who greeted him.

Kiba bowed stiffly from the waist. "Lady Tsuki would like a word with you."

"What about Matahachi? I don't think he'd like that idea," said Saizou, curling his lip.

Kiba's expression did not alter. "He left a moment ago for Tokyo."

Tokyo. Probably that meant that Matahachi was convening with a government official, or even the Prince-Regent himself.

"Fine," said Saizou. "Her room?"

Kiba nodded. "Second floor."

The three floors above the first each contained one large room and a bathroom, Saizou remembered clearly. It was not a particularly large home for a daimyo, but he had grown up here. It was his. And the thought of another man whispering into the Prince-Regent's ear, attempting to tear it away...

Saizou closed his eyes for a moment, just long enough to put his mind back on the right track. Tsuki wanted to talk to him now that Matahachi was gone, which meant she had felt a conversation impossible in Matahachi's presence. That, at least, was promising.

He descended the stairs behind Kiba to the second floor, where Kiba knocked on the door. "Saizou," he announced, glancing at the samurai. Saizou wondered if the bodyguard's face could hold anything other than that grim, almost-neutral expression for more than a few seconds.

Tsuki's voice came, muffled, through the door. "Come in."

Kiba pushed the door open and stepped aside, letting Saizou enter the room past him. Tsuki's room was not much different from the one Saizou currently shared with Shi—the colors were different, and a shelf held books and trinkets Saizou did not give more than a cursory glance.

Tsuki turned around and hurried up to Saizou, stopping a few feet away. She searched his face in a moment that seemed to last much longer. At least five years longer; a heartbeat for every minute Saizou had not been here, keeping her safe.

Her face softened and seemed to open, a sunflower touched by the light, but when she spoke, all she said was, "You have to be more careful."

Whatever he had expected her to say, that was not it. Saizou took a mental step back, trying to figure out what direction she was coming from. "If you're talking about Matahach—"

"Do you know where he went just now?" she demanded, putting her hands on her hips. The softness disappeared from her face, melting back into irritated angles. "Tokyo. Do you know why?"

"Probably to petition the Prince-Regent for my domain," said Saizou quietly. He knew if he spoke any louder, there was a good chance his temper would run away with him. In this current situation, that would end up with Kiba attacking him and Tsuki never giving him another chance. He clasped his hands behind his back and squeezed them together.

"Exactly." She squinted at him. "You should be more concerned about his current position."

"I am concerned."

"Well, then you should have been concerned *before* you attacked him."

Saizou shifted and glanced over his shoulder at Kiba, who had shut the door and was standing in front of it with his arms at his sides. "He told you about that?"

"No. Kiba noticed the signs. His shirt had clearly been grabbed, and there were red marks on his collarbone. Not to mention the looks he gave you all evening. I thought he was going to stab you with his chopsticks."

Kiba was more than a bullet shield, then. He had eyes and a brain, and he used them. Saizou pushed his tongue against his cheek before he said anything else. "What do you suggest, then?"

"I suggest playing it safe when you're called to the palace tomorrow."

"What makes you think I'll be called to the palace tomorrow?"

"I know Matahachi, that's what. I know the way he and the Prince-Regent work. They'll want to get this domain out from underneath you before you realize it's happened, and do you know why?"

"You're going to tell me," said Saizou. "I won't bother guessing."

She snorted lightly. "You could find out at the hearing tomorrow, if you'd rather wait."

Saizou sighed. "Tell me now."

Her smile would have been smug, were it not shadowed

with regret. "It's your mines, Saizou. We found out about it a few years ago. It's the reason the Prince-Regent put Matahachi in charge of Akita."

Saizou. The first time she had spoken his first name since he arrived. The first time in five years, and it was about this.

"The mines have never brought in enough profit to draw that much attention," said Saizou. "They're enough to keep the domain on its feet."

"They used to be."

"Did they find something? A larger vein of gold?"

Tsuki rubbed her forehead with her index finger. "Not just a vein. A river of it. Matahachi has kept it quiet for the Prince-Regent, and that's why he's here. Matahachi keeps the secret, and the Prince-Regent amasses wealth no one knows about it and uses it to his own ends."

A river of gold in his mines. The generations before Saizou had not found such luck there, and to think it was discovered during his mandatory service years—it was enough to wrangle a deep-seated groan of frustration from his throat. He pressed the heels of his hands against the sides of his head for a moment, processing the information. "What exactly is the Prince-Regent using this for? Do you know?"

Tsuki shrugged one shoulder. "Everything, most likely. He has assassins and bodyguards and a personal army."

"The men haven't been conscripted?"

"No. Those who serve the Prince-Regent are exempt from entering the Emperor's service. It makes it easy to find people willing to flock to his side, since nobody wants to leave their friends and family to fight someone else's war in another country."

Saizou folded his arms and tilted his head back, gazing at the ceiling. "If the Prince-Regent wants Matahachi to be here instead of me, then I doubt I'll be able to hold on to the domain."

"That's...actually what I wanted to talk with you about, specifically." Tsuki glanced at Kiba, then back at Saizou before pressing on. "This domain is in fairly good condition. The people get more to eat and trade more successfully than most." She hesitated. "And the reason for that is the Prince-Regent's interest."

Saizou blinked once, not sure he liked where the conversation was heading. "Get to the point."

Tsuki cleared her throat and said, "I don't think you should fight for the domain."

Saizou stared at her. Not fight for Akita, for his home? "You want me to leave it in Matahachi's hands? Tsuki, don't be—"

"Matahachi might be less than wonderful, but he isn't a cruel man," Tsuki interrupted, taking another step forward, close enough to reach out and touch Saizou if she wanted to. "The Prince-Regent is. If he thinks the domain is in danger, he will turn the lives of every serf who lives here into a living hell. He gets what he wants, and if for some reason that proves difficult, he makes sure no one else can have it, either."

Saizou swallowed a sharp reply. *Breathe. Once. Twice. Three times. Now speak.* "Before I think about what you just told me, you have to answer a question."

She nodded briefly. "What?"

"What are you doing here? Are you engaged to Matahachi? Are you some kind of live-in companion?"

Tsuki's expression of caution turned into one of anger and disgust. "Live-in companion? Please, Saizou, are you twelve? Am I honestly the kind of person who would trade sex for a safe place to live? Give me a break."

"I don't know you," Saizou said sharply. "I used to. The

Tsuki I used to know would never ask me to act like a coward and not fight for my home."

"I'm not asking you to act like a coward!" Tsuki planted her fist in the center of Saizou's chest and pushed, not hard enough to send him backward but enough to leave a faint throb. "I'm asking you to make a sacrifice for the thirteen hundred people who work on your land. Give it to Matahachi, and they won't suffer. Fight for it, and I guarantee you the Prince-Regent will make them pay for your mistake."

Everything around Saizou melted away, leaving only the meaning behind Tsuki's words.

*Don't fight.*

*Give it to a stranger.*

*Your mistake.*

Shi's voice came through the intercom. "Captain?"

Saizou could not find the voice to answer him, but Tsuki spoke instead. "Go talk to him," she said. "We're done here."

She gave Saizou one more glance before turning and striding across the room, entering the bathroom and closing the door shut behind her. She did not slam it, but the gesture sent aftershocks through Saizou.

Kiba opened the bedroom door, indicating that Saizou could now leave. As he moved through the doorway, Saizou realized Tsuki had not answered his question, had not explained what she was doing here.

As if reading his mind, Kiba said, "Lady Tsuki is not here because she wants to be, samurai. Don't think she is."

Saizou ground his back teeth together before asking, "Then why is she here?"

Kiba's lips pulled apart just enough to reveal a hint of teeth. "She told you. The Prince-Regent does whatever he wants with whatever, and whomever, he wants. She was a housewarming gift for Shigure Matahachi."

Housewarming gift.

Tsuki.

The girl who had pestered him about his sword and asked if she could train alongside him had been treated like a slave and handed over to a man she did not know.

"I hope," said Kiba, an edge in his voice, "that you will understand her point of view a little better now. She would be very unhappy if she knew I had told you."

So she had evaded answering the question on purpose. "Thank you."

He stepped out onto the landing just as Shi came down the stairs, his mask back in place but his silver-blond hair still dripping with water. "What were you doing?"

Saizou walked past him, back up the stairs and into the guest room, where he sat heavily on the bed and stared at the floor.

Several minutes of silence passed before Shi finally said, "All right, time to talk."

"Kiba informed me that Tsuki wanted to talk, so that's what I did."

"Hmm. About?"

Saizou rubbed his face with both hands. "She wants me to hand my domain over to Matahachi."

An expression of blank shock on Shi's face, and Saizou explained as concisely as he could. When he finished, he stretched out on the bed and closed his eyes for a few long seconds.

Quietly, Shi asked, "What are you going to do?"

"Shower," said Saizou, getting up again. He shut the bathroom door and turned the hot water on, allowing the streams to flow over his face, washing the dust from his skin. If only it could wash the blood out, he thought; and it was not the first time.

*Give it over.*

*Turn away from your home.*

*Leave.*

*Everyone will be safe.*

He leaned his forehead against the tiled wall and shut his eyes.

He would not be sleeping tonight.

The fate of his world rested on his shoulders, and if he made a wrong move, it would all shatter.

# FIVE

THE ENVELOPE ARRIVED via bike messenger early the next morning. Saizou was awakened by Shi, who had gotten up before him and had been downstairs when the message arrived. The envelope was thick and glossy, with Saizou's name embossed in gold on the front. Upon opening it, he found a summons written in elegant hand-lettering.

*Lord Saizou Akita, you are hereby called to the Palace of the Sun at high noon. You will appeal for Akita Domain directly to Prince-Regent Mamushi, who will personally oversee your case and make a fair and wise decision regarding the ownership of the Akita Domain. Failure to respond to this summons will result in the automatic forfeit of Akita Domain. Hail the Sun.*

Saizou sat on the edge of the bed, reading and rereading the note until Shi plucked it from his grasp and said in a dramatic voice, "You've been summoned."

Saizou rubbed his hands together and nodded.

"At least we expected it. It's not like they took you by surprise."

"Don't give me optimism right now. It doesn't work on

you," said Saizou, standing. Even that motion felt difficult, as if he weighed three times more than he had the night before, or gravity had shifted and begun pressing him down.

"Sorry." Shi handed the envelope back and opened his pack. He began pulling out clothes.

Saizou watched for several seconds before saying, "Don't tell me you're dressing up for this."

"You really think the Prince-Regent is the only one who'll be there? You'll have all eyes on you, captain. You need to look worthy of a domain, whether you should have to or not."

"I don't have anything formal," Saizou said. "I'm assuming Matahachi put my belongings in storage, if he didn't burn them on a bad day."

"I guessed as much," said Shi, and flung a long, leather Nehru jacket at Saizou. "Wear that. At least it's in better shape than the clothes you have."

Saizou turned the jacket around and held it up to himself. "You seem to have forgotten the fact I'm five foot eleven."

Shi glanced up, his eyes narrowing. "And?"

"You're five foot seven."

Shi folded his arms and leveled a challenging stare at Saizou. "It will fit you. If you don't like the fact it doesn't reach your feet, deal with it. The arms are long enough."

"If I wear this, what will you wear?"

"Don't be such a woman, Saizou. They won't be looking at me, and if they do, it's not like they ever look beyond my face."

Tsuki's voice came over the intercom with a single word. "Breakfast."

"Speaking of women," said Saizou.

Shi blinked at the intercom. "Don't tell her what I said." He crossed over to the door but paused and turned around when he noticed Saizou made no move to follow. "You waiting for a second call?"

"I'm not eating." Saizou ran his hands through his hair and stood up. "You go."

Shi leaned against the door with his shoulder and tucked his free hand into his pocket. "What are you doing if you aren't eating?"

Saizou gave him a tired look. "Thinking."

Shi regarded him quietly for a moment. "You going to be all right?"

"I'm not going to jump off the roof," said Saizou, with a small smile. "If that's what you mean."

"Have you made up your mind about the hearing?"

*Give it over.*

*Mistake.*

"Go eat," said Saizou. "I'm going for a walk."

Shi gave him a lingering look before opening the door and walking down the stairs. Saizou gazed at the landing through the doorway before following, but he did not turn into the kitchen when he reached the foyer. Instead, he left out the front door, walking between the two posted guards, who said nothing.

Saizou put his hands in the pockets of Shi's jacket and walked slowly away from the house. He did not stick to the road; instead, he veered right, taking his time, strolling up over the nearest hill, where he stood beneath the bare, gray branches of the trees and looked at the domain spread out in front of him.

No songs rang from the mines, although he could hear the faint, metallic ringing of work floating over the crisp breeze. Black smoke rose from chimneys and mingled with dust from the mines, smudging the storm-swollen clouds above and turning everything into a grim, bleary haze.

*I'm asking you to make a sacrifice for the thirteen hundred people who work on your land. Give it to Matahachi, and they won't suffer. Fight for it, and I guarantee you the Prince-Regent will make them pay for your mistake.*

He sighed, his warm breath meeting the cold air in a white cloud that quickly dissipated.

Thirteen hundred people, some of whom he had grown up alongside, with faces he knew as well the palms of his own hands. Was Tsuki right? Was the Prince-Regent so tyrannical that he would crush these people to make a point?

*Lady Tsuki...was a housewarming gift.*

He remembered the raw, barely suppressed anger on Kiba's face as the bodyguard uttered those words. Slowly, Saizou sank to his knees, unable to remain upright under the weight of the matter pushing him down. He ran his hands over the dry, brown blades of grass and closed his eyes.

The weight of his decision threatened to suffocate him. He had to choose, and he had to choose before he walked into the Palace of the Sun at noon.

———

THE PALACE of the Sun was set in the heart of Tokyo; a square mile of shining glass buildings off which the pale winter sun reflected like walls of diamonds. It was called the Palace Mile, and in the very center was the Great Hall: a pagoda of black and red, like some underworld temple dedicated to the Prince-Regent himself.

Saizou and Shi rode up to the front gates, which were guarded by two machine-gun turrets and a dozen guards, each armed in faceless armor. The armor was also black and red, designed to resemble samurai armor from centuries before, but the differences were obvious—everything was semi-robotic, allowing for easy, enhanced movement and bodily protection. Each of them held a six-foot white staff decorated with engravings and buttons near the middle and top. Saizou had seen similar weapons on the warfront—they were reizaa-naginata, with a deadly blade on either end if you pushed the right button.

Saizou and Shi were allowed to pass through the gates after announcing their identities to the faceless guard. A faint network of red lines covered them as they drove through the gate-scanners. They kept riding until they reached the tree-lined courtyard, where they were quickly surrounded by two dozen more of the robot-suited samurai. Their reizaa-naginata were turned on and blazing in various shades of crimson. The Prince-Regent seemed to like the color, Saizou thought as he and Shi lifted their hands.

One of the soldiers stepped forward, and through the mask, his human voice snapped, "You are carrying blades longer than thirty centimeters. Please remove your katanas and set them on the ground."

Saizou reached back and removed his katana from the sheath strapped to his back. Slowly, he drew it out and held it, pointing the blade down, before dropping it. Shi did the same, but he did not drop it like Saizou—he half-tossed it, watching the blade clatter to a stop at the commanding soldier's feet, the blade inches away from his boots.

"Please dismount your vehicles," said the soldier, his only reaction a slight twitch of his head toward Shi. Overhead, a crow gave a throaty laugh and lifted away from the stark white branches of the twisted winter trees. Saizou glanced up, watching as the bird's black feathers caught the sun for a brief, glinting moment before it disappeared over the top of one of the buildings.

Saizou threw his leg over the motorcycle seat and stepped off.

"Follow me," the soldier stated before turning and striding away at a rapid pace toward the Great Hall rising like a black shadow in front of them.

Saizou glanced at Shi, who drew closer and said under his breath, "We're walking into an enemy camp full of reizaa-naginata, and we have a wakizashi each."

Saizou blew out a deep breath and muttered back, "Try to relax. Remember, we also have brains and diplomacy on our side."

"No," grunted Shi. "*I* have brains and diplomacy. You only have me."

Saizou smiled a grim smile as they followed the palace soldiers up the steps and under the grand arch. It resembled a dragon, thousands of intricate scales winding from its tail to its mouth full of sharp, golden teeth.

The Grand Hall was aptly named. Eight pillars rose on either side, guiding the straight, wide path to the Sun Throne. It was not named the Sun Throne simply because of the Prince-Regent's self-appointed title; the throne itself was designed to resemble the star for which it was named, with symmetrical flames spreading away from the center seat.

Palace soldiers lined the way, standing between the pillars, but they were not the only ones gathered. The Hall was full of curious onlookers and men bearing the pendants and robes marking them as bakufu officials.

It was darker inside the Hall than it was in the gray sunlight outside, and there was a chill in the air that was not entirely related to the temperature. The only light was that which filtered in from the open door, but it was not dark enough for torches to be lit or lights to be turned on.

The Sun Throne was on a raised dais, with steps on either side leading up to meet in the middle. Although he was too far away to clearly make out the details of his face, the Prince-Regent's reclined posture was clearly calculated to appear as languid as possible. His back was straight, his legs crossed, and his head lowered to direct a narrow, burning gaze at the men who approached.

Two other figures were clearer, more in the forefront, and they were so bizarre that Saizou found himself staring at them rather than the Prince-Regent, trying to assess who they were and why they were there.

The first figure sat on the top stair to the Prince-Regent's left, and the first thing Saizou noticed was the leash running from the thick leather collar around his neck straight to the Prince-Regent's right hand, where he gripped the leash in a tight fist.

The man wearing the collar was a strange sight, if 'man' was the right word. He was nearly androgynous and hairless, his too-wide cheekbones nearly as sharp as his bared teeth. His large, too-far-apart eyes were narrowed not at Saizou but at Shi, who regarded him with a neutral expression. The dog-man growled deep in his throat and shifted from a sitting position to a crouch, as if prepared to leap at either of the newcomers. He wore no clothes, but the cold did not seem to bother him at all. Nothing about him was quite right. Quite human.

The other figure stood on the Prince-Regent's right, tall and slender, with his hands folded in front of him and his head tilted to the side. While not as strange a creature as the dog-man, he was a curiosity if only for the mask fitted around the lower half of his face. It looked like a cross between a gas mask and a muzzle: a sleek, elegant thing still somehow barbaric when attached to a human's face. He wore a split skirt over close-fitting leggings and boots, and a sleeveless jacket that went high up his neck was cropped high enough to display his lean, hard stomach. His detachable sleeves were open carriers for knives—a long, thin blade decorated each of his forearms, and even more circled the sash around his waist.

"Lord Saizou Akita, Prince-Regent," called a voice from the back of the Hall. Saizou did not bother to turn and look at the announcer as he added, "And Shi Matsumoto."

The Prince-Regent leaned forward then, into what dim light filtered back to the throne. His face was sharp, his hair long and unkempt, unlike the rest of him. Everything else about him seemed impeccable, sleeves gathered at his wrists, boots that reached his knees, everything black and close-fitting except for the red gloves on his hands.

"The Sun did not summon anyone named Shi Matsumoto," he stated in a soft, womanly voice.

Saizou had expected something sharper to match the snake-like appearance of the speaker.

The Prince-Regent lifted a hand and waved it, gesturing for Shi to move away from Saizou and stand on the sidelines.

Shi glanced at Saizou, and the look held both encouragement and warning. *Watch yourself. Stay in control.*

Saizou gave him an almost imperceptible nod, and as he did so, a movement on the left caught his eye. For the first time, he noticed Matahachi standing amid the officials, his eyebrows slightly raised, his lips pressed firmly together. There was something almost like concern on his face, but Saizou had no doubt that the concern was not for him.

He returned his full attention to the Sun Throne and sank to one knee, lowering his head in deference to the

Prince-Regent. "Hail the Sun," he said, with fervor he did not feel.

"You can stand up," said the Prince-Regent, boredom and interest mingling paradoxically in his tone. "You just returned from China, didn't you? Liaoyang Province, I believe."

"I did, Your Highness."

"And you returned, it seems, with an interesting souvenir."

It took Saizou only a moment to realize the Prince-Regent was referring to Shi. Fighting a fresh burst of hot anger, Saizou took a deep breath and replied, "He saved my life in Liaoyang, Your Highness."

"Really? How noble of him. What happened to his face?"

The question was so unexpected that Saizou was sure he had heard incorrectly. "Your Highness?"

"Something must have happened to it. No matter how interesting a mask is, it's still a mask. Masks cover things. What's wrong with his face?"

Saizou clenched his hands into fists and said, as evenly as he could, "A war injury, Your Highness."

"Bad, was it?"

*He is the Prince-Regent, the younger brother of your Emperor. You owe him your loyalty and allegiance. Running up to the dais and punching him in the face is not the Way, no matter how tempting it sounds.*

He could not bear to look at Shi. "He is still recovering, Your Highness."

"And you? Did you sustain any significant injuries during your time in Liaoyang?" The Prince-Regent leaned farther forward. The dog-man's black eyes glinted, and he shifted closer toward the stairs, but the Prince-Regent tugged absently on the leash, jerking him back a few feet.

Saizou realized his wary bewilderment must have been

obvious, because the Prince-Regent said, "Never mind the Dog. He won't attack unless I order him to. Now answer my question."

"With all due respect, Your Highness, I don't see what possible injuries have to do with my domain." The words left Saizou's mouth, tainted with more anger than he intended.

The Prince-Regent leaned back and lifted his hand again, this time to silence the shocked murmurs that arose from the gathered crowd. "Your Sun commands you to answer," was all he said.

Saizou clenched his jaw. *Breathe. The behavior of others does not dictate your own.* "I did sustain injury, yes. Your Highness."

"You look remarkably well. You aren't wearing a mask, for instance." The Prince-Regent laughed a little.

"Not all injuries are visible on the surface, Your Highness."

"Ah." Suddenly, the Prince-Regent's eyes narrowed into slivers of cold, hard calculation, all mirth and mockery temporarily swept away. "You are mentally impaired, then."

*You left yourself wide open for that, you idiot.*

"No, Your Highness; *impaired* would imply that I can't function like a normal person."

"So, you can function, then?"

"Yes, Your Highness."

"Hmm." The Prince-Regent rested his chin on a red-gloved hand. "Then maybe you would be so kind as to explain why I received a report stating that both you and your companion were carrying illegal weapons within city limits—and before you protest, I should add that I'm fully aware of the fact you both kept those illegal weapons until several minutes ago."

*He's attempting to trap you. He wants to force your hand. Keep a level head.*

"We weren't aware they were illegal until we were confronted by Commander Haka, Your Highness. After that, we still weren't certain."

The Prince-Regent's eyebrows drew together. "Even after he assured you they were illegal and told you to get rid of them?"

"It was somewhat difficult to believe, Your Highness." He didn't add his argument with Shi earlier that morning, in which Shi had stated with characteristic stubbornness that he was not removing his katana unless the Prince-Regent himself ordered it to his face. "I take the word of sober men. Commander Haka was clearly—"

Shi shifted into Saizou's peripheral vision, and he stopped short, glancing at his friend. Shi shook his head, ever so slightly.

Saizou studied the Prince-Regent. There was no kindness on that eerily flawless face, no mercy. He had already decided Saizou's fate, and lordship of Akita Domain was not included in the deal.

*River of gold.*

*Give it up.*

*Coward.*

*Sacrifice.*

*Thirteen hundred people.*

"Your Highness." Saizou sank to both his knees and placed his palms on the ground.

Intrigue filled the Prince-Regent's voice. "What are you doing?"

Saizou bowed, his forehead just inches from the cold stone floor. "I will not contest the ownership of my domain."

The Prince-Regent's voice was thick with suspicion. "You must have a condition, Saizou. What is it?"

Saizou lifted his head and straightened, resting his hands

on his knees. "Release Lady Tsuki from her position with Matahachi."

Matahachi glanced quickly at the Prince-Regent, who did not return the look. Instead, he leaned back and laughed, a genuine, mirthful laugh.

"Are you in love with her?" he asked, around fits of giggles. "She's quite beautiful, I'll give her that. More beautiful even than some of my own pastimes. However, I'm afraid my dear Matahachi is quite fond of her, and he wouldn't want me to give her up. Your Tsuki stays right where she is."

*He tried to force your hand. Now try to force his.*

"Then I'm afraid I'm going to have to insist my domain be returned to me."

A cruel smile cut the Prince-Regent's face. "That would be much easier for you, I think, if you weren't under arrest, effective immediately. You and your friend," he continued, raising his voice for all to hear, "for the possession of illegal weapons after a clear warning." He lifted a hand and pointed toward Saizou and Shi in a sweeping line. "Take them away. Congratulations, Matahachi—Akita Domain is yours now. Although," he added, with another laugh, "I suppose it should be re-christened now, don't you think?"

Saizou's vision blurred, and everything around him faded, leaving only the clear-cut hiss of the Prince-Regent's laughter. As palace soldiers closed in on him, the only sensations he felt were the red heat of his boiling blood and the feeling of his own hands taking hold of the nearest reizaa-naginata.

# SIX

FOR A MOMENT, the only thing Shi could see was his captain. He held the reizaa-naginata in his hand, the laser edge glowing a bright, bloody red and two bodies fallen in front of him, no blood pooling from their severed, cauterized heads.

His face was too pale, his eyes too wide, gleaming with reflections of mindless anger driven by a simple fact: the injustice had taken its toll, and he had snapped. It was not for the first time, but it would not end with two bodies if Shi did nothing to stop it.

The Prince-Regent rose to his feet. "He resisted arrest and murdered two of my guards," he cried, flinging a tattoo-encircled finger at Saizou. "Kill him and the Deaths-Head!"

Shi sighed and pulled his wakizashi smoothly from his belt. He turned on the nearest soldier and jammed the short sword through the soldier's neck, in the soft, bendable rubber just under the soldier's upper jaw. It was a calculated move he could not use twice; so Shi left the wakizashi there and grabbed the reizaa-naginata from his hands as the soldier fell over.

He flicked the button, switching the blade on, and ran

across the hall to Saizou's side. Saizou whirled to face him, the blade of his reizaa-naginata stopping six inches from Shi's neck.

Shi looked at Saizou's bloodless face and said in a calm voice, "We should leave before we both die."

Saizou blinked once, and his eyes came into focus, taking in the sight of the Prince-Regent's soldiers converging around them from the direction of the throne. Even in his haze of berserk anger, he was level-headed enough to realize they were outnumbered if they did not get out right that instant.

"Go," he said, breaking into a run.

Shi heard an inhuman cry behind them, an animal howl from a man's voice, and ran faster, swinging the reizaa-naginata and cutting a burning line across the chest of a soldier who raced around the door.

Saizou turned around and carved a fiery arc in the air, searing three more soldiers who reached the top of the stairs just in time to die.

"The motorcycles," he shouted at Shi.

Shi raced down the stairs, in spite of the fact he knew it was a futile attempt at escape. Even getting that far was pure luck; they were outnumbered probably a thousand to two, and even if a miracle pushed them through the front gates, every officer, bounty hunter, and mercenary in the nation would be looking for them.

Shi was halfway across the courtyard when he heard foot-steps behind him, and he spun, slicing the reizaa-naginata low through the air to cut off the opponent's legs, but he missed. This one seemed to anticipate the move and instead jumped into the air, twisting over the pole of the weapon and slamming into Shi with his full weight.

Shi recognized the mouthful of sharp teeth grinning down at him; the Emperor had released the dog-man. He wondered, with a flash of sharp concern, if the muzzled man had been sent after Saizou, or if Saizou had been flooded by soldiers and was already dead, or if—

But there was no time; Shi rolled just as the dog-man's teeth snapped together where Shi's throat would have been half a second before. These quarters were too close for the reizaa-naginata; Shi let go of it and punched the dog-man in the face.

The dog-man crouched a few feet away and slowly tilted his head to one side: a predator studying his prey, waiting, daring it to make a move.

The motorcycles were close, but Shi knew they would not have enough time to reach them and turn them on. He delivered a spinning kick to the dog-man's face, his boot cracking against the side of the creature's head. The dog-man grabbed his leg and raked his fingers down it, and the sharp, tearing pain brought something to Shi's attention—the dog-man did not have fingernails; he had claws.

A human with claws and sharp teeth, and all the mannerisms of a feral animal—what was the Prince-Regent thinking? What had possessed him to think this was a good idea?

The dog-man sank his claws farther into Shi's calf and yanked him to the ground. Shi twisted and grabbed the reizaa-naginata he had let go of, but before he could use it, the dog-man was on his back, and Shi cried out in pain as the dog-man's teeth sank into his shoulder and pulled a mouthful of flesh free from his bones.

Suddenly, the pressure was gone from his back and there was a high yelp from the dog-man. Shi pushed himself up with one hand, blood gushing down his arm, spilling across the smooth stone, and someone grabbed his other arm.

"Don't faint yet," said Saizou's voice in his ear.

Shi blinked, trying to chase away the blackness closing in on his vision. "The bikes aren't started," he said, but the words had barely left his mouth before a familiar low, rumbling sound reached his ears.

The men turned to see their motorcycles tearing across the courtyard toward them, riderless.

"That's weird," said Shi. "I have the keys." He felt like he was floating, a balloon untethered and drifting away, but he had to stay grounded. He had to stay focused; otherwise, he would become a liability. A liability would endanger Saizou.

"Doesn't matter," said Saizou, as the motorcycles roared to a sudden, precise stop in front of them, the new-era gravity-balancers keeping the bikes upright as they idled. "Come on."

"Where are the soldiers? Where is everyone?" Shi asked as Saizou pulled him around to the side of one of the motorcycles.

"One of the security grids came on. They're trapped behind the phoenix-arch."

Shi shook his head. He was tired. Tired was dangerous. "Someone's helping us."

"We'll figure it out later. Can you ride?"

Shi clumsily mounted his motorcycle. "Not for long."

"Follow me." Saizou mounted his own bike and turned it to face the courtyard gates.

Shi did as he said, revving the engine and following Saizou as his captain took off toward the gates. *Phoenix-arch grid. No keys in the ignition. Whoever you are, keep helping. Get him out safely.*

They roared through the courtyard gates, and as they did, Shi heard the gates slam shut behind them with a thunderous boom. So far, so good.

But Shi groaned when he saw the obstacle ahead. *Way to go, Shi. You jinxed it.*

Palace soldiers were lined up, blocking the front gates: two rows, maybe sixty bodies, their white, faceless figures pointing guns directly toward the approaching escapees.

In front of the soldiers stood the muzzled figure who had stood beside the Prince-Regent, and in each hand, he held the long, thin knives previously sheathed in his sleeves.

"I think our luck's run out," Saizou said aloud.

"Can't," Shi replied grimly. "We never had any."

"See you later, I guess," said Saizou, crouching lower over his handlebars.

Shi lifted the corner of his mouth in a partial smile that was all he could manage. "Optimistic of you."

Over the roar of wind in his ears, Shi heard the muzzled figure scream in a robotic, monotone voice, "FIRE."

As useless as it was, Shi braced for impact.

He did not mind death. Not this way.

Nothing happened.

Heads bent immediately, stunned at the guns refusing to fire. The muzzled figure did not hesitate at the delay. He broke into a run, heading straight for Saizou's motorcycle with strides longer and more powerful than Shi had expected.

Shi accelerated as hard as he could and drove straight for the muzzled man.

The figure changed his course, his hand flashing, and a knife sliced through the air. Shi ducked, the blade whistling as it flew past his ear.

Saizou roared past. "Straight ahead!" he shouted. "Don't stop!"

Shi settled deeper into the seat as soldiers leaped out of the way, useless without guns.

Shi's heart sank when he saw the front gates up ahead were closed, an impenetrable wall rising to block their way. *Come on,* he thought, his mind revolving the words in a frantic prayer. *Come on, come on, come on.*

A thousand feet away, closing rapidly.

Neither of them slowed down.

Nine hundred feet.

Seven hundred feet.

Five hundred—

A sliver of light appeared where the black gates met, widening inch by inch. They were opening, but they were not opening fast enough.

*Move it. Move it faster.*

Four hundred feet.

Three hundred feet and the gates were still only open a foot and a half, creaking and groaning like a house being torn apart by a high wind.

Two hundred feet.

*Kuso.*

Shi had always figured he would die violently, yes, but not pulverized like a bug on a windshield.

Suddenly the doors flew open, as if whatever had been restraining them had snapped. They slammed against the walls, sending tremors through the ground like the aftershocks of an earthquake.

Saizou raced through just ahead of Shi, who did not stop to ponder the improbability of their escape from the palace. There would be time enough for that later if he managed to stay awake.If nobody raced out behind them.

*Stay awake. Stay awake...*

# SEVEN

A FEW MINUTES LATER, Saizou glanced over his shoulder. Shi slumped forward over his handlebars. The blood dripping from his shoulder spit into the air as it landed on the front tire.

Saizou did not know how bad Shi's injury was, but he needed help and he needed it as soon as possible. Hospitals were not an option, and neither were medical clinics. It would be hard enough to stay hidden and out of sight as it was.

He turned left into a smaller side street, checking again to make sure Shi was still with him. He slowed. "Can you make it?"

Shi lifted his head a few inches and nodded, but there was a glassy look in his eyes that put Saizou on alert. He had seen that look many times—Shi had a few minutes, if that, before he lost consciousness. Losing consciousness on a motorcycle was a bad idea.

Saizou swept his gaze across both sides of the street. The buildings were tall and worn by the weather, still wet from the heavy rainfall the night before. Broken neon signs flickered in barred windows.

The tires of Shi's motorcycle squealed against the damp pavement as the vehicle swerved to the side. Shi straightened, shaking his head.

Saizou's eyes landed on a sign that read *INTOX Bar & Lounge*.

"Pull over," called Saizou. "Pull over at the bar."

Shi squinted and slowed down, pulling up alongside the decrepit building. Light glowed through the filmy windows in shades of purple and green.

Shi began to dismount his bike, but his legs gave out. Saizou caught him just as he collapsed, unconscious.

*Ah, shit.* Saizou hefted Shi up, doing his best to cover Shi's bleeding shoulder from view. Supporting Shi was awkward when trying to make it look natural; he shoved the door open and quickly stepped inside, hauling the other man's body as naturally as he could.

The light was dim except for the colorful spotlights over the windows and bar, and the place was surprisingly crowded, considering the time of day. Then again, Saizou thought briefly, maybe it wasn't so surprising. Too many people were jobless and hopeless these days. Drowning your troubles in alcohol could seem like a pleasing idea, even as early as noon.

A small red sign caught Saizou's eye, pointing toward the restrooms. Nobody stopped to look as he half-dragged Shi across the room, which Saizou counted as a small blessing. If they could make it in and out of the bar without any trouble at all, it would be a full miracle.

He shouldered the bathroom door open and pulled Shi inside, setting him on the floor, glad to see it was surprisingly clean, considering the location and appearance of the place. He leaned Shi's back carefully against the wall and locked the door. Working as quickly as he could, he opened Shi's coat and shirt, blowing out a breath when he saw the nasty, gaping wound. Blood bubbled inside, like lava in the crater of a volcano. Shi either needed stitched up or cauterized, and neither seemed like a viable option.

It was two steps to the sink where he filled his cupped hands with water and used it to rinse the blood away from Shi's shoulder. At the very least, he could clean it, and they were in the perfect place for alcohol. He could sterilize it too, at least partially.

He yanked the borrowed Nehru jacket off and tied it, awkwardly but firmly, around Shi's shoulder before he got up. He prayed nobody needed the bathroom before he got back.

Shutting the door quietly behind him, he moved quickly through the crowded space toward the bar. "Excuse me," he said to the bartender's back.

She turned around, and Saizou found himself staring at the first gaijin he had seen since Liaoyang. Her bright-blue hair and pale skin were purple under the lights. He guessed she was in her mid-twenties, although it was harder to tell where foreigners were concerned. She lifted an eyebrow and said in fluent Japanese, "Wow, you look like you've had a rough day. What can I get you?"

"Sake," he said, taking a deep breath. He had already been triggered once that day, and people had died as a result. The presence of one gaijin would not affect him. He was determined not to let it.

"Straight up?" She picked up a glass, but her mouth twisted suddenly when she looked closer at him. Leaning forward, she wiped two fingers across his cheek before he could pull away. His stomach lurched when he saw the sticky red substance she was now inspecting.

He would never be used to the forward, impersonal

behavior of foreigners, but that was the least of his concerns as he watched her study her hand. She then wiped her fingers off on a paper towel. "So who's bleeding?"

"Just get me the alcohol," Saizou said in a low voice.

The light overhead slowly changed from purple to green, washing her in a sickly light as she raised a pierced eyebrow. "Look, fella, you want a drink, you tell me who's injured."

"I will jump over this counter," said Saizou, curling his free hand into a fist while the fingers of his other hand squeezed the handle of his wakizashi, "and take what I need. If you give it to me before that happens, I'll buy it like anyone would."

"Urgent, huh?" She reached under the counter, and Saizou braced, but instead of drawing a gun, she withdrew a green bottle of sake and popped the lid. She glanced at a shot glass, but instead she set the bottle on the counter in front of Saizou. She did not let go of it.

"I saw you come in with your friend," she said, just loud enough for him to hear. "He looked awful, and this isn't exactly a clinic."

Saizou knew that if he looked down at his knuckles they would be white with the strain of gripping the handle of his sword. "What do you want?"

"Well." She smirked softly. "You must be running from someone, if you're using a bar bathroom in place of a hospital."

*She's going to report you. You have to get out of here.* He turned around and almost ran into someone who had approached silently behind him.

The figure was startling; a nightmarish patchwork of skin and machinery cobbled together in the shape of a human. It looked like a river spirit had been violently merged with a junk-yard. He registered the creature in pieces: Paper-white skin. Long paper-white hair. Mechanical right eye made of blue light. Black lines running from ear to mouth as the thing spoke; a genderless voice that sounded like someone speaking through a long plastic tube. "Is something wrong, Honey?" the thing asked, unblinking eyes focused on Saizou. "You pushed the panic button."

"Oh, there's no panic," said the bartender, waving a hand.

Saizou ground a curse between his teeth and swallowed it. She *had* done more than grab the bottle of sake. "Get out of my way." He moved to push past the newcomer, but the man-crea-ture-thing grabbed his arm, and Saizou was astounded at the amount of pressure applied. He staggered at the unexpected, crushing pain.

"If there was no panic," the thing continued, its unblinking gaze still focused on the bartender whose name was apparently Honey, "then why did you push it? It is called a panic button because it is intended for times of panic, not mild concern."

"Seiko," said Honey, twisting the bottle around on the counter, "when have you ever known me to panic?"

"Never, and that is why your decision to install a panic button still confuses me."

"All right, then we'll change the name and call it a *mild concern* button. Does that help?"

"It does make more sense, yes," said Seiko, its gaze still unblinking, boring into Saizou.

Saizou had had enough. In a fast, fluid motion, he drew his wakizashi and pressed the blade against Seiko's side. "Let go."

"Honey?" asked Seiko calmly, its grip still casually crushing Saizou's upper arm.

Saizou sliced into Seiko's torso. The cut felt bizarre, like stabbing a soccer ball. No blood leaked through the gash.

Honey sucked in a deep breath and snapped, "Hey! I'm

gonna have to repair that! Do you know how hard it is to find quality synthetic skin around here?"

Seiko turned his head farther than anything humanoid should be able to and gazed down at the cut across its lower back. "Not much damage. It will take less than two hours of repair work."

"Yeah, but it's two hours I didn't plan on spending with you."

"I'm sorry," said Seiko pleasantly. "What should I do with this man?" It indicated Saizou with his free hand.

"I think he has a friend bleeding out in the bathroom," said Honey, leaning her elbows on the counter. "I guess I'll go help, so you can guard the door."

"I always guard the door," said Seiko. It blinked finally, and Saizou felt strangely relieved even as he re-sheathed the wakizashi. It had been a stupid idea to use it in the first place. "It's my job."

"I don't mean guard it like a bouncer. I mean guard it like someone who's preventing the Shinsengumi from getting in. Keep people from coming in instead of throwing them out."

Seiko's expression remained perfectly blank, but the thing tilted its head as if curious before releasing Saizou's arm. "Yes, Honey."

"Thanks." Honey hopped over the bar with a small metallic box in her left hand. "Come on, guy," she said, gesturing with her free hand.

Saizou took a deep breath and strode next to Honey toward the bathroom. The door was still shut, thank God. Shi had not moved; he was slumped to the side, and blood had completely soaked through the sleeve tied around his shoulder.

Saizou locked the door behind them and knelt by Shi,

smacking his friend's face lightly. The only response was for Shi's head to slide a few inches farther down the wall.

"How long ago did this happen?" asked Honey, tossing her head to flick her long blue ponytail over her shoulder and out of the way. She opened the metal box, revealing a mess of first aid supplies crammed into the small space.

"Not long. Twenty minutes."

"It looks like an animal attack, but an animal attack in the city doesn't make much sense."

Saizou glanced quickly from Honey's hands, rapidly removing items from the box, to Shi's face. "If the bleeding isn't stopped, he's going to die."

"Yeah, I can see that," said Honey. "Is he strong?"

"Very."

"Cool. He's got a good shot. So," she continued, pulling something that looked like a staple-gun from the box, "you must've really ticked the Prince-Regent off."

"I don't know what you mean," said Saizou tersely.

"Pffft. Please. This had to be the Prince-Regent's Dog, right? Explains why you're hiding in a bathroom instead of going to a hospital, too." She untied the sleeve from around Shi's shoulder and grimaced. "Nice."

When Saizou did not answer, she continued. "I saw him once, the Dog. He was outside the palace with some of the Prince-Regent's wannabe samurai guards. I guess they must have been looking for something. I feel bad for him, you know? Like, the guy was probably a normal little kid and now he's that."

Saizou remembered the look of pure, feral hatred on the Dog's face and shook his head. Reducing a human to that exis-tence...it left a bad taste in his mouth, even if he didn't exactly feel bad. He couldn't, not when the Dog had torn up Shi like this.

"I'm going to dissolve something in the wound, but don't let it bother you." Honey picked a small plastic case out of the box and unscrewed the lid, tapping a white pill into her hand. "It's going to disinfect the area."

"Bartender and doctor," remarked Saizou, glancing at the locked door. "Just hurry up."

"Definitely not a doctor, I just pick up some things. Sometimes people come through the bar with no money, so they haggle a drink out of me and I haggle interesting things out of them. This whole first aid kit came from a guy who wanted more alcohol than he could afford." Honey made a *blech* noise before placing the pill in the center of the crater made in Shi's shoulder.

The pill began to fizz, like Alka-Seltzer dropped in a glass of water. Shi's eyes did not open but his shoulder twitched, then his entire torso spasmed with the sensation. Saizou crouched down and pushed against Shi's chest, keeping him upright.

Honey clicked her tongue. "Sorry. That's probably normal. At least it looks like it's working."

Saizou gave her a sharp look.

"I'd never used it before," she told him, glaring defensively. "But hey, look. It also slowed the bleeding down. Don't give me that sour face."

"How is a pill supposed to stop the bleeding?" Saizou demanded, pushing his weight against Shi, who continued to convulse as the pill dissolved.

"Cayenne pepper. Super helpful that way. Even stops internal bleeding if you swallow it."

*Cayenne pepper?* No wonder Shi's body was reacting so

strongly; even a person's subconscious would have to react to a pain that intense. He was glad Shi was not awake to have the full experience.

Something beeped, and Honey reached into a pocket hidden in her patchwork cargo pants. She withdrew a small electronic device with a flashing blue light. It seemed to consist solely of that light and one button, which she pushed and said, "Yeah, Seiko?"

"The Shinsengumi are here," said the odd neutral voice. "They are demanding I let them in."

"Send the goons away."

"It is not a goon, it appears to be their commander."

"Haka?" said Saizou, stiffening. Shi's convulsions had subsided, and he was now limp again, his breathing shallow but steady.

"That's the one," said Honey with a sigh. "He's harder to deal with than the rest of them." She pushed the button again. "Keep them at bay, but try not to be suspicious."

"I think," said Seiko, "that might be impossible. Commander Haka is always suspicious. Do you want me to try and alleviate the suspicions he already has?"

Honey grinned. "Give it your best shot. I'll be out as soon as I finish with these guys."

Honey put the device back into her pocket and looked at Saizou. "I'll give you some extra supplies, but I can't finish this. Do you have somewhere safe to go?"

"We'll find somewhere," said Saizou. "Just because I let you take care of his wound doesn't mean I trust you."

"Fair enough." She closed the lid of the first aid kit and handed it to Saizou. "Take this. I can get another one. Seiko and I will try to keep the Shinsengumi off your tail for as long as we can, but Haka's sharper than he looks and he thinks better than he talks. He might be high on stardust, but honestly, I think that actually helps him do his job."

"I'll remember that," said Saizou. *Stardust.* That must the cause of Haka's unnaturally pale eyes and bad balance. He had never heard of the drug, but he tucked the mental note away.

Honey stood up. "The back door is around the other side of the bar; you'll see the sign. Once you're outside the bar, you're not my problem, okay?"

"Fine." Saizou took the box and tucked it into his sword belt. Why she was helping, he had no idea. Her reasons were her reasons, and he was in a hurry. He grabbed Shi under his arms and hauled him to his feet, propping him up against the wall.

Honey turned away from the door. "You got him?"

"I've got him."

Honey slipped out the door, and Saizou followed, struggling to keep Shi upright. He caught a glimpse of the bar's front door as he moved behind the bar, saw a flash of pale eyes and lank black hair and Seiko's back barring the way.

He saw the sign pointing toward the back door and uttered a quick prayer, *keep the Shinsengumi at the front door and not around the back,* before pushing the door open with his shoulder, tightening his grip around Shi's chest and pulling him through the space back into the cold winter air.

Just before the door groaned shut behind him, he heard Haka shout something unintelligible, and the sound of chaos. The Shinsengumi were in the bar.

Haka's voice came again, screaming this time. "OUT THE BACK! LOOK OUT THE BACK, NOW! GO!"

# EIGHT

THERE WERE no Shinsengumi standing outside the front of the bar; they had all poured inside and Saizou could only hope they didn't notice him through the filmy windows. He dragged Shi over to the first motorcycle and took the key out of his pocket, half-expecting the bike to come alive on its own. It remained still, waiting for him as he hoisted Shi up in front of him and wrapped an arm around his stomach to keep him from falling over.

He took off, spinning the motorcycle back around the way they had come and roaring away at a speed too fast for the narrow streets. Rain drizzled from the sky, and the bike tires spun fresh mud, turning the broken pavement into a slippery obstacle course. Saizou held on tightly to Shi and did not look back, sure he would see the entire Shinsengumi task force on his tail.

His decision not to look back faded at the sound of an engine growling, louder than his, and he risked a brief glance over his shoulder.

The vehicle chasing him was neither a car nor a motorcycle

but some cross between the two, a long machine with four wide wheels set close together and only one seat in which sat Haka. The wind whipped around his vicious face, and Saizou faced forward again, determined to lose him.

Shi lifted his head, shaking it a little, and then every muscle in his body stiffened. Saizou glanced at the back of Shi's head and said in a loud voice, "Hang on!"

"To what? You should have put me on the back!"

"I couldn't hang on to you that way! Grab onto something," Saizou shouted, wrenching the motorcycle to the left. The bike swerved dangerously, tires skidding, but righted itself as Saizou sped down the side street.

The Shinsengumi were all over Tokyo, as were security cameras and scanners and informants. Outside the city limits would be safer—at least there he could find somewhere to rest and take care of Shi before they decided their next move.

The drizzle hardened into a heavy rain, and Saizou blinked rapidly, trying to clear the water from his eyes. He heard the roar of Haka's engine and hissed under his breath, *"If you don't want us caught, God, then get him in a wreck."*

It was not the most Christian prayer he had ever prayed, but he meant it with every fiber of his being. Shi gripped the smooth metal of the handlebars, keeping out of Saizou's way, and bent forward, keeping his head down.

Saizou made a sharp right and used the opportunity to glance back at Haka one more time. The vehicle was still following, half on the sidewalk, half off it. It crushed carts and boxes in its path and sent people running, but Haka hardly seemed to notice. His pale eyes were wide, his white teeth flashing in a wicked grin. He was a speed-demon with an order out for Saizou's arrest.

Saizou gazed down the street in front of them. It ended in a few thousand feet, intersecting with a busy street, and he clenched his jaw. A busy street would make things infinitely more difficult—but, he realized, it would make things even more difficult for Haka. His vehicle was wider and larger, less agile.

With a small smile, Saizou charged into traffic, the stream of cars having stopped for a blinking red light. He wove in and out of the idling vehicles, ignoring the cries and stares of passengers who shouted, "Hey! What do you think you're doing?" or "Get off the road, crazy bastard!"

"They're calling you names," said Shi, just loudly enough for Saizou to hear him.

"I've heard worse."

"Green light!" barked Shi, and Saizou glanced up at the traffic light. The cars around him began to move again, picking up speed and attempting to part around Saizou, mingling lanes and honking angry horns trying to get him out of the way.

"Get out of the city, Saizou," said Shi, with a loopy laugh. "You're dangerous."

"And you're still out of it. Hang on tight and shut up."

Saizou turned left again, off the main road—beyond the buildings were trees, and beyond the trees were mountains. The mountains were a better, safer bet than the city.

He glanced into the right rearview mirror. Haka was no longer there, no doubt caught in the flow of traffic somewhere behind him. Saizou caught a flash of something bright cardinal-red on the rooftop to the left, but it disappeared in the same moment he glanced up.

Saizou made several quick turns in succession, winding through thin streets and alleys, attempting to avoid as much traffic and as many cameras as possible until he reached the city limits. He would not use any highways; he would take a dirt path, if he could find it—anywhere that wasn't monitored. He was good at sneaking. At hiding. Ambushing.

No doubt the Prince-Regent would throw a dragnet over the city and surround the perimeter if he hadn't already, but Saizou couldn't think about that now. If they ran into more Shinsengumi, then they ran into more Shinsengumi, and he would deal with them.

———

HAKA SLAMMED both fists down onto the dashboard of his seikoju.

He was going to kill somebody—no. Not somebody. He was going to hunt those samurai down and kill them, specifically. The first time, he had let them off with a warning. Now he was thrilled to have a warrant out for their arrest. Arrests could get violent. Deadly, even.

Haka backed his vehicle up, forcing pedestrians out of the way. The painful clarity inside his skull was beginning to cloud, and with the cloudiness came the beginnings of a headache. Still, it would be a few more hours before the effects of the stardust had completely worn off. His vision was beginning to grow less sharp, the colors to fade in brightness and intensity.

It would last until his shift ended, not that his shift ever truly ended. And now with these two samurai on the loose—

He lifted his hand to his mouth. His wrist was encircled with a standard-issue Shinsengumi walkie-talkie, a simple two-way affair with a range of up to ten miles. Into the speaker, he said, "They're heading out of the city. I want drones up and ready to fly by tonight."

"Sir, we only have two in the Greater Tokyo Area, the rest are—"

"I don't care," Haka snapped, waving a woman out of the way with his hand. These people and their carelessness—honestly, if he ran into someone, it wasn't even his fault. "Pull the drones from Chiyoda and Shinagawa. Have them ready by nine o'clock."

"Yes, sir!"

Haka gripped the handlebars again, cursing under his breath with every word he knew. The Prince-Regent was furious but refused to say why. Haka's only instructions were to catch Saizou Akita and Shi Matsumoto and to use any means necessary.

And he had lost them, thanks to a crowded street.

*Shimatta.*

He drove back to the station, his blood boiling and his head pounding. Of all things, of all people—two washed-up war veterans. This headache was their fault; maybe it had nothing to do with stardust. It was them. All them.

Haka swore again and parked the *Seikoju* on the street in front of the office. He noticed all other vehicles were gone; no doubt they were currently being used in a manhunt for the so-called 'Lord' Akita and his crony.

He shoved the doors open and strode inside. Not only was his head killing him, so was his back. It was always something; something pushing him just to the edge of what he could take without screaming at everyone.

Haka tried to restrict screaming to only the most urgent of circumstances. If you took to screaming every command or request, people would eventually stop listening to you. The quieter you were, the more people listened to you, which was very backwards, he thought, but unfortunately, it was the way it was.

*Oh, gods, I need another shot.*

He threw open the door to his office and crossed the room, pulling out the chair, but before he could sit down, the restricted telephone line on his desk rang like a strangled bird. He wanted to let it ring until it stopped, but that would push the limits of his luck. They were strained enough as it was. He lifted the phone off the hook at the first ring and put it to his ear.

"Commander Haka," he said, without bothering to list the office or precinct. Very few people could get ahold of this line, and they all worked for the Prince-Regent.

"Have you caught them yet?"

He recognized the monotone, robotic voice on the other end. Kirikizu, the Prince-Regent's killer-slash-thief, among possible other things.

Rumors abounded.

Haka smiled tensely. "We'll have them caught in forty-eight hours. The drones have been pulled from Shinigawa and Chiyoda and will be ready—"

"Just because the Prince-Regent has given you forty-eight hours does not mean you should test his generosity. He would prefer Lord Akita and Shi Matsumoto to be caught before then."

Haka rolled his eyes. "Yes, well," he began, but cut himself off. "Of course. The Prince-Regent should see them both in prison before tomorrow evening."

"Don't roll your eyes," said Kirikizu in flat tones.

Haka pulled the telephone away from his ear to give it a startled look before putting it back. "I would never do such a thing. Also, how did you know I did?"

"I heard it," said the assassin and hung up, a click signaling the end of the call.

Haka slammed the phone back down on the receiver and leaned back in his chair. He blinked rapidly, clearing his swimming vision. The Prince-Regent would have what he wanted, and if not, Haka would personally feel the consequences.

He lifted his walkie-talkie to his mouth. "This is Commander Haka. Collect five blood samples from the bathroom at that bar and bring them to the station."

"Yes, sir," a voice crackled in response.

Haka pushed his chair back and hurried out of his office, heading toward the underground level. He typed in the password for the door and pulled it open as soon as it beeped. As he descended the stairs, he called, "Otter! Get the mutts ready for a manhunt."

# NINE

THE BRIDGE WAS OUT.

Saizou rested his feet on the ground and leaned back on the motorcycle seat, studying the damage. A tree had fallen over at some recent point, smashing the middle of the bridge to splinters. The break was roughly six feet wide, from what Saizou could tell—too wide a gap to drive over, even if he gained momentum. If the motorcycle fell through, it would plummet roughly eighty feet below and be dashed to pieces against the moss-covered boulders below.

Saizou nudged Shi's ribs. "You awake?"

"Yes, I'm awake," snapped Shi—or rather, he attempted to snap, but he lacked the energy to make it sound really convincing.

Saizou gave the back of Shi's head a concerned look and dismounted the motorcycle. "I'm going to have a look. Stay here."

"You drove us up a mountain to a broken bridge." Shi slumped over the handlebars, resting his forehead on his arms.

"You don't last five seconds without me. I can't even pass out around you."

Saizou ignored him and approached the bridge. It was quiet here, a few miles up the mountain. Even the trees seemed to be watching, leaning down and anticipating his every move. A branch snapped somewhere, and overhead a flock of birds fussed in the branches with dozens of high, clamoring cries.

Saizou stepped out carefully onto the bridge and peered over the side. He had miscalculated the depth of the chasm below—eighty feet was too shallow. It was closer to a hundred. *Perfect.*

He turned around and headed back to Shi, who had not moved. "We'll have to go back and find another route."

"How big is the gap?" mumbled Shi, without lifting his head.

"A little over four feet."

"We can jump it." Shi tilted his head, his cheek still resting on his arm, but one eye visible.

"You can't even walk. I wouldn't fantasize about clearing a four-foot gap just now," Saizou pointed out.

"You could probably make it. Or for heaven's sake, just get some wood and fix the gap temporarily."

Overhead, the flock of birds suddenly flew out of the trees, chattering excitedly until the sound faded and they were gone.

Saizou turned around with a sudden uncomfortable feeling brushing along the back of his neck.

A man stood on the other side of the broken bridge. Saizou could not make out the expression he wore, but his stance was still and observing, his head lowered. With his long white coat swaying in the breeze, he reminded Saizou of a heron standing in the shallows, waiting for a fish to swim near.

Saizou said nothing, and the moment of silence stretched

thin before the other man asked, "Do you need help?" He raised his voice to be heard, but he did not shout. Saizou had the distinct impression the man would like Saizou to say no, they didn't need help and could make it just fine.

"Just say yes," said Shi, lifting his head a few inches. "I don't much care about your pride or mine at the moment."

Saizou called, "Who are you to ask?"

Shi groaned and rested his head on his arms again.

"If you do not need help, say so."

He could not exactly say that. "My friend is injured."

The man strode closer, reaching the break on the other side of the bridge. "How badly?"

"He needs taken care of," Saizou retorted, wondering what this stranger's game was. "What more do you need to know?"

The man stood for another long moment, so still he could have been a lifelike sculpture. Then he said, "I will help you cross the bridge, but you will have to take care of the motorcycle yourself. You can take care of your friend at my place."

"Your place?" Saizou rubbed the fingers of his right hand together, grounding himself. He was too twitchy and he knew it, but he had no idea if this was the appropriate time or not. This man might simply want to help, like the bartender, or he might be waiting to kill them. "Where is it?"

The newcomer jerked his head slightly back up the steep path behind him. "Not far."

Saizou heard a thump behind him and turned to see that Shi had slid off the motorcycle onto the ground. His eyes were open, but he blinked once, slowly, and they drifted shut. Saizou jogged over and lifted him off the ground, shaking his uninjured shoulder. "Hey, Shi. Wake up."

The stranger spoke again, his strong voice carrying across the distance. "Make up your mind."

Saizou stared down at Shi and took a deep breath. "Fine." He turned and strode back to the bridge. "Do you know how much weight the bridge can hold?"

"Not much, toward the break," said the stranger. "Just pass your friend over carefully. When you want to cross, you can simply jump."

The thought of physically handing Shi over to someone Saizou didn't know was an odd one, but he shook his head once and stepped gingerly across the bridge toward the demolished center. "Careful with him," he instructed, careful to spread his weight as evenly as possible as he approached the break.

"Don't worry," said the stranger dryly. "I won't drop him."

Saizou leaned as far forward as he felt he safely could, and the stranger reached out, grabbing Shi's torso as it slumped forward. Quickly, he pulled Shi back away from the edge and half-dragged him back to where the path met the beginning of the bridge.

Then he set him down and regarded Saizou with a narrow look on his sharp face. "I'll take him back," he said after a few long seconds, and hoisted Shi over his shoulder. "Hide the motorcycle. Don't want anyone seeing it, even though I'm sure you left clear tracks. Get rid of those, if you can." He turned around and began to walk away, up the steep path.

Saizou stepped forward, torn between covering his tracks and leaving his unconscious friend with a stranger. "Where do I find him when I'm done?"

"At the monastery," said the stranger, without bothering to glance back at Saizou. "Not far up ahead."

*Monastery?* "You're a monk?"

Now the man turned around again, bent slightly over with the weight of Shi, but not as far as Saizou would have expected. Whoever this man was, he was not weak, and he had carried people over his shoulders before. Saizou had seen inexperienced men attempting to help others and simultaneously being detrimental to their own efforts. *A soldier?*

"Winter," the stranger said finally, a hint of annoyance in his voice. "You can call me that. Hurry, hide the bike." Then he continued on his way, trudging around a curve and disappearing behind a thick stand of bamboo trees.

Saizou hid the motorcycle well. He considered letting it drive over the cliff into the rocks below, but when he and Shi left, they would probably need to move faster than they could on foot. He drove it half a mile back down the mountain and into the woods, where the trees were not thin bamboo but thick and large, with plenty of leaves already padding the forest floor and more yet to fall.

He laid the motorcycle on its side on the far side of the largest tree and buried it underneath a large pile of leaves, then gathered several long branches with leavers still clinging to them. He pulled the branches behind him as he walked back up the path, dusting the distinctive motorcycle tracks away as thoroughly as he could. It seemed futile, considering anyone with half a brain would know the motorcycle had not simply vanished, and therefore, if anyone was looking, they would continue up the path. Still, even a half-measure was better than no measure.

He reached the bridge, tossed the branches over the side, and ran for the break, clearing the gaping space in a running leap. The wood creaked beneath him as he landed on the other side with only a few inches to spare, and he jogged quickly across, just in case.

The bridge held, and he gave it one last look before hurrying up the mountain path.

———

TECHNICALLY, the underground level of the Shinsengumi station was a basement—or it had been, back when it was still part of an apartment complex. It had been converted years ago and now functioned as both a dungeon and a kennel. A dungeon for prisoners, although prisoners were rare and elusive things these days as the Prince-Regent preferred to have suspects and variables removed before they caused problems. One the right side of the dungeon were three cells, all currently empty. On the left side, farther down the hall, were the cages. They were not much different than the cells; all were square and roomy, with a drain in the center for when things got messy. The only real difference were the occupants.

Those cages held the mutant animals created to the Prince-Regent's requested specifications. Large, hulking beasts with grotesque muscles, twisted features, and six legs for maximum strength and speed: some with switch-like tails, some with three or four eyes, and all disgusting, in Haka's personal opinion.

They were dangerous, too, of course, ruled by the growl in their stomachs more than the brains in their thick skulls, and it took someone with a special touch to oversee them, much less control them. Haka knew of only one person who had the ability to make them listen, and by all appearances, she was unlikely.

"Otter," Haka bellowed, reaching the bottom of the stairs. "Otter!"

"Shhh!" The fierce hiss reached him from a distance. "Lower your voice, for crying out loud! No, wait, crying out loud cancels the whole 'lower your voice' thing. I'm in Violet's cell."

She knew damn well he didn't know their names. In a loud whisper, he asked, "And that cell is?"

"The last one, Commander," the loud whisper replied, with an added "Geez."

Haka frowned and walked down the hall, keeping as far away from the cages as he could. Mutts watched him with snarling mouths and claws scraping across the stone, sending chills darting up and down his spine.

*Violet.* What in the hells made the girl think naming a monster *Violet* was fitting? Otter was a crazy little monster herself. Haka found himself across from the last cage and walked over, staying a good three feet away from the door. The iron bars were as thick as his forearm, and the beast inside was kept chained to the wall at all times when it wasn't set with trackers and electric collars to keep it in check. Strangely, the measures did nothing to lessen his apprehension.

He moved his fingers through the air, as if playing an invisible piano. "Otttterrrr," he sang softly, watching the darkness between the bars. "Where are you?"

"In the cage," the girl whispered, still invisible to his naked eyes. There was a chance he could have seen her if his stardust high was still going strong. As it was, his eyes had probably returned to their normal deep brown, and his eyesight had returned to normal along with them. "I'll be out in one second. Don't raise your voice."

"Why not?" Haka hissed in annoyance.

"You make them jittery, Commander. How many times do I have to tell you that?"

A large black shape moved within the shadows, and three gleaming lights blinked and disappeared again. Haka backed instinctively another foot, every nerve on edge. How he hated it down here in the dark, with the monsters.

He felt a tremor in his right hand and squeezed it into a fist. *Stardust. I need more stardust. Curse the Prince-Regent and his stupid boy toy.*

Otter's silhouette appeared on the other side of the door, and Haka tensed as the girl opened it and quickly slipped through, shutting it behind her and locking it with a hefty iron key.

Haka eyed the key. "We should update to electronic locking mechanisms."

"No," said Otter, shaking her head. "If we get a power outage or something, they could get out. If that happened, they'd probably eat half the Greater Tokyo Area, and then they would get indigestion."

"Oh," said Haka. At least Otter was a sensible kind of crazy.

"What did you want?" she asked, tucking the key into her belt. Each cell had a different key, and she wore all eight of them in a row. Haka guessed they must weigh two pounds or so altogether.

"Hey," said Otter, snapping her fingers. She looked up at him, watching closely with large, keen eyes in a face that looked much closer to fifteen or sixteen than her actual age, which was...somewhere around twenty. Haka had a habit of forgetting unimportant details.

He leaned back and knocked her hand away, although it was farther away than he had thought and she had to mimic his leaning back to avoid getting hit in the face. "I need the mutts prepared and sent out as soon as possible."

Otter scratched the bridge of her nose and sighed. "Why?"

"Because I ordered it."

She continued to stare at him until he said, "Orders from the Prince-Regent. Two fugitives need found."

She ran her hands through her short-cropped hair and clicked her tongue. "Fine. Do you have something for them to smell?"

"One of the fugitives is injured," said Haka. "I ordered blood samples. I assume," he added archly, "that should be good enough."

"Blood samples? That might be a little too good, even." She grinned, but when Haka did not respond, she cleared her throat and said with exaggerated solemnity, "Yessir, Commander. Does 'as soon as possible' mean—"

"As soon as possible," Haka interrupted. He put up with Otter's idiosyncrasies and disrespectful attitude, although in truth, he was almost afraid that if he didn't, she would sic the mutts on him. "As soon as the blood samples are in and you..." He took a breath and nodded toward the row of cages. "Do whatever you do to get them ready."

"You could stay and watch," Otter offered.

Haka gave her a sharp look, noted the mischievous glint in her eyes, and leaned down until his face was just inches away from hers. "Don't push me."

She watched him for a long moment, unblinking, before lifting a finger and pressing it against his chest. Then she pushed, and just as quickly tucked her hands behind her back. "Never again, Commander."

Haka straightened and narrowed his eyes, but before he could give her a stinging reply, a bolt of knife-sharp pain cut through his skull and stole his vision. The ground rose up to meet him as he collapsed to his knees with a sound between a growl and a shriek, and he dug the heels of his hands into his forehead, cursing everything he knew. *Stardust,* he thought in fractured pieces. It was not a clear thought so much as a driving need. *Stardust. I need it.*

"Commander?"

He heard Otter's voice, broken into shards by the hammer in his head, and he reached out, pushing her away as soon as his hand came into contact with her shoulder.

A chorus of inhuman voices rose around him, snarling, barking, howling, and he screamed back at them, at himself, at Otter.

The noise was the last thing he remembered.

# TEN

"*SHIMATTA!*" the man at the table swore. He leaned back, rubbing a thick hand over his bald, tattooed head.

Tsuki leaned across the table, pulling her winnings toward her. She knew better than to make any kind of glib remark about winning; these were not safe people, and they were already pissed at her victory.

"I think we should play again," said the third player, a skinny man with several gold teeth. "I can read you now, girlie."

She smiled briefly. "Thank you, but I'm done for the night."

He grinned, teeth twinkling in the florescent light. "Not even a private game? Just the two of us?"

The tattooed man narrowed his eyes. "You'd better go home to your mommy, *Gabyoo*. If anyone's going to show this lady a private game, it's me."

"I don't think she likes you."

Tsuki stood up. "I really do have to go, but I'm here fairly frequently if you ever feel like playing again."

Kiba sighed and folded his arms across his chest. He often went unnoticed, standing in the corner and half-obscured by the haze of cigarette smoke that filled the room with the smell of burnt paper. If Tsuki had her way, he wouldn't be at the gambling pit; he would be covering for her back at Akita Domain—which, he supposed, would soon be renamed Shigure domain.

It was a suggestion she had given up mentioning three years ago, directly after she began her streak as a hustler. "Hustling isn't hustling if it's for a good cause," she had told him. The 'good cause' truly *was* good, mainly the feeding of starving peasants who slaved in the gold mines. They were better taken care of than most domain serfs, but that did not amount to much these days.

Kiba knew full well that half the reason Tsuki won these games was because she distracted her opponents, the vast majority of whom were unintelligent men and therefore susceptible to the wiles of a beautiful woman.

He occasionally suggested that she rein herself in a little more, and usually, she ignored him. Tonight, at least, she seemed to be taking his advice to heart.

Being her protection might not always seem rewarding to anyone looking in, but from his perspective, it was more than enough.

Tsuki pushed her chair back with the toe of her boot and stood up. "I hope I see you again next week," she told the players, and crossed quickly over to Kiba's corner. "Another win," she said, presenting the money with a smile. "Congratulate me."

"I'd feel more congratulatory if I was surprised," he replied, watching the two men at the table. They were glaring at each other like wild animals arguing over a fresh kill, and it amused him. "As it is, routine doesn't surprise me."

"Heavens, Kiba." She clicked her tongue. "What's the matter? Are you bored?"

"Boredom would be a nice change."

Tsuki began to tuck the money into his belt. She preferred not to carry it herself—she had the good sense to know that an attractive young woman carrying obvious money was a tempting target, particularly in less-savory parts of Tokyo at night. "Keep this safe for me."

"Don't I always?"

She gave him a skeptical squint. "Just because you're my bodyguard doesn't mean you need to become the stereotype, you know. You could loosen up. It wouldn't kill you."

"No," he agreed, "but it might kill you."

She looked like she might argue, but to his relief, she thought better of it. "All right," she said after a moment. "It's time to leave."

"I think it is," Kiba agreed, noticing Tattoos and Teeth watching Tsuki closely from the table. They were standing now, and Teeth was shuffling the cards back and forth in his hands as he leered in Tsuki's direction. Tattoo was scowling at Kiba, like he had just noticed him and was sizing up supposed competition. Kiba was often mistaken for Tsuki's lover or husband, which usually suited the situation just fine. This probably wasn't one of those cases.

Tsuki saw the look on his face and asked in a low voice, "Do you think they'll be trouble?"

"I think everyone can be trouble."

"I revise my earlier statement about you needing to loosen up, but you could develop a better sense of fun."

"You worry about my sense of fun," he said flatly. "I'll worry about keeping you alive so you can indulge in the same behavior again until you face the consequences."

"I never have to face my consequences," she said lightly. "That's your job."

Kiba frowned, even though he knew she was joking. "You aren't funny."

"I'm a little funny."

"About as funny as your two new boyfriends. Let's go." He gave Tattoos and Teeth one more glance before following Tsuki out of the small room and shutting the door firmly behind him. They made their way out of the den to the alley where their motorcycle was waiting.

Tsuki waited for Kiba to mount up before she sat down behind him, wrapping her arms around his waist. "Do you think..." she began, then stopped.

He turned his head. "Do I think what?"

"They'll be fine, won't they?" she asked finally. "Saizou and his friend."

"If you thought they would be fine, you wouldn't be asking me."

She made a small humming noise. "I'm allowed to worry about them," she said after a second. "Saizou means a lot to me, even if I can't...I can't act how I want around him. And now he's gotten himself outlawed, not that I'm surprised, and it's..."

"He and his friend survived five years of war," said Kiba, turning the motorcycle and riding out of the alley onto the vacant street. "I'm sure they can handle themselves. Your main concern should be Matahachi."

Tsuki was quiet for a few minutes. "I don't say this as often as I should," she began, but Kiba interrupted her.

"It's my job," he said. "Nothing more."

A lie to himself, and a lie to her.

And if she knew it was a lie, she said nothing; only held on tighter and stayed quiet.

———————

OTTER STOOD BY THE COT, her arms folded over her chest as she watched Commander Haka sleep. It was probably a creepy thing to do, but the station was empty and leaving him alone felt like a bad idea.

She sighed and dropped to a crouch a few feet away. Loudly, she whispered, "Commander? Commander, can you hear me?"

His eyes remained shut. She poked him in the arm. Not even a twitch.

Otter scratched her hands vigorously through her hair in frustration. "Idiot," she said daringly. She was certain he had really passed out in the dungeon, but whether or not he had awoken and was testing her—well, that was different. He was unpredictable in what he chose to do, which also made him interesting. At least in her opinion. "You're a lanky, wasted, strung-out idiot who needs to eat more and shower once in a while, because you look like a glassy-eyed hobo."

His only response was to part his lips slightly and release a quiet, strangled breath. Otter frowned and straightened. He wasn't faking it. "You need to stop doing this. It's unhealthy. Plus, it looks bad." She reached out and felt his forehead with the back of her hand. His skin was clammy and cold. "You feel like you've been stuck in a freezer and I had to thaw you out."

She looked down at his left arm, which was hanging over the edge of the cot, and gingerly lifted it up, folding it across his stomach. "I'm not your nanny. You're a grown man, drugs or no drugs."

She licked her lips and put her hands in her pockets, gazing down at his face. He had such an elegant face—or it would be elegant, if it wasn't quite so gaunt and pale all the time. The main effect of stardust, she knew, was the deadening of fear. It made people bold to the point of stupidity, and he took more of it than anybody she'd ever met.

"What are you so afraid of?" she asked softly. His eyes roamed under closed lids, and he turned his head to the side, grimacing at something in his sleep. "You're going to kill yourself, and it won't be my fault. In fact, I'll come to your funeral and say I told you so—no, I'll compose an entire song called "I Told You So." The lyrics will consist entirely of me singing 'I told you so.'"

"No." Haka's moan was quiet, his eyes still shut. It was not directed at her, but Otter jumped at the sudden sound.

"No what?" she whispered.

He groaned "No" one more time and then fell silent again, as still as a corpse. Otter placed her hand over his mouth and waited until she felt breath, warm and faint, against her palm.

"One day," she said softly, swallowing hard, "you're going to fall down and you're never going to get back up."

# ELEVEN

SAIZOU NEARLY WALKED past the staircase. The mountainside had been carved away around weathered stone steps, twisting up and away on the left of the trail. He glanced ahead and shook his head once. If the stone steps were wrong, he would go back.

Bamboo grew close, encroaching on either side of the steps as he jogged up them. Now and then he glanced over his shoulder and to either side, unnerved by the quiet around him. After a moment, he saw the remnants of a statue. He had no idea who it had once been; the stone was blackened and covered with moss, half of it crumbled into pieces on the ground.

Saizou turned in a circle and realized he was in what might have once been a courtyard. More stone was visible through the tangled grass and shrubbery, and up ahead, he saw two pillars holding up a building, the shape of which was hard to make out beneath the overgrown trees and moss that obscured any details.

He reached back for his katana, but his hand swept

through empty air. With a muffled groan, he remembered that his sword had been left at the Palace of the Sun. He drew his wakizashi instead and crossed the courtyard. The front doors of the eerie building seemed intact, and the rice-paper covering the wooden frame was in good condition, if a bit faded.

As he reached the third step, the front doors slid open and Winter stood there, giving Saizou an expression that was less than welcoming. He stepped aside and gestured half-heartedly with a hand; his only welcome was, "I'll take you to your friend. And you don't need the sword."

"That's what everyone seems to think," said Saizou. His words had more of a bite than he intended, and he said hastily, "It's been a long few days." He bowed, even though the other man was facing the opposite direction. "Please forgive me."

Winter turned around again and sighed through his nose, looking Saizou up and down with a critical, unpleasant expression. His face reminded Saizou of a hawk or a lizard, not unhandsome, but sharp. He had the look of a man who had seen a lot of the world and didn't much care for it.

"Your tongue is yours, to form your own words, and I don't care what those words are," said Winter finally, "as long as they are minimal and don't waste my time."

Saizou squinted, trying to feel out an appropriate response to the other man's statement. "So...an apology is a waste of time?"

"Yes," said Winter. "You can stay on the steps all day, or you can come inside, but choose."

"So you're the kind of person who likes company, then," said Saizou, hurrying up the rest of the steps and striding inside.

"No," said Winter, closing the doors behind him.

Saizou cleared his throat. The situation could hardly get more awkward so he only said, "That...I was—"

"Being sarcastic," said Winter flatly. "I assume. Follow me."

Saizou rolled his eyes and turned on his heel to follow the man, whose long strides led him from the plain foyer down a thin hall. He made barely a sound on the smooth wooden floor. Dim light glowed through the rice-paper walls, but Saizou saw no shapes or silhouettes to indicate that anyone else was living here.

"What is this place?" he asked. "It doesn't look like a monastery."

Winter did not stop or look back. "Why are you whispering?"

Whispering? "I didn't realize I was."

"It isn't a library, so there's no need to whisper." Winter stopped near the end of the hall and pulled two more doors open. He gestured Saizou into the room with a hand.

The room was empty except for Shi lying on a mat with a blanket across his lower half and a bandage wrapped around his shoulder and across his chest.

"I took care of him," said Winter, "but he'll need rest. I won't bother asking why you didn't go to a hospital."

Saizou began to speak, to come up with a quick explanation, but Winter held up a hand. "I don't want to hear it. You should know you were followed."

Saizou glanced at Shi and lowered his voice, as Shi possessed the rare talent of remembering what his subconscious overheard. "Who? Why didn't you tell me before?"

"There was no point," said Winter. "I don't know who it was. I had never seen them before. You should pay more attention to your surroundings."

"We can't stay there, then," said Saizou immediately, but

before he could walk toward Shi and wake him up, Winter grabbed his arm.

"Your friend is stable, but if you move him, I doubt he'll remain that way."

Saizou narrowed his eyes. "That's what someone would say," he said slowly, "if they wanted to keep us here. For all I know, we weren't followed. Or you're working with whoever did follow us, for a reward or for the law, I don't know. Let go of me. We're leaving."

Winter's mouth twitched below humorless eyes. "You're a suspicious man."

"Suspicious enough to survive. Unhand me."

"Suspicious, but not inherently violent." Winter tilted his head to one side. "If you were, you would have hit me already." In a slightly gentler voice, he repeated, "You were followed. I don't know who followed you. Your friend needs rest. I do not lie. You can mistrust me if you like, but your friend will suffer for it if you do."

He released Saizou's arm and lifted his hand, as if glad to be rid of the contact. "I'm not going to keep you prisoner, however. If you are still here by evening, go through that room." He pointed to the doors at the end of the hall. "The room on the right is the dining room. At least you'll have some dinner."

Stiffly, he turned and strode down the hall the way they had come, the hem of his long coat swirling around his ankles.

Saizou slowly crossed the room and knelt next to Shi. "According to Frostbite over there, I can't move you." He sighed and rubbed his right hand over his face, groaning softly into his palm. He dragged it down and eyed Shi. "I don't know if he's telling the truth, but..." As the words left his mouth, he realized with absolute certainty which was more important to him: Shi's definite safety or Shi's uncertain safety.

There was a possibility Shi could heal and recover here if they remained.

There was a possibility Shi could be injured further if they left the place.

*Your friend will suffer for it.* Winter's warning echoed in Saizou's head.

He stood up. Looking down at Shi again, he said, "I'm going to scout around outside and see if I can find whoever followed us. If someone really did." He reached the doors, but paused when he saw a shadow on the other side.

Quietly, he drew his wakizashi and reached for the door on the right. He flexed his fingers, making sure his grip was not too tight for close-range use, and he flung the door open, stepping forward and putting the blade against the girl's neck.

*The girl?*

Startled, Saizou narrowed his eyes at the girl who stood in front of him. She wore a sweater so thick and large it threatened to drown her, but her red-brown hair and wide eyes were clearly visible. She sank farther into the folds of the sweater, her gaze not on him, but the handle of his sword.

Her skin was as white as her sweater, and in her hands, she clutched a tray set with a wooden box, a towel, and a bowl of water.

From somewhere within the depths of the sweater came a small squeak, and Saizou blinked before pulling the blade away and lowering it. "Who are you?" he demanded.

She said nothing, but her eyes flicked to the room behind him. She lifted the tray, and he noticed the ripples in the bowl of water. He had frightened her so much that her hands were shaking, although she did not drop the tray and run down the hall, which was impressive.

He sheathed his sword, feeling like more of a failure than

he had all week, and reached out to steady the tray. "I'm sorry," he said gently. "I didn't know anyone else was here. I was startled, that's all."

She nodded, one quick movement, like a sparrow, and let him take the tray. She hurried past him into the room and pointed to the floor beside Shi.

Obediently, Saizou set the tray down and straightened again, watching as the girl settled down on her knees and opened the box.

"Are you here to help him?" It seemed obvious, but her lack of speech made him wonder if he quite knew what was happening.

She nodded and began to unwind the bandage around Shi's shoulder with small, nimble hands.

Saizou rubbed his forehead. "Didn't the monk just put that bandage on?"

She lifted a small silver pot the size of a teacup out of the box and removed the lid. It held a thick, clear substance that smelled like a salve.

The girl glanced up at him, and then made a shooing motion toward the door with her hands as if to say, *You were leaving, so go.*

Nothing about the girl whispered *enemy*—not her aura, not her behavior, and certainly not her size. Saizou rubbed his jaw and nodded, reassuring himself before he left the room. He did not close the doors, but he had the feeling Shi was in safe hands.

As he stood outside the room, he closed his eyes and released a deep breath. "Maker-Lord," he prayed, his voice so quiet it was barely audible to his ears, "please heal Shi. Make him be all right. He's had worse than this, so all I ask is that you take care of him." He glanced sideways at the open door once more and added, "Obviously, I can't keep him safe. I don't like to leave it to you, but it seems I don't have much of a choice. So, please, take care of him well." He bowed slightly at the air and hurried down the hall, through the foyer, and back into the frozen air.

It smelled like snow, but nothing fell from the sky. A pale blanket of thick, gray clouds covered the sky, and Saizou took in a breath of sharp, clean air before jogging down the steps. He took his wakizashi in hand, scanning every shadow and corner as he moved through the courtyard.

*I do not lie,* the monk had said, and against his cautious judgement, Saizou believed him. The man had not looked interested enough to bother with lying.

He moved quietly, keeping to the exposed stones instead of the frost-stiffened grass. He stepped around the retaining wall, scanning the trees. When he saw nothing, he continued walking. The farther away he got from the ancient building, the farther away he was from any kind of help or shelter.

Nothing drew an enemy out of their hiding place like making yourself look vulnerable and exposed—even if, Saizou knew, that did not always work quite as planned. He had to appear cautious, but no more cautious than a man double-checking the parameter. He whistled a few strands of an old song under his breath and fell silent again, not wanting to waste his breath. He reached the bottom of the staircase and continued down the winding path toward the shattered bridge.

Who could have followed them? He had been careful, constantly looking over his shoulder, making certain. *Well, you weren't certain enough.* Worry always clouded his judgement—it was his most defining flaw in battle and the reason why he had never made any rank higher than captain, no matter how often he was praised as a leader.

He could hear General Isao's voice in his head as he walked, not harsh, but reprimanding nonetheless. *A leader who cares for his soldiers is a good leader, but a leader who cares more for his soldiers than for victory can only go so far. You will not be promoted until you learn the most unfortunate lesson.*

Saizou had bowed deeply, grinding his teeth until he thought they would turn to powder. *Please tell me the lesson, General.*

He could remember the look on General Isao's face—a sudden sharpening, a fierce light— vicious, with just a hint of regret. *Every victory flag is red.*

Saizou stopped at the beginning of the bridge and looked over his shoulder, casting a sweeping glance across everything he could see. It was the stillness, he realized, that put him on edge. The winter birds were silent, and there were no animal cries in the distance. The only sound was the slight breeze.

He lifted his wakizashi and watched the pale winter light glint off the fine edge. "Come out where I can see you," he said in a loud voice. "To be honest, I'm too tired for hide-and-seek."

A laugh split the air, loud and half-crazed. "That's disappointing," a male voice boomed. "I like games."

A tall figure emerged from the trees across the bridge, his all-black clothing separating from the shadows where he had previously gone unnoticed. The man reached up and pushed his hood back, revealing a shock of wild, neon-red hair.

His face split in a wide, white-toothed grin, and he lifted a hand, motioning with his fingers as if to say, *Come at me.* "Who told you I was here? Was it the monk?"

Saizou regarded him in silence, trying to form an idea of the man's threat level. He was well over six feet—tall for a Japanese man—and very broad-shouldered, but he carried no weapon. He remembered the brief glimpse of red on a rooftop in Tokyo, and he couldn't keep a faint smile away from his mouth.

"You followed us out of Tokyo, didn't you?"

"Yes, I did."

"Any particular reason? Are you a bounty hunter? Strange kind, with no weapons."

The man spread his arms and said, "According to my father, you don't need a weapon if you were born one."

"Size is not necessarily a weapon," Saizou pointed out.

"Speak for yourself," said the stranger, pushing his tongue against the inside of his cheek and winking.

Saizou rubbed his thumb along the bridge of his nose. "Why?" he asked finally. The stranger did not seem unfriendly, but Saizou did not relax the grip on his wakizashi. A relaxed enemy was either confident for no reason, or confident for a good reason.

"Why did I follow you?" The other man rotated his head and shrugged his shoulders, loosening up for something. "You're all over Tokyo, man. Or at least you should be, by now."

*All over...?* "What do you mean?"

"The name's Shotgun, by the way," said the stranger, rubbing a hand through his wild red hair as if it wasn't electrifying enough already. He pointed a finger at Saizou. "To answer your silly question, you're the deposed Lord Akita. The guy who went berserk and killed a bunch of palace guards before escaping, along with your friend in the..." He stopped pointing and waved his hand in front of his face instead saying the word *mask*.

"So you know who I am," said Saizou, pacing slowly back and forth in front of the break in the bridge. "Am I supposed to be impressed?"

"Impressed? You probably should be. Mainly, I just want

you to be curious." The giant stranger leaned forward and grinned again. "Don't you want to know how I came by all that information?"

"I *am* curious," said Saizou. "Curious enough to cut the information out of you if you don't tell me. Stop playing around. I don't care if you like games. I don't."

"Eh, that's disappointing." Shotgun stretched his arms over his head. He seemed incapable of simply standing still, Saizou noticed. He was like a hyperactive child in an overgrown man's body, and Saizou knew full well the damage a hyperactive child could do when left unchecked. "But okay."

Saizou lifted his head and spun his wakizashi absently, waiting. "Well?"

Shotgun stepped forward, but the bridge groaned beneath the weight of his tall frame, and he glanced down. The wood near the break on his side splintered more.

Without thinking, Saizou snapped, "Move back!"

Shotgun jumped back just in time. Six more planks creaked and splintered, falling away from the bridge and crashing down the ravine to the bottom, where the underbrush swallowed them from view.

The gap between them was now nearing ten feet, and Saizou tilted his head back, watching the other man. "Be more careful."

Undaunted, Shotgun pressed a fist into his hand, but it was not a bow. Instead, his knuckles cracked so loudly that Saizou heard them.

"That," said Shotgun, "gave me an idea!"

"Does it involve you telling me what I want to know?" asked Saizou flatly.

Again Shotgun winked. "It will if you win."

"I don't want to fight you."

"I hate to remind you, but a minute ago you were ready to... what was it? Cut the information out of me? I didn't tell you everything I know. I know how much money you withdrew from the bank, what you bought with it, and where both motorcycles are. I also know a fun fact concerning dear Commander Haka and what he's up to, but that's just a bonus. The cherry on top." He pointed to his head and made a clicking sound with his tongue.

Saizou opened his mouth to ask Shotgun how he knew, but he stopped himself. "You want me to fight you?"

"That's about the size of it."

Saizou put his free hand on his hip. "With ten feet between us, I suppose."

"Nah." Shotgun stepped off the path, and Saizou watched as the taller, younger man grabbed a bamboo tree and bent it back, pulling and then pushing it toward the ground. He gave it a final shove, and the tree cracked free of the trunk.

Shotgun then stretched the length of the tree across the break in the bridge until it reached the other side. He slid it a few feet farther for good measure, then proceeded to do the same thing three more times until there was a sizeable—if unsteady—bridge between bridges.

Finally he broke another tree; this one was a sapling, slender and as long as Shotgun was tall. He walked back to the bridge, plucking the leaves away, and set the stick down. Leaning against it, he said, "Here's the idea, but it's not for the faint of heart."

Saizou twisted his mouth, but said nothing, allowing Shotgun to continue. He had waited this long.

"You get yourself a branch," explained Shotgun, gesturing actively with his free hand. "I try to get to your side and you try to get to mine. Whoever makes it without falling to his death wins!"

"You're crazy," said Saizou.

"Sure," said Shotgun, lifting the pole and twirling it over his head like a baton. "Is that a yes?"

*I need to know where he got his information and why he followed us. And if he really has information about Haka's plan...* It was a good thing Shi wasn't here. He would have hated this.

"Let me get a tree," said Saizou, lowering his blade. As he walked off the path, Shotgun's raucous laughter followed him.

# TWELVE

HE WATCHED the Prince-Regent hunch over the desk, holding the phone to his ear. "Do whatever you have to. When you find who it is, bring them to me. I want to look at their face with my own eyes before the week is out. That gives you three days, do you understand? You have one day left to find the samurai and three days to find the criminal making you all look like idiots. Oh, you do understand, do you?"

The Prince-Regent slammed a palm down on the desk. "If you understand me so well, then repeat what I just told you." He paused, listening with an arched eyebrow. Then he sniffed. "Fine. If you fail me, remember who controls your drug supply, hmm?" He paused once more, probably to listen to Commander Haka's *Hail the Sun*. Then he set the phone delicately back on the receiver and took a long breath.

He straightened, kneading his hands into the small of his back, and said, "As if those two idiot samurai weren't enough, now some so-called 'rebel' hacker is playing with the imperial video feed."

"I'm sure the criminals will be dealt with, Prince-Regent."

"Of course. How is the Dog?"

"Taken care of, Prince-Regent."

"He wasn't injured seriously?"

"He has a thick skull. According to the physician, he has a slight concussion and some bruising, but nothing that should concern you."

"Nothing that should concern you, what?"

"Nothing that should concern you, Prince-Regent."

The Prince-Regent turned around. His upper lip trembled, as if to form a snarl, but he smiled instead and drew closer, his hands still clasped behind his back. "Sometimes I think you are the only subject I can trust," he said softly, standing a few feet away. "You don't let me down. Do you?" His eyes widened suddenly, his tone rising. "Do you let me down, when I'm not looking?"

"What do you think, Prince-Regent?"

The Prince-Regent took one long stride forward and stopped just inches away from the other man. They were the same height, and the Prince-Regent's dark eyes shone intense with scrutiny.

He released a quiet sigh. "No, Kirikizu." He smiled. "My deadly flower, you will never betray me. Do you want to know why?" Before the other man could answer, he urged, "Ask me why."

Kirikizu paused, listening to the monotone buzz of his own breathing in and out through the muzzle. He was used to it by now, in the way a person got used to chronic pain or bad vision. It was simply part of his being. "Why, Prince-Regent?"

"Because I've been good to you," the other man said, a confident smile on his face. "I'm well aware that I treat others with...well, I believe poets would call it 'an iron hand.' Sometimes respect demands cruelty, and cruelty demands respect.

But you...you're different. You've always been so different from the rest." He lifted a hand, brushing two fingers across the high curve of Kirikizu's cheekbone. "Have I ever told you that? How grateful I am?"

For a moment, Kirikizu said nothing. The white-hot elixir of rage and fear boiled through his veins, constricting his throat and squeezing his lungs.

He heard himself say deliberately, "I live to serve you, Prince-Regent. You know that."

"Yes. Which is why I have another command for you."

Kirikizu regarded the Prince-Regent with a neutral expression, carved from years of experience. Showing emotion in front of the Prince-Regent was tantamount to threatening your own life, especially if it was the kind of emotion he did not want to see. "Command me, Prince-Regent."

"I'm beginning to doubt Commander Haka's skill." The Prince-Regent rubbed his forehead, kneading a headache with his fingertips. "They recovered a good amount of blood from one of the veterans, and I've ordered his mutts released tomorrow. If they recover nothing, I'm sending you after them."

"Lord Akita and Shi Matsumoto?"

"Saizou Akita is deposed. I don't want him referred to as *Lord* from this moment on. Make sure everyone knows it." The Prince-Regent combed his fingers through his long hair and paced in a slow circle.

Kirikizu watched him in silence. He had seen his surroundings more times than he cared to count. He was familiar with the marble walls and floor, the golden sun emblazoned over the wide bed, the reflective gold-plated ceilings so clear you could see your reflection.

The color gold made him sick.

"Prince-Regent?" he prodded finally.

The Prince-Regent tilted his head back and stared at the black ceiling. "My Lord."

"I'm sorry?"

"Call me *My Lord*. You know how much I like hearing you say that." The Prince-Regent straightened and gave Kirikizu a smile that would have seemed kind if his face were capable of such a thing. Instead, his smile was a twisted, insincere expression that sent a thin shiver down Kirikizu's back.

"My Lord," said Kirikizu. The stiffness in his voice did not translate through the muzzle. At least the contraption served that useful purpose.

The Prince-Regent made a pleased *hmm* noise that dragged on a few seconds too long. "You may leave. I'll have word sent."

Kirikizu bowed from the waist and turned to go, but the Prince-Regent's tattooed hand landed firmly on his shoulder. In a low voice, the Prince-Regent coaxed, "One more time. Say it."

Kirikizu did not turn around. "My Lord."

The Prince-Regent squeezed his shoulder for a long moment before allowing his hand to slide away. "Now go."

Kirikizu did.

———

BEFORE SHI COULD WONDER what had happened or why he was lying on his back staring at an unfamiliar ceiling, the pain in his shoulder reminded him of the details.

A dog-man had tried to bite his shoulder off, they had ridden into the middle of nowhere on a motorcycle, there was a broken bridge, and someone else...he didn't remember much after that. He could recall a few snatches of a conversation he had not been part of—Saizou speaking with the stranger in the off-white coat.

Off-white coat...

Ah, his shoulder hurt.

With his good arm, he pushed himself halfway into a sitting position and squinted around the room. It was minimalistic and old-fashioned, with traditional paper walls and a bamboo floor. The only decoration appeared to be the mat underneath him.

He looked down at his shoulder. It was well-bandaged, but a bandage did nothing to stop the pain. He ground his teeth and sat up the rest of the way, searching for his jacket. It was too cold to go without it now that he was awake.

The doors slid open with a whisper, and a girl stepped into the room, or he assumed it was a girl. Her top half was obscured by a pile of white blankets. He moved to stand up and help her before she tripped over her own feet, but one of her hands shot out and motioned for him to stay where he was.

"Do you need help?" he asked politely, watching in bemusement as she approached him and dumped the blankets beside the mat in an unceremonious heap.

"No," she said. "I've got it."

"I see that now." Shi eyed the blankets, then the girl. She was pretty, he thought—or maybe *cute* was the right term. "Nice sweater," he added, and then mentally slapped himself. *I shouldn't be allowed to talk when I'm not fully cognitive. Who knows what I said to Saizou. I probably talked about puppies.*

"Thanks," said the girl. She sat on her knees and tucked her hair behind both ears. "You're probably wondering where your jacket is. I cleaned it and hung it up to dry in the kitchen. I couldn't hang it outside, obviously. It's too cold. But I thought you would probably want these blankets or something, because the weather honestly isn't conducive to going around half-naked."

Shi blinked. "No," he said. "It isn't."

The girl continued, "On a scale of one to ten, how much does your shoulder hurt?"

"Seven."

"Seven. I was expecting an eight. Still, I'll give you some more salve in an hour or so, once the salve already on the injury has dissolved. There's no point in doing it now. Aren't you cold? Take a blanket." She pushed the top blanket toward him, and when he took the edge, she dragged another blanket around behind him and wrapped it gingerly around his shoulders.

Suddenly feeling very mothered, Shi asked, "Where am I, exactly?"

"Old Shinsei Monastery. From what I gather, you passed out near the broken bridge and Winter brought you back here."

"Winter," repeated Shi. "The monk?"

"He isn't exactly a monk. *Priest* is a more appropriate term, I believe."

"Shinto? Buddhist?"

"Christian."

"A Christian priest?"

"That's what I said." She reached out and felt his forehead. Her hand felt cold, almost icy. "Hmm."

"Hmm?"

"You have a slight fever. Nothing too horrible; your injury isn't infected, although I can't say I would be surprised if an infection did take hold. It looks nasty."

"It was," said Shi.

"What kind of animal was it?"

"A human one."

"I don't believe humans are animals," the girl said, tucking her legs underneath her. "We're far beyond that. Although, I do believe animals have souls. Obviously not the same kind of souls that humans have, but still souls none-theless."

Shi was unsure how he should respond to that, so he only said, "Mmm."

"I'm sorry," she said, fluttering her hand like a bird. "I don't always talk to people, but when I do, I can't seem to stop."

"I don't mind," said Shi. At the very least, her chatter distracted him from the pain in his shoulder.

"Really? That's sweet of you, truly. So what did you mean by a *human animal*?" She leaned forward, her eyes wide and intrigued. Her sweater covered her chin, but her mouth was pursed, like she was forming another sentence and just hadn't spoken it yet.

"It was a man with sharp teeth and claws," said Shi, attempting to keep the explanation simple.

The girl quirked an eyebrow, and she reached her hand up to feel his forehead again.

"That's what it was," Shi insisted, ducking slightly to avoid the contact. Her hand brushed his hair instead, and she smiled and gave it a ruffle for no discernable reason.

She smoothed her palm over his hair one more time and then retracted her hand again. "I like your hair."

Shi cleared his throat and glanced at the doors, wondering where Saizou had gone. As if sensing his thoughts, the girl said, "Your friend left, but he'll be back since you're here. He hasn't been gone more than an hour, so worrying is completely unnecessary."

"Why did he leave?" asked Shi curiously, pulling the blanket around his chest to block as much of the cold air as possible.

"I didn't ask, I only watched him leave."

"Ah."

"Are you hungry? The soup will be finished soon, and you're welcome to have as much as you want. There's always more than enough, in case guests drop in."

A brief smile touched Shi's face. Her mannerisms were shy, but her questions were forward and open. It was nice to have someone to talk to, he realized—someone who wasn't Saizou. No matter how much you loved a person, one person was rarely enough. In case she was planning to leave if he said *yes*, he stalled and asked, "Are you a guest?"

"I was, at first. Although, I suppose...technically, I was more of a stray than anything else."

Shi remained silent, waiting for her to continue.

The girl leaned back and asked curiously, "Do you really want to know, or are you just being polite?"

"I'm curious." Shi smiled again. "I promise."

"Because there's no need to humor me. I'm well aware—"

"I'm not humoring you."

She smiled and reached up, tucking the neck of her sweater back up around her chin. "My parents left me at an orphanage when I was young. Typical, right? They were nice to me there, but I didn't like it, so I ran away. Winter found me on the bridge when I was eleven."

Shi wanted to ask how old the girl was, but he knew from experience that asking a woman's age usually resulted in their total, frigid silence. Instead, he asked tactfully, "How long ago was that?"

"I'm twenty-one, and yes, I look younger, and yes, I talk a lot, which—for whatever reason —people seem to equate with youth. Although, I take it back; I only talk a lot to people I feel like talking to. I think I said that before."

"You said something like that."

She smiled and stood up, brushing invisible dust off her

knees. "Do you want to eat in the kitchen, or should I bring dinner here? You know what, never mind. I'll bring it here. You should lie down. I'll be back in a bit, so try to get some rest."

She left, shutting the doors behind her, but not all the way. She left them open a few inches, and Shi listened to her footsteps shuffle quietly away until he could no longer hear them.

He bowed his head and sighed deeply. Automatically, he lifted his hand to adjust his mask, but his fingers brushed nothing but bare skin.

He jerked his head up and looked at the patterned rice-paper doors.

The girl had not mentioned his face. Not even once.

# THIRTEEN

SAIZOU HAD VERY little experience with staff-fighting. He could handle a naginata, but only when absolutely necessary—his strengths were with the katana, rifle, and bow. Still, Shotgun seemed genuine when he said he had information Saizou wanted, and if this was the only way to get it, then he would use a staff.

He just needed a strategy.

He hefted the bamboo pole and strode back to the bridge. He put one foot on the bamboo trees Shotgun had laid down from one side of the broken bridge to the other—they wobbled dangerously, and from the other side, Shotgun laughed.

"Better than nothing, but not by much." He swung his bamboo pole over his head. It whistled through the air, and he lowered it, tapping the ground with the end. "You ready?"

"Explain the rules to me again," said Saizou. If he died doing this, Shi would spit on his grave for all eternity, and he would be completely justified.

"Sure. Whoever crosses that first wins." Shotgun pointed to

the bamboo bridge-between-bridges. "The loser loses, obviously. If you fall over the cliff and die, it's a forfeit."

"I'm glad you cleared that up."

Shotgun threw back his head and unleashed another boisterous chuckle, but when he lowered his head again to face Saizou, every trace of mirth was gone. His mouth quirked, but it was a twist of determination. He narrowed his eyes and crouched, gripping his pole with both hands.

He was waiting.

Well, they had to start sometime. "Go," said Saizou.

Shotgun needed no further urging. With a throat-shredding roar, he charged the bridge, his head lowered like a bull. From the way he gripped his pole, Saizou guessed rather than swinging, he was planning on ramming the pole into his stomach or chest, thus pushing him back out of the way.

Saizou smiled, twisted his pole, and inserted it vertically between the middle two trees stretching across the gap. Shotgun noticed the move, but he was already halfway across, and it was too late. Saizou leaned on the pole with just enough weight that it separated the four trees, pushing two away on either side and cracking open a wide space in the middle.

Shotgun shifted his balance and stared at Saizou with wide eyes and a shocked expression, but no amount of compensation could keep him upright. His foot slipped, and he fell to the side, but his reflexes were faster than Saizou expected. He dropped his own pole as he pitched over the side. His reaching hands caught one of the bamboo poles, and he held fast with a shout.

The trees dipped in the middle and rolled from side to side, threatening to roll over the side completely. Shotgun grunted, gripping the slender trees as his knuckles turned white and his eyes narrowed, focusing every effort on not plummeting to his death.

Saizou lifted his pole out of the gap and set it down on the solid wood. "Does this mean I win?"

"You crazy bastard," said Shotgun, through clenched teeth.

Saizou took a step forward. "You won't make it to this side without my help. I won. Yes or no?"

"Yes," panted Shotgun, heaving himself a few inches farther up.

His grip would not hold much longer, Saizou could see that. His weight would either snap the trees or pull them over the edge. The thin trees weren't enough to hold the weight of two people, but he could hear the weight of the wood creaking and knew the whole thing would fall apart if he didn't do something first.

"Slide toward me," Saizou instructed, reaching out a hand and motioning Shotgun toward him. "Use your hands and get as close to me as you can."

"You got me into this mess," Shotgun pointed out. "Really don't need your help." His words were confident and unbothered, but his voice was strained. A sheen of sweat already glazed his skin, and that meant time was short before Shotgun's palms became slick. The bamboo was smooth as it was; there was no way someone with sweaty palms could hold on for long.

*Be calm. Talk him through it. He's been taken by surprise; he didn't expect this. He's still trying to catch up.* "You're a big guy," said Saizou, his voice steady. "Bamboo poles are only so strong, and one of them isn't going to hold you. Even if you swing up on it, there's a good chance they'll snap. If you slide this way, I'll help you up. I give you my word."

Shotgun gave him a long look, his muscles straining through his jacket as he fought to keep a grip on the only thing between him and a fall to the rocks below.

"Even if you think I'll push you right back over, what's the point?" Saizou continued. *Listen to me, you idiot.* "You're going to die right here either way."

As the words left his mouth, the pole in Shotgun's grip bent, and a thin crack appeared beneath his fingers.

"Fine," Shotgun grunted quickly. He took a deep breath and swung his legs toward the other side of the bridge, giving himself momentum. He swung his body and slid his hands, moving with agility that surprised Saizou, given his size.

The crack in the bamboo grew wider, and as Shotgun reached a point about three feet away from Saizou, it cracked in half. The fibers in the middle tore, and Shotgun's arm shot out, wrapping around another tree with lightning-fast reflexes.

The halves of the bamboo pole crashed through the foliage and landed somewhere below.

Saizou leaned forward as far as he could and grabbed a fistful of Shotgun's sleeveless jacket. "Your left hand," he instructed. "Grab my arm with it."

Shotgun groaned. He breathed out through clenched teeth and took hold of Saizou's forearm, and Saizou pulled him toward the edge of the bridge.

Another loud crack split the air, and Shotgun let go of the other pole completely, grabbing Saizou's other arm. Saizou leaned back, trying to balance the sudden extra weight as the second pole snapped into three pieces and rolled away over the edge.

Shotgun moved like a side-winding snake, twisting his torso, then his hips up over the side of the bridge, pulling Shotgun as far to safety as he could. He fell back when Shotgun let go of Saizou completely and half-stumbled, half-jogged a few more yards to the path and sat down hard.

Saizou stood up, but pressed his palms against his knees and leaned over, shaking his head. When he straightened and eyed Shotgun, the younger man was leaning back on his hands, chest heaving, and his grin was inexplicably back on his face. It was not the expression of someone who had just survived a near-death experience.

Shotgun leaned forward and pointed at Saizou, shaking his head. "I have to admit, that was smooth."

"What was?" asked Saizou, watching the other man carefully.

"Your one-eighty. First you cheat and try to kill me, then you act like some kind of paramedic or rescue squad. You're an interesting guy."

"I didn't cheat," said Saizou, "If that's what you're implying. The rules, as laid down by you, stated that whoever got to the other side first won. I didn't feel like leaving my side, and you agreed to the rule change when I proposed it a minute ago while you were dangling over a ravine."

Shotgun rubbed his hands back through his wild, cherry-colored hair. His throaty laughter turned into a sigh, and he gave Saizou a bright smile. "All right. Fine, you won. Might not have been fair, but at least it was square." He stuck his right arm out.

"Am I supposed to pull you to your feet or shake your hand?" Saizou asked, still scrutinizing the other man.

"Help me up," said Shotgun. "Duh."

Saizou strode forward and took Shotgun's hand, leaning back and pulling him to his feet. Shotgun rose to his full height, several inches taller than Saizou with at least six inches of electric hair adding to it.

"Thanks," said Shotgun, and he grinned.

Saizou did not see the punch coming until it slammed into his face like a sledgehammer. He reeled back until his back rested against the stand of bamboo trees behind him, white lights flickering across his vision.

"That's for the pole trick," said Shotgun, wiping his sweaty palms off on his pants. "I would have beaten you if you hadn't pulled that stunt."

Saizou cupped his hands over his face and breathed slowly, trying to clear the sharp, pounding pain from his skull.

He heard Shotgun again, but this time his voice held some concern. "*Oi*, are you okay? Hey, it didn't hurt that much, right? It's not like I shoved your nose into your brain."

Saizou lowered his hands and levelled a flat, black glare at the other man. "There is such a thing," he said slowly, "as losing with dignity."

"Don't have any," said Shotgun, as relief blossomed across his face. "Hey, for a second there, I thought I'd killed you."

"That was quite a punch," said Saizou, blinking rapidly.

"My mom always told me I didn't know my own strength," said Shotgun apologetically.

"I can see why she said that."

"You sure you're okay?"

"I'm fine. I've had worse."

"Caught you by surprise, yeah?" Shotgun grinned again. "I'd say I'm sorry, but I'm not." Immediately, he added, "So I promised you information, you earned it. But even out here, I don't like the idea of sharing sensitive info. Drones and shit, you know. There's a monastery not far up the trail, right?"

It was probably nearing dinner, Saizou realized, recalling Winter's invitation—if Saizou was still around to take him up on it. "There is. Come on."

"I like you, man."

Saizou sighed.

———

MATAHACHI SAT at the dining room table, his legs crossed as he studied the document in front of him. It was paper, not digital; the Prince-Regent was taking every precaution with Akita Domain. Soon to be Shigure domain, once he signed the agreement.

Matahachi held his calligraphy brush between his fingers a few inches above the table and let the end slowly fall to the surface. Then he slid it back up and let it drop again, a continual *tap, tap, tap* as he thought.

All he had to do was sign his name on the line, write the brushstrokes and be done with it. The domain he had worked for would be his, officially and irrevocably.

He recalled the questions Lord Akita had asked him at the dinner table the previous night—was it really only the previous night? Was that possible?

Lord Akita's plan to make him talk had been obvious, but he supposed it was what he would have done in the other man's stead. Idly, he wondered what it would feel like to serve five years in another country, surrounded by blood and death, only to find your home stolen away upon your return.

Stolen.

It was not stolen. He had been given the keys temporarily, and the position was about to become permanent. He should have no misgivings, no regrets. Everything was legal, with the Prince-Regent's blessing. He would be Lord Matahachi.

He lifted his brush and wrote the first kanji symbol. *They would be proud,* he thought, *if they were here to witness this. I do this for you, Father. I will be forgiven, in time.*

He wrote the last symbol and lifted the brush away. He watched the black ink dry, wrinkling the crisp paper.

"So you signed it, then."

Matahachi looked up and saw Tsuki standing in the door-way. Her hands rested on her hips, and she wore displeasure like a perfume, subtle but obvious.

"Of course I signed it." He pushed his chair away from the table and stood up, lifting the piece of paper with two fingers and letting it hang like laundry, drying in fresh air. *If only it were clean.* "Did you think I wouldn't?"

"Maybe I harbored a ridiculous hope that you would urge the Prince-Regent to give control of the domain back to the person it belongs to," she said, shrugging.

"Why do you care so much?" Matahachi lowered the sheet of paper and bent it in half, sliding his fingers along each sharp fold. "You haven't seen each other in years."

"I practically grew up with him. I care about him."

"The way you speak sometimes makes me wonder exactly how much of a child you are," Matahachi said, and his voice was harder than he expected. He strode around the table and across the room and took hold of her wrist. With his other hand, he held up the now-folded paper. "What man, having cared for something year after year, would relinquish it for a stranger?"

"I would rather be a stranger than a thief."

Matahachi hissed, a sharp intake of breath, and searched Tsuki's face. "Think that way, if you wish to," he said, after a threadbare moment. He glanced at her mouth; his gaze often found its way there if he did not work to keep it elsewhere. "But if I were a thief," he continued, straining to keep his voice from snapping again, "I would have stolen more than this domain."

She said nothing, but her face grew more shuttered, harder to read even than usual.

"Would it be stealing?" Matahachi asked, his voice fading to a near-whisper. "To take what is mine? Yet I haven't." He tightened his grip on her wrist, just for a moment, before releasing it. He lifted his hand and, instead, brushed his thumb against her chin. It was a brief taste of her, barely the brush of a feather—but Tsuki turned her head away from it, her eyes narrowing into glimmers of dark fire.

Matahachi's hand hovered in the air for the length of one breath before he let it fall to his side. "I take what is given to me," he said softly. "And nothing else."

As he walked around her, he glanced down at the paper in his hand. It was crumpled, crushed in his fist.

*What honor I do or do not have—it doesn't matter. I do not do this for myself. I do this for my family, to save their honor. Not mine. I do not need her blessing; I do not need her permission. Lord Akita forfeited his right to this domain.*

*I am not a thief.*

*I am not a thief.*

*I am not.*

# FOURTEEN

"AHHH, SOMETHING SMELLS GOOD, EH?"

Shi got to his feet as the unfamiliar voice boomed through the monastery. He gripped his shoulder and shuffled out of the room and down the hall, into the foyer. He stopped short and blinked once at the person Saizou had apparently dragged in with him.

Bracelets dangled around his wrists, and chains hooked around his belt, his jeans, and his boots.

"Hiya," said the stranger.

Shi looked at Saizou. "Who...?"

"It's a long story," said Saizou. "He says his name's Shotgun."

"That's because it *is* my name," said the stranger. "Ask anyone." He bowed briefly to Shi, grinning broadly.

Shi gave Saizou a frown and crossed the foyer, where he squinted at Saizou's face. "Your nose is bleeding."

"It was bleeding. It's stopped now." Saizou reached up and wiped his nose with a finger, glancing down at the drying blood smeared across it. "I'm going to go wash up."

"Saizou," Shi began, but Saizou only said, "I'll be back in a minute" and walked down the hall where, apparently, there was a bathroom Shi had not noticed.

Shi turned to face Shotgun and gave him another quick study. He had deep-set eyes, a wide mouth, and a strong nose—bold features, to say nothing of the hair.

Shotgun held up two hands and formed a square with his thumbs and index fingers. "You want that film developed?"

Shi tried to think of a response, but Shotgun waved a hand as if swatting a fly and said, "I know. I'm hard to look away from, but I think you've got me beat there." He motioned to his face. "What happened? Did you faceplant on a land mine?"

Shi's hand twitched, and he curled it into a fist, but he swallowed a growl and said coldly, "I'm guessing you're my junior."

"Yeah? I'm twenty-five. You?"

"Thirty-three," said Shi. "My point is, watch your mouth."

"Sensitive about the face?"

Fortunately for Shotgun, Saizou's voice snapped from behind Shi just then. "Hey, if you want to eat, then watch it."

Shotgun held up both hands in surrender. "Sorry." He bowed again in Shi's direction, deeper than the last time. "Really, I'm sorry." He gestured toward his mouth. "My sister used to say the filter between my brain and mouth never got installed."

Shi grunted and turned around to give Saizou a sharp look. He jerked his thumb toward his room and left the foyer. He heard Saizou tell Shotgun he would be back shortly before following him down the hallway. Shi pulled the doors open, stepped inside, and shut them behind Saizou.

"Talk," said Shi. "You said it was a long story, so condense it. Who is he, where did you pick him up, and why is he here?"

Saizou was silent for a long moment. Then, as if he had put

all the pieces of a puzzle together in his mind, he said evenly, "He followed us from Tokyo and seems to want to help us. He likes games, so before he would give me helpful information, he wanted me to fight him. I won, but we didn't want to discuss sensitive information in the open, so I brought him back here. Hopefully, the monk doesn't mind."

"What kind of sensitive information?" Shi demanded. He drew closer to Saizou and lowered his voice. "We've been outlawed, captain. We can't just drag every stray so-called informant off the street."

"One person does not count as 'every stray so-called informant,'" Saizou interrupted, holding up a hand. "And I'm convinced he does know something that could help us. He knew what happened inside the Palace of the Sun, and he has information on Commander Haka."

"If he's telling the truth," said Shi darkly.

"I think he is.'"

"For a suspicious person, you seem very trusting."

Saizou opened his mouth, but he shut it without saying anything. He turned in a wide, slow circle around the mat on the floor before facing Shi again. "Maybe you're right. I don't trust him, but he's..." He cleared his throat and glanced at the opposite wall.

A pit opened in Shi's stomach, and he rubbed the back of his neck with his left hand. His right shoulder was in too much pain to consider moving his arm. "He reminds you of them, doesn't he?" he sighed. "Your soldiers."

"He's just a kid who seems helpful," said Saizou. A new edge had crept into his voice; letting Shi knew he had hit the right mark. "It's not like I'm planning to drag him behind us everywhere. He'll give me the information tonight, and we'll leave tomorrow."

"You can't leave yet, are you crazy?"

Shi turned around and saw Fumiyo stepping into the room. His jacket was neatly folded and hung over her arm, and in her free hand she held his mask. "They're clean and dry, but you can't leave yet." She gave Saizou a sharp look as she handed the jacket and mask to Shi. "He's not in a good condition. I still need to dress and bandage his shoulder. It could get infected still or start bleeding again. He needs to stay here for a few more days at least, all right?"

Saizou's eyes were wide, a look of mild shock on his face. "She speaks?"

"Yes, she speaks," said Shi, and gave Fumiyo a small smile. "The trouble is getting her to stop once she starts."

"You don't seem to mind listening, anyway," snipped Fumiyo. She gave Saizou a dark look before returning her attention to Shi and adding, "Dinner's ready. I don't know what Winter will think of the new person you brought in, but I suppose he'll have to feed him now."

With that she stepped out of the room, leaving the door open behind her.

———

SAIZOU FELT a little apprehension as he followed Fumiyo into the dining room. A long, low table sat in the center of the room, and pillows lined the floor on either side. Saizou crossed his legs and sat down at the far end, and Shi settled down on his left. Fumiyo ducked out of the room into the kitchen, and Shotgun strode in and sat down comfortably opposite Saizou.

He noticed Shi pick up the chopsticks at his place and begin tapping them on the table, a sure sign he was unhappy or upset but refusing to say any more about the subject. Shi pointedly did not look at Shotgun but kept his head bowed, his disfigurement once again covered by the black leather mask.

Fumiyo stepped out of the kitchen, balancing a tray that carried four white bowls. She set a bowl down in front of each of the men, then one at the empty place on Shi's left. She left the room, but Winter entered this time with another bowl and sat down at the other end of the table, as far away from everyone else as possible.

Saizou looked down at the contents of his bowl—warm white rice with butter and shredded meat. It was a simple meal, but as he placed the first bite in his mouth, he realized he had eaten nothing since the night before, and his stomach welcomed the plain meal more than any banquet.

Shotgun bowed toward Winter, who barely glanced up and only nodded slightly in response. "So you're a monk?" asked Shotgun, gathering a large bite and shoving it into his mouth with gusto.

*Come to think of it, he hasn't mentioned what he is,* Saizou thought, looking at Winter with rekindled interest. He had the mannerisms and attitude of a warrior, but he lived in a remote monastery with no one for company but an eccentric girl. He offered help and gave it when required, but without the kind warmth monks usually displayed.

"I am not a monk," said Winter.

"Oh?" Shotgun separated a large piece of meat from his rice. "What are you, then?"

"Nothing which concerns you."

"I thought you were a priest," said Shi.

Shotgun lifted his eyebrows, interested. "Priest, huh? What kind? Shinto?"

Winter gave a slight shake of his head. "Christian."

Saizou straightened and stared at Winter. "You're a Christian?"

"I am," said Winter with a faint sigh. He levelled a direct stare at Saizou and asked, "Is that surprising?"

"I find it surprising," said Saizou. "I adopted the Christian faith during my time in Liaoyang."

"Interesting," said Winter, and for the first time, he looked as if he really was interested. "Why did you choose it? It's hardly popular."

Saizou cleared his throat and leaned back, suddenly feeling as if the blood had been drained from his veins and replaced with white-hot anxiety.

Shi still did not look up, but he said, "That's his business, not yours. Priest." He said the last word with an almost vicious intonation, but his face was neutral as he placed another bite in his mouth.

"I see you are very protective of your friend," said Winter, with no emotion in his voice or face to betray what his true thoughts were, "but I was speaking to him, not you."

Shi set his chopsticks down beside the bowl, aggression radiating from his very aura.

Saizou cleared his throat and gave Shi a significant, darting glance.

After a few seconds of silence, Shi bowed toward Winter and said, "I'm sorry."

Saizou knew the reaction would not have been so immediate if Shi hadn't already gotten ahold of himself, and he relaxed. Usually Shi was the one reaching out a hand to steady Saizou's volatile temper, but there were times when the tables reversed, and Saizou was never sure when they were beginning to do so.

Winter regarded Shi gravely for a moment before speaking

again. "I seem to have put you off somehow. You have my apology."

Shi said nothing. He only lifted his bowl closer to his face and ate in silence, concentrating entirely on moving his chopsticks from the bowl to his mouth.

"Fumiyo," said Winter, "did you take care of his shoulder?"

Fumiyo tugged the neck of her sweater down around her chin. "I did, but they're planning on moving out tomorrow, and he can't be moved that soon. I need to keep taking care of it, for goodness' sake. Please tell them so."

Shotgun eyed her curiously and pointed his chopsticks in her direction. "Are you a nurse? A doctor?"

Fumiyo's eyes widened at his sudden attention, and she yanked the neck of her sweater back up, as if attempting to hide from his gaze.

Shotgun blinked. "What did I do?" He glanced from Saizou to Winter and back again. "Was it something I said?"

"She's a selective conversationalist," Saizou told him. "She doesn't talk to me, either."

Fumiyo sank even further into the depths of her sweater. She lifted her bowl to her mouth and scooped in a huge mouthful, then set the bowl down. Her cheeks bulging like a chipmunk storing before a frost, she stood up and bowed before shuffling quickly into the kitchen and closing the doors behind her.

Shotgun lifted his open chopsticks, squinted through the gap, and snapped them shut in the direction Fumiyo had left. Abruptly, he said, "Can we talk in front of him?" and nodded toward Winter.

The lack of manners surprised even Saizou. He leaned back, wondering what to say to the stranger. This was Winter's monastery, and Shotgun was the guest, not the owner. He watched Shotgun's eyes flicker from Winter to the table, and a faint expression of disgust crossed the red-haired man's face.

"There I go again." He sighed, raking his fingers through his hair until it stood up even more than before. "I swear by heaven, I don't do these things on purpose."

"Insult me all you like, intentionally or unintentionally," said Winter in his dry, neutral voice, "but do not pretend heaven has anything to do with it."

Shotgun's mouth fell open as Winter rose to his feet in a fluid, graceful motion. He lifted his bowl, gave a polite, shallow bow to Saizou, and left through the kitchen, the same way Fumiyo had.

Shi relaxed visibly with the monk's absence; his back straightened, and he lifted his head, his burning gaze directed at Shotgun. "You said you have information, and now you have privacy. Get it over with."

"It's like everyone hates me, it really is," said Shotgun, shoving a large bite into his mouth and pushing it over to his cheek. Around the mouthful, he added, "Commander Haka's pulling drones from positions over the city and sending them out tonight. Also, I guess they picked up blood from you some-where, because they logged it in, which means they'll be sending the mutts out."

"Mutts?" Saizou leaned forward. "Clarify."

"Mutts. Mutated animals. Big, mean, ugly, good at tracking people down. Like me, but not human." Shotgun grinned and finished chewing. "They'll smell the blood, have everything they need, and find you pretty quickly, I'd guess. I've seen them work before."

"In what situation?" asked Saizou. The way he saw it, there were two options: either Shotgun was a very bad Shinsengumi spy, practically handing his position as a spy to Saizou on a silver platter, or he was a very good one, and he hoped Saizou would see his blundering incompetence as innocence.

Well. There was a third option. Maybe Shotgun was actually innocent, and he wanted to help.

The third option was unlikely.

Shotgun's face clouded, and for the first time, he seemed uncomfortable. "It was a long time ago. They were hunting someone down. Caught them too, although I don't really want to talk about it, so don't ask."

"All right," said Saizou amiably. He knew trauma when he saw it. "I won't. Tell me, how do you know all this?"

"Because he's a Shinsengumi spy," muttered Shi.

Shotgun threw back his head and howled with laughter for a long, loud moment. He wiped his eyes with the heel of his hand and grinned at Shi. "Me? You think I'm a spy? With this hair?" He pointed to his head to illustrate his point. "I have the tact of a rhino, I've been told many times. I'd make a lousy spy."

"That's what every spy would say." Shi set his empty bowl down and placed his chopsticks across the top.

"Yeah, well, then I'd be a lousy spy all over again, wouldn't I? Geez. I ran across rooftops—do you realize how many somersaults I had to make to follow you here, just to help you?"

Shi rolled his shoulders back, preparing to rebut Shotgun's remark again, but Saizou quickly intervened.

"Answer my question," he said politely. "Please."

Shotgun heaved a loud sigh and leaned back. "I have a friend. Mad hacker skills."

"The Shinsengumi employ hackers," Shi pointed out.

"Not like this one, they don't. It's like her brain is a power outlet connected to every webstream in the universe. Oh, and she believes in aliens. Doesn't really matter, but anyway. She's pretty stable, for an asylum escapee."

Saizou blinked and traded incredulous glances with Shi.

"I know, I know," said Shotgun, smiling widely. "Sounds like a bad movie or something, but I'm telling the truth. You can meet her, if you want. Actually..." He scratched his head. "You probably should. She can get you a safe place to stay. This won't be safe once the mutts find you."

"You're here, too," said Shi.

Shotgun nodded enthusiastically. "I am. I am."

*Does he always have this much energy,* Saizou wondered with a faint smile, *or is he just having a particularly good day?* He supposed it could be leftover adrenaline from the kid's near-death experience, but he didn't seem ruffled enough to be experiencing this much of an aftershock.

"Do you think we have until morning?" Saizou asked, pushing aside all variables and asking the most pressing question.

Shotgun cocked his head to the side and squinted. "Probably. I can't make any promises though."

"Fine." Saizou stood up and nudged Shi with his knee. "Come with me. We have to talk."

"My opinion is no," said Shi, but he stood up reluctantly anyway.

Shotgun unfolded himself and stood uncertainly on the other side of the table. "What about me? Where do I go?"

"Anywhere," said Saizou. "Just don't leave."

Shotgun grinned. "I'll be on the roof."

Saizou lifted a hand in acknowledgement and strode out of the room, closely followed by Shi. To risk taking Shotgun's offer, or to ignore it and get by on their own...each option had problems and sub-problems, and he had a few hours at most to solve them.

# FIFTEEN

SHI FOLLOWED Saizou into his room and shut the doors. He turned and looked at Saizou for a long moment, until Saizou said, "What's on your mind?"

"You," said Shi. "And your...."

Saizou's eyebrows drew together. "My what?"

Shi reached up and rubbed his cheek, sliding his fingertips between the mask and his skin. He didn't feel like taking it off, but there were times when the scar felt tight and uncomfortable, and there was nothing he could do about it.

"Shi," prompted Saizou.

"Let me gather my thoughts, captain," Shi snapped. He blinked, taken aback at his own ferocity, and offered Saizou a slight bow in place of an apology.

Saizou folded his arms across his chest, the irritation in his voice replaced with concern. "What's upsetting you?"

"I understand you're upset about your domain," said Shi, trying to keep his voice calm and even. He rarely snapped at Saizou—it felt disrespectful, and the anger made him uncomfortable. "But you need to clear your head."

A shade passed over Saizou's face. "Is that so?"

"It is."

"Tell me what I've done," said Saizou, "that you disagree with."

Shi noticed the other man begin to rub his fingers together, and he considered ending the conversation before it took a darker turn, but they could not afford the time. "Bringing him here, for one thing."

"Who? Shotgun?"

"Did you bring someone else and fail to mention it?"

Saizou sighed and touched his forehead briefly. "The information he gave us was helpful. Unless you think he was lying, which I'm not leaving out as a possibility."

"But we have no way of knowing," Shi pointed out. "And when are we supposed to find out? When we arrive at the destination he gives us and it's a trap?"

Saizou clenched his hands into fists and raised them both, as if preparing to deliver a double-blow to Shi, but he only held them there until he lowered them a few seconds later. "Do you...do you have a better idea?" he managed, obviously struggling to remain civil.

Shi was used to his temper and his behavior and so did not step back, even though Saizou's hands remained clenched and threatening. "I think we need to get out of here as soon as possible."

"I already said we're doing that."

Shi hesitated. "I think we need to take the girl with us. The monk too if he wants."

"The girl?" Saizou's eyebrows rose. "Why?"

"You know as well as I do that if the Shinsengumi have a way to find us, they won't turn around and leave if they don't find us here. They will question, torture, and maybe kill them. I don't know. I think the monk could handle himself as well as anyone, but the girl?" Shi shook his head. "We can't drag danger to their front door and leave them to deal with it while we run and hide. I refuse."

"Refuse," Saizou repeated, rubbing his chin. "And if, as you pointed out, Shotgun is walking us into a trap? Then do we bring the girl and the monk into that same trap with us?"

Sudden pain shot through Shi's shoulder, and he winced, grinding his teeth against the sensation. "At least if they came with us, there would be four of us instead of two."

A frown formed between Saizou's eyebrows, but he nodded. "I'll go talk to Shotgun."

"In an hour," said Shi. "If you don't sleep at all tonight, that means three days without it."

"I'll be fine," said Saizou shortly.

Shi moved, blocking him again. "I've seen you running on three days without sleep, captain."

Saizou's dark eyes glimmered with irritation and a hint of amusement. "I can't be that bad," he began to protest, but Shi interrupted.

"I need you fully functioning." Gently, he reminded Saizou, "You got us outlawed, remember? You can't afford to miss this much sleep. Just take a rest for an hour. I'll be here."

"You're injured. I'm not taking the mat."

"I'm been sleeping; I don't need more."

Saizou paused, and Shi could physically see the excuse attempts crossing Saizou's face and getting immediately vetoed when he realized none of them were good enough. He took a hitched breath and sighed. "One hour of rest."

"One hour. I'll wake you if you don't wake yourself."

"Don't worry," said Saizou. "I'm not going to sleep."

———

OUTSIDE IN THE COLD AIR, on the moss-slick tiled roof, Shotgun rose from a crouch and straightened. He pressed his hands into the small of his back and listened to three satisfying clicks as he put it in—he had probably twisted it earlier, hanging off the bridge like that.

He licked his lips and said quietly, "I told you they wouldn't trust me."

"Stop complaining. It isn't just you they don't trust. They don't trust anyone," said the distracted female voice in his ear.

Shotgun touched the earring on his earlobe. It hooked over the swell of his ear and inside it, just far enough that he could hear Riza well even in the faint, frigid breeze. "Sounds like they might still come with me, if I'm lucky."

"I wouldn't hold my breath."

Shotgun grinned. "I make my own luck, so let me worry about that. Are you still broadcasting the feed from the palace?"

"From the minute they walk into the hall to the minute they burst dramatically through the doors, yes."

Shotgun let out a deep, satisfied breath. Up here, the world was spread out underneath him, dizzying and glorious. He could see treetops miles away swaying back and forth, rustling like a chorus of whispering voices, and beyond those, the lights of the city—fireflies in the darkness.

"Tell me the truth," he said coaxingly.

"What," said Riza flatly.

"You left the palace gates shut longer than you had to, right? It was a publicity stunt, wasn't it?"

"Brat," said Riza. "Get off the roof, or wherever you are,

and don't call any more attention to yourself than you have to. You need to seem trustworthy."

Shotgun pressed his hand over his heart. "I'm insulted that you think I'm not."

Riza snorted, and the connection went silent with a click.

————

GUNFIRE.

An explosion flashed white, and blood rained down from the sky.

*"Please let me wake up. Captain! Please let me—"*

Saizou opened his eyes. His arms were stiff, locked at his sides like a corpse dead for a day. The muscles in his throat constricted as he tried to make a sound. His heart hammered, wanting to get out; he felt like prey, but he could not move and couldn't run from the predator.

Something moved on his right, and Shi appeared, the sight of him just comforting enough that Saizou got a foothold, a tighter grip on his own mind.

"It's all right, captain." Shi reached around Saizou's shoulders with his left arm, his right still curled toward his abdomen, and helped him sit upright. Saizou felt his fingers begin to regain their ability to move, but the rest of his body was slower in catching up. His throat loosened and he began to breathe, one attempt at a time.

"Sorry," he managed, closing his eyes, a vain attempt to erase the memory from his mind, to keep it from coming back in dream form the next time he tried to sleep.

"It isn't your fault, captain."

Saizou flexed his fingers. They shook in the blue light

filtering through the rice-paper walls, trembling like a child's when they imagined a monster under the bed. He said nothing.

"Saizou." Shi's voice cracked like a whip. "It isn't your fault. Everyone suffers in war; you are no different than countless others. Stop beating yourself up."

Saizou shook his head once, then again, then harder. *Go away,* to the dream. *Go away, go away.* "He was in pain. So much pain, I couldn't—"

"I know, captain. You did what you could."

"What I could? I led him there. I put him where was."

"Listen to me," said Shi in a hard voice. "Casualties happen in war. That's the way it works. You saved as many lives as were destroyed by the enemy. Not many leaders can say that."

A small part of Saizou knew Shi was probably right. There was logic in his words, obviously not every casualty was his fault. War meant death; there was no way to have one without the other.

But when he thought of Corporal Ayu, staggering towards him with half his body missing, blown apart by the enemy...

Something cold touched his face, and he reached up, wiping a tear away with the palm of his hand. "I know you're right," he said finally. *Explosions...*

He remembered Shi, throwing his body in front of Saizou.

He remembered the blast.

But....

"You never told me," said Saizou suddenly.

"Eh?"

Saizou nudged Shi's good side. "I can sit now. You can stop playing furniture."

The ghost of a smile touched Shi's mouth, and he sat with his legs crossed where Saizou could clearly see him. "So? What didn't I tell you?"

"Why you saved my life. I would be dead if not for you, but you never told me why you did it. I don't think I ever asked."

Shi said nothing for a long moment, until Saizou looked up to see if he had heard. He gave his friend a probing look, searching his eyes, his body language for any kind of clue as to what he might be feeling.

"Why are you asking now?" questioned Shi, his deep voice strangely muffled in his throat. He did not hunch over or glance in a different direction; he did not try to avoid the question, but it was obvious he wished Saizou had not asked it.

Saizou rubbed his hands over his face and sighed. "I don't know. Maybe because I don't...you've followed me since Liaoyang, and I don't understand why. You call me *captain* even though we've been discharged. I'm the reason..." He glanced at Shi's face, then down at his hands as he slid his palms together. "You never talk about yourself. Is it because I don't ask?"

"It's because I'd rather you didn't," said Shi in a low voice. "You don't need to know about me."

Saizou hesitated, debating whether to press the issue or not, but he could tell now was not the time. "One day, Shi."

"Fine," said Shi, getting to his feet. "But it's been almost an hour. If you are awake, you can go talk to Cherry Hair and decide our next move before we're swarmed by mutts."

# SIXTEEN

KIRIKIZU STEPPED through the doors of Shinsengumi Station just as the moon broke through the haze of clouds over the city. It was a dingy, gray building, clean and minimal, but old. After walking through the front door, Kirikizu was greeted by a small square room with no seating area. To the right was a reflective wall—he pressed his fingertip against it and watched his reflection's fingertip meet the real one. He was being recorded. Had there been a space between his finger and the reflection, he would have known it to be simple plexiglass.

There was a door in the reflective wall, but instead of knocking or waiting for someone to appear, he opened it. Unlocked. *Messy.* Then again, the state of things was no surprise, not with the residing commander being the wreck he was. He had no discipline.

Computer screens cast an eerie blue glow across six unmanned desks, and Kirikizu gave them a disapproving glance. At least one person should be here. He took one more step but stopped as a small figure stepped out of a door to the left, just down the short hall, and came scuttling toward him.

He recognized her, the girl who handled the mutants in the dungeon. He could remember that she was named after some furry animal, but not which one specifically.

The girl hurried toward him, but only seemed to notice his presence when she was three feet in front of him. She stopped short and stared. Even her short, jagged hair seemed to rise on end, an animal with her hackles raised.

"What—" She stopped herself and gave a brief, bouncing bow before continuing with, "do you want, my lord?"

His reaction was immediate, knee-jerk. "Don't ever," he intoned coldly, "call me that again."

She knitted her eyebrows together, but only bowed again, her hands clasped together. "I'm sorry. Are you here for Commander Haka?"

"Yes. Where is he?"

"He isn't here." She scratched her head and smiled sweetly. She had the face of a small child but the husky voice of a woman, and he noticed the pitch of her voice rise with the word *he*.

"Where is he?"

She cleared her throat. "He's out with a few of the officers. They're doing something with the drones, I don't know. I'm just the zookeeper."

Kirikizu's lip curled in a sneer hidden from her view by the muzzle he wore. "Is he really," he said softly.

"He is, actually."

Kirikizu swept a critical, probing glance around the room. The officers were gone—she might be telling the truth. The Prince-Regent had ordered drones to be sent out. However...

"Why weren't you in the dungeon?" he asked, looking down at her with a neutral gaze.

She glared. "What does it matter to you, my—" She caught herself. "What does it matter to you?"

He glanced at the door she had come out of. "So," he said, and started toward it with long strides.

"Hey!" He heard the note of desperation in the woman's voice and played the possibilities of her next move in his mind. Either she would attempt to stop or distract him with her words, or as small as she was, she might even throw something at him.

She took the first option. "Hey," she said again, and then bellowed, "Commander!"

The door flew open, and Commander Haka stumbled out, catching himself just before slamming into Kirikizu.

"You," he said, drawing himself up as gracefully as possible, his eyes wide and his irises frosted over with the effects of stardust. It was recent, too, by the look of him—Kirikizu guessed he had been injecting himself when Otter came out of the room.

"Were you perhaps asleep on the job?" asked Kirikizu archly, stepping away from Commander Haka just in case the other man suddenly lost his balance and pitched forward onto him.

"No," said Haka, tossing lank black hair out of his eyes.

Kirikizu drew a hissing breath. "Your negligence is worse than I thought."

"It wasn't negligence," snapped Otter. "He was coordinating the drones in there."

Commander Haka tilted his chin up, and for a second, Kirikizu thought the other man's eyes would roll back in their sockets. Instead, he blinked once, and a soft smile curved his mouth. He rolled his head to one side and hitched his shoulder as if working out a muscle kink before purring, "I don't need help. If that's why you're here."

"Your entire task force seems to be missing," said Kirikizu. He had seen the effects of stardust many times, and the sensual euphoria people had after taking the drug. He despised it. "Where are they?"

"I sent them out to look for the Prince-Regent's fugitives, where else?" Haka's smile was smug, but his eyes were cold and calculating despite the fact he was, very obviously, wasted.

"It's doubtful Saizou Akita and his companion are still within city limits," said Kirikizu. "Your task force will have to go outside its jurisdiction, which is why I'm here."

"Jurisdiction is relative," said Haka, waving a hand, giving Kirikizu a glance that was both scathing and skeptical.

Kirikizu ignored the remark. "I'll be taking one of your mutts with me."

"Oi, excuse me?" Otter stepped forward again, her face pinching in a glare. She looked at Commander Haka. "Can he do that?"

Commander Haka's drugged eyes held a knowing gleam. "If it's in the Prince-Regent's interests, of course he can do that. After all, Otter dearest, everything he does is to make sure the Prince-Regent is...hmm. Satisfied."

Kirikizu heard every exhale through the filters on his muzzle, but he could not feel his lungs expanding or shrinking. *Breathe.* He forced himself to feel it, to make himself aware. To place himself back in the moment, where he had control over his next action. He waited a few more seconds, standing absolutely still. Regaining control. Finally, he said, "I will be taking your best tracker. See the girl gets it ready."

"The girl's name is Otter," said Haka.

Otter. That was the animal. "I don't care."

"Do as he says," said Haka, with a quick jerk of his head.

Otter growled and stalked between them toward the

dungeon door. She yanked it open, leaving no question as to how she felt about being ordered about, and let it slam behind her.

Haka folded his long-fingered hands together, false politeness coating his words. "Can I get you anything else?"

Kirikizu would have liked nothing better than to see Haka fired and replaced, but he knew full well the Prince-Regent's reasons for keeping him on. The Prince-Regent had him in the palm of his hand, thanks to endless supplies of stardust, which he could withhold at any time if he so chose. On top of that, Commander Haka was not entirely useless—there were times when he was downright competent. It was easy to mistake his sloppy, slimy demeanor for lack of ability.

Kirikizu wished the man *did* lack ability. Then he would have grounds for approaching the Prince-Regent with the suggestion of Haka's release.

"I'm going to wait out back," said Kirikizu. The mutts were released into an enclosed courtyard through which the only exit was a rusted liftgate leading out onto the streets. He assumed Otter would be resetting their tracking chips and ensuring they were still controllable via collar. The Dog wore a similar thing; Kirikizu knew how it worked well enough.

"Shall I escort you?" Haka leaned heavily against the wall behind him, obviously too off-balance to stand straight for terribly long. His grin was eerily self-aware. It was like he was saying *I know I'm a wreck but I have the favor of the Prince-Regent. There's nothing you can do about it.*

Kirikizu squeezed his left hand into a fist. The motion triggered a device inside his sleeve, and as soon as he felt the slender knife slide into his grip, he drew back his arm to throw it.

Haka flinched, and Kirikizu sneered before lowering the

knife. "Don't forget, Commander." He laced the word *Commander* with all the loathing he felt. "You and I each wear a different leash, but they are both held in the same hand. And it just so happens," he added, lowering his voice to a simmering whisper, "my leash is longer than yours."

He spun the knife as he turned away from the other man and strode down the stairs into the dungeon. He did not bother to look at the mutts waiting to be sent out; he walked across the spacious dark room and down another, smaller hall. He pushed the door open and entered the stone courtyard.

Otter was already there, standing in the shadow of a beast nearly twice her height. Dark purple-black skin stretched over sculpted muscles. Six legs shifted restlessly, and two tails whipped the air like a cat waiting to pounce.

As Kirikizu approached, the monster lifted its broad, flat head and bared a double row of teeth; eight eyes gleaming, deep-set, from its face.

"This is Violet," said Otter, turning to face Kirikizu. She had one hand on Violet's collar—a thin affair, just one wire encircling the creature's neck with a pendant plugged into a glowing implant on its chest. "She's the best one we have. I'll control her from here."

Kirikizu noticed she was watching him closely, judging his reaction to the beast looming over her. "She needs to smell something of their scent."

"Well, if you have something, let me know. We were supposed to have blood samples, but they haven't arrived yet."

Kirikizu plucked a thin vial from his belt and unscrewed the lid. "This will work."

"Is that the blood?" Otter held out her hand, and Kirikizu dropped the vial into her palm. The young woman turned the vial over and glanced sideways at him. "Where did you get this if we didn't even get the vials yet?"

"One of them lost quite a lot of blood in more than one location. Give it to her. We need to leave now."

She curled her lip, but Otter took the vial and turned around to face Violet. She tapped her finger against the underside of the beast's chin. "Open up."

The monster's mouth opened with a throaty growl. Otter poured half the vial onto Violet's tongue before pouring the rest onto the ground in a thin, red trickle. Violet snapped her mouth shut and lowered her massive head as she sniffed the traces of blood on the pavement.

"That should do it." Otter tossed the vial back to Kirikizu and looked slightly disappointed when he caught it. "She's faster than you, obviously. If you didn't bring the right transportation—"

"I did."

She shrugged. "Fine. Take her, then." She pointed at the liftgate. "Out that way. I'll be monitoring. Please," she added, with a short bow from the waist, "be careful with her. She's my baby."

The monster lifted her head and unleashed a hellish bay, her voice ululating until it sounded like not one monster, but an entire pack about to wreak havoc on the city.

Kirikizu crossed the courtyard and gripped the liftgate handle. It resisted, rusted from the rain, but it came free as he pulled upward.

Otter sighed, then pointed at the gate. "Go."

With a deep huff, Violet trotted out the gate. Kirikizu followed the monster out of the courtyard, up around the station where he had parked his vehicle.

Commander Haka stood by the front door, and while he

stepped farther back into the shadows when he saw Violet, the streetlight caught his eyes, and they gleamed like a cat's as he watched Kirikizu mount up.

"Itterashai," sang Commander Haka softly. *Safe travels.*

Kirikizu bowed his head politely.

Violet howled.

# SEVENTEEN

EVERYTHING ON TELEVISION WAS BOLLOCKS.
Bloody Japs with their bloody sumo wrestling and their exaggerated reality shows. Oscar stretched out on the bed and picked up the remote, deciding to flip through channels one more time and see if anything interesting had come on within the last sixty seconds.

Probably not, but it was worth a try. He could go out on the town, of course; Tokyo was renowned for the amusements it offered, but he had one more lecture to deliver the next morning, and he should probably use common sense and get some sleep.

He tucked one arm under his head and glanced around the hotel room. It was expensive: the wall to the right of the massive bed was made entirely of glass, looking out on the city. Tokyo was a mass of glittering lights and colors: blue, red, orange, and green twinkled like Christmas lights.

Christmas was soon...well, he would be home by the twentieth. Mum would not be able to rag on him for missing another year, and that was something.

He changed the channel again, and a blurry image stretched across the screen. It was two men, standing in a courtyard. *Are those corpses in front of them?* He pushed himself up and leaned forward, squinting at the screen.

*Absolutely, corpses.*

Decapitated, too, it looked like. "Well, laser naginatas or whatever you call those will do that," Oscar told the screen. "Which is why you should keep them out of the reach of bloody criminals."

Red kanji moved across the bottom of the screen, and he caught a few words of it: *attention* and *run*. Fortunately, a few seconds later, English phrasing replaced the kanji and proclaimed in red block letters, ATTENTION. DEPOSED LORD SAIZOU AKITA AND COMPANION SHI MATSUMOTO WANTED FOR POSSESSION OF ILLEGAL WEAPONS, RESISTING ARREST, AND MURDER. REWARD: 100,000 YEN FOR SAIZOU AKITA. 50,000 YEN FOR SHI MATSUMOTO.

They included a phone number after the announcement, but Oscar did not bother to write it down. He was here for a conference, not to keep his eyes peeled for fugitives. Besides, he made enough money as it was. More than enough, really; he didn't know what he was going to do with it. Fund his own lab in the future, maybe—splice monkeys all day if he wanted to.

He crossed over to the window and looked out, listening to the television murmur in mingled Japanese and English. There were bits of Chinese here and there, too. He had never bothered to learn another language, even when he could have. He didn't have to when most countries spoke English anyway.

He watched his reflection smirk, but the smile faded and he rubbed his eyes. Jet lag. He had flown in a week ago and he still had jet lag.

"Doctor Oscar Sleiman, the youngest in his field at just thirty years old," said the television, and Oscar blinked. He turned around and stepped halfway across the room, peering at the television.

"Oh, look," he remarked to nobody, "there I am. Finally, television worth watching, eh?" He glanced around the empty room and shrugged. Oh, well.

The footage was from the lecture he had given that morning on the ethics of bioengineering, particularly the controversy over whether or not an engineered sentient being possessed a soul.

"Ah, well," said the small, grainy version of himself, and Oscar shook his head. "Flustered, Oscar," he said aloud. "Must work on that. There's always some twit going to ask you irrelevant sensational questions."

On the screen, Oscar said, "That's not really something I consider much, actually. I'm a doctor, not a priest. I work with the more, ah, physical aspects of a thing."

The crowd laughed politely but whether it was at his humor or his awkward reply, Oscar could not tell.

The camera panned once again to the middle-aged woman who had asked the question in the first place. Her auburn hair was pulled back in a French twist—he vaguely remembered seeing her deep in a discussion with Yoshida Tagomi, the world's foremost authority in genetic splicing. *Right. Her. The nosy hag.*

She touched the back of her neck, as if fixing her hair. It looked impervious, probably could have withstood a hurricane-force wind. "But doesn't that raise inquiries of a moral and ethical nature?"

The Oscar on television blinked once before leaning toward his microphone. "I'm sorry, but this is a convention for science." He laughed a little and glanced toward the camera briefly. "Now anyone with an actual question, please feel free to—"

Oscar picked up the remote and switched the television off before pinching the bridge of his nose and sighing. It was the 'actual question' remark that had brought up all this controversy. *Is he really a self-centered ass? Is he just under pressure?* What did it matter? He wasn't an actor or a singer or some glitzy celebrity parading around a stage; he was a scientist, for the love of—

Someone knocked on the door.

*Oh, brilliant.* They couldn't have picked a better time, no, of course someone knocked just before he was about to go to bed. Why not?

Muttering under his breath, he crossed over to the door. He did not bother to make himself look professional again; at this hour, an untucked shirt and unbuttoned cuffs were perfectly acceptable.

He leaned a shoulder against the door and shouted, "Who is it?" Lower, he added, "Don't you people have bedtimes?"

"Imperial Guard," said a voice on the other side of the door. "Open up."

Oscar jumped back. *Imperial Guard? Bloody hell.* "I haven't done anything!"

"Open the door, Doctor Sleimann."

Oscar ran his hands through his hair. Imperial Guard at his door. What could he have done? His passport was good, the trip was fully funded—

"Open the door!" barked the voice, obviously fed up.

He didn't want to have to pay for damages if the Imperial Guard broke down the door to an expensive hotel room, so Oscar unlocked the door and stepped back as six imperial guards strode into the room, their sleek samurai armor gleaming under soft striplights in the ceiling.

The foremost guard stepped forward and removed his helmet, tucking it under his arm. "Oscar Sleimann, yes?"

Oscar blinked. The guard looked like a bloody ten-year-old. "That's me, but I think you probably have the wrong man. I'm here for a science conference, right? Haven't done anything except lecture and eat at some truly terrible restaurants."

"You have a PhD in bioengineering and another in biotechnology, this is correct?" the guard continued, staring straight ahead as if he had been ordered not to look Oscar in the eyes.

"Everyone knows that, mate," Oscar pointed out, glancing at the other five guards. "Am I a bomb threat or something?"

"We need you to come with us," said the guard. "If you please."

"I bloody well don't please!"

The guard hesitated. Apparently, he had not been prepared for that response. Oscar pointed at the door. "Look, mate, until you come back with a proper arrest warrant or whatever you boys use, I'm not taking a step outside that door."

Another guard stepped forward without removing his helmet and said, "The Prince-Regent wishes to see you."

"Yes," said the first guard, clearing his throat. "It would be in your best interest to accompany us." He bowed from the waist and stepped back, watching Oscar carefully, as though he might suddenly decide to leap out the window.

"My best interest," Oscar repeated. He laughed briefly and rubbed the back of his neck, casting another glance at the guards standing around him in a half-circle. "You know what's funny, is the fact I don't get that feeling."

"Please, Doctor Sleimann," said the first guard. "The Prince-Regent demands it."

"Yeah, I heard you the first time." The door was the only exit, and it was totally blocked. Imperial guards were, from what he gathered, ruthless in the service of their so-called 'Sun,' and he was probably either leaving voluntarily or bound and gagged.

Bound and gagged would look terrible on television, really. "Well, when you ask nicely like that, it seems a bit rude to refuse, really."

The guard bowed again. "Your cooperation is most welcome. Hail the Sun."

"Hail the bloody Sun," said Oscar.

———

SAIZOU STEPPED into the courtyard and turned to look up at the roof. A tall silhouette stood framed against the stars, but he jumped down to the slick stone ground as soon as Saizou said, "Get down here."

"Thought it over, captain?" Shotgun asked, lifting his right hand in salute.

Saizou smiled briefly. "You're a risk, and probably a bad one."

"I've been told that a lot." Shotgun grinned and then sighed, rotating his head and bouncing his shoulders up and down, loosening his muscles. "So are you going to take me up on my offer or not?"

"We're going to," said Saizou.

Shotgun let out the beginning of a whoop, but Saizou raised a hand and cut him off. "If we get there and it's a trap, or if you've been lying in any way—"

"You'll kill me?" Shotgun interrupted. He chuckled. "Fine. Fair enough."

"I won't kill you," said Saizou. "I'm done spilling the blood of boys. I'll be disappointed in you, is all."

The grin faded from Shotgun's face, and he blinked rapidly. Licking his lips, he said, "Hey, I'm not that much younger than you are."

"Younger is relative," said Saizou, kicking a frozen chunk of snow. It slid several yards before slowing to a stop near Shotgun's left boot. "There's a condition."

"What? On you coming with me?"

Saizou nodded.

"Okay," said Shotgun. "What?"

"I'm inviting Winter and the girl to come with us. It won't be safe here once the Shinsengumi arrive."

Shotgun opened his mouth to protest, but no words left his mouth. He stared at Saizou's face for a long moment and slowly scratched the back of his head. "Ahhh, fine."

"We'll leave in fifteen minutes."

"What about that motorcycle you hid? Can we take that?"

"There are five of us," said Saizou. "I'm giving the motorcycle to Shi and the girl. You and I can walk. Winter, too, if he agrees to come."

"I don't like him," said Shotgun in a loud whisper, as if informing Saizou of a great secret. "Cold-blooded bastard. What do you think of him? You know taking two extra people is a risk for me, right? I don't even know if we can trust them."

Saizou watched Shotgun's nervous expression for a moment before asking, "Why do you trust me?"

"Why? I saw you running from the Prince-Regent, that's why. I know you need help."

"And that's the only reason? Suppose it was an elaborate plot. Suppose the Prince-Regent wants to catch you and whoever you're working with. This would be a good way to do it, don't you think?"

A look of surprise and uncertainty came over Shotgun's face. "That would be stupid. That's...yeah, I don't believe it."

Saizou smiled.

Defensively, Shotgun added, "I'm not a big-time criminal like you are."

"Am I big-time?" asked Saizou, amused.

"You think you aren't?"

"I'm just curious." Saizou breathed out and watched the fog dissipate. It was freezing out here. He needed warmer clothes, but he couldn't exactly dash back to his domain and get them.

No, it wasn't his domain.

Not anymore.

Not for a little while longer.

"Curious about...?" Shotgun prompted, hugging himself and watching Saizou closely.

Saizou rubbed his hands together. "You want to help two people you've never met. This tells me that you aren't afraid of the law, probably because you're already on the wrong side of it."

"Okay," said Shotgun, with new wariness in his voice.

Saizou continued. "You're working with someone else, also probably an outlaw. If the two of you want to help us, it probably means you have a plan and you need our help. I doubt you'd put yourself in more danger just to lend a helping hand."

"Hey," Shotgun began, but Saizou was not finished.

"You not only want our help, but you also need it. What do you need it for? That's what I'm curious about."

Shotgun was silent for a long moment after Saizou finished. He shifted his jaw from side to side and opened it widely before snapping it shut so hard Saizou heard his teeth clack together.

"I don't suppose I could wait and tell you when we get there?" said Shotgun finally, with a grimacing smile.

"You can," said Saizou. He stepped closer, stopping a foot in front of the taller, younger man. He wondered what he should say, what he should add, if he should make another threat. But he chose nothing; instead, he patted Shotgun's arm and walked past him, back up the steps.

"Oh," he added, pausing at the top, "the next time you listen in on a private conversation, don't give away the fact you did it. Only Shi calls me *captain*."

He went inside, leaving Shotgun standing, wide-eyed, in the courtyard.

# EIGHTEEN

SAIZOU WANDERED THROUGH THE MONASTERY, searching for Winter. He saw no sign of Fumiyo—with her disposition, she might well be hiding behind a shelf somewhere. He did not want to intrude on anyone's privacy, but he had told Shotgun they would leave in fifteen minutes. He had to convince Winter to come with him, or at least allow him to take the girl.

He could not leave innocent people behind to suffer for his presence.

The monastery was divided into four hallways, each leading to a different corner of the building, as far as Saizou could tell. He had already been to the dining room and kitchen corner, as well as the corner with personal rooms.

He took another hall, to the left of the foyer, and found himself confronted by two doors at the end. He pushed them to either side and looked in. The room was larger than any other he had seen in the monastery, with a smooth wooden floor and a wooden rack hanging from the far wall. The rack held several katanas, a wakizashi, several staffs, and a naginata.

Winter sat cross-legged in the center of the room, his eyes closed. Across his knees rested a long katana, with a blade three feet from tip to hilt. Even from this distance of fifteen or so feet, Saizou could see that the blade of the katana had been tampered with—the small, golden good-luck idols had been removed, and it had been re-bound with black string. In the center of the handle was a silver cross.

"What do you want?" asked Winter, without opening his eyes.

Saizou bowed from the waist, not just out of convention, but because it seemed necessary. He felt as though he had invaded a moment of personal meditation or prayer, which perhaps he had. "I apologize."

"What," repeated Winter, "do you want?" He opened his eyes now and turned his head, giving Saizou a grim expression.

"May I come in?"

Winter nodded once.

Saizou stepped into the room and shut the doors behind him, in case Fumiyo was hanging around anywhere within earshot. He felt he should explain the situation to Winter first, before the girl heard it.

He sank to his knees and leaned down, pressing his palms to the floor. "I'm afraid I have unintentionally put you in danger."

Winter breathed out through his nose and lifted his chin. "What makes you think you have done this?"

This was a gamble, and Saizou knew it. He had already been through the possibilities in his mind, and whether he told Winter the details depended on what he said next. "Let me ask you something. You have said you are a man of God."

Winter looked down at the blade across his knees. He said nothing.

Saizou continued, "Are you bound by the law of God or the law of the nation?"

A brief, frosty smile touched Winter's face and was gone. "An interesting question," he remarked. He wrapped his fingers around the handle of his sword and lifted it, cutting through the air and resting the blade behind him. It was a hold designed to cut someone standing behind you, but he only rested the tip on the floor. "You're an outlaw, then."

"I have the feeling you already knew that."

"With the condition your friend is in, you would have gone to a hospital if you weren't. In fact," Winter continued, "you are about to tell me that the Shinsengumi, or worse, will possibly track you here. If they find this place, they will torture and kill myself and Fumiyo to get to you."

Saizou tapped his index fingers on the floor. "And if I said that, what would you say?"

"I would ask you to go on." Winter lifted his left hand in a *keep talking* gesture. "What more is there to add?"

"There's a chance Shotgun knows a safe place."

"No place is safe," said Winter. "Some places are just safer than others."

"I would ask you to come with us. Both of you. I'm responsible for bringing this on your heads, and this is the only way I can apologize."

"By asking me to leave this monastery," said Winter. He lifted his gaze and looked at the opposite wall, unblinking. "Do you know why I'm here, Akita? I am not a monk, and yet I live in a monastery. Are you curious as to why?"

"Yes," Saizou admitted, "but you seem private."

"I am private. I lived alone, until I took in Fumiyo. Sometimes she stays hidden for days. The only way I know she is still residing here is the fact food disappears. I like to be alone. I prefer it."

*Where are you going with this?* Saizou watched the older man closely, waiting for him to speak again. When he did speak, Winter's voice was hard and brittle, his jaw muscles clenched, cutting lines to his cheekbones.

"I am...atoning. Or I hope to. Through meditation and prayer, and the..." He glanced at Saizou, and his mouth twitched. "The somewhat begrudged helping of strangers in need."

"You're making up for something you've done in the past." Saizou nodded. They had to leave, sooner rather than later, but curiosity kept him where he was. "I can understand that."

"I'm not sure you can," said Winter flatly. "You were a soldier, that much is obvious. A leader, if I'm not wrong."

Saizou cleared his throat. He was unused to being observed, and it was unnerving—particularly by a semi-priest gripping a three-foot blade. "A captain. Yes."

"You killed men."

Saizou lifted his hands from the floor and pressed them against his knees, gripping them until his knuckles turned white as bone pressed against skin. "Of course I did."

"So did I." Winter's voice was softer than before; Saizou strained to hear it. "Many men." He straightened his shoulders and tilted his head, casting a straightforward, stone-cut stare at Saizou. "But never in the service of my country."

"An assassin?"

"A mercenary. Which, unfortunately, bears no honorable distinction."

*If he didn't fight in the war...* "You weren't conscripted?"

"I was not."

"You aren't a priest or a monk—how did you escape conscription, if not for those?"

"They came looking for me," said Winter. "They left after a brief discussion. Now," he continued, pointedly moving beyond that subject, "I will see to Fumiyo. If she wishes to accompany you, then please take her."

*Just Fumiyo?* "You aren't leaving?"

"No," said Winter.

"You must realize the danger—"

"I do," Winter interrupted. He unfolded his long limbs and got to his feet, holding his katana halfway behind his back as if still prepared to slash an unseen enemy in half. "However, I took you in."

"You showed us hospitality," Saizou argued, also standing. He took a step closer to Winter. "You don't owe us anything. If you come with us, you'll be in less danger than if you remained here."

"The Shinsengumi will find this place and search it." Winter shook his head once. "They do not frighten me."

"They should," said Saizou. "They are not the Shinsengumi I remember. They are ruthless. Their commander should be locked up, not giving orders."

Winter crossed the room in three impossibly long strides, his face less than a foot away from Saizou's. His angular eyes were blue, Saizou noticed; an odd thing to take in at a time like this, but blue they were. Deep, near black, but brighter in certain shades of light.

Uncomfortable at the proximity, Saizou stepped back, wary. He expected sharp or angry words from Winter explaining the sudden reaction, but instead, Winter only said, "I know the Shinsengumi commander. I will deal with them when they get here. You take your friends and Fumiyo away from here."

"I can't leave you here in good conscience," said Saizou, clenching his hands into fists. "I don't even like you, but I take responsibility where I should take it."

Winter's laugh barely made a dent in the silence. "You feel responsibility for me?" He lifted a hand and placed it on Saizou's shoulder. He pushed, but it was a brief and strangely gentle gesture—that of a brother or a comrade. "Worry about your friends." He dropped his hand and stepped past Saizou. "I can take care of myself."

———

"HEARD THEY ESCAPED, TOO."

"Where'd they go?"

"Nobody knows. Everyone says they're still at large, even with that video footage being plastered everywhere I look. Have to give them credit for that, what with all the resources the Prince-Regent has up his sleeve. People are saying they're heroes for spitting in his face like they did."

"Eh. They'll get caught sooner or later. What do you want to bet they're forgotten in a week?"

"They're veterans, just returned from war. It's making people mad, you know. Everyone has got a loved one fighting. They can relate."

"Who can't? Still, I bet they're forgotten as soon as they're caught and executed."

"Wouldn't bet on an execution—his Royal Highness is also royally pissed. He's probably given orders for them to be shot on sight."

"Nah, that's too fast if they've got him angry. I call torture.

Skinning alive, maybe; no, he'll probably boil them alive and broadcast it over every available station."

"I don't like those blanket broadcasts. Kids turn on the television and they see that? Kids see enough these days."

"That's the truth."

The elderly men returned to their drinks and fell silent, drowning their speculations in alcohol, and Shimo slowly turned around on the barstool, scanning the bar. *Where's he gone?*

He slid off the stool and walked casually across the crowded, haze-filled room, searching for his brother. If this place had a back room, he was probably there. Well, there or one of the bathrooms.

Shimo never touched alcohol when on a job; it dulled his sense of smell. Now, however, in a crowded bar, he lifted the bottle of sake in his hand and took a long swallow of the clear, burning liquid. Too many people, smelling like sweat and smoke and alcohol and sex and chemicals...

He took another swallow and headed toward the back of the bar, casting a backward glance over his shoulder at the door. The cybernetic bouncer was watchful and stronger than it looked. Just twenty minutes ago, it had thrown a rowdy drunk man out the front door with one hand.

He saw the sign for the bathrooms and turned the corner. There was only one bathroom, apparently; that made it easy. He kicked it with his foot. "Virgo!"

There was no response, not that there would be. If his brother was in the middle of something, he would ignore Shimo even if he stood outside yelling for an hour. He knew this from personal experience.

He tried the handle and found it locked. He clicked his tongue against his teeth, took another drink, and leaned against the door, listening. He heard a breathy, female moan, and a male voice laughed and asked, "Do you like that?"

Ah, yes.

Virgo was in there, all right.

*Too bad for him.* His information was too hot to stand around holding.

Shimo tilted the bottle into his mouth and finished the last of the sake. He looked at the door for a long moment—knocking or calling, those would be ignored. Ah, well. He raised his hand and smashed the bottle against the door, shutting his eyes as glass splintered everywhere. He called his twin's name again. "Virgo!"

Less than two seconds later, the door flew open and Virgo fell out, shards of glass crunching under the soles of his boots. He was half-naked, which was normal—he hadn't even bothered to put a shirt on that morning—but his belt hung unbuckled and his shoulder-length hair had obviously been toyed with. At least his eyes were wide and alert.

"Shim—" he began, but he looked down at the glass and the panic left his face. "What the hell, Shimo," he said flatly.

Shimo smiled sweetly and nodded at the pretty, blushing girl who appeared behind Virgo, looking as embarrassed as she was bewildered. To Virgo, he said, "We have another job if we want it."

Virgo lowered his kohl-smeared eyelids and gave Shimo a narrow look. "Can it wait?"

Shimo crossed his arms. "Yes, it can probably wait."

"Good," said Virgo, preparing to close the door again, but he paused when Shimo added, "It's a big one."

Virgo planted his hands on his hips. "Ah-huh. How big?"

Shimo held up both his hands and pulled them apart until his arms were spread out.

Virgo rubbed his mouth. "Well, *kuso*," he sighed. He turned to the girl behind him and wrapped his arm around her neck, pulling her toward him and giving her a loud, open-mouthed kiss before releasing her and turning back to Shimo. He kicked a few shards of glass out of the way and walked past his brother.

"This had better be good," he warned. "And when I say *good*, I mean better than what I just ditched for you."

"You'll live." Shimo turned and followed him back toward the bar. He used to feel a surge of sympathy for whoever Virgo chose to bestow his ever-changing favors on, but he was too used to it by now and the surge was hardly a twinge.

Virgo leaned against the bar, put two fingers in his mouth, and whistled at the bartender. "Two of those cute little bottles of sake," he said with a wink.

Shimo glared at him, even though he knew winking was a reflex for his brother and not an act of conscious thought. "I already had a bottle. I don't want another one."

Virgo nudged Shimo's arm with his elbow. "Ah, that works out well then, because it isn't for you. No. It's for me."

"Oh, for the love of—you don't need another one. You've already had two."

Virgo turned, leaning just one elbow on the bar, and held up two fingers. "Two," he said, and held up two more, "and two makes four. See, I can do math." He glanced past Shimo, and a lazy grin curved his mouth. "Hey. You've got another one on your tail."

"Another what?" asked Shimo, even though he was afraid he already knew.

"Another guy who thinks you're a lady."

Shimo growled and began to spin around, but Virgo caught his arm. "Hey," he said, clearly suppressing a laugh, "leave him alone. If he walks up, I'll set him straight. No use getting ourselves thrown out if he's only looking, right?"

Shimo leaned his elbows on the counter and swore under his breath. It had happened since he was a child—consistently being mistaken for a girl. It was his slender build and feminine face; he knew that. He was praised for his "pretty lips" and willowy figure by half the people he ran into. It was only when he spoke that they realized the mistake they had made. Usually, they backed off. If not, Virgo took care of it before Shimo had time to fully react.

"You should get a girlfriend," said Virgo. "That would take care of this problem."

"It would give said girlfriend a new one," sighed Shimo.

"Lame excuse."

"I'm too busy for a girlfriend, and you know that."

"About to be busier, too, I think. Tell me about this job, yeah?"

"You know that feed of the two vets escaping the Palace of the Sun?"

Virgo adopted a shrewd expression. "Yeah."

"A hundred and fifty thousand yen if we bring them both in."

Virgo slammed both hands down on the counter. "Perfect. We'll head back to the motel and get our stuff as soon as I finish these drinks."

———

AT THE OTHER end of the bar, two men sat watching Virgo and Shimo. At first glance, they did not look unusual. Both were in their mid-thirties with long hair and long coats. Like many men in the city, their eyelids were heavy with kohl and they sported piercings in their ears. Still, Honey noticed, they exuded masculinity in the way they held their mouths, in their posture.

They had one bottle of vodka and two shot glasses between them, but they had stopped drinking and were observing the brothers instead.

Interesting.

She had served them earlier, but she had not paid much attention to them. They seemed to prefer observation to making themselves the life of any party. They could be trouble, or they could be nothing. She decided to see for herself.

"Hey, fellas." She paused wiping the counter with a rag and gave them both a friendly smile. "You want another one?" She nodded at the bottle.

The man on the right, with the sad eyes and pursed lips, smiled. "Ah, I appreciate it, but no. This is probably more than enough."

He had a dimple and a surprisingly open manner, considering how brooding he had looked a few seconds ago. He either was pretending, or he just had a homicidal resting face. They were both plausible options.

"You're cute," Honey told him with a wink. "It would be on the house."

He smiled again and leaned back, stretching. He had been sitting there for quite a long time, Honey realized. Just sitting and watching. "Really, thank you, but no."

"What about your quiet friend?" She nodded toward the other man. His face was long and lean, the shape of his lips curled into a natural look of skepticism.

The first man nudged his companion with an elbow. "Yuu?"

Yuu hardly seemed to notice; he flicked a glance at Honey and resumed watching the brothers across the bar.

"Guess he doesn't," said the first man.

Honey clicked her tongue against her teeth. "If his name is Yuu, what's yours?"

"Kido." He bowed his head a little. Almost overly polite, but it seemed more like good manners than anything else. As he bowed his head, his hair fell away from his collar, and Honey saw a glimpse of a heavily detailed snake tattoo, curling up to under his ear.

She made sure her observation was unnoticeable, and she smiled breezily. "It's very nice to meet you, Kido. I'm Honey."

He inclined his head in response.

Honey continued. "I don't think I've seen you in here before. Have you...?"

Another shake of his head. "First time. We'll probably be back."

"Your accent is a little different. Are you from Tokyo?"

"New Kyoto."

"Ahhh," said Honey knowingly. "I've never been there. Too close to the border right now for my taste."

"I wouldn't visit," Yuu spoke up in a gritty voice that did not match his face. He gave Honey a frown. "Gaijin aren't welcome there."

"I'll keep that in mind," Honey replied, skimming over his remark. If he was surprised at her lack of reaction, he did not show it.

Kido gave him a slight, disapproving twist of his mouth. To Honey, he said, "I'm sorry for his behavior. He's never had many emotions. Something in his brain, I don't know exactly what."

Yuu grunted.

"Don't you worry." Honey smiled. "I've seen enough of the really horrible to know when someone's just mildly irritating."

Again Yuu grunted, and Kido chuckled. He tapped a ring-laden finger on the counter before pushing his stool away. "Thank you." To Yuu, he said, "Come on, let's go."

Yuu stood up and pushed his stool back against the bar. He paused, then picked up the half-empty bottle of vodka before turning and following Kido out the door. As they walked past Seiko, he turned to give Honey a quizzical look. She motioned him over with a finger, and he crossed to the bar, leaning forward to be heard over the noise.

"Yes, Honey?"

"Have you seen those two before?"

"No."

"You sure?"

He blinked once. "Of course I am."

"If they come in again, let me know."

He tilted his head a calculated two inches to the right. "Is something wrong? Would you like me to go after them?"

"No, don't worry about it." Honey chewed the side of her lip and glanced at the brothers at the other end of the bar. "They were watching the pretty boys over there in an interesting way."

"Could it be defined as harassment?"

Honey snorted softly. "Hardly. I think they might be bounty hunters, but one of them had a snake tattoo up his neck. It looked like he was trying to hide it."

"Yakuza?" Seiko guessed.

"Maybe."

"Is this a problem?"

"Mm...no. But they're interesting. If they come in again, let me know, will you?"

"Of course, Honey."

"Oh, by the way." Honey circled around Seiko and lifted up the back of his shirt, studying the bloodless gash near the top of his belt. "I need to get this fixed."

"I feel no discomfort," said Seiko, folding his hands.

"Yeah, yeah, I'm aware, but it's like getting a scratch on something you love, you know? If you can fix it, you fix it."

Seiko turned his head to eye Honey, his face carrying its usual blank curiosity. "Do you love me, Honey?"

She reached up and pushed the back of his head. "Don't be stupid. You don't even know what love means."

"Just because I lack the ability to love you does not necessarily mean you lack the ability to love me," Seiko pointed out.

"All right. I love you, but not in a romantic kind of way. I love you like a friend, and also like an art project I'm really proud of, okay? Don't let it go to your head."

"I do not think I could."

"Fair point. When we get home, remind me to fix you, please. That gash is really bugging me."

"Noted. I will tell you if the two suspicious men return, and I will remind you to fix me tonight. Is there anything else?"

Honey grinned. "Not that I can think of."

He turned to face her. "If you're through?"

She patted his arm. "I'm through. Thanks."

"Honey?"

"What?"

Seiko said, "You are fully aware of the fact I cannot love you."

Honey raised an eyebrow. "I know, babe. Remember, I'm the one who fitted the hollow half of your skull with gadgetry."

"I cannot remember that, and you are well aware—"

"You know what I meant," said Honey, slightly exasperated. She knew it was not Seiko's fault—nothing about his current state was his fault. Except, of course, the explosion that had killed him. "I know you can't love me. That's okay."

"I know," said Seiko. "But I do care about you, as much as I can."

"Oh, yeah?" Sometimes she wondered whether, through some weird trick of science or biology or maybe even a miracle, he retained some kind of emotion. This was one of those times, and she couldn't help but push him toward a faster answer. "What way is that, Seiko?"

"I could not say."

She smiled. "Just go back to the door, okay?"

"Does that upset you?"

The pretty boys were leaving; Honey noticed them make their way toward the front of the lounge. Oh, well. She could find someone else nice to look at. Even Seiko was nice to look at, in a bizarre and unsettling way. "Does what upset me?"

"My lack of reciprocation."

"Umm....no," Honey assured him. "I'm a mechanic. I'm used to working with machinery that doesn't love me back. If a car up and said, 'I love you, Honey,' I'd freak out."

Seiko's eyebrows drew together a fraction, and his expression twitched; the briefest flash of something. It might have been a glitch. "Be careful, Honey. It's dangerous for you if you hold the yakuza's interest."

"I don't think it's me they were interested in." Honey nodded toward the door. "It was Virgo and Shimo, those brothers who just left."

Seiko stepped closer and bent down, lowering his voice. "You may forget, we also helped criminals escape the law. Even if the yakuza are not a problem, the Shinsengumi could decide to view our actions as abetting the escaped soldiers. If that happens, I will be fine. You may not be."

Honey leaned back and narrowed her eyes at him. "Are you feeling all right?"

He straightened, blinking. "Yes, I feel perfectly fine."

"Okay," she said slowly, continuing to give him a narrow-eyed look. "Just checking."

He sighed and folded his hands together. "Honey, you are a strange person to work for."

She rolled her eyes and made a shooing motion with both her hands. "Oh, go back to the door."

# NINETEEN

THE INTERCOM BUZZED. Hiro reached across the desk and pressed the button, his gaze still focused on the report in front of him. "What?"

"Kido and Yuu just got back. They have something to tell you."

Hiro tapped his pen against the paper. It was better to keep important information away from anything digital, whenever possible. Once substance became zeroes and ones, it was a free for all. Anyone with the quickest fingers and the most back doors could take whatever you gave them, by secrecy or by force.

Hiro only uploaded extremely specific things, for an extremely specific reason.

When he wanted them to be stolen.

He rotated his shoulders and leaned back on his stool. He preferred stools to chairs—they were easier to pick up and throw in a fight. Not that he had ever had to fight with a stool, but he was suspicious by nature and the trait revealed itself in strange ways. "Let them come in."

The door buzzed open, and the two men walked into the large, empty room. It was just a converted storage space, with no windows and two doors. An entrance and an exit. Hiro's desk and computer were across the room at the far end, near the exit.

"Hey, boss." Kido approached first, his hands in the pockets of his long coat. Yuu strode behind him, glancing around the room like he had never seen it before. "Guess what we picked up at INTOX?"

"Too busy to guess," said Hiro, tapping his fingernails on the desktop. "Just tell me."

Kido grinned. "The Prince-Regent's splashing those two veterans over every screen in the city. A couple of bounty hunters are going after them."

Hiro folded his arms. "I fail to see how this has any bearing on my life or my business."

Yuu tossed his hair out of his eyes and said, "It's not a small reward."

"Look." Hiro placed both of his hands on the desk and leaned forward, giving them both an intense, narrow stare. "You want to play at bounty hunting, do it on your own off-time. I have more important things to do. We don't need the money. Tokyo's bringing in even more money than New Kyoto, so if you want to chase down two outlaws, that's your hobby. Get out of here and stop wasting my time."

"Harsh, boss," said Kido, but Hiro could tell he was not upset. Neither was Yuu, but then Yuu never was. He was the least emotional person Hiro had ever seen, which made him especially useful for nastier jobs. As two disgruntled, displaced ronin, Kido and Yuu usually made an efficient and helpful duo.

"Get out," said Hiro, jerking his chin toward the entry door.

"See you tomorrow," Kido said affably.

Yuu said nothing; he only turned and followed Kido back out of the room. The door closed, and the sound echoed around the room.

Hiro frowned and sat down on the stool, propping one leg up.

An eerie whistle danced through the air, and a round, blue light flashed across Hiro's computer screen. He flicked the monitor on, and suddenly his workspace was awash in blue light. "What do you want now?"

"I have a little job for you," sang a female voice through the speakers on either side of the screen. No image appeared, but the blue light continued to pulse, hypnotic and annoying. "Nothing tough or fancy, I promise."

Hiro snorted. "Last time you promised nothing tough or fancy, it was fitting someone with new fingerprints. That might sound easy to you, but to me, it was a pain in the neck."

"And it's such a pretty neck," cooed the voice. "Look, I'm sorry, but when I say nothing fancy, I mean it. I just need you to put a few people up."

"I hope by *up*, you mean hang them from the ceiling in plastic bags," said Hiro lazily. "Otherwise, no deal. I can't afford that."

"You're the head of Tokyo yakuza," was the reply. "I'm rolling my eyes right now, by the way."

"I know what I am. And what I am is under scrutiny, head of Tokyo yakuza or not. My position doesn't matter, there are a dozen punks who would be happy to take my place the second I start to look more prey than predator."

"Sweet thing," said the voice, "have you looked in the mirror lately? It doesn't get more predatory than you."

Hiro grunted. "And appearance is overrated."

"I could talk about your appearance all day, but I really do need you to do this one tiny thing for me."

"One tiny thing," He rubbed his chin, then shook his head. "No."

"You realize I can just tap into the Prince-Regent's network and alert him to the fact you've been skimming off his cut. Right? You realize this?"

Hiro curled both his hands into fists and slammed them down in front of the screen. He tried to speak, but all he could manage was an angry growl that turned into a defeated sigh. "People on the same side are supposed to work together better than this."

"I think we work together very well; I don't know what you're talking about," the woman retorted. "Now just listen. A few people are going to come to you sometime later tonight, and I need you to hide them."

Hiro glanced at the exit door. "Here?"

"Please," the woman said. "There are plenty of hiding places. It's the *docks,* for heaven's sake."

"Hiding places, maybe, but not with my boys everywhere."

"I'll leave that part up to you."

Hiro shut his eyes and lifted his face toward the ceiling.

"Are you praying for patience? Guidance?" the voice prompted. "Mmm...a tractor beam?"

"I'd pray for Yomi itself to help me if it would get you off my back."

"As much as I'd like to be on your back, I'm afraid I have to go now. Just be on the lookout for a bunch of weird-looking people. One of them will tell you I sent him. He has very red hair, and he's taller than you."

"How many people are there?" Hiro demanded, straightening. "You said a *few,* not a *bunch.*"

"It was just going to be three, but there might be a couple more. I'm not sure."

"Riza," snapped Hiro, "you'd better be able to vouch for every one of these people. I might like to screw the Prince-Regent over, but not if it means I get skinned alive and hung on a wall."

"I can vouch, I can vouch," said Riza, but her voice was just doubtful enough that Hiro uttered a low, animal sound of frustration and shook his head, hair swinging over his shoulders.

"Just deal with them nicely."

"Don't hold your breath," said Hiro.

———

OSCAR HATED TWO THINGS MOST: being kept in the dark literally and being kept in the dark figuratively. And since he had been blindfolded the whole car ride and nobody would tell him where they were taking him, he felt justified in his attitude when he said, "I hope you all rot in hell."

Something sharp jutted into his ribs, not hard enough to make him fall, but enough to make him angrier. "Watch it," he snapped. "Wanker," he added under his breath.

Someone shoved him, and his shoulder ran into a wall. "Oh, so that's how it is? Bastards. You really think—"

The blindfold was pulled off, and he blinked rapidly at the sudden blaze of florescent blue light. He did not know what he had been expecting, but it wasn't a concrete room that looked like a...

"Hang on," he said, squinting at the tall, steel shelves, the long metal tables, and the jars of suspicious-looking liquids. "This is a lab. Why would you bring me to a rutting lab? Sorry, mate, I don't do the common cold, and frankly, I wouldn't even give a rat's arse if you had Moschkowitz Syndrome gutting you from the—what the bloody hell is he doing here," he finished, eyeing the figure who had just walked in through the door behind him, flanked by two guards. "Is that who I think it is?"

"Yes," said the guard behind Oscar. He had been fairly polite since the hotel, although Oscar didn't know if he was the shover or not. He was betting it was the other one, the second guard, who had also removed his mask.

They both held their masks tucked under their arms, and they bowed deeply from the waist as the Prince-Regent clasped his hands behind his back and smiled.

"Doctor Oscar Sleimann. It's an honor to meet you."

Oscar's heartbeats picked up speed. "Yes, well, I'm sure it's marvelous to meet you and all, but this—"

The guard on the Prince-Regent's left moved toward Oscar, but the Prince-Regent held up a hand and stopped him. "I'm sure you have other places to be," he said, with surprising patience.

"I do, actually," Oscar began, but he was cut off again.

"I need you to build something for me, if you would be so kind. I believe you're the only one who can."

Oscar folded his arms, but the gesture was not so much defiant as it was to hide his shaking hands. He did not even ask what it was the Prince-Regent wanted him to build. "And just how long is this supposed to take, exactly?"

"That," the Prince-Regent purred, "depends entirely on your motivation."

# TWENTY

IT WAS NOT Saizou who convinced Fumiyo to come with them; it was Shi. The girl packed a bag and scuttled past Saizou with her head down, out the front door into the courtyard where Shotgun was waiting.

"You'd think neither of them had ever seen a member of the opposite sex before," grunted Shi.

Saizou watched the girl, bundled up to the eyes, then gave Shi a curious look. "She's taken to you like a fish to water."

"Then she's a deep-sea fish and likes it salty, because I didn't do anything special." Shi walked out ahead of Saizou, his left arm curled around his torso to prevent movement.

Winter approached from behind, his footsteps soundless but his voice as sharp as a well-cut blade when he said, "Take good care of her."

Saizou nodded, eyeing the other man with a brief pang of regret. "You're certain you won't come with us? If Shotgun is right, Commander Haka is more of a threat than he seems."

"I can take care of him." Winter's blue eyes gleamed coldly in his stone-set face.

"What makes you so sure?"

"I have dealt with him before, as I believe I stated once already. Go on, quickly." He nodded toward the open doors.

There was no point; the strange non-priest had said his part, and Saizou knew there was no point in pushing the matter any further. "Take care of yourself."

"Go," snapped Winter, but it was not an angry snap, and his face softened into the shadow of a smile before Saizou turned and jogged out the doors and down the stairs.

The courtyard was slick with a thin layer of ice, but he and Shi knew how to deal with ice. Winters in Liaoyang were bitterly cold, and comparatively, this winter was gentle.

"I already got the motorcycle out," said Shotgun helpfully as they strode down the mountain. He slapped branches out of the way, glaring at the twigs that reached out and attempted to entangle themselves in his hair like wayward fingers.

Saizou nearly asked "When?" but didn't bother.

"Shi and Fumiyo will take the motorcycle," said Saizou, looking pointedly at Shotgun. "You and I will walk."

Shi opened his mouth to protest. Saizou was prepared to interrupt him and insist, on no uncertain terms, but to his surprise, Shotgun interrupted them both.

"That's chivalrous and all, but we don't have to walk." Shotgun grinned. "My contact has transportation waiting for us just below the far end of the broken bridge."

"Which we still have to get across," said Saizou, "and which will be tricky enough, given Shi's shoulder."

"Quit worrying about me, would you?" growled Shi. His mask could not cover the tight line of his mouth or the strain in his neck. He was in pain, but Saizou knew he would never let on. Not unless it became truly unbearable, and he doubted it would reach that point. Shi had survived far worse damage, and his face bore witness to that.

Fumiyo pulled her sweater up to her nose and tucked an arm around Shi's side. Her voice was muffled when she spoke, but Saizou heard "Lean on me" and shook his head in wonder. The strange girl had taken a liking to Shi, that was certain, but why? He had known Shi for a full year before they spoke more than a few sentences back and forth; the man was too quiet to judge after one meeting.

He was too quiet to judge after thirty meetings, really. Four years, and Saizou was still realizing just how little he knew about his brother-friend.

"So what's your contact's name?" asked Shi.

"She calls herself Riza." Shotgun whacked another branch out of the way. "And she's a genius, I know that much. She managed to broadcast your daring escape from the Palace of the Sun all over Tokyo for twenty-four hours before the Imperial Security Service stopped her."

"You sound proud of her," said Shi.

"I guess." Shotgun scratched his nose. "She's kind of like my grandmother, you know? Hovering. Always there. Sending me money when I need it. Plus, she's alive," he added, gesturing toward the sky with his right hand, "which makes her infinitely better than my biological grandmother."

"Any idea how we're going to get Mr. Mask across the bridge?" Shotgun asked as they came around the bend and saw the obstacle looming in the distance. "I've done it a few times but he probably can't do it the same way."

"Bamboo poles, like last time," said Saizou. "How did you get across before?"

"I pole-vaulted," said Shotgun.

Fumiyo gave him a startled look.

"I didn't want to walk across a makeshift bridge," the red-haired giant said defensively. "I had a bad experience."

"It wasn't that bad," said Saizou, hiding a smile.

"Aha-ha-ha," retorted Shotgun flatly.

"I'm not pole-vaulting," said Shi.

"You'd die," said Saizou.

"So would you."

"Point taken."

Fumiyo pointed at Shotgun. "He'll pole-vault, we'll go across a bridge. Stop making a fuss out of nothing."

Saizou's eyebrows shot up, and he traded wide-eyed looks with Shi, who said, "Good."

"She speaks!" exclaimed Shotgun, flinging a pointed finger at Fumiyo.

The girl's eyes narrowed into thin slivers. "Stop talking to me."

Shotgun shook himself like a wet dog and clapped his hands together once. "That's me in my place."

Saizou edged across the bridge to the broken edge as soon as they reached it. He peered down at the drop, then stepped back. "It's slicker than it was before," he said. "We'll have to be more cautious."

Shotgun waded into a stand of bamboo trees and came back out dragging a nine-foot pole behind him. He pressed his weight on it, bending the length to see how it would hold. When it proved solid, he walked past Saizou and gave the far side of the gap a critical eye.

"It's not too slick. Piece of cake."

"You fall, you die," said Shi, shrugging his good shoulder.

"See you on the other side," said Shotgun, and without another word, he jumped up and soared through the air like an Olympian, landing on the other side with unexpected grace. He stood very still for several seconds before bringing both hands into the air. "Woooo-hooo!" he howled, spinning around and turning both fists into rock n' roll gesture. "Your turn!"

It did not take Saizou long to find fallen trees and stretch them across the gap; Shotgun helped from the other side.

When the makeshift bridge was ready, Saizou crossed halfway and then turned around, gesturing to Shi. "Come on."

Shi glared. "It's my arm I can't use, not my legs. I don't need help." He nudged Fumiyo forward with a quieter, "Go ahead."

Saizou bit back a sigh and walked carefully across. Arguing would get him nowhere. "All right." To Shi, he added, "If you fall, it's not my problem."

"Never has been," said Shi, watching Fumiyo as she dashed across the bridge like a startled rabbit.

Saizou blinked. "I'm not sure you even touched the wood," he remarked.

In a barely audible whisper, Fumiyo said, "I don't like heights." She glared up at Shotgun as if his height personally offended her.

"I only grew until my feet touched the ground. Geez," he said, rubbing a hand through his wild hair. "Blame my parents."

"Where's this transportation you promised?" Saizou asked, snapping his fingers to grab Shotgun's attention.

"Around the bend," said Shotgun, and he took off with long-legged strides. Saizou and the others caught up to him and found him standing in front of Saizou's motorcycle and something that looked like a punked-out robotic four-wheeler.

"Cool, isn't it?" asked Shotgun.

"If by cool, you mean *likely to fall apart*," Shi grunted.

"Don't underestimate my contact's skill in choosing which vehicles to steal," said Shotgun, patting the side of the stolen four-wheeler. "If she picked this one, she picked it with good reason."

"I don't trust most people I meet," said Shi. "And I never trust people I've never met."

"I haven't even met her," said Shotgun, turning around and settling down onto the four-wheeler.

Saizou held up a hand. "What do you mean," he asked calmly, "you haven't even met her?"

Shotgun pursed his lips, and his eyes darted to the right, clearly searching for a way to retract or explain his statement. "It's not like I don't know her."

"But you've never met," said Saizou. "Is that right?"

"Technically," Shotgun began, but Shi stepped forward and interrupted.

"Forget him, captain," Shi snapped, his teeth bared like a vicious dog. "He's probably undercover Shinsengumi."

Shotgun straightened his back and seemed suddenly taller and broader than before. "Hey," he snarled, but before he could get any farther a strange look crossed his face. He reached up and touched his earring. "I didn't—"

Saizou strode forward and took hold of the earring. It was not attached through a piercing, only hooked around the swell of Shotgun's ear, so he wrenched it away from Shotgun's head without a second thought and hooked it over his own ear. "Who is this?"

"You could have waited half a second," said a woman's voice. "I was telling him to give it to you."

"Then talk," said Saizou brusquely. He glanced down the path. The mountain stretched out in front of them, frozen and wreathed in frost, tilted down like a roller-coaster. "And don't waste my time."

He glanced at Shi, who watched him through the mask

with unblinking eyes. Fumiyo stood just behind him, sending withering glances at Shotgun, who leaned his elbows on the handlebars and scratched the side of his head.

"Hi! I'm Riza," said the voice. "I'm assuming you're Saizou."

"Yes," said Saizou.

"Captain of the White Cobra guerilla unit in Liaoyang province, honorably discharged after a nasty injury and severe post-traumatic stress disorder, recently deposed daimyo of Akita Domain, and son of nobles—this is quite a resume, precious."

Saizou stiffened. "How do you know all that?"

"How do I know anything? Zeroes and ones. Would you like to know a little about Shotgun? I know the boy can be less than personable, but he tries harder than people deserve. The Prince-Regent wiped out his whole family—you can believe me when I say he has no more love for the beloved "Prince of the Sun" than we do."

"I don't believe you," said Saizou, "but it's nothing personal."

"I know it isn't, pet," cooed Riza. "Now listen. You can stay in direct communication, if you like. I'm assuming you stole Shotgun's earring, and he can do without it. Ask me anything you like; I'll probably answer, but I can also tell you that the Shinsengumi are out looking for you."

"How close are they?"

"Eh...not terribly. The one you really have to watch out for is Kirikizu."

"Who's that?"

"Tall, mid-length hair, has the lithe body of a dancer, looks like a BDSM advertisement?" Riza made a sound somewhere between a purr and a growl. "Just my type if he wasn't attached to the Prince-Regent. The PR isn't my type whatsoever."

Saizou recalled the figure standing beside the Prince-Regent during the hearing, and again at the gate. "How dangerous is he?"

"On a scale of one to ten?"

"Sure."

"Twelve. Thirteen, maybe. If you need clarification, I'd put you at a twelve."

*He's as dangerous as I am.* A line of heat swept up Saizou's spine, and he glanced down the path again, half-expecting to see Kirikizu's form watching from the trees. *Maybe more so.* "If this goes badly thanks to you, I'm going to skin Shotgun alive."

Shotgun's mouth fell open. "Why?"

Wryly, Riza said, "Something you're good at, apparently. But I wouldn't worry; I'm not that attached to him. If anything goes south, you can keep him."

The sudden coldness coming from such a warm voice startled Saizou, but he kept his gaze steady in Shotgun's direction and said evenly, "We're following you."

"I'm so glad you said that," said Riza, "because this was a tragic waste of three minutes. Get on the bikes."

# TWENTY-ONE

HAKA STARED up the mountain path with narrowed eyes, his fingers curled around the handlebars as his knuckles pushed white against his skin.

A voice crackled through his radio. "Commander?"

Haka licked his dry lips. "What is it, Lieutenant?"

Lieutenant Takuan's signal was weak, but audible. "Your signal says you've left the city. Why is that?"

Haka rolled his eyes and reached back, pulling his hair into a tail at the nape of his neck. "That's because I've left the city, moron."

"I don't suppose I should inquire as to why," drawled the lieutenant.

"I'm chasing down a lead." He shifted his jaw to one side. The path stretched in front of him, daring him to ride it up to the end, to what he knew was waiting. "Don't you have a job to do?"

"This is my job."

"Focus on something other than me. That's an order."

"Yes, sir. Should I tell Otter you'll be out all night? Again?"

Haka switched off the radio. He didn't need questions, and it was none of Lieutenant Takuan's concern where he was or what he did. If he didn't come back, the reason was a good one —he would be too dead to make it back to the precinct or home.

---

KIRIKIZU MADE A SHARP LEFT, following Violet's sudden turnaround as she angled back toward the city. She was no longer howling; she flew over the ground as swift and silent as a bullet. So they had been in the mountain, as he had suspected; but they were leaving now, looking for a better place to hide. He had no doubt that Commander Haka would take the monastery angle, searching for the man whom Kirikizu most suspected of hiding the fugitives.

Let the Shinsengumi handle a cold lead.

The Prince-Regent's Hand would finish the job.

---

FUMIYO WEIGHED SO little that Saizou kept reaching down to make sure the girl's arms were wrapped around his waist. He had kept Shotgun's earring, waiting for Riza's voice to make another irritating remark or say something helpful. She had been silent since they passed into Tokyo again. They left any decent part of the city behind, and business high-rises brightly lit with neon colors gave way to dark concrete apartment complexes.

Saizou tapped the earring, wondering if he had lost the connection. "How much farther?"

"Not much."

She sounded very relaxed, and it put Saizou on edge. "How much farther, specifically?"

"You're heading to the shipyard. The docks."

"What?"

"You know the place. It's where all the ships come to dock?"

Saizou shook his head, wishing he could be rid of the voice but not willing to give the earring back to Shotgun. "I know it's a good place to dump bodies in the water."

"I know war makes people suspicious, but you really are something. And also, burying people in water is a bad idea unless you wrap them in a tarp. Decomposing bodies tend to release chunks over time and chunky water looks bad."

Saizou frowned. "Don't change the subject."

"Don't take that tone with me, young man; I was exactly on the subject. Turn right."

Saizou turned right, knowing Shotgun and Shi would follow his lead. He hated feeling blind; he could be leading Shi into a trap, and he wouldn't know it until it closed in around them. Every sense on alert, he rode through the narrowing alley and came out the other side in full view of the docks and the black, moon-gilded sea.

Two dark, looming shapes were tied up to the docks. Fishing boats, from the look of them.

"You can stop now," said Riza.

Saizou slowed to a stop, his headlights illuminating the damp concrete ground. The space was open: an alley behind, the sea to the right, a hill curving up around a building to the left, and large storage units several hundred yards ahead.

Open, but prime for an ambush.

Shotgun pulled up next to Saizou, the engine of his four-wheeler growling like a hungry predator. Shi's back was ramrod-straight, and he caught Saizou's eye.

"I don't like this," he said.

Just as Saizou's fingers curled around the hilt of his wakizashi, Shotgun said, "Company. That must be him." He pointed, and Saizou leaned forward, squinting at the figure walking toward them from the direction of the storage units.

"Is this our contact?" Saizou asked, watching the figure grow closer, still too far away to make out anything distinct. "Riza?"

"Just don't stare at him," was the response Saizou could only take as an affirmative. "He hates that."

Saizou glanced at Shi. "This is him," he said, and both drew their wakizashis simultaneously, still not trusting Riza or her contact.

"Whoa, he's on our side, guys," said Shotgun, but Saizou and Shi dismounted their vehicles and ignored his protesting.

"We'll find out," said Saizou.

The figure stopped just outside the ring of light created by the vehicles' headlights. He did not appear to be armed, but that did not necessarily mean anything. Saizou had met plenty of people who had no need for weapons. From the way this one walked, he had a degree of confidence. He was not afraid, but he was wary, keeping himself at a smart distance from the others.

"Did Riza send you?" the figure asked in a flat, baritone voice.

"Yes," said Shotgun.

The figure grunted and lifted a hand, just visible. "Come with me."

Walking into a situation blind was not only unpleasant, it

was moronic. Knowing it was their only option—other than taking their chances—increased Saizou's anger.

"Show us your face," said Shi.

The figure paused and turned back toward them, his lean silhouette still just out of clear sight. He chuckled briefly before stepping into the ring of light. "Show me *your* face," said the albino, his white skin and scarlet eyes awash in a yellow glow. He smiled at Shi, his lips parting just enough to show sharpened, reptilian teeth.

Saizou nodded to himself; Riza's instruction not to stare made sense. "My name is Saizou Akita."

"I know," said the albino. "Now come with me before my boys see you. And turn those lights off," he added, turning away from the headlights and walking away.

"He turned his back on us," said Shi in a low voice. "He must be confident."

"Either he's hidden fugitives before," said Saizou, "or this is a trap."

"We could run."

Saizou shook his head once. "No. We follow him, and if he proves false, we kill him."

———

THE MONASTERY DOORS WERE OPEN.

Haka drew his katana. Winter did not use guns.

Not anymore.

He stepped across the threshold and, in a voice somewhere between a snarl and a howl, cried, "Winter!"

The doors at the far end of the hall slid open as Winter pushed them apart. He stood in silence for a moment that stretched and grew and swelled, until he said, "What do you want?"

Haka felt his fingers tightening around the hilt of his sword. A tight grip made for choppy movements, he knew that. Yet he could not relax his grip any more than he could feel nothing at the sight of the man across from him.

Haka cut through any meaningless courtesies and said, "The fugitives."

Winter's mouth was a grim line, his gaze set in stone. He said nothing.

"They were here. Your silence tells me as much as anything." Haka took a step forward. "Where did they go?"

"You brought no reinforcements," Winter observed in a voice so even it was nearly monotone.

"I came alone."

Winter grunted. "Then you did not come for the fugitives."

"I knew they wouldn't still be here." Haka took one more step forward; slowly, carefully, the curved blade of his government-issued katana pointing toward the other man.

"You have no proof they were ever here," said Winter calmly, "but you're welcome to search. Something might turn up."

"No." Haka's mouth smiled even as his heart curled in on itself. "It wouldn't."

Again, Winter said nothing. He did not move; no expression crossed his face. He was a tall, emotionless statue.

Even now. Nothing had changed.

For a moment, Haka also stood still, but it was not the stillness of stubborn determination. He was still because he could not move.

He cleared his throat and tossed his hair from his eyes. He was not afraid. He had taken enough stardust to ensure that.

There was no fear, but stardust did nothing against other flaws. It did nothing against open wounds.

Winter glanced at the wall to the right, then at the floor, and once again levelled his gaze at Haka. "The Shinsengumi is welcome to search this place, I've already told you. So search."

"There would be no point. You know as well as I do."

"Knowing a thing is pointless has rarely kept you from doing it," Winter replied. The muscle in his jaw clenched as he lifted his chin and added, "If you aren't going to search, then leave this place. Run back to the precinct and write a report."

"I could arrest you under suspicion." Haka's voice left his throat as a hiss. It surprised him, but he clung to it and hissed again, "If I chose to do so."

"But you won't."

Haka drew back. "You don't know that."

"I do know." Winter began to walk toward him, his strides slow and methodical. "I know you don't have it in you. You lack the heart, you lack the courage, and you lack the conviction to follow through on anything you know is right, and you lack what it takes to stand up to anyone with the ability to hurt you."

Haka's laugh was brittle, breaking in his ears. "You think now, after everything, you have the ability to hurt me? I live in the real world, brother; I uphold the law while you hide away in the mountains, alone, professing a God you don't know and atoning for your sins by doing nothing."

"You uphold nothing. You drag down everything, and you crawl in the presence of worms. You are no brother of mine."

How Winter's voice could hold such loathing while his face remained empty, Haka did not know, but he was incapable of the same coldness as he snarled, "You are under arrest for suspicion of aiding and abetting fugitives, and if I have to bring every officer in Tokyo up here to do it, I will."

"You needn't worry." Winter's coat brushed against Haka's as he walked past him, toward the open doors. "I'll come."

"You won't—"

"You may hold me for twenty-four hours in your western-ized jail," spat Winter. "I'll wait patiently until that time is up, and then I will come back here." Winter looked over his shoulder, his eyes cold and narrow in his angular face. "Let's go. I don't care to drag this out any longer than is necessary."

———

AS THE VEHICLE turned down the mountain path, now carrying two passengers instead of one, Virgo cocked his head to one side and said, "Looks like the Shinsengumi's taking the priest for interrogation. Which means the fugitives are no longer at the monastery, which means I was right."

"They came up the mountain," Shimo insisted.

"I believe you, but it's possible they came back down."

The bounty hunters each straddled a Scorpia X60 bike; off-road two-wheeled vehicles that resembled flattened motorcy-cles, equipped with a 'tail' that curved up from the spine of the bike. Shimo's bike-tail was equipped with a net, and Virgo's was equipped with an automatic machine gun. The surface of each Scorpia was carefully coated with Kameleon, a military-grade camouflage coating made from millions of tiny, color-sensitive cameras that changed hue to match their surroundings.

The Shinsengumi commander and his prisoner had missed the brothers completely.

"Either they came back down or kept going," said Shimo. "We should search the monastery anyway. I might pick up something useful."

"Right." Virgo pulled out of the tree line ahead of his twin.

"We have to get to the fugitives before the commander does or we don't get a paycheck."

"We're doing fine," said Shimo, pulling up alongside Virgo. "This much money would be useful, but we'll survive without it."

Virgo only revved his silent engine and took off, leaving his brother to catch up.

# TWENTY-TWO

"YOU FAILED to mention the contact was Yakuza."

"I didn't think it was necessary," said Riza. "You can give the earring back to Shotgun now. He gets lonely without me."

"I don't think so."

"He does, too."

"I don't think I'm giving the earring back to him," Saizou clarified. "I don't like working through a middleman."

A loud sigh threatened to deafen him. "Fine. Just keep following Hiro and do whatever he tells you."

"He's Yakuza. He can't be trusted by outsiders."

"He can't be trusted by insiders, either. He's helping outlaws fleeing from the Prince-Regent. You think his underlings would be happy if they found out he's jeopardizing their standing with the royal house?"

Saizou had considered the possibility Hiro was working alone, but he had dismissed the idea because it didn't make sense. He told Riza his opinion, keeping his voice low so Hiro couldn't overhear him. "What's in it for him?"

"Personal satisfaction."

"He has a grudge against the Prince-Regent too?" Saizou asked, incredulous.

"What, you think you and the Lone Ranger are the only ones?"

Saizou glanced at Shi, whose jaw was firmly set as he walked slightly behind Saizou and Shotgun. Fumiyo stayed firmly next to him. From the look of it, she might have adopted him permanently.

"The Prince-Regent lets the Yakuza trade in drugs and worse as long as he gets a large cut of the profit," murmured Saizou. "Why would he want to mess that up?"

"I contacted him because I found some suspicious activity in his secret account." She clicked her tongue. "He was skimming the Prince-Regent's profits and funneling the money toward forging fake passports and identities for outlaws attempting to flee the country. Satisfied? Now, there are no cameras in your area; where are you right now?"

Saizou glanced around. "We're headed away from the ships, toward the storage units."

"It's probably where he'll hide you. His underlings probably won't think to look for you there."

Saizou watched at the albino ahead of him. Nothing about the gangster's appearance suggested a heart, let alone a heart that large. "Are you sure that's what he used the money for? He could have lied to you."

"For heaven's sake, cupcake, I wasn't born yesterday. I verified it."

"Why are *you* helping us?"

"Sorry, the Q and A session is over for today. I'm going to shut down and get some sleep, and so should you. You're as safe as you can be for the night. Tell Shotgun I said sweet dreams," said Riza, and the connection went silent.

Saizou flexed his fingers before balling his hands into fists. *As safe as you can be.* He had heard more reassuring words in his lifetime, but it was better than nothing. Right now, it was all they had.

———

"SOOO."

Haka glanced up from his desk. Otter leaned against the doorframe, her arms folded. Her short, shaggy hair was pulled back in a barely-there ponytail, and she watched him with one eyebrow raised.

"That's 'sooo, Commander' to you," he said, pointing a pen at her.

"Sooo, Commander," she said dutifully, waving one hand in the air, "what's with the new prisoner?"

"He's a prisoner. That's all you need to know."

Otter snorted and crossed over to the desk. "I'll call you *Commander*, but I can quit any time I please and it would take ten men to replace me."

Haka cleared his throat and avoided eye contact. She was right, but he hardly felt like admitting that out loud.

"Well?"

Never before had anyone batted their eyelashes at him with so much sarcasm. Haka rubbed his hands over his face and looked at the screen. All he had to do was click *send* and the report would be gone, filtered through to the Prince-Regent...

"I can hire ten men." He glanced away and clicked the button before he could stop himself. He switched the computer off and stood up, doing his best to pretend Otter wasn't there.

Her eyebrows rose even further. "Oh, it's like that, is it? Fine. I'll just tell the Prince-Regent's Hand that *you're* putting Violet up for the night."

Haka drew himself up to his full height in defiance but said quickly, "It's an ex-mercenary who might know where the outlaws are."

Otter frowned. "What makes you think he knows anything?"

"He as much as said so. Now," said Haka, stepping around the desk, "stop bothering me."

"Bothering you is my right. It makes up for all the times I baby you or drag you to your cot or put sleeping pills in your tea."

Startled by the last part of her sentence, Haka tripped over the wastebasket and caught himself just before he crashed to the floor.

With a fierce chuckle, Otter reached down and picked up a crumpled piece of paper that had rolled next to her foot. "Do you need help there? Commander?"

"No," snapped Haka, adding firmly as he got back to his feet, "clean that up." He swept carefully out of the room.

Otter tossed the piece of paper back into the wastebasket and scooted it around the corner of the desk, where the commander would be less likely to trip over it.

"Half-brained drug-addled moron," she muttered, casting a glance around the room to make sure everything was in order. Although *order* was a very fluid thing where the commander was concerned, and it wasn't her job to keep his office clean anyway.

The door opened, and she turned, expecting Haka, but it was Lieutenant Takuan instead. "Ah, Otter. Where's the Commander?"

Otter shrugged. "Beats me. He tripped over the waste-basket and left in a huff."

"Oh," said the lieutenant, not at all surprised. "Any idea where he went?"

"I don't know. He seems a little upset."

"More than usual?"

"He's usually stressed, high, and delusional," Otter told him. "But right now he seems stressed, high, delusional, *and* worried. I think it has to do with the prisoner he brought in earlier."

"The priest?"

"Yeah."

"I just gave him dinner. He seems like a fairly calm fellow."

Otter shrugged and glanced at the computer. Commander Haka would have sent in a report unless he forgot, which had happened more than once. But if he *had* sent one, all she had to do was turn the computer back on, log in with the commander's information, and find out what had upset him.

"No," said Takuan.

"Drat," said Otter, and left the room behind him.

———

VIOLET HAD LOST THE SCENT. Her gallop had become a lope, then a prowl as she lowered her head to the pavement.

Kirikizu rode slowly to the left of her, his gaze divided between the monster and the alley ahead. Mutts were supposed to be unstoppable, but apparently Violet's sense of smell was not as keen as he had hoped.

It was well past dark, and the air was damp with the promise of either rain or snow. It might be cold enough for snow, and Violet gave every indication of being a semi-reptilian creature. Perhaps it had grown too cold for her.

"Violet, back."

The creature spun around and raced back down the alley, the way they had come.

Kirikizu was far less eager to return.

———

"I'M SORRY, could you repeat that?" Oscar leaned forward. He was seventy percent certain he had heard the Prince-Regent correctly. He was also one hundred percent certain he wished he had misheard.

"Either you can do it or you can't." The Prince-Regent shrugged one shoulder. His silken robe slid halfway down his arm, but he did not bother to fix it. Oscar wondered for a wild half-moment if the Prince-Regent was acting seductive on purpose.

Gracious.

Oscar glanced at the guards on either side. Their masks were back in place, emotionless and frightening. Or they would have been if he didn't know they looked like high schoolers underneath. "Well, I mean," he began, then stopped.

The Prince-Regent watched him with glittering eyes, demanding an answer.

"Look, mate—I mean, Your Highness," Oscar said, running a hand through his hair, "you've got the wrong guy. I'm not Victor Frankenstein, right? You're asking me to make a thing, a person, from spare parts. From other people." He shook his head vigorously. "That's insane. That's ludicrous. What would you even do with it?"

"The toymaker doesn't ask the child how he'll play with the toy." The Prince-Regent smiled and smoothed his long, black hair over his bare shoulder, combing it with sharp fingernails. They were painted gold, Oscar noticed. Probably real gold. "Please say yes. Please."

Oscar had a brief vision of the Prince-Regent chewing him to shreds with his perfectly white teeth. "Do I have a choice?"

"Of course you have a choice." The Prince-Regent's eyebrows drew together, his tone wounded at the question.

Oscar rolled his eyes. "Do or die, right?"

"I mean." The Prince-Regent laughed. "I'd choose the former option, but the decision is up to you. You have three seconds." He put his hands behind his back, watching with a look of narrow curiosity. "One."

*Okay. Okay, think of the options. Obviously, you don't want to die. That would be tragic. On the other hand, consider the consequences—*

"Two."

*Think, Oscar, think. The consequences of this—this thing— it's wrong, isn't it? It has to be wrong, so there you have moral problems and ethical problems, obviously—*

"Three."

"Wait!" Oscar's voice snapped through the lab, louder than he intended.

"Ooh." The Prince-Regent raised an eyebrow. "Why?"

"I'll do it. I'll bloody do it. Just...ah, I'll need some things. And an assistant."

The Prince-Regent hummed a note of consideration and gestured at the two guards nearby. "Will one of them do?"

"Someone with medical training would be better," said Oscar, grimacing at the thought of untrained hands around his work.

The Prince-Regent's statuesque face had adopted a look of sudden annoyance, and Oscar added, "Fine."

"Wonderful." The Prince-Regent stretched his arms over his head. "I'm so excited."

# TWENTY-THREE

HIRO LED them to a storage unit the size of a boxcar. It had seen rough weather, from the look of the dented exterior and peeling blue paint.

Hiro lifted the door and pushed it up, motioning toward the black interior. "In."

"Whaddya got in there?" Shotgun asked, peering in. "Tigers?"

"It's empty," said Hiro. "You'll be safe for the night."

"Is there any light?" asked Fumiyo. The question was obviously for Hiro, but she glanced at Shi as she said it.

"There's a lantern in the back. I need to hide your vehicles so either get in or leave." Hiro put one hand on his hip and motioned them toward the interior of the unit with the other.

"Come on," said Saizou, stepping inside and crossing the twenty-foot space to the back. He caught the glint of moonlight on glass and found the lantern, switching it on to illuminate the interior.

This seemed to be enough of a comfort to Shotgun, who sighed and followed Shi and Fumiyo inside.

Hiro said nothing more; he closed the door behind them, and as it hit the ground, Fumiyo jumped.

"Nice guy," Shi remarked, sitting down with a sigh. "Big talker."

"Do you think he was hiding something?" Shotgun asked, a note of anxiety in his voice.

"No," said Saizou, although he was wondering the same question himself. There was no real reason for him to trust Hiro, or Shotgun, or Riza. But this was a question of survival, and he had done things far worse and far more dangerous for survival before. "Get some sleep," he told Shi as he also lowered himself to the ground. It was cold and hard, but there was a pile of blankets and a few packets of dried food shoved in one corner.

Fumiyo picked up two blankets and gave one to Shi, while she wrapped herself in the free one until only her freckled nose was visible. Shi glanced at her and a brief smile touched his face as he cushioned the blanket behind his shoulder and leaned back against the wall.

Shotgun did not sit. "I don't like this," he said, drumming his fingers on his biceps.

Saizou picked up a food packet and tossed it to the gangly, red-haired giant. "Eat that and get some sleep. You'll still be alive in the morning."

The packet bounced off Shotgun's stomach, but he caught it before it hit the ground, with a sarcastic, "Thanks, Dad."

*The Prince-Regent wiped out his whole family.* Saizou recalled Riza's words and watched as Shotgun crouched down. The younger man ripped the packet open with his teeth and tilted his head back, letting the contents pour into his mouth.

Shotgun lowered the packet and coughed, thumping his

chest a few times before shaking his head. "It fizzes," he choked in a strangled voice.

Saizou rubbed his mouth, trying to disguise a smile. "You should probably have checked for instructions."

"Probably, but it's not bad. Tastes like orange." Shotgun flipped the packet over. "Ah, 'add water.'"

"We don't have any water," said Shi, his voice thick and faint with sleep. His eyes were closed, but he had not removed his mask. Though Fumiyo and Shotgun had both seen him without it, he did not want his disfigurement flaunted, Saizou guessed.

A sharp slice of guilt gutted him for the thousandth time. He knew Shi's injury was not his fault, not technically. But if he removed himself from the equation, if he had not been present, it would never have happened. He could not remove that knowledge.

As if reading his mind, Shi grunted, "Go to sleep, captain."

"We can't all go to sleep," Saizou pointed out. "I'm fine."

"Hey, I'll keep watch," Shotgun volunteered, sitting in the middle of the floor and leaning back on both palms. "I won't be able to sleep anyway."

Fumiyo gave him a scrunched glare from within the shadowy depths of the blanket.

Shotgun flapped his hand at her. "You can trust me."

"We don't know that," said Shi, his eyes still shut.

"Fine, don't trust me. Trust my claustrophobia."

The kid had claustrophobia? Damn. Saizou shifted to look more directly at Shogun. "I didn't know. Sorry about this."

"I'm not going to hyperventilate and die," said Shotgun, even as his eyes darted from wall to wall. "I just can't relax."

Saizou knew he had to decide whether to trust Shotgun while they slept. But rather than relying on Shotgun's claustrophobia, he decided to trust the fact that both he and Shi were light sleepers. If Shotgun made a move, they would wake up.

Saizou drew his blade and rested it across his folded legs. "All right," he said evenly, tipping his head toward Shotgun. "Goodnight."

"Night," said Shotgun, lifting a hand as if waving Saizou goodbye. "Sleep tight."

Before Saizou closed his eyes, he saw Shi open his own eyes and give him a long look.

Saizou shook his head slightly. *I'll be fine.* He knew his limits, and while he was in the habit of ignoring this knowledge, he was now an outlaw on the run and he knew he needed strength.

Shi blinked once, then closed his eyes and leaned his head back against the wall.

Saizou let out a deep breath and did the same.

———

HAKA STOOD in front of Winter's cell with his arms folded across his chest. Neither of them had moved for the past twenty minutes, and Otter couldn't resist the urge to poke Haka in the ribs as she walked past.

He jumped, cutting a curse in half with, "What do you want?"

Otter nodded toward the prisoner. "Is this your interrogation technique? Just curious. Where'd you learn it? Was it at the academy, or during that childhood you supposedly had?"

He blew out a *pfft* and looked away from her. "Neither my childhood or my interrogation techniques are any of your business."

"No," she agreed. "Nothing is, apparently."

Haka sniffed. "The mutts are your business. The prisoners are mine."

Otter cocked her head to one side as a faint roar made its way through the prison walls. "Sounds like Violet's back."

"Oh, good. Your star pupil is home."

"So's your best friend ever," she reminded him. "If he's back this quickly, I doubt he found anyone. At least when he's in a bad mood, it's hard to tell," she continued, watching Haka's face. "It's not like he can give a whole lot of inflection with that muzzle of his. He's also a lot more self-controlled than you are, so—"

"Are you done?" Haka interrupted.

Otter grinned. "Yes. I have to go bring Violet in. Oh, but, Commander?"

He sighed and put his hands on his hips. "What?"

She poked his ribs and ran, fairly sure he wouldn't bother chasing her. He never did, she thought with a sigh, but then, he had bricks for brains.

She walked past the mutt cages and opened the door to the courtyard. Kirikizu had just pulled up, and Violet loped ahead of him, straight toward Otter.

She held up a hand and barked, "Stop!"

Violet halted and lowered her massive head to the ground, asking for permission to come inside. Otter walked up and scratched the side of Violet's neck, eliciting a pleased thrum from the massive creature.

"No prisoners, huh?" She watched as Kirikizu dismounted his vehicle.

He walked past her. "Your mutt lost the scent."

Otter bit back a sharp retort about Kirikizu's own incompetence and the punishment he might receive from *his* master.

She enjoyed tormenting Kirikizu because he enjoyed tormenting Haka, but she was never cruel.

She had the gut feeling Kirikizu had experienced enough cruelty already.

He never said anything about it, but she knew the rumors that floated around as well as anyone else. Rumors that the Prince-Regent favored Kirikizu for more than his skill as a killer. Some rumors suggested the Prince-Regent had used Kirikizu when the assassin was still a child, but some rumors suggested Kirikizu offered himself to the Prince-Regent as a way of staying in his favor.

Otter never believed the latter rumors. The lower half of Kirikizu's face might be masked, but his eyes were not. They were not the eyes of a gold-digging schemer with no self-respect; they were the eyes of someone in pain, someone determined.

They were not so different from Haka's eyes.

When Haka's eyes weren't glazed over with stardust, anyway.

Otter sighed and followed Kirikizu inside, whistling for Violet.

———

KIRIKIZU HAD EXPECTED Haka to be in his office, but he was just past the cages, staring into a cell. Surprisingly, there was a prisoner inside.

Haka turned around as Kirikizu approached, and his face twisted into an immediate display of disgust. "I see you return empty-handed."

The jab was petty, and Kirikizu brushed over it. "Who is the prisoner?"

"The monk who lives up in the mountains."

"He isn't a monk. He doesn't wear the right clothes."

Haka waved a hand. "Whatever. He fancies himself a man of God, and I have reason to believe he gave the fugitives shelter."

"Was there any sign of them?"

"The fugitives?" Haka shook his head.

"Did you *check?*"

"Of course," Haka snapped, but his eyes darted toward the monk as he spoke.

"You didn't check."

"I know Winter. He wouldn't leave evidence even if he had."

"Winter," Kirikizu repeated, looking at the prisoner. The man sat on the cot with his back against the wall, his eyes closed. His back was straight, his face was set. He gave no indication of being alive, except for the steady rise and fall of his chest as he breathed. "That's his name?"

Haka nodded once.

"How do you know this man?" Kirikizu gestured toward Winter, watching Haka closely.

Haka licked his lips, although they did not look dry, and he blinked twice before saying, "He has a history with law enforcement."

It was a good reply, but Haka was a poor liar. "I'd like to see any records you have regarding this previous history."

"He has nothing to do with you," Haka snapped. "This is not your jurisdiction."

Kirikizu calmly replied, "Shall I ask the Prince-Regent for a warrant?"

Haka's pupils shrank, and he brushed his bangs out of his

face, tucking them behind his ear. Still, his response was surprisingly defiant. "He is my prisoner. The interrogation is mine. I'll be sure and pass along any information I gather."

Beneath his muzzle, Kirikizu's mouth curved in a faint smile. It was intriguing when the commander showed some backbone. "I'll be back tomorrow morning. I expect a detailed interrogation report to hand to the Prince-Regent."

Haka's lip curled. "Fine," he sneered. "But leave me to my interrogation. You should go back to the palace. The temperature is supposed to drop well below freezing tonight, and we can't have the Prince-Regent getting cold."

"Commander!"

Otter's voice snapped through the frigid silence that followed Haka's taunt. Kirikizu did not turn as the girl hurried toward them, stopping at Haka's side and hissing, "Do you *want* to get reported?"

Kirikizu knew the rumors tethered to his name. He knew Haka lacked the usual filter between his brain and his mouth. In spite of that knowledge, Kirikizu felt the pain of the verbal wound as Haka's sneer curved farther, knowing he had driven his point home.

In an even, quiet voice he said, "You should listen to the girl, Commander. You are many things. Irreplaceable is not one of them."

"You're threatening an officer of the law," Haka said, taking a step closer. He was only a foot away now, his glassy eyes cutting into Kirikizu's, trading cut for cut. "I could arrest you, but the Prince-Regent wouldn't like it." He lowered his voice and said softly, "Go on. Go home. Come back with your warrant tomorrow. I'll have your report ready."

Self-control was Kirikizu's strongest suit, but in that

moment, he chose not to employ it. He brought his fingers together and lashed out with his right hand. His hand struck Haka's throat and withdrew so quickly even Otter didn't notice it until Haka sank to one knee, struggling to breathe.

Kirikizu walked up the stairs and shut the door behind him.

## TWENTY-FOUR

SAIZOU LEANED his head back against the wall, which rang with a faint, metallic thrum. Shotgun had dimmed the light so they could all sleep, but he kept the light with him near the front of the storage unit. The weak glow barely reached Saizou's feet; and beyond was pitch black.

Shi's bulldog voice came out of the darkness. "Can't sleep?"

He sighed. "No. You either?"

"No."

"Why not?"

"No reason."

Saizou looked at the dark shape that was Shi, a few feet away. He glanced at Shotgun, who still faced the door, and lowered his voice. "Your shoulder that bad?"

"It's fine, captain. I just can't relax."

"What about the girl?"

"She's asleep in the corner. She snores."

Saizou peered through the blackness. She couldn't be terribly far away, but he couldn't hear her. "She does?"

"I turned her head, and that seemed to stop it."

There was a slight strain in Shi's voice. It was barely notice-able, but Saizou caught it as Shi shifted, the metal on his jacket scraping the wall. "Let me have a look at your shoulder."

"I said it's fine."

Saizou raised his voice enough so Shotgun could hear him, but he kept it soft enough he hoped not to wake Fumiyo. "Shot-gun, slide the light over here for a minute."

Shotgun blinked, startled out of some reverie, and shoved the lamp across the floor of the storage unit. Saizou set it next to Shi, whose face stared at him, grim and immovable.

"I'm fine," said Shi again, leaning forward as if to move out of the light.

"So you've told me," said Saizou, pushing firmly against Shi's good shoulder. "Now I need to see for myself."

"Cap—" Shi began, but Saizou lifted a hand.

"No," he said, pulling Shi's jacket down around his elbows. He gingerly began to unwind the bandage, attempting not to cause Shi any further discomfort.

"You need kids," Shi muttered.

"I agree," said Saizou, "but they'll have to wait. Consider yourself the trial run."

"Practice on Shotgun."

"You have many distinctions, my friend, but the largest is the fact you're injured and he isn't." Saizou lifted the light and brought it closer to Shi's wound. As the glow illuminated Shi's shoulder, it also illuminated the sheen of sweat on his face.

Saizou frowned and ran a rough finger across Shi's fore-head. "You're sweating."

"It's hard to breathe in here."

Saizou took a deep breath. The air was fine; the unit was

large enough to give them plenty of air for a few hours, and if they ran out, they could lift the door a few inches. "It's not that hard."

"Shut up," said Shi. "Are you going to check the injury or talk?"

Saizou shook his head once and peered closer at the wound. It had been well-sewn, the stitches neat and precise, but the injury was a large and vicious one that would no doubt become a crater of scar tissue if it healed well enough.

*Another injury for my sake.*

He cut off that line of thought. Shi could read him too well, and he didn't need the man feeling worse than he already did.

"I don't see any signs of infection," said Saizou quietly, pulling Shi forward to inspect the back of the injury.

"Don't mind me," said Shi with a longsuffering sigh. Then, with slight hesitation, he said, "It could have been poisoned, I suppose."

Saizou's heart sank as his mind spun. "His teeth? That would poison him. I doubt there's much logic behind that."

"He could be immune to it."

"Highly unlikely. Stop being paranoid."

"That's *your* shtick, not mine."

"That's why it looks bad on you." Saizou shook his head and leaned back, wishing there were antibiotics on hand. He could ask the albino for some the next time he saw him.

"I told you I was fine," said Shi. "Re-bandage me. I can't do it myself."

Saizou twisted his mouth and gave Shi an exasperated glance before re-binding the bandage around Shi's shoulder.

"I feel sorry for him," muttered Shi, as Saizou finished tying the bandage in a secure knot.

"Hey, El Capitan," Shotgun hissed, "you about done with the lantern?"

Saizou slid it back, leaving their end of the storage unit in total darkness again.

Saizou looked in Shi's direction. "You feel sorry for who?"

"The Dog who relieved me of half my shoulder. Maybe I should thank him. It was probably weighing me down."

Saizou couldn't help a brief smile at his grim companion's black sense of humor, but he said, "I've never seen anything like him before. Him. It. Whatever he was."

"It was a he," said Shi quietly. "I saw his eyes. There's someone in there, buried deep. I wonder how he became that way."

"I wonder that the Prince-Regent isn't criticized for having such a creature."

"He's the Prince-Regent," Shi scoffed. "I assume those who criticize him end up as negative examples for anyone else who would follow suit."

Saizou bowed his head and was silent. His silence stretched long enough that, after a while, Shi said, "Are you asleep?"

Saizou shook his head, then remembered Shi could not see him. "No."

"Ah."

"It seems..." Saizou caught his breath and released it heavily. "It's hard to believe how far..."

"The mighty have fallen?" Shi supplied, with the hint of a smile in his voice. He sighed; Saizou heard him stretch out, heard the soft, metallic bang as Shi leaned his head against the wall. "I know. I suppose the Prince-Regent was just waiting to leap at the Emperor's absence. It's interesting we never heard much about the Prince before the Emperor left for China, though."

"He was too busy lurking in the shadows, I suppose."

"This much planning must have taken most of his time. I rarely even saw him on television appearances."

"I heard he was disgraced in the eyes of the Empress Dowager."

Shi cleared his throat softly. "It's no surprise, then."

"What isn't?"

"The Empress Dowager's sudden heart attack. What was it, a year ago?"

Saizou nodded again. "I suspected an unnatural death, but I didn't yet...I didn't consider the Prince-Regent."

Shi snorted softly. "You should have."

"I should have," Saizou agreed, but the subject felt too heavy then. He was already bone-weary, and the Prince-Regent's machinations threatened to exhaust him completely. "She's taken quite a liking to you."

"Who, sweater girl?"

"Fumiyo, yes."

"It must be shocking," Shi grunted. "That someone takes a liking to me."

"If I recall correctly, I've been the only one," said Saizou, adopting a teasing, superior tone.

"I thought it was the other way around."

"Was it? I get confused." Saizou tapped the side of his head. "The war, you know."

"Mmm," Shi affirmed. He nudged Saizou's arm. "Get some sleep, captain. I'll wake you."

"You need sleep as much as I do."

"I need sleep," said Shi, "but not as much as you do. You haven't slept half as much as I have this past week. Please, captain. Sleep."

*Please* was not a word frequently found in Shi's vocabulary, and Saizou felt obliged to give in. He opened his mouth to protest, but shook his head and slid down, letting his head rest on the floor. "Don't let me sleep too long."

"Sleeping men don't speak."

"I thought it was *dead* men."

"I can't hear you."

———

TEETH and red tongues and wide eyes ringed with white. Claws and snarling and it hurt, it hurt so much. These weren't dogs, they were demons—and he had unleashed them on himself. He had killed himself. He was dying.

Haka sat up, flinging his blanket onto the floor. It was too constricting; he needed to breathe. He gripped the sides of the cot with both hands until needles of pain shot through his fingers.

*Ugh.* He shook his head, trying to clear the cobwebs from his skull. What had happened last night? He glanced around the office.

The Prince-Regent's portrait was hung crookedly.

How long had it been crooked? Had the Prince-Regent's Hand reported that, too?

The Prince-Regent's Hand.

His remarks from last night flooded back to him, and Haka doubled over with a groan. *I didn't...*

"You did."

Haka raised his head and stared blearily at the open office door. Otter stood there with a plain white mug of something hot in her hand. The steam curled toward her face, and she took a deep breath. "Coffee? I thought you might need it."

"How much did I say last night?" He accepted the offered cup of coffee and took a sip. It burned his tongue, and he hissed, holding the cup away from his face.

"Is it too hot?" asked Otter innocently.

Haka gave her a dark look. "Is this retaliation or what?"

"Retaliation?" Otter clicked her tongue. "What on earth would I retaliate for, Commander? I'm not the one you accused of having an affair with the Prince-Regent."

"It's not like it's a secret." Haka blew steam across the surface of the cup before bringing it cautiously back to his mouth and taking a gingerly sip. He licked his dry lips and cleared his throat, still trying to wake up. Morning was never his favorite time of day. Then again, he wasn't sure any time of day was his favorite. All were equally prone to negative experiences.

"Still," chided Otter, "it was uncalled for. He doesn't want to do it."

Haka grunted. "How do you know that?"

"Please, Commander. He's never looked the slightest bit happy." She pointed two fingers and brought them closer to his face, then proceeded to poke his eyelids the second he blinked. He yelped and leaned back, glaring at her. "It's in his eyes," she added as he took another sip of his coffee.

"No excuse for being a pervert."

"Ah. Of course not. Force is never an excuse," said Otter, rolling her eyes. "Heaven forbid he's forced into a position he hates, unlike the upstanding Shinsengumi commander who upholds the law while high and can't walk ten feet without falling over a piece of furniture. That's a choice."

"Falling over furniture isn't a—" Haka began, but Otter cut him off.

"Taking drugs is a choice," she said, narrowing her large eyes at him. "And you know it. He's a victim. You're just pathetic." She kicked his foot and curled her lip. "Drink your coffee."

Haka stood up, staggering half a step before regaining his balance. He was still in yesterday's clothes: boots, leather pants, a wrinkled tee shirt. His jacket must be somewhere...ah, it was hanging over the back of his desk chair. "Any news on the fugitives?"

Otter shook her head. "No."

"And the prisoner?"

"Lieutenant Takuan gave him breakfast, but I don't think the priest has touched a bite of it. He just sits on the cot with his eyes closed and doesn't move, like a rock or something."

Haka snorted. *The prisoner.* "That sounds like him."

Otter turned toward the door, but hesitated. "Commander..."

Haka glanced up. "What?"

"Can I ask you something?"

He lifted the key from around his neck and unlocked the top right desk drawer. "What?"

"You know him, don't you? The prisoner."

Haka paused, the drawer pulled halfway out. Without looking at Otter, he said, "No. He's just a source of possible information."

"Right."

Still focusing on the drawer, Haka lifted a hand and made shooing motions at the girl. "Scram, Otter." He listened to her footsteps head toward the door, but they stopped, and he glanced up. "I said scram," he repeated.

Otter scratched the back of her head, her hair sticking up

all over like a disgruntled porcupine. "Do me a favor and don't ever play poker, Commander. In fact, just don't gamble at all. You can't even look at someone when you're lying to them."

"I'm not lying," he said defensively. Too late he realized he had glanced away from her as he said it.

"Ha," she said humorlessly. "I know you know him. It's the only reason you haven't interrogated him yet. Which also means you don't hate him."

Haka pulled out a vial of stardust and slammed the desk drawer shut. Otter did not jump at the sudden noise, but she flinched. "He," Haka growled, "is none of your concern. This has nothing to do with you. Don't overstep your boundaries, Otter."

She opened her mouth to speak, but he lifted a hand, this time cutting her off. "Get back to your demons."

"So you can get back to yours?" asked Otter, pointing toward the vial in his hand.

Haka took a step around the desk toward her, and she scurried around the corner, out of sight. Haka sat down on the corner of the desk, gazing at the vial in his palm. The liquid drug was thick and pale, like bottled tears. It caught the light and glittered faintly inside the glass as he rolled the vial between his hands.

Someone knocked on the door.

"I told you to get back to the mutts," Haka snapped, looking over his shoulder.

"I'm guessing Otter was here, Commander?" Lieutenant Takuan replied, lifting his eyebrows.

Haka sighed and rubbed his eyes. "Yeah. What do you want?"

"You slept here again?"

"Izanagi's balls, yes! I'm wearing the same clothes I wore yesterday, too. I haven't showered, I haven't had a full cup of coffee, and I haven't even shot up yet. I haven't seen the prisoner this morning, I don't have an update on the fugitives—is there anything else you'd like to know, Lieutenant?"

If he was affected by the outburst, Takuan didn't show it. "It's seven A.M., and I would expect a visit from Kirikizu sometime before noon, so you might want to shower and put on a fresh change of clothes before then. Finish your coffee. Don't shoot up. I don't have an update on the fugitives, either, and dealing with the prisoner isn't part of my job."

Haka scowled. "I'm glad my birth mother isn't here. I couldn't stand having two."

"I pity her, wherever she is," said Takuan gravely. He took a small white pill out of his breast pocket and crossed the room, dropping it into Haka's coffee. Haka watched it dissolve in a small pocket of bubbles. "What is that?"

"Something to clear your head and help you wake up before everyone else arrives at the precinct," said the lieutenant. "There's a fresh change of clothes in your locker."

"My clothes?" asked Haka, taken aback.

"Yes. You left them at our house the last time you were there, so Mayumi washed and pressed them and gave them to me to give to you. That woman does everything."

Haka leaned his head back and groaned. "I take it back; you're more like a high-class nanny."

"I thought I would be serving my country when I joined the force," said Takuan with a straight face. "But no."

Haka picked up his coffee and stalked past the lieutenant, out the door and down the hall to the locker room and the shower. It was empty and silent, the official work day not starting for another half an hour. He tossed his clothes into the bin and took a brief, cold shower, the water washing away the remains of sleep. What little he'd had of it, at least.

He wrapped a towel around his waist and padded across the cement floor to the double sink, where he stared at his reflection in the wide, scratched mirror.

The overhead lighting was harsh and luminescent, filling under his cheekbones with shadow and glaring off his pale lips. With his long, wet hair clinging to his back and shoulders and the hollows under his eyes bruise-purple, he looked like a ghoul risen from the depths of a cemetery. Even the earring gleaming in his right ear seemed like a stolen artifact.

"There you are!"

Otter's voice broke his caustic observations, startling him so much that he whirled around and ran his hip into the edge of the sink.

Otter actually winced. "Okay, I'm sorry for that one."

"This is the men's locker room, Otter!" he barked, pressing a hand against his throbbing hip.

She gave him an odd look. "I know that."

He levelled a *So what are you doing here?* expression at her.

"Oh," she said, "we just got a call. Apparently, Kirikizu got permission to interrogate the prisoner himself and he'll be here around ten. I thought you'd want to know."

*Oh no.* Haka pushed his hair out of his face and straightened. "Fine."

Otter looked him up and down. "I can see your ribs. And for the millionth time, I'm not going to ask you about your scars, because I know you won't answer me."

"Yes," said Haka, "thank you."

"Your muscles won't last forever if you don't eat, you know."

"I know."

"Nice towel, though," she added.

"Will you get out?" Haka snapped.

Otter grinned and hurried out of the room. It wasn't until the door closed that Haka noticed his previously empty coffee cup had been refilled.

# TWENTY-FIVE

*EMPTY YOURSELF.*
  *Empty yourself.*
  *Empty yourself.*
  *Empty yourself.*
  *Empty yourself.*
There were no thoughts in Winter's mind, nothing clouding the space. He stared at the backs of his eyelids and did not think. If he thought, he would feel. If he felt, he would lose the only upper hand this situation offered him.

He heard the door open, followed by footsteps slowly descending the stairs. The steps flattened out, coming toward him, and stopped outside the cell.

Winter opened his eyes. His little brother looked back at him, his hands hanging at his sides like he didn't know what to do with them.

"So you aren't eating?" Haka shifted his jaw, a hard sneer on his face. "Why not?"

Winter remained silent, refusing to reply.

"You're going to stay this way, then? Not talking? Not even to me?"

Winter shut his eyes and let out a quiet breath. *Empty yourself.*

He heard Haka snap his fingers. He heard him say, "I can't —I'm not sticking my neck out for you."

Calmly, Winter said, "I don't need your help."

The door rattled like it had been struck. "No. That's right, you never did. You were always like this."

Winter kept his eyes shut. "Like what?"

"Alone. Even when I was next to you, you were alone. I see nothing has changed, except maybe your clothes. Where are your swords?"

"I have no use for them," Winter replied, resting his hands on his knees. *Empty yourself. Empty your—*

"So, what, you had your fill of killing and decided you could become someone else? You thought you could change just because you wanted to?"

"That's the only way any of us change," said Winter. "Because we decide to." He was doing his best to keep his voice even, to remain calm and cool even as his pulse beat quicker and his blood grew heated. "I wanted to change, so I did."

"You think you can become someone else because you let your weapons fall?" The bars rattled again. "You're a bigger fool than I am."

"Perhaps." Winter did not move, but he opened his eyes. "But you seem content to remain a fool. That is what separates us."

Haka was gripping the bars of the cell door, his eyes darker than the day before. The filmy, glassy sheen had faded. He was sober, Winter realized. In this moment, at least, he was his own man.

"You," Haka hissed, "think you're so far above me. You always did. You may have changed your profession, brother, but you're the same thing you always were. You aren't a man. You're a cold-blooded reptile if you're anything. A snake who dreams of humanity."

"I would rather be a snake who dreams of humanity," said Winter, clenching his hands into fists, "than a human sacrificing his freedom for slavery at the hands of a drug and a tyrant."

Haka spat into the cell. "I hope you drive your God away." He straightened, stepping away from the bars. "You've already done it to everyone else."

———

HAKA SLAMMED the dungeon door behind him.

He heard something fall over and glanced toward the desks where the officer assigned to secretary duty for the day had just dropped a stapler on the floor.

"Sorry, Commander," he apologized, picking it back up and setting it carefully by the edge of the desk.

"You're new," said Haka, after a brief moment of recollection.

The officer stood up so quickly his chair rolled into the wall. He bowed, trying to inconspicuously reach behind him and pull the chair back. "Officer Shun. Um...I've been here for three months, Commander."

Haka blinked. Three months and he still didn't recognize the man's face? That was awkward.

Officer Shun apparently knew better than to point it out, because he added quickly, "I have a forgettable face. Nobody remembers it. Even my mother sees me sometimes and asks, 'are you my son?' That's how forgettable it is."

Haka felt his mood darkening with each new word as Officer Shun tried to smooth the situation over. "Be quiet," he snapped. "Has there been any word from the Prince-Regent?"

"Not yet," Officer Shun began, but the phone ringing interrupted him. He lifted the receiver and barked, "First Precinct, Shinsengumi Officer Shun speak—" He paused and glanced at Haka. "The commander is here. Would you like to...yes. Of course, here he is."

Officer Shun held the receiver toward Haka and whispered, "It's the Prince-Regent's Hand."

Haka snatched the telephone and held it to his ear. "What do you want?"

Kirikizu's voice was annoyingly calm as he replied, "There has been a change in plans. I'm arriving in half an hour. See to it the prisoner is ready. And, Commander?"

Haka ground his teeth but asked, "Yes?"

"I will need an assistant. That girl, Otter."

"What the h—"

Kirikizu hung up before Haka could finish his incredulous question. Haka did not bother to put the receiver back where it belonged; he tossed it onto the desk, nearly knocking over Officer Shun's coffee cup.

Officer Shun obligingly scooped the telephone up and set properly in its place. "Bad news, sir?"

"Where is Otter?" Haka demanded. "The short, scary girl?"

"I know who she is," Officer Shun stammered, "she's with—she's with the mutts in the courtyard, I think. I think, but I'm not sure."

Haka turned and went back the way he'd come. He had given Winter a warning. That was as much as he could do.

———

OTTER SENSED Haka's presence before he came into view. She caught a glimpse of him around the corner, half-hidden, eyeing Violet like a cat eyeing a large dog. Otter lifted a hand toward the mutt and said, "Ayyyet!"

Violet sat, her eyes intent on her trainer.

"Good girl," Otter cooed, putting a hand on Violet's nose. Without looking away from the mutt, she lifted her voice and said, "It's all right, she won't bite. Probably."

Haka emerged, glaring and giving Violet a wide berth. "You need to put that thing away."

"Her name is Violet, for the five hundred and seventy-seventh time, and we aren't done with her session. If I don't keep up with it, she gets—"

"Kirikizu will be here in half an hour, and he wants you to assist him in his interrogation."

"What?" Otter's yelp startled Violet, who jerked her head back. The sudden motion was enough to send Haka leaping six feet in the opposite direction, his body poised as if to leap over the wall separating the courtyard from the alley.

"Sir," said Otter, raising her hands and clucking to Violet in more soothing tones. "I'm a mutt trainer. That's my job. I'm not an assistant or an interrogator or an assistant interrogator."

"He knows that."

"Then what does he want me for?"

Haka shrugged. "I didn't argue."

"Of course you didn't," said Otter blackly.

The commander sneered defensively at her and backed

away from Violet, heading back the way he had come rather than move around her the other way and enter the station through the rear door. "Consider it a new part of your job."

Otter knew other living creatures were sensitive to changes in mood, particularly moods of hostility and aggression, so she took a deep breath and forced herself to relax. "Yes, sir, Commander Haka, sir."

"Behave," he warned her, before walking around the corner. She listened to his retreating footsteps until she heard the courtyard gate swing closed.

Then she looked at Violet and said, "I need a raise."

Violet snorted in agreement.

———

SAIZOU DID NOT SLEEP DEEPLY enough to dream that night. He opened his eyes when he heard a hollow pounding and a muffled voice saying, "Open up."

Shotgun sprang to his feet and eyed the door. "Sounds like him."

"Just open it," said Saizou, standing.

Shotgun bent down and hauled the door up. Hiro stood outside, even more intimidating in full morning light. He had a pale hand raised, blocking against the weak sunlight filtering through the clouds. In his other hand, he held a plastic bag, which he tossed onto the floor near Saizou's foot.

Fumiyo stirred, waking up with the noise and eyeing the Yakuza boss with all the suspicion her face could hold. Under her breath, Saizou heard her whisper, "What does *he* want?"

She had spoken quietly, but Saizou saw Hiro's red eyes, pink in the daylight, slide a fraction to the side, his gaze flickering to Fumiyo and back. "That's food."

Saizou's mouth twitched, but he gave Hiro a shallow bow. "We appreciate your generosity."

"You call shoving us in an oversized box generosity?" Shotgun cracked his knuckles. "If we don't get outta here soon, I'm—"

"You're what?" Hiro interrupted, skepticism written all over his pale face. "You should be grateful you're alive. I could have turned a friendly welcome into a trap and killed all of you without raising a finger."

"Yeah," Shotgun retorted, "I'm real grateful and all, but—"

This time, Saizou interrupted him. "Watch it," he said sharply. "This man has done nothing but help us. I'd like to keep it that way."

Shotgun crossed his arms and leaned back against the wall, his stance wary and annoyed. "Fine."

"Your friend doesn't look well," said Hiro, his gaze travelling past Saizou.

Saizou turned, and his pulse quickened when he saw Shi had not stood up, or even opened his eyes. He was slumped in the corner, his head resting against the wall. His skin was ashen, covered by a thin film of sweat.

Fumiyo was at his side in an instant, checking the side of his neck for a pulse. "It's weak," she said, her voice pitched with panic. "He's alive, but Mr. Hiro is right. He's really sick."

"Whatever injury he has may have gotten infected," said Hiro. "We can take care of it once I take you to a new safe house."

"What?" Shotgun barked, straightening. "You're just bouncing us from one safe house to another? What's the point? Saizou, we don't need this guy."

Hiro clasped his hands in front of him and regarded Shotgun with an icy calm. "Thus far, your safe house has been temporary. However, I'm sure I could find a much smaller, far more permanent safe house, roughly six feet deep and slightly longer."

Shotgun's eyebrows drew together. "Are you threatening me?"

"Yes," said Hiro.

"Shotgun," Saizou began.

"I still say we don't need this guy," Shotgun declared, cutting Saizou off. "We're wanted enough as it is, we don't need to get mixed up with the Yakuza too. Don't know why I didn't think of it earlier."

"The Yakuza are regarded warmly in the current political climate," said Hiro, his voice still even, his words clipped. "Patriots are not."

"If you aren't a patriot, why are you helping us?" Shotgun demanded, his lip curled as he took a step closer to the albino.

"Since knowing my motive does not affect you in any way," Hiro replied, "it isn't necessary for me to tell you." He turned back to Saizou. "I'll bring pharmaceuticals for your friend, but there is nothing further I can do until we've moved. It's too dangerous here. You must stay quiet and wait until I hear from my contact."

"Yo, tell her to hurry up, would you?" Shotgun snapped. "It's not like we need a five-star hotel. Can't be that hard to make reservations."

Hiro continued to look at Saizou for a long moment, and Saizou could see the albino making a decision. He decided not to stop him; Shotgun could use the lesson.

Not a half-second later, Hiro spun gracefully to the side, his body tilting as he unleashed a high kick that collided with the side of Shotgun's head, knocking the taller, younger man to the ground.

Hiro moved gracefully out of his spin and strode back to the door, which he pulled down behind him. It hit the ground with a hollow bang, and for a moment, the only sound was that of Shotgun, coughing and pushing himself onto his hands and knees.

"Bastard," said Shotgun, gingerly feeling the side of his head. "Ow."

Saizou picked up a lantern and turned the light to the brightest setting, then crouched beside Shi. He pulled the bandages away to inspect the wound. It still showed no signs of infection. Maybe a slight redness, but with a mass taken out of your shoulder like that, it was to be expected.

"I don't think it is," said Fumiyo, lifting one of Shi's eyelids. Exposed to light, Shi's pupil shrank inside his brown iris, but he made no sound and did not move. "I think he was poisoned."

"You can see the effects of poison in a wound," said Saizou, curling his hands into fists. *Not poison. Please, don't be poison.*

"Not all poison," said Fumiyo.

"How do you know this?"

"My parents were doctors," said Fumiyo, her tone more brisk than Saizou had yet heard. "I know some things. How was he injured again?"

"The Prince-Regent's Dog-man. Bit him in the shoulder."

"I hope he got indigestion," said Fumiyo, pushing a lock of Shi's silvery hair away from his forehead. "We need an antidote. If the Dog is venomous but lives with the Prince-Regent, they definitely have an antidote handy. I don't know whether it's an immunity or an antidote, but we need to find out, and soon."

"Today?"

"Within twenty-four hours."

Saizou raked his hands through his hair. They were shaking, and he balled them into fists again, trying to steady his nerves. Shi had not survived guerrilla warfare and disfiguration in another country only to die from a bite back home.

But how could he find an antidote from a creature that lived inside the palace?

It didn't matter how. He had to figure it out.

Saizou rose to his feet and faced Shotgun, who was on his knees, looking a little dizzy. "You stay here with Fumiyo," he instructed. "Feed Shi, if you can."

"Where do you think you're going?" Shotgun demanded, his voice chiming in with Fumiyo's near-identical cry of, "Where are you going?"

"To help Shi," said Saizou, crouching down and lifting the door of the storage unit.

"Hey, what if you don't come back?" Shotgun demanded.

"Go to the safe house and figure things out."

Shotgun swore softly and climbed to his feet. "Yeah, just hurry up, all right?"

Saizou glanced back at Fumiyo. "Don't kill him."

"Her?" Shotgun barked a brief laugh, but the sound faded when he caught sight of the dark glare glittering in Fumiyo's eyes as she looked at him. "Thanks for the instructions."

*Hang on, Shi.* Saizou closed the unit door behind him and broke into a quiet run, heading east, away from the docks.

# TWENTY-SIX

TSUKI CLOSED her eyes and let the cool breeze wash across her face. A thick blanket of dark clouds blocked the sun's warmth, but the chill felt somehow cleansing.

She did not hear Kiba climb out onto the roof as well, but she sensed his arrival before he settled down next to her, crouching by the edge of the roof.

"What's chasing you this time?"

Tsuki opened her eyes and sighed. "What do you mean?"

"You only come onto the roof to escape something. Has Matahachi been bothering you?"

Kiba's voice always carried an edge, but Tsuki detected the edge was slightly sharper with that question. "He always bothers me, but he didn't do anything specific, if that's what you're asking. I came here so I wouldn't have to think."

Kiba arched an eyebrow, and Tsuki's mouth twitched. "I will not be accepting remarks about my thought process at this time."

"Whatever you like."

"Thank you."

The breeze carried the sound of metal pinging against rock. The mine was nestled against the base of a mountain a mile and a half away. Akita Domain spanned a thirty-mile circumference. It was not large, as domains went, and most of the land was flat, with at least ten miles taken up by marsh and rice fields.

But any domain that housed the base of a mountain was regarded with a special kind of awe, lingering superstition from previous centuries remaining in various forms. Tales of yokai and oni remained alive and well in stories among the lower classes.

Villagers used to claim the Akita Domain was protected by a magnanimous spirit who blessed the domain with wealth and kind rulers, but now the whispers claimed the spirit had been killed by a demon, or perhaps the yokai had simply decided to move on and leave Akita Domain behind.

"Do you believe in spirits, Kiba?" Tsuki asked suddenly, leaning back on her palms. A shaft of pale, white-gold sunlight filtered through a thin patch in the clouds, shining across the scene of bare trees in the distance.

"What kind?" he asked, still crouched and ready to spring up, his elbows resting on his knees.

"Yokai. Oni. Angels, demons."

"I might."

"What about fate? Do you believe in that?"

"You're too young to have an existential crisis."

She smiled. "I wouldn't call this one existential. It's pretty garden-variety."

"Mmm." He settled back on his heels. "And what caused this garden-variety crisis?"

She hadn't planned on telling Kiba any of this; he had enough to concern himself with as it was, but if he found out by other means, she knew what would happen. He would be hurt she hadn't told him, although she knew he would never say so. "I told Saizou not to fight for Akita Domain."

Kiba looked over his shoulder at her and said nothing, waiting patiently for her to continue. When she said nothing, he spoke. "You knew it would harm the people if he fought for it."

A knot untied itself in Tsuki's stomach. He understood. Of course he did. "Yes. Still, I feel...partially responsible. He's an outlaw. God only knows where he is, and some of that is my fault."

"You knew it would happen."

"You don't go easy, do you?"

He gazed out at the horizon. "What does fate have to do with this?"

"Do you remember the story you told me once? I must have been nine or ten."

"I don't remember ever telling you a story," said Kiba, frowning.

Tsuki smiled and leaned forward as the breeze increased in strength, pushing her hair away from her shoulders. Kiba's long ponytail blew back in the breeze, too, and Tsuki shifted closer to his back. "It was about a time-traveler named Yuki."

"You're making this up."

"You know I can't make these things up; I have no imagination." Tsuki took the elastic out of his hair and ran her fingers through it, combing out the wind-made tangles.

"I doubt that." Kiba tilted his head back as Tsuki began to braid his hair. It was tradition, a near-ritual Tsuki had begun as a child, when Kiba was first assigned as her bodyguard. His hair had always been long and thick, and endlessly fascinating for a seven-year-old girl. As she grew older, his hair became a comfort of sorts—a link to security, something to do connected to someone she trusted. Twenty years later, it still helped put her mind at ease.

"Did this time-traveler also leave the listener hanging?" Kiba prompted.

Tsuki smiled. "Yuki wanted to fix everything."

"Mmm," grunted Kiba. "She sounds like someone else I know."

"If you thought I didn't know you modelled her after me, you were deluded," said Tsuki. "One day, she came across a man caught in a fox trap. His foot was badly injured, but he pleaded with Yuki. 'I have a wife and daughter,' he told her. 'If I'm late for dinner, they'll worry. If they come looking for me, they may be caught, too.' So Yuki helped him out of the trap and went on her way."

"This can't be headed anywhere good," Kiba interrupted.

"It's your story," Tsuki reminded him. "Shut up and listen. Two nights later, she came across a small house. She was hungry, and willing to trade work for food, and so she went up to the door and knocked. When nobody answered, she opened the door and saw the man she had saved from the fox trap."

Kiba frowned, his head angled toward her just a fraction.

Tsuki finished the braid and let it fall against his back. "He held a bloody knife in his hand, and the bodies of his wife and daughter were strewn across the floor. Blood coated the walls."

"I had poor judgement when it came to age-appropriate stories," said Kiba, leaning forward, his elbows resting on his knees. "And I really don't see why Yuki needed to be a time traveler for this story."

Tsuki laughed. "I never really thought about that. The story left an impression on me, though. You said to be careful, because sometimes what I thought was help was really interfering with fate. If Yuki had ignored the man caught in the fox trap, his wife and daughter would have lived. And yet, ignoring someone in need seemed evil to her, so she helped him and unwittingly abetted an even greater evil."

For a long moment, Kiba was silent. Then he said, "You wonder if you should have left Saizou alone when he came here? If perhaps you interfered rather than aided."

"I think it's a possibility that scares me. He might have had a chance."

"He had no chance, and you know that as well as I. A war-ravaged daimyo, returning from a long absence? Long absences create speculation. His case was over before it began."

"Maybe it was." Tsuki shifted forward, once again beside Kiba. She tilted her head back and took a deep, cold breath. The stars gleamed overhead, fixed against the dark sky. "Wherever he is, I want to help him."

"That will be difficult, with Matahachi keeping such a close eye on you."

"His eyesight is hardly perfect. If it were, we would have been arrested for what we do in the city on a weekly basis."

"I think we may need to enlist someone to find Saizou and his compatriot if you wish to help them."

Tsuki quickly turned her face toward him. "Who do you have in mind?"

"The one spirit I'm certain is real," said Kiba, rising to his feet in a single, fluid motion. He did not offer Tsuki a hand, and she would not have taken it, for she leaned back and performed a perfect kip-up and landed on her feet.

"Dramatic," said Kiba.

"I learned from the best." Tsuki flung an arm toward the stairwell. "Shall we?"

———

KIRIKIZU STEPPED into the 12<sup>th</sup> Precinct and was even more underwhelmed than usual. Empty take-out cartons sat across the abandoned front desk. The floor needed to be swept, and even the blinds were avant-garde, the slats half-open.

He was fairly sure this was Commander Haka's version of 'cleaning up' for his arrival, and he would not have been surprised in the least to discover every inch of the disaster was completely intentional.

"Sorry about the mess," said a female voice, and Otter's face appeared behind the desk. Kirikizu stepped forward and looked down. She had been sitting in the chair all along, leaning back far enough that her small form was completely invisible from the door. "It's Lieutenant Takuan's day off."

She blew a large, pink bubble between her teeth and popped it with an expert smack.

Kirikizu focused on the sound of his breath, filtered through his mask, rather than his annoyance. "Where is the prisoner?"

"In the dungeon. Where else would he be?" Otter tucked her feet underneath her and stood on the seat of the chair. From there, she hopped onto the desk before jumping off several feet in front of Kirikizu. "Follow me."

Now he knew the mess was deliberate.

Kirikizu followed Otter down the hallway, but just as she reached the basement door, she stopped. "Hey, why did you request my assistance? You know it's not my job, right? Plus, you're not a surgeon. It's not like you need a nurse. If you want to rip a guy open and watch him bleed to death, it's okay. Not like you're going to ask me for forceps or a sponge."

"I require your assistance," said Kirikizu. "That is all you need know."

"Geez," said Otter, opening the door. "Helpful much?" She descended the stairs, shouting, "Hey, Commander! The Hand is here!"

Haka strode into view and stood near the bottom of the stairs, his arms folded. He looked even worse than usual, like the rest of the place; even in the dim dungeon light, the commander's skin was sallow and his starlight-bright eyes appeared to have sunk further into his skull.

"Bad night's sleep, Commander?" asked Kirikizu patronizingly.

Haka lifted his hand, forming an offensive gesture, but Otter grabbed the front of his jacket and began to walk, tugging him along with her.

Kirikizu tilted his head and watched as the small young woman hauled the gangly commander farther down the corridor, whispering words too quiet to catch. In his idle moments, Kirikizu sometimes wondered if Otter really ran the precinct, using Haka as a malleable, operational front.

But this was not an idle moment, and there was work to do. Kirikizu faced the cell that held the prisoner. Winter did not look overly concerned, if he was concerned at all. He sat on his knees in the middle of the room. He might as well have been sleeping.

Kirikizu tapped the bars with a finger, and Winter opened his eyes.

"Ah," said Winter blandly. "I assume you're the one supposed to wring answers out of me. I've been looking forward to this."

"Most people don't," said Kirikizu.

"No," admitted Winter, "but the sooner you start, the

sooner you realize I know nothing and the sooner you either kill me or set me loose to contact my supposed partners in crime."

"Hm," said Kirikizu, as close as he ever came to a sound of amusement. "Otter."

"Coming!" Louder, he heard her hiss, "Just stay out of it and let him get this over with, okay? Geez."

"I don't care what he does," said Haka, without bothering to keep his voice low.

"Good. Fine." Otter strode over to Kirikizu, but he only listened to her approach. Something else had caught his eye— Winter lifted a hand and ran it through his hair. It was not a worried gesture, not a nervous tick.

But he had used his left hand.

Kirikizu tilted his head, watching Winter's left hand, and then he studied Haka, standing down the hall. Just a moment before, he had also gestured with his left hand.

Haka's attitude about the prisoner had been out of character for the man since he was arrested.

Interesting.

"The prisoner looks incredibly unharmed," said Kirikizu, clasping his hands behind his back.

"Once we found out the interrogation was your job, we didn't bother with it," Otter explained.

Kirikizu nodded, but rather than entering the cell, he said, "I'll be back in a moment."

"Where are you going?" asked Otter, as Kirikizu turned and moved back up the stairs.

"To make a call."

# TWENTY-SEVEN

THE DOOR OPENED and the same baby-faced guard who had arrested him walked into the lab and set down a covered plate. "Your meal is here."

"Is that so?" Oscar cast an exaggerated glance at his bare wrist. "Amazing how you keep track of time like that. It'd be so useful if there was a bloody clock around, but, no, you people seem bent on keeping me away from the time. Good thing I have you chaps around to make sure I know when it's time to eat!"

The guard hesitated. "Are you all right, doctor?"

"Oh, fine, fine." Oscar realized he couldn't angrily roll his sleeves up, since he had done that several hours ago. Instead of that gesture, he picked up a plastic slider from the nearest table and threw it directly over the guard's head. "Wonderful! Ecstatic! Brilliant!"

The guard backed toward the door. Oscar found this hilarious, considering he had no weapons training and the guard carried some kind of modified sword he no doubt knew how to use.

"How many days has it been, if I may ask?" questioned Oscar, crossing his arms and attempting to look calmer. "Or should I just ask which meal is this, since they all seem to consist of rice and meat like I'm a common prisoner?"

The guard hesitated. "Breakfast," he said finally. "It's breakfast."

"I'll be honest," said Oscar after a moment, "I didn't really expect you to tell me."

The guard glanced at the door. "Don't worry," Oscar continued, his anger softening just enough to allow him to say, "it's not like I'm going to tell the P-R. Not sure we could communicate anyways; I don't speak jackass."

"You're on camera," said the guard blandly.

Without looking up from the meal, Oscar gestured toward the corner of the wall that afforded the best view of the lab. "Right there."

"Whoever's on duty can—"

"There's no audio feed. Trust me, someone would have arrested me yet again if they could hear the names I've been calling the P-R for the last...how long's it been?" Oscar held up a hand. "No, wait, you can't tell me. That's fine. You know what would be even more fine? A fork. I've had it up to here with these bloody chopsticks."

"I'll see what I can do," said the guard, turning back to the door.

"Wait," Oscar interrupted and pointed toward the enormous, steel freezer door behind him. "I can't find any in there, so." He slid the paper across the table and jabbed at the meal with his chopsticks. "I need samples from these three animals. Get them right."

———

KIRIKIZU DESCENDED THE STAIRS AGAIN. The call had taken half an hour. He had commandeered the computer and sent a DNA sample, looking for a match. When it returned positive, it changed his entire interrogation plan.

People thought interrogations and torture were the same thing.

They were not.

Torture had three uses: punishment, example-setting, and sadistic pleasure. Torture could be vicious and pointless. When torturing someone, you could use any method you liked. If the victim passed out, you let them wake up again or woke them yourself before starting again.

Interrogation was far more delicate; the difference between a finger painting and an original Hokusai. There were things you could and could not do. The subject had to remain alert, functioning well enough to correctly answer questions but too desperate to lie.

Anticipation was key. In fact, to Kirikizu, success in any endeavor was fifty percent anticipation, be it pleasure or pain. Making someone wait for pain, they envisioned all kinds of gruesome things, often dreaming up more creative measures than Kirikizu ever did. Sometimes, the subject talked even before Kirikizu began any actual interrogation.

This time, it would have to be a little different.

He reached the bottom of the stairs. Haka was doing pull-ups on the bars of an empty cell, and Otter was rattling off some kind of shopping list.

"—expensive coffee, you're going to have to shell out if you don't want the gross kind." She broke off as Kirikizu approached. "You were sure chatty up there."

"Secure the prisoner," said Kirikizu, nodding toward Winter.

Haka dropped to the ground and turned to face Kirikizu. "Who was that? The Prince-Regent?" When Kirikizu regarded him in silence, Haka said, "Did he want to know what you were wearing?"

Kirikizu's complete lack of reaction seemed to surprise Haka, because he lifted an eyebrow and said, "Usually, you at least clench a fist at jabs like that."

"I'm not concerned with your petty attempts to rile me," said Kirikizu.

Haka's eyes narrowed, but before he could say anything else, Otter said, "Commander, the prisoner?"

Haka brushed past Kirikizu and entered Winter's cell. Kirikizu watched, aware he was under observation from Otter. Winter was proving a very demure prisoner. He did not struggle once as Haka chained his arms to the wall with only a few inches of space between the manacles and the stone.

"Get me a chair," said Kirikizu.

Otter sighed and jogged past him, up the stairs. Kirikizu walked toward Winter's cell and stood outside as Haka tested the chains, then turned toward the cell door.

"Satisfied?" he asked, looking bored.

It was a farce, Kirikizu knew that now. The Shinsengumi commander's apparent lack of interest in the prisoner was an award-winning performance. The DNA test had proven that much.

"Quite," said Kirikizu.

Sounds of loud, metallic screeching rang through the dungeon as Otter came back down the stairs, dragging a metal chair behind her. She took her sweet time, letting the chair clank down each step, groaning against the stone.

When she reached the bottom, she set the chair down and crossed her arms. "Happy?"

Kirikizu smiled mentally at the similarities between Haka and Otter, without allowing the expression onto his face. "Put it in the cell, on the opposite side."

"Gonna throw shade at him first?" Otter rolled her eyes as she dragged the chair into the cell.

"Out of the cell now," said Kirikizu, stepping toward the cell door.

"Do this, Otter. Do that, Otter," she quipped, but it was half-hearted, and she cast a concerned glance at Winter's impassive face before exiting the cell.

Haka attempted to follow her, but Kirikizu struck. He brought his elbow back on Haka's face hard enough to send the commander staggering back into the cell. Kirikizu removed the key from the lock and slammed the door shut, enclosing himself and Haka in the room with the prisoner.

Before Haka had time to recover, Kirikizu wrapped an arm around his neck and dragged him back to the chair, where he slammed him down, pushing a knee into his stomach and removing the handcuffs from Haka's belt.

Otter shrieked through the bars, yelling questions and curses at Kirikizu as he secured Haka in the chair.

The whole affair had taken roughly eight seconds. Haka shook his head, his enlarged pupils dilating with his rapid breathing.

"What in hell's name do you think you're doing?" Haka snarled, trying to pull away from the chair, but Kirikizu had made sure Haka's arms were entwined through the rungs on the back of the chair and then handcuffed, making the chair and the commander inseparable.

He was not secure enough to go to work on, but he soon would be. Kirikizu drew a thin length of chain from his belt. It was roughly six feet long and much stronger than it looked, helpful for lashing out or strangling.

He put a foot down on Haka's right boot, making sure the other man couldn't move too much, and proceeded to chain Haka's feet to the chair, then hook the chain up through the handcuffs.

"Too much movement and you'll fall over," said Kirikizu, stepping back again.

"What are you doing?" Otter screamed from outside the cell.

"Proceeding with the interrogation," said Kirikizu, unbuckling each of his sleeves. He tossed them on the ground and began to remove the various instruments he kept in them, laying them across the sleeves like a set of surgeon's tools.

He lifted his head and met Winter's direct, frozen gaze. The older man's blue eyes were cold enough to draw all warmth from the room, at once broken and sharper than before. He was also done playing any game with Kirikizu.

"If you lay a hand on him," said Winter softly, "I will kill you. Perhaps not today or tomorrow, but I will do it."

"You'll have to get in line," shouted Otter, ramming her elbow into the bars.

Haka spat a mouthful of blood onto the stones and laughed, but it was directed toward Winter, not Otter. "You gave up on violence, remember? I wouldn't want you to break your precious oath of cowardice."

Kirikizu tilted his head. Haka seemed to equate lack of violence with cowardice, while Winter equated lack of violence with righteousness. It proved two different mindsets; Haka's was that of a bully, stemming from innate fear of vulnerability. Most likely he had been a victim during his formative years.

Winter's mindset was that of a stereotypical Champion, willing to take the brunt of a blow to protect the weaker without deliberation.

This would most likely prove more effective than he had hoped.

# TWENTY-EIGHT

KIBA DROVE THEM TO CHIYODA, a run-down section of
Tokyo on the city's outer edge. The pale winter sunlight had
slowly hidden itself behind a cover of dark clouds, threatening
snow. As they entered the city limits, Kiba slowed down to
thirty miles an hour, driving quietly through streets long ago
emptied by the war. Barren concrete buildings stood vacant
and broken, lining streets badly in need of repair.

Tsuki had always correlated yokai and their kin with mountains, with trees and fresh air and nature. This was the last
place she would think of a yokai inhabiting, which made it a
clever place to live in the current climate.

If the Prince-Regent heard of a living yokai, he would hunt
it down until he found it, and only God knew what kind of
duty would follow a mandatory capture and conscription.

A firefly floated past, and as Tsuki turned her head to
follow it, others caught her eye, swirling through the mist.

Mist that had no right to appear in an urban neighborhood
on a cold winter morning.

The neighborhood began to darken the farther they rode.

The mist grew thicker, no longer transparent but dense, like riding through a swelling storm cloud. Kiba leaned farther forward, peering through the darkness, the headlights of the motorcycle lighting the way just enough to keep going.

When Tsuki finally spoke, her voice was muffled in her ears, dampened by the mist. "Fireflies in the city?" As she spoke, one of the tiny, illuminated creatures flew past her face, followed by a dozen more. They were everywhere—pinpricks of light in the surrounding gray.

"It's one way to tell when you're near a yokai-kin," said Kiba. He sounded three miles away, even though his face was less than a foot away from Tsuki's. "I thought you knew that."

"You failed in my education."

"Educating you was not my job. Safeguarding you was."

Tsuki smiled. She had learned more applicable lessons from Kiba than she ever had from her various teachers and tutors.

Kiba slowed the motorcycle down to a stop. "Here we are."

Tsuki looked up at the looming apartment building. A single light shone through a cracked window three stories up. "This yokai of yours," she began.

"He's not mine," Kiba interrupted, "and he's a kitsune. You should know before you meet him."

"Aren't kitsune all women?" Tsuki felt a heady thrill in spite of herself. Even those who believed in yokai and yokai-kin widely regarded kitsune as fables. The mountain fox-spirits whose number of tails increased their power were legends, said to have been created by rice farmers who saw things in the mist. Mist which may not have been entirely natural.

"Most," said Kiba. "Not all."

"Let me guess," said Tsuki, keeping her voice low, "he's the only resident for miles."

"He likes to keep to himself."

"Then what makes you think he's going to care about my request?"

"I never said I thought he'd care," said Kiba. "We may need to bribe him."

They left the motorcycle on the sidewalk and approached the rusted fire escape. The metallic ring of their footsteps echoed dully as they ascended. Tsuki swatted lightly at a firefly circling around her head.

"I cannot believe you've known a *kitsune* and you never told me," she hissed softly, glancing up at the yellow light pouring through the solitary window.

"He prefers anonymity," said Kiba, climbing up to the second floor.

Tsuki glanced at a window and saw only dust coating the glass. A firefly floated out of a crack between panes. "What else can you tell me about him?"

"Tell you about whom?"

The new voice echoed over Tsuki's head several times before fading away.

"Kiba!" the voice rang out, hollow and reverberating. "It's been a long time, you old son-of-a-gun! However, I do have to remind you that I don't enjoy visitors. Never have. You *know* that." It would have been a threatening remark had it not sounded so much like a complaint.

"Sorry," said Kiba, climbing up the last stair and stepping aside to let Tsuki through.

Light spilled around the figure leaning out of the window, but as Tsuki stepped around Kiba, the angle shifted, allowing her to see the mysterious speaker.

The kitsune lowered his hands from where he held them

cupped around his mouth and gave Tsuki a wide Cheshire smile before propping his chin on his hand. "So," he said.

Tsuki stared. She wasn't sure what she had expected, exactly, but copper hair and a floral shirt were not high on the list.

"Underwhelmed?" said the yokai, stifling a sudden yawn.

For once, Tsuki had no idea what to say.

The yokai grinned then and held out his hand. "Hi, Underwhelmed," he chirped, suddenly cheerful. "I'm Nix!" Immediately, he added, "Come on in, you two! I have tea," before ducking back inside and shutting the window.

Tsuki slowly reached for the doorknob, but paused and said, "Is he really a kitsune?"

"Yes," said Kiba.

"You're sure?"

"Very sure."

The door opened before Tsuki could turn the knob, and Nix ushered them both inside with enthusiastic force. He shut the door behind them, turning the deadbolt and pulling the chain across before bouncing over to the two-burner stove.

The entire apartment was one tiny room, with the exception of a bathroom. A mattress sat on the floor in the far corner in place of a bed, and since there was no closet, Nix seemed perfectly content to fling clothes wherever he felt like it. The kitchen barely had enough room for one person, but he moved with the grace surety afforded, spinning and snatching two cups from where they hung from nails on the wall.

Tsuki stepped back toward the other side of the apartment, moving around a lightbulb hanging from a string.

Nix leaned around the corner. "Sorry about the digs," he apologized, waving one of the cups in the air. "I like to keep it simple."

"Oh, please, don't apologize," said Tsuki, still attempting to process the situation.

"You're too polite," said Nix, with a wide smile. The teakettle began to whistle, and he promptly set the cups down on the counter and filled a small, clay teapot with boiling water. "So, tell me, what brings you kids to my humble abode?"

Kiba smiled a rare smile. "I have not been called 'kid' in a very long time. Especially not by someone who appears younger than I am."

Nix chuckled. "Yes, well, if I looked as old as I was, two things would happen. One: I'd be dust, and dust is really very hard to manage. Two: I wouldn't be calling you two *kids*, I'd be calling you whippersnappers, or youngsters, or infants, or possibly the equivalent of unrelated great-great-great-great-great-great grandchildren."

Tsuki liked him immediately, and she wondered if that was wise. Kiba hadn't said anything about trusting Nix, only that he might help, but still, it was hard not to like him. "What should I call you? Nix-sama?"

"Oh no! None of that. Eugh." He shuddered. "Just Nix is fine. All these prefixes and suffixes and what-have-you fixes; it's enough to give me a headache."

"I take it your kind don't use formal speech, then?" Tsuki leaned forward, intrigued.

Nix lifted the teapot and swished it in careful circles, holding the spout and the handle. "Oh, we have our own linguistic behaviors, but let's just say they aren't the same as yours." He paused, and the swaying lightbulb flashed across his eyes as he studied Tsuki. Abruptly, he said, "Whatever it is, I can safely say the answer is no."

Tsuki removed a hand from her pocket and tucked a strand

of hair behind her ear. "What makes you think we're here to ask for anything?"

"Darling, please." He tapped the side of his head. "I see much more than meets the eye. One of the perks of being a kitsune. Which, coincidentally, is how I know that *you* are as dense as a—"

"With all due respect," Kiba interrupted, straightening, "the favor is not without compensation."

"Oh, isn't it?" asked Nix, and resumed swirling the teapot. "And what makes you think I need compensation?"

Tsuki squinted at her surroundings. It hardly felt like the home of someone who didn't need any kind of assistance.

"I see that look on your face, sweetheart," said Nix, pulling Tsuki's attention to him. "You're thinking the word *squalor*, and let me tell you that this is not squalor. This is a home. Have you ever seen a fox den? This is practically spotless."

"I didn't," Tsuki began, but Nix gave her a knowing wink and said, "Please continue, Kiba. Compensation?"

"Matahachi Shigure," said Kiba.

Tsuki whirled around, her pulse suddenly pounding. "What?"

Nix's wide grin thinned into a sly smile. He poured pale green liquid into each cup and set the teapot down before handing the cups to Kiba and Tsuki. "What about Matahachi Shigure?"

"He'll be handed over to you."

Tsuki could only stare, trying to grasp the pieces of a puzzle she hadn't known existed until just now.

Nix had adopted a shrewd expression that worried Tsuki. It held none of the kitsune's previous warm cheer. With this expression, she could easily believe the youthful face hid a thousand-year-old powerful entity. "Congratulations," he said finally, "my interest is piqued!"

Tsuki held up a hand, as if stopping oncoming traffic. "Before this conversation goes any further...Kiba? Why would Nix want Matahachi?"

"Oh, pish tosh," said Nix with a sniff, "it's my business. No need to worry!"

Kiba looked very much like he wanted to continue avoiding the subject but couldn't bring himself to. "I made Nix's acquaintance thanks to Matahachi."

"Whoah, whoah, whoah. Excuse me!" said Nix. "Let me tell the story, because that's a tragically bad opening line and it's a riveting story that deserves better."

Kiba sighed and stepped back toward the wall, allowing the kitsune to continue.

"Thank you, dear," said Nix primly. "See, it's like this: Matahachi took something very important from me, and I want it back."

Kiba held up one finger. "That," he said, "was not good storytelling either."

Nix cocked his head to one side. "Oooh, you're right. In fact, that was terrible storytelling," he concluded. "But my point is made! And the young lady honestly doesn't need all the gory details."

"Tsuki Shimabukuru," said Tsuki, wishing with mounting urgency that they hadn't come here.

"I know who you *are*, kiddo."

"Please do as she wishes and use her rightful name," said Kiba, setting his cup on the counter.

"Ack. No fun." The kitsune sighed heavily, then snapped his fingers. "Oh, by the way, I've thought it over and I agree to your terms!"

Tsuki's stomach sank, even though she still had no idea what was going on. "You don't even know what we wanted. Want."

"No," said Nix sweetly, "but I don't think I need to. You give me Matahachi after I help you out, and everything will be golden. But now that you mention it," he added, scratching the side of his head, "what is the job?"

# TWENTY-NINE

"I KNOW you can't feel physical pain."

Kirikizu's muffled, buzzing voice cut through Winter's haze.

His mouth and throat felt as if a sandstorm had swept through. He could not remember taking a breath through the last half hour. He lifted his eyes to the Prince-Regent's Hand as the other man said, "Fortunately, your baby brother can." There was a brief pause. Then Kirikizu said, "Look at him."

Winter shut his eyes and tried to swallow, but there was no moisture in his mouth. His ears echoed, not with Haka's screams, but with the moans that continued long after Haka's voice had grown too exhausted to continue.

"Winter," repeated Kirikizu coaxingly, "look at him."

Winter opened his eyes. It was the sight he had fought against his entire life, the sight he had made sure he would never have to see. Haka bound and unable to move, his skin slick and ashen with pain he no longer had the strength to vocalize.

There was no blood. There were only needles. First an

injection in the neck, and then longer, more flexible needles. One in Haka's throat, up under his jaw, and Kirikizu had cut open Haka's shirt to insert another needle in Haka's stomach.

"I'm going to make a phone call," said Kirikizu, tapping the needle inserted in Haka's neck. Haka breathed out, his voice barely a whimper. "These two needles are targeting the nerve clusters found in the pharyngeal plexus and the splenic plexus. I'll be back in five minutes. I'd rather not have to continue this, so please think things over."

He left the cell, closing it behind him. He did not need to lock it with both prisoners bound, but he did so anyway. Winter listened to Kirikizu's footsteps fade and the sound of the door closing.

"Haka!" He leaned forward as far as the chains would allow, although he could not help. Fifteen feet stretched between them. "Haka, look at me."

Haka shut his eyes and leaned his head back, swallowing around the needle in his throat. He spoke, but it took Winter several seconds to realize Haka had hissed, "Go to hell."

"Where did the girl Otter go?" Winter asked, ignoring his brother's remark. "Is she bringing someone to get you out?"

Haka only moaned and leaned his head back again, his eyes shut.

"I will fix this." Winter shook his head, furious with himself. He had played the part of passive prisoner, thinking he was the only card in Kirikizu's hand. Thinking it would not matter, because he could not feel physical pain anyway.

"You can't fix yourself." It barely sounded like a voice, just a scratching whisper forming words. Haka choked on a strangled laugh. "Forget it."

"You might have spared yourself this pain had you at least pretended to interrogate me," Winter snapped. "Your lack of action spurred him to get answers to questions he never would have asked otherwise." The last word had no sooner left his mouth than Winter wished he could take it all back.

A strange light gleamed briefly in Haka's eyes just then, as though someone had taken a knife to his back. "You've never—never forgiven me for it," he garbled, a realization dawning on his face, quickly smothered by a twist of his mouth.

Winter lifted his gaze to once more include his brother. "Forgive you?"

"The dogs." Haka swallowed again, painstakingly slow. "I saved your *life*." He choked on what would have been a laugh. "You hated me for it. Still—still do."

Winter had never thought of it that way, never equaled a young boy's foolish actions with hate. Haka's accusation struck his core, blindingly painful in its bewildering accuracy.

"You are a depraved fool," Winter whispered, surprised by the sound of his voice: calm, quiet, frigid. The opposite of everything he felt. "You sold your soul that day. Why should I forgive that? No one stole it from you."

Haka blinked rapidly, as if trying to figure out the meaning behind Winter's accusations. Suddenly, his face transformed from confusion into raw, unfiltered hurt. "I took it for *you!*"

"Because you were a whining coward who couldn't gather up enough courage to do something brave without it! Your life in ruins is hardly my doing." *Do not look away from him.* Winter looked away. "Do not blame me for your decisions."

Haka shifted his jaw, not so much an expressive gesture as an attempt to shift the needle protruding from his throat. "You always were dif—difficult to please," he rasped. Something glistened low in his eyes, before slipping down his gaunt face. Tears.

*I never thought I would see his tears again.*

*I prayed I would never see his tears again.*

"I hope they catch up to you one day," Haka continued. There was a broken piece in his voice, a crack caused by something other than the needle. "And I hope they rip your throat out and leave you to rot."

And in his mind, where Haka could not overhear, Winter prayed for it to be so.

———

"IF THE DOG IS VENOMOUS, there has to be a cure. If the dog is venomous, there's a cure. If the dog is venomous, there's a cure. There has to be a cure." Saizou cupped his hands in front of his mouth, blowing warm breath between his palms before rubbing them together.

The palace loomed in front of him, lit only by the neon strips wrapped around the tops of each building in the Palace Mile. The palace guards were black silhouettes, their reizaa-naginata glowing dimly, set in standby mode to conserve power.

He sized up the wall. It was tall, the stone just smooth enough to make climbing up and over difficult. He ran quickly through his options—could take one of the tall reizaa-naginata from the nearest guard and vault over, or he could attempt to gain enough momentum and jump. Taking out a guard risked noise, but Saizou favored that option. He had taken out more soldiers than he cared to think of, and very few had ever had time to cry out.

He chose the guard standing on the other side of the nearest corner. They were spaced out thirty feet apart. He drew a knife from the sheath on his arm and took a deep breath, steadying his nerves. There were very few places in a suit of palace armor where a knife could penetrate; an inch of rubber between the lower half of the neck and the jaw was the only opening, and it was hard to see in the dark.

*God, don't let me miss.*

Saizou threw without hesitation. There was no sound but a faint hiss as air released from the suit of armor, and Saizou ran forward to catch the guard before he pitched forward onto the ground. He removed the rest of the man's weapons and placed them on the ground below the wall. Carrying an unregistered weapon beyond the walls could trigger an alarm and end his rescue operation before it began.

He took the reizaa-naginata and glanced both ways. So far nobody had noticed a difference in the blackness, but if someone saw the dim glow of the reizaa-naginata moving around uncharacteristically, it would bring at least a dozen guards down on him. He found the correct button and switched the power off completely. Total darkness was slightly less suspicious than a wildly waving light.

He stepped back, looked once more at the wall, and used the weapon to launch himself into the air and onto the wall. He did not go over it; he caught himself on top of the wall and waited. If a guard was directly below him on the other side, landing unprepared and without aim would be a terrible idea.

He peered over. There was nobody directly below. The Prince-Regent did not seem overly concerned with protection inside the walls, although no doubt he would after tonight. Saizou doubted sneaking into the palace would be this easy again once the breach was discovered, but he hoped he would never have another need to repeat this night.

His second problem presented itself: he did not know where the Dog was kept.

He needed to ask for directions.

———

"HE ENTERED THE PALACE." Shimo watched the scene from a distance, the engine of his Scorpia purring quietly.

"He's got a pair, I'll give him that," Virgo's voice crackled through the radio-bracelet.

"How is it on your end?"

"Quiet. Nobody's come in or out of the shipping container, and none of the Yakuza goons have noticed anything."

"This kind of luck won't last long."

"I know," said Virgo. "If our Number One Fugitive was desperate enough to am-scray and go to the palace, it's got to be urgent. I'm betting Masked Guy's injuries were worse than we thought."

"And yet he's getting help from inside the palace?"

"Yeah, that's weird. I...wait. Remember that scene from the footage? When they fought their way out of the palace, the Dog was there. I'll bet you a new tattoo Mask was bitten."

"So this man is going for the antidote?" Shimo whistled low under his breath.

"Oh, he's got a big pair," Virgo reiterated. "Solid gold."

"He won't make it out alive."

"He'd better, or that's half of our reward money. Let him get the antidote, and we'll catch them all together when he comes back."

"Sounds good." Shimo began to lower his wrist, but Virgo's voice came through again.

"I'm going to the bar to get something to eat."

"It's irresponsible to leave your post," said Shimo without surprise.

"I'm hungry."

"You mean you can't go more than six hours without getting a drink or getting laid."

"A meal, bro. I'm getting a meal. Those other things are just a bonus. I won't be gone more than an hour, and I'm leaving Birdie here to keep an ear out. I'll leave my bracelet on; let me know when our guy escapes the palace. Or if all the alarms go off."

Shimo twisted the microphone on his bracelet, cutting the connection until another call came through, or he made one himself. If they lost Saizou, they lost at least half the reward, possibly more. It wasn't like they exactly needed it; the last criminal they tracked down had raked in enough to keep them comfortably afloat for a month or two. But the reward for Saizou could give them enough money for six months, and if they factored in Saizou's compatriot, well, that could be a year of high living.

Still, Shimo had never felt a pull toward high living, unlike his brother. Virgo simply couldn't resist an expensive drink or five. The most expensive everything, that was what he liked. It was too bad he never had anything to show for it. Shimo sometimes wondered whether Virgo ate the money he made, since he never saw where it went. Virgo didn't even buy half his own drinks; he was more than happy to let someone flirtatious buy him whatever he liked.

Shimo settled back. Might as well get comfortable. Saizou could be a while. If he ever came back out at all.

———

SOMETHING BUZZED SOFTLY outside Matahachi's door.

Matahachi closed the book he was reading and set it on the nightstand before crossing over to the door and opening it. A

dragonfly, an inch long with gossamer wings, fluttered in. Matahachi closed the door again, holding his hand out expectantly.
Obediently, the dragonfly landed on his palm and Matahachi
pressed the tiny blue dot on the dragonfly's back.

With a mechanical buzz, the insect went stiff.

Matahachi deftly twisted the tail, detaching the back of the
tiny drone from the front. He proceeded to plug the "tail" into
a small round port on his computer, and as soon as a window
popped up, he pressed *play*.

# THIRTY

THE CRANE PERCHED atop the roof of the Prince-Regent's House. It had formerly been known as the Emperor's House, but the building was in the center of the Palace Mile and the Prince-Regent had taken it for himself. The Crane approved. After all, who knew when the Emperor would return? It was fitting that the Prince-Regent should take over more than just his brother's country.

The cool night breeze brought sounds of city traffic along with it. The outskirts of the city had fallen quiet as the war progressed, particularly at night. It was safer to stay indoors. But here, in the center of the city, citizens continued their daily lives as if night never fell, losing money at casinos or private gambling clubs, drinking their worries away in neon-lit bars, or taking a night shift so they could support their loved ones.

The Crane looked down at the roof beneath her and ran an index finger over a smooth red tile. The Prince-Regent's Hand was away, and Mamushi's safety now fell to her. It would always be this way, if she had any say in it, but none of her arguments or coaxing could convince the Prince-Regent to put his human plaything in second place.

It was ridiculous.

A faint sound caught the Crane's attention. She knew that sound well enough. A body hitting the ground. She slunk to the other side of the roof and peered down. There, in the blacker shadows by the base of the building, she could just see the edge of a white suit of armor.

She dropped lightly to the ground and crouched by the fallen guard. She reached for a pulse but lowered her hand when she saw the unnatural angle of the guard's neck.

The Crane straightened. She should sound the alarm. She knew that.

*Or...I could track the invader down and dispose of them without making a commotion of it.* The Prince-Regent needed his sleep, and even if the invader took out a few more guards on his way, a consolation gift to their families, if they had any, would cover the inconvenience.

After all, she thought wryly, it would be silly to pass up an opportunity to prove herself, and the intruder was heading away from the Prince-Regent's House. He was no assassin, then; the life of the Prince-Regent was in no danger.

The intruder, however...he obviously didn't realize how much danger he was truly in.

*How fun.*

———

SAIZOU FOLLOWED what information he knew about the Palace Mile. The foremost buildings facing the front gate were the Emperor's residence—or now, he supposed, the Prince-Regent's. There were servants' quarters, barracks, the kitchen, and the Main Hall. Toward the back, the buildings became more scattered, housing the Prince-Regent's private guard, his amusements, the magazine, the weapons house, and, he hoped, the Doghouse. Or wherever he was kept.

He didn't want to call in Riza's help, but he knew he needed it. Saizou took the ear cuff he had commandeered out of his pocket.

Riza might be asleep. Any sane person would be.

He placed the cuff around his ear. "You'd better be there."

Silence.

He flicked the cuff with two fingers. "This isn't Shotgun,? this is Saizou. Wake up."

"Isn't there a fugitive curfew?" Riza's voice came through the speaker, loud and clear. "Don't you people have bedtimes?"

"You don't seem to."

"I'm the exception to every rule. What do you....oh. My goodness. Saizou, dear, why are you inside the Palace Mile? Wait, don't tell me. It has something to do with the living bunraku doll."

"His name is Shi," Saizou hissed, pressing his back against the wall of the kitchen. It was dead inside; the cooks wouldn't be awake for a few more hours, although breakfast would be prepared before the sun came up. "I need you to tell me where the Dog is kept."

"Oh, you do, do you? I'm already busting my ass to keep you from getting caught, and you want my help waltzing back into the reach of the Prince-Regent? Hilarious."

"If you think the Prince-Regent's reach is limited to within the palace walls, you're a fool." Saizou glanced left and right. It wouldn't take long for someone to see the trail of bodies he was leaving behind, no matter how he tried to hide them.

"You have a real gratitude problem, are you aware of it?"

"Tell me where the Dog is."

Riza's loud sigh nearly deafened him. "Fine," she said. "See that building toward the back-left corner? You should have a clear line of sight from where you're standing."

Saizou was hardly surprised that Riza's ear cuff doubled as a tracking device. "I see it."

"The Dog is probably there."

"Are you positive?"

"I repeat my gratitude remark, but I'm going to give you a warning anyway," said Riza. "That's also the Royal Poisoner's residence."

Saizou tried to wrap his head around the idea of a Royal Poisoner. The concept was simple enough, but the fact the Prince-Regent blatantly employed one without hiding it, that was startling. "The Poisoner keeps the Dog in his house?"

"Lots of people have pets, dear."

"Most pets aren't human beings."

"And to think you were only gone for a few years. I really thought a guy who's skinned people alive before would be less naïve," said Riza.

Saizou said nothing. He couldn't think of anything to say.

When she spoke again, Riza's voice was surprisingly soft. "But you didn't harden over there, did you? Not all the way. That must be...tough. Sorry."

"I have all I need from you. Thanks." Saizou reached up to remove the ear cuff, but Riza interrupted him.

"I'm not a pessimist," said Riza, "but optimism does me no good, either. There's a whole country of hard facts you're going to have to face up to if you want to survive. Personally, I like you as much as I like anyone, and I'd like to see you pull through this."

"Why?"

"It'd be good for national morale on a revolutionary level," was Riza's breezy reply. "So keep your head down. The Poisoner created the Dog's venom, so there's probably an antidote floating around in that building somewhere, but be careful. He takes his job pretty seriously."

"So the house is probably full of poisoned booby-traps," said Saizou dryly, then nodded once. "Got it."

"Stay safe, doll. And be careful. One-Eye is a lot more dangerous than he looks."

Saizou removed the cuff and placed it in his pocket again. Then he raced toward the Poisoner's house.

It was a long sprint, but Saizou was in good shape and he worked hard to maintain himself. Stamina and strength were often the only things between life and death, especially in these times.

Light glowed dimly through the closed shutters of a window on the side of the small outbuilding. Apparently, the Poisoner was still awake.

The sound of approaching footsteps interrupted the formation of Saizou's plan. He took a step back and made a running leap, gripping the nearest corner of the low-sloping roof. He pulled himself up and over, then flattened his body against the tiles.

Below him, the guard walked past without so much as a glance up.

Routine, thought Saizou. Always more counterproductive than efficient. People grew bored with routine, and they grew lazy. Sloppy.

For once, he was glad of routine.

As soon as the guard walked out of sight, Saizou crept to the other side of the roof, careful not to slip on the smooth tiles. He wasn't exactly dressed for shinobi activities, but he would make do. He dropped to the ground behind the building and found himself face-to-face with the back door.

It would be locked, he thought, and it was, but locks were of little consequence. He switched the reizaa-naginata on and cut through the wood, searing the lock away from the rest of the door. Lasers, as it turned out, were very effective lock-picks.

He stepped inside, leaving the weapon in his hands in the *on* position.

The interior of the building was less sinister than he had envisioned. Plants grew across the walls and twisted around indoor trellises. They spilled out of pots and lined the shelves, along with bottles and flasks and boxes of all kinds. It felt more like a medieval apothecary's shop than a poisoner's home.

He moved carefully around a shelf draped with ivy, the leaves so dark they were nearly purple. Careful not to touch the plant, he avoided bumping into the long table overlaid with measuring cups, spoons, knives, and bowls covered with thin cloth.

Above him, something hissed. Saizou ducked and glanced up at the same time.

A long, impossibly thin snake was lowering itself from the beam over his head. The reptile was a bright, venomous green, and its tongue flickered in and out less than two feet from Saizou's face.

*You've dealt with venomous snakes in China. You can't use the weapon in your hand; you may not be quick enough and it would anger the snake. Back away slowly. Make no sudden movements.*

Carefully, Saizou took one step back, still trying not to touch the dangerous-looking vine growing across the shelf to his left.

Immediately, the snake darted forward, a warning strike so close Saizou felt the brush of its tongue.

"I wouldn't move, if I were you," said a calm voice. "Nor would I speak. She's very sensitive to strangers."

Saizou dared not move his head far, but he glanced out the corner of his eye and saw a young man shut the partition door behind him and stand there, his hands in his pockets. A patch circled his head and covered one eye, a morbid accessory for someone so young.

*This must be One-Eye.*

The young man smiled. "You must be Saizou Akita. I had the feeling you'd come back when I saw pieces of your accomplice stuck in the Dog's teeth."

Saizou's stomach twisted, but it was hard to keep his eyes on the human and not the red, unblinking gaze of the snake swaying in front of him.

He saw the young man nod toward the snake. "She's a *Trimeresurus Stejnegeri*, if you're interested. You may have encountered her family before, actually. She was imported from China. Shaowu, Fukien Province, specifically. And yes, she's extremely venomous." He held up a small glass bottle. "Her glands carry a hemotoxin that, if it enters your bloodstream, probably feels something like a hot iron under your skin. It's incredibly painful. The pain lasts up to twenty-four hours, in fact. Longer than the effects of most snakes."

The snake lowered itself several more inches and blinked once, apparently willing to ignore One-Eye and focus completely on the intruder.

"It's necrotic," One-Eye continued, tapping one finger on the lid of the bottle. "The infected skin and muscle will turn black as it dies. Some people can survive more than one bite, but not without severe injury. More than one bite, and...well, I don't know anyone who's lived through that."

Saizou swallowed. "You talk too much."

He leaned back as the viper struck forward with lightning speed, just missing his face. As she drew back, recoiling from the strike, Saizou jumped back and swung the reizaa-naginata forward in the same motion. The glowing blade cut through the beam and the viper in half.

Two pieces of wriggling snake fell to the floor, writhing like worms on a hook.

One-Eye said nothing, but he turned slowly and looked at Saizou with a stare just as cold and unblinking as that of the still-twitching viper. Then he looked at the door, put two fingers to his mouth, and whistled.

# THIRTY-ONE

THE DOG LEAPED over the table, his clawed hands—fingers too long—outstretched, his face twisted in a sharp-toothed snarl. His attack was soundless and instant, slamming into Saizou, missing the red blade of the reizaa-naginata by the span of a hand.

The Dog was heavy, his body a mass of muscle and animal strength. His teeth snapped together above Saizou's face as Saizou struggled to lift the unwieldy reizaa-naginata with one hand.

The Dog wrapped his hands around Saizou's neck and began to squeeze with brutal speed. There was nothing human about his attack other than the use of his hands; he wasn't strangling like a human. There was nothing but the urgency to kill, kill, kill, and Saizou pushed any idea that the Dog was part human out of his mind. He did not fight like a human; he would not treat him as one.

Saizou let the reizaa-naginata remain on the floor and brought his hands to the Dog's face, pushing his thumbs into the Dog's eye sockets.

A sharp growl rumbled in the Dog's throat, his grip on Saizou's neck tightening, pushing harder. Saizou dug harder, his thumbs pressing impossibly far into the slippery holes. Anyone else would have backed off by now, would have been terrified of going blind, but he might as well have been beating his attacker with a piece of cardboard.

Black spots invaded his vision. Saizou took a deep breath through his nose, unable to draw any air through his mouth, but the air could not reach his lungs. He let his hands fall from the Dog's face, let his body go limp.

Just as the last pinprick of light began to fade from Saizou's unblinking eyes, the Dog let go. The noise he made had no humanity in it; it was a growl that ended in a chirp.

Saizou's hands shot out; he curled his fingers around the Dog's thick black collar and twisted. The Dog howled, trying to wrench free, but Saizou held firm and hauled the Dog's head back, strangling him.

Across the room, One-Eye whipped around like he'd been slapped. "Dog!" he snapped, his voice high with shock. "Get him! I said *get him!*"

The Dog twisted to the side, thrashing so wildly Saizou was amazed his neck did not snap under the pressure. His breath came in wet, strangled gasps, but his clawed hands scrabbled across the ground, seeking a foothold.

He stopped.

His low, chirruping growl became a purr.

Then the Dog grabbed the reizaa-naginata, the blade still searing the floor, and swung it in a circle back toward Saizou.

Taken by surprise, Saizou let go of the collar and jumped, the blade slicing through the air where his legs had been not half a second before. He staggered back toward the wall, off-balance. The Dog spun around as spines rose from his back, from his arms, and he hissed before launching the reizaa-naginata at Saizou's head.

Saizou dropped, reflexes the only thing that saved him as the laser-blade seared through the wall and stuck halfway out, embedded.

It would take too long to pull back out; the weapon was now useless to him. Saizou jumped up and rolled across the table toward One-Eye, who made a dash for the door.

He was not fast enough.

Saizou grabbed his shirt, yanked him back, and wrapped an arm around his neck. Then he placed his fingernails against the young man's throat. "I'll kill him." His voice sounded strangely rough in his ears as he met the Dog's wide-set, wary gaze. The creature dropped back to all fours, his odd-limbed hind legs propelling him as he paced back and forth, watching. Uncertain. Searching for the right move.

Saizou pressed his fingertips farther into the soft flesh of One-Eye's neck.

Most people assumed weapons were necessary for the worst kind of injuries, that you needed a gun to riddle someone full of holes, that you needed a knife to cut someone's throat. Lies. The human body could do as much. It could do worse, if you had the stomach for it. One-Eye made the Dog's decision for him. "Down," he ordered, his heartbeat throbbing against Saizou's fingertips. "Down!"

Reluctantly, the Dog sank into a crouch, a row of viciously sharp teeth bared as he watched Saizou.

"Give me the antidote," said Saizou calmly, unmoving. "The one for the Dog's venom."

"What makes you think there is one?" One-Eye's remained calm in spite of his pounding heartbeat. Saizou almost admired his collectedness.

But he did not have time to waste. Shi was suffering, maybe dying. Saizou prayed that Shi continued to suffer—anything, as long as he held out long enough.

"Don't play coy with me," said Saizou softly. "Give it to me."

One-Eye's breathing grew heavier, either from fear or the pressure of Saizou's fingers digging into his throat, it was hard to say. "If I tell you where it is, the Prince-Regent will kill me."

"If you don't tell me where it is, I will kill you. Giving it to me might buy you five more minutes."

One-Eye swallowed. Then he tried to throw his head back into Saizou's chin.

Saizou had been expecting it and gripped a fistful of One-Eye's hair, wrenching his head back, exposing his throat even more.

"Fine," Saizou hissed, and dug into the poisoner's neck. Blood seeped out around his fingernails as they punctured the skin.

One-Eye cried out, his visible eye widening. "Wait!" he gasped. "Wait!"

Saizou stopped, his fingers buried halfway in the flesh of the poisoner's throat. "I don't have time for games."

"The bottle I—the bottle—" One-Eye's strangled voice wasn't enough; he pointed toward the overturned table. Saizou saw an amber-tinted vial sitting on the table amid the rest of the tools.

"How do I know it's the antidote?" Saizou squeezed, just enough. If he put any more pressure, if he dug any deeper, he could kill the poisoner, and he couldn't. Not yet. "How can I be sure?"

A whimper.

A sheen of tears glistening across the poisoner's eye, his face twisted in pain and fear.

And one of the tears fell, landing on the ground, leaving a tiny damp stain.

Suddenly Saizou felt it; felt the warmth of the young man's blood, felt his own human fingers puncturing another human's flesh and muscle. The pulse of another person hammering against his hand.

*He's a life. He's a life.* White light pulsed across Saizou's vision. *Not an obstacle. Not just an obstacle. He's a life. Look at him.*

*Look at him.*

Saizou's hands began to tremble. He released One-Eye's hair and realized he could not let go of the poisoner's neck. His hand was stiff, frozen in place. Stunned, Saizou gripped his own wrist, forcing his hand free, his fingernails out of One-Eye's throat.

One-Eye stumbled forward, falling to the ground as he clutched at his throat, wheezing desperately for air. Panicked. He was so young. Twenty-two, twenty-three maybe.

Maybe—

A strange sensation—pressure, out of nowhere, stabbed Saizou's left side. He looked down and saw four slender, silver talons embedded in his ribs.

The talons were attached to a hand, and an arm, and a placid female face.

As he fell to the ground, he heard a distorted voice laughing darkly. "Sweet dreams."

———

KIRIKIZU LEANED against the tiled wall and let the warm spray of water rain down on him. He was not physically tired; interrogations were never tiring, as he never opted to beat his prisoners. Beatings rarely achieved anything but extra stubbornness on the prisoner's part. No, he wasn't physically tired.

And yet he was exhausted. He had left Haka and Winter where they had been all day—one tied to a chair, the other chained to a wall. Leverage. It was the most effective form of torture, and the strongest acid to his conscience.

Some people had others they would die for. That was something special. Something precious, even, or so it seemed. People could endure incredible amounts of pain for someone they loved. Loved ones brought out the hero in people.

They also brought out the weakness.

It was almost cruel, an irony like that. Yet it was an irony that he sometimes idly—stupidly—wished he could experience. Even for thirty seconds.

But that kind of attachment was impossible, and family... what was family, anyway. He did not even have a proper name. Only a word to describe a gash, an incision.

That was all he deserved.

He tilted his head back and let the water run across his bare face. It felt so good to remove the muzzle, to let air and water touch his smothered skin. He tried to relax his mind along with his body. It did not last long.

He heard the door to the shower room open, and he stiffened. He looked over the short wall separating the shower from the rest of the room, used only by the Prince-Regent's elite guards. He could have used the Prince-Regent's bathing room; it was far more lavish, far more luxurious. He never did, and he only used the shower room after hours, when the Prince-Regent's guards were asleep.

Kiko walked around the corner. Her soft boots, made for climbing and gripping, made no sound on the concrete floor.

Kirikizu turned the faucet off, and the water stopped with a faint squeak. He glanced over at the ivory sink; his towel was flung across it, his muzzle sitting atop the fabric. Too far away.

"Don't stop on my account." Kiko leaned against the shower wall, an easy smile playing across her face. It would have been a soft, pretty face if her large eyes were not so sharp and malicious. She laughed a little, her voice twisting into a jeer. "It's not like I haven't seen you naked before."

Kirikizu looked at the floor, taking a moment to collect his emotions and place them safely in the vault where they belonged. He would let whatever she wanted to say roll off his back like he always did.

Like everything always did.

He lifted his head and ran his hands back through his hair, pushing it out of his vision and keeping water from dripping into his eyes. Then he gave her an expectant, patient expression.

"I guess that's your version of asking what I want?" she asked, although she knew perfectly well.

His raised one eyebrow slightly. He had no patience for her, and she knew it. But she also knew that he could not respond to anything she said.

Not while his muzzle remained fifteen feet away. If he said anything without the sound filter the machinery inside the muzzle provided, she could die and he would be punished.

Badly.

Killing the Prince-Regent's best friend could get even his Right Hand killed.

Kiko folded her arms, looking perfectly comfortable. "What

time did you get in? Oh." She flicked a finger in his direction. "Don't answer that. Late?"

He maintained his neutral expression. He was very good at it, but right now he felt himself working harder than usual to keep it there. It was more of a strain without the muzzle hiding half his face. He clenched his jaw and did not bother to loosen it.

She knew she had aggravated him already.

"Late, then. Oh well." She smiled again, her eyes gleaming. "In that case, you should know that I caught someone very important today."

She was here to gloat over something. Kirikizu rolled his eyes a fraction and turned the flow of water back on.

He saw the flash of indignation cross her face, but she had already told him not to stop on her account and could say nothing against it without contradicting herself. She settled back against the partition. "I wanted to be the first to tell you. It was Saizou Akita."

Kirikizu froze.

She chuckled at his expression. "Oh, that's right," she said dryly. "Weren't you trying to uncover his whereabouts all day? That's a shame. Well, at least you spent the day doing something you're good at."

She had never beaten him in one sparring match, never beaten him in one fight, but he knew the size of her jealousy, and it recognized no bounds. Not in the Prince-Regent's bedroom and not here, except here the Prince-Regent was not present to tell her to stop.

He released a soft breath, letting it blend into the sound of the water, and began to soap his shoulders and chest. Ignoring her was a pretense, however, and she knew he was listening.

"Looks like maybe my Prince will finally put us in our

rightful places," said Kiko, lifting a finger and studying the blade that ran across the top of it. The entire length of the blade was sharp, but only the very tip contained a paralytic neuro-toxin. Kirikizu had felt its effects several times before. "I would serve him better as his Right Hand, and you...well, you work best underneath him."

He felt a reply surface in his throat and lodge there, just before it translated into sound. Just before it killed her.

He pressed his palm against the wall and took a deep breath, trying to push the reply back and smother it into silence.

"I know the truth hurts you. I would apologize, but you know I'm not sorry."

He glanced at the woman, who acknowledged his look and smiled. "Do you want to know what I think?" she continued.

He did not want to know what she thought. He did not care. Or if he did...no, he reminded himself. He didn't care what she thought. It was what she said that caused the most pain, and she had grown up in a palace. There was no better training ground for verbal war.

Especially when she knew her adversary was handicapped.

"I think that you don't enjoy your work enough. I would enjoy it if I were in your place. My Prince deserves a better Right Hand than someone as emotionally compromised as you, and you're well aware of it. You might take orders well, but you take no pleasure in it."

*Stop talking. Stop talking, stop talking, stop—*

"You don't deserve to be his Right Hand. You may be able to fool my Prince, but you can't fool me. I see right through you. You're using him to keep yourself safe, don't think I don't know it."

He wanted to laugh.

He wanted to vomit.

Instead, he patiently, quietly placed the bar of soap back and turned and watched her, waiting for her to continue. To run out of words.

If she saw the hot glint in his eyes, she said nothing about it, but she did hesitate for a moment. Then she said, "Anyway, my Prince wants a personal report, and you should know that your position is in danger. You could always leave. I'd even cover for you," she added, with a fierce, quick smile that faded into an almost pleading expression.

Slowly, deliberately, Kirikizu shook his head.

Kiko's expression melted into one of barely suppressed rage. "You've been his Right Hand long enough," she said in a sharp, low voice. "It's my turn now, Kirikizu."

He turned the water off and crossed the room. He lifted his muzzle to his face and turned back toward her. Then, in a voice just as sharp and low as hers, he said, "Get out."

Kiko turned and stalked out of the room. As the door shut, the sound echoing across the tiled ceiling, Kirikizu tore the muzzle off and threw it against the wall.

# THIRTY-TWO

VIRGO LEANED COMFORTABLY against the back of his seat, his stomach pleasantly full as he ran his finger in a circle around his palm. Birdie, his fist-sized drone, flew in a lazy circle overhead, following the same pattern.

"Hey."

Virgo twisted his radio bracelet and held it next to his mouth. "Hey, what?"

"I don't think Saizou Akita is leaving the palace any time soon."

Virgo straightened and snapped his fingers. The thin glove he wore controlled Birdie's movements when any pressure was applied, and the drone froze, hovering in place. "Why not?" he demanded. "Was he captured?"

"I think so, unless he managed to make it back to your location in record time."

Virgo peered down at the storage unit currently housing a handful of fugitives. It had been quiet for hours—no movement, no sound except the water lapping against the wood of the dock and the looming ships. "He's not here, but nobody has left, either."

"At least we have them still closed up, but we're going to have to forget about this one. If the Prince-Regent has him, there's no point in hanging around."

"No, you're right. Get back here; they'll probably sweep the area looking for anything suspicious."

"I'm already gone, heading your way. Do you want to call it in, or should I?"

Virgo sighed. "I'll call it in, don't worry about it. Just get back here and stay low."

"See you in an hour."

Virgo lowered his arm and groaned. Losing a target was one thing. Losing that target inside the palace was another, especially when their employer seemed keen on said target not falling into the wrong hands.

The Prince-Regent definitely had the wrong hands.

Virgo punched the numbers into the square blue console in front of him. It was a specialized section of the Scorpia's dashboard, modified by himself with illegal parts. It could make calls if they were brief and within thirty miles.

It only worked if the other party had the counterpart piece of technology, however. Virgo usually gave that counterpart to their current client. If they got busted, it was untraceable and he could always acquire the parts to make another. It was a glorified walkie-talkie, really, but it worked well enough for calls to people who weren't Shimo. Plus, Virgo could cause it to self-destruct, his favorite feature.

He tapped his fingers against his thighs, waiting.

There was a brief click, and his client's voice, foggy with sleep. "Hello?"

"We lost the target."

Silence reigned for several long seconds while Virgo

watched the storage unit and made sure nobody else slipped through his fingers that night.

"And where," asked the client finally, "did you lose him?"

"Well, he snuck back into the palace and didn't come out, so there's not much we can do about it."

Then the voice on the other end, frustrated and resigned, asked, "And the others?"

"Those eggs are still in one basket. But they probably won't be for long. Once they realize Saizou's missing, they'll move somewhere else if they have any sense at all."

"Hm," said the voice. Then, "Follow them."

"We're bounty hunters, not bodyguards," said Virgo, shaking his head. "You want us to follow and watch from a distance, you pay for the time."

"Fine," said the voice, clipped and icy. "Just do as I say. You'll be well compensated, you have my word."

"We're not talking spare change here. We're talking five thousand yen to keep up this spy nonsense."

"I'm aware of your monetary needs, and I'm fully willing to meet them. Even if you do overcharge," said the voice. There was another click as the client hung up.

Virgo shut the communication screen down and once again settled back against his seat. Five thousand extra yen for a little extra cloak to the dagger? He grinned and pressed his fingers against his mouth, then blew a kiss at the full, orange harvest moon overhead.

"Goodnight," he sang softly, and slid his finger against his palm in a line toward the storage unit. Birdie would alert him to any movement. For now he could rest.

———

BEFORE THE FIRST BOMB, the loudest thing Shi had ever heard was a tornado siren.

His family had always lived on the outskirts of Matsuda Domain, with the job to oversee the breeding and selling of the domain's cattle. The tornado siren was positioned, like all warning sirens, in the center of the domain. One day, Shi had been chasing a runaway bull and was near the tornado siren when it went off. His ears rang for twenty-four hours.

The pain left sooner.

From that moment on, his hearing was muffled. Just enough to make it a constant aggravation, a constant strain. He found himself having to work to hear any conversation, having to pay attention to expressions and body language over voice and tone. He had to rely on more than inflection and cadence now; everything was important. Every shifting glance, every twitching hand.

When he was conscripted, everyone thought he was intuitive, that he was a people-reader. That he had some special insight or cared more than the average person. The truth was, he just paid better attention than most. It was because of this idea, that he was good at reading micro expressions or seeing the truth under layers of lies, that he was assigned to Captain Akita's guerilla task force.

He had not thought much of Saizou upon meeting him. His eyes darted too much—here, there, sizing everything up with this startled, half-afraid look.

It put Shi on edge. Saizou also seemed too withdrawn to be a captain. Quiet, self-contained, bordering on self-absorption. He was shifty, flighty—like a deer with its head constantly lifted, ears pricked, listening to every little sound. Brusque and short-tempered. Thought himself too good for the company he was forced to keep.

It wasn't until their first field operation that Shi saw the man behind his first impressions.

One of the older guerilla soldiers assigned to White Cobra, the name given to Saizou's task force, had returned to their jungle camp with news: the governor of Liaoyang Province was travelling in secret that night, down back roads, while his decoy took the main road, accompanied by most of the governor's private guard. Most attention would be focused on the decoy, who no doubt would not survive the night.

Liaoyang was an important province in the war. Wealthy and densely populated, it was a well-known trading hub that sent supplies across half the nation, supplying enemy soldiers with food, clothes, ammunition, and even women.

The governor was a relatively clever man, but more importantly, he had political connections and a private guard of two hundred well-trained soldiers. It would be more effective to seize him, ply information from him, and hold him for possible ransom than to kill him.

The plan was simple: ambush the caravan, kill the small accompaniment, and snatch the governor. A basic, uncomplicated first move for a novice task force. It would be a good way to cut their teeth.

Shi had barely spoken ten words to Saizou when they set out that night; he did not care for the captain, and the captain seemed too engrossed in his own thoughts to bother initiating conversation.

There were eight of them in the task force: Captain Akita, Lieutenant Shota, and six soldiers with no official rank. If they were caught, they had no serial number, nothing to identify their position. They could be anyone, and they could die as no one.

They pulled their masks up around their mouths and noses,

their faces smeared with sticky black paint, and waited in the trees above the road.

It was well past midnight when the palanquin approached, carried by four muscular men and guarded front and back by eight guards to each side. Shi never worried that they wouldn't be able to take them—each man on this task force had been chosen for their skill, and he had seen all of them display their prowess with gun, sword, halberd, knife, and throwing star. Everyone, that was, except Captain Akita.

Shi had glanced at the opposite tree. The captain was sitting with one leg propped up, watching the road, a Ganosuke rifle with precision extensions held in his hands.

Next to him, one of the younger men—a mouthy South Korean named Kyung-Ho—whispered, "Dude, a palanquin. Those things are ancient. Why didn't they bring a four-wheeler? Or horses? I don't get it."

Shi reached up and adjusted the mask over his mouth and nose. He couldn't wait to take it off—in the thick, humid air, it threatened to activate his claustrophobia. "Anything with an engine would be too loud. It would give them away," he whispered in a voice so low he could barely hear himself. "If they're heading to Shenyang, the road is too dangerous for horses."

"It's not like the guy doesn't have two legs. He could walk."

"He's a governor," said Shi.

From his perch, Saizou lifted his head like a startled bird and hissed, "Shhh."

"Yessir, Captain, sir," muttered Kyung-Ho.

Captain Akita lifted one hand, telling everyone to prepare. The procession was almost below them, the guards looking intently at every bush and tree trunk, everywhere but in the trees above them. Even if they did happen to glance up, chances were they would see nothing. Dressed in black clothing, hardly daring to breathe, the men in the trees were invisible in the darkness.

Captain Akita brought his fist down in a forward chopping motion.

Shi drew his sword and leaped from the tree. He landed on the palanquin, the sudden weight throwing the bearers off-balance. They staggered, and the palanquin bearing the governor fell sideways, tipping over the edge of the path and down several yards into the thick tangle of vines and leaves.

The governor's guards were obviously prepared for an attack, but it was a habitual kind of preparation. They had not really expected an attack here. It was not an ideal place for an ambush, which ironically had made it an excellent spot for one.

One of the palanquin-bearers jumped onto the fallen box and attempted to shove Shi off, but Shi ducked and turned, drawing his sword across the other man's body. His newly-sharpened blade cut deep enough that he wondered if he had cut the bearer in half, but he did not stop to look; he jumped off the palanquin and brought his sword down across one of the guards attacking Kyung-Ho.

The bullets from Saizou's gun made no sound, but Shi saw their effectiveness as the governor's guards dropped one by one, like marionettes with the strings cut.

Even in the middle of fighting, Shi was impressed with the captain for the first time. It was excellent aim: every target was moving, melting with the shadows. Even with no light to guide him, the captain shot and killed and shot and killed again.

Then the battle sounds fell silent, and Shi turned in a circle, expecting more opponents, more of the governor's guards. Instead, there were twenty bodies on the ground in various positions of death: crumpled, splayed, cut into pieces.

Shi lifted his sword and beheaded the twitching man at his

feet. As the head rolled several feet away, a sound cut the thick silence, more effective than any blade.

Somewhere nearby, a child was wailing.

Shi could never quite remember how Saizou got there first. He was sniping from a tree, but when Shi ran down into the underbrush where the passengers of the palanquin had fallen, Saizou was already there.

He did not have his gun. He was crouched on the ground, the tall, thick plant stalks half-obscuring his legs and the body of the governor.

"Is he dead?" Shi ventured, looking left and right, sweeping the ground for any sign of a child.

The captain had ignored him. Had not even turned his head.

Shi sighed and pulled his mask down around his neck. He bent down and checked the governor for a pulse.

Nothing. The fall from the palanquin had broken his neck.

"He's dead," said Shi, answering his own question.

The others, still standing above them on the trail, shouted down. "Who's crying?"

"Is it a baby?"

"Shit, the governor's dead?"

"*Kuso!* We really messed this up."

Shi was about to call up something in agreement, but as he rose from his crouch, he saw another body, flung several yards farther. It was a woman—the governor's wife, judging by the finery of her clothes. Perhaps his concubine or mistress.

Shi did not need to check her for signs of life; her stiff pose and pale, unmoving face told him enough, but still he crossed over and checked, to be completely certain.

"They're both dead." Shi kicked the tree trunk the woman had fallen against.

Groans and curses, fainter now that he was farther away, reached his ears. This was their first mission, and they had failed it completely.

"Did a baby get thrown out of the palanquin?" This query came from Kyung-Ho, his hands cupped around his mouth.

Shi walked toward Saizou, re-sheathing his sword as he did. "Captain?" *Don't tell me the sight of blood makes him squeamish.* "We need to find the child if there is one. We can't leave it out here."

As if in agreement, another faint, infantile cry came from somewhere nearby. Shi strode quickly to the right, searching.

Then he saw her. She wore a tiny red dress, and her hair—so much hair for such a young thing. Done in pigtail braids.

Saizou was bent over the splintered corner of the palanquin. The corner that was crushing the baby.

"Captain!" Shi barked, amazed at Saizou's lack of motion. "She's still alive, sir. We need to lift the—"

Saizou held up a hand. It was a sudden, sharp motion, like a snake striking forward in warning.

Shi felt rage, then. Rage at the captain's refusal to speak to him, rage at his stillness. He strode forward and reached out to grip Saizou's shoulder, to wrench him back and lift the palanquin himself if he had to—

But he stopped, his hand no more than six inches from Saizou's shoulder.

The corner of the palanquin wasn't on top of the baby. It was in her. The infant was all but severed, and the weight of the wood was the only thing holding her together.

Again, the baby cried. It was a weak sound, but to Shi, it was louder than the tornado siren that had rendered him half-deaf.

It was the loudest thing he had ever heard.

From above, Lieutenant Shota called down, "Captain! What are your orders?"

Then, for the first time, Saizou spoke directly to Shi. "Tell...." He swallowed. His breath shook as he pushed through and said, "Tell them to gather anything useful. If anyone is still alive enough to be helpful, we'll take them back."

Shi cleared his throat, trying not to look at the baby. Trying not to listen to the weak, horrible sounds she was making as the life bled out of her.

Her dress wasn't red, he realized.

Her dress was white. Her blood was red.

"Captain?" Lieutenant Shota called again.

Shi looked up. "One minute."

Saizou did not turn his head or look up at Shi, but his voice was loud enough when he snapped, "Do as I said."

"Captain—"

*"Do as I said."* Saizou's voice pierced the humid air, causing the soldiers on the incline above to step back, as if his voice alone could wound them.

Shi turned and strode back up the incline, using the tangled mass of vines to pull himself up onto the path again. "If anyone is still alive, we're taking them back to base. Gather anything useful."

"What's going on down there?" Lieutenant Shota demanded, stepping closer, his eyes narrowed.

"Yeah." Kyung-Ho gestured off the trail. "Is the captain signing adoption papers?" He grinned. It was a garish expression, and Shi was filled with such sudden loathing that he turned away. He would rather look down at the expressionless face of a corpse than tolerate a smile.

"Do as the captain said," Shi answered softly.

Lieutenant Shota raised his voice. "You heard him! Captain's orders. Gather—"

An infantile whimper rose to a shriek, then fell into silence. It was too fast; so fast Shi wondered if he had misheard.

He turned around, stepping toward the edge of the path.

Saizou had begun to walk back up, using the vines as footholds rather than pulleys. Shi reached over to help pull him up over the edge, and as he did so, he saw the child: limp, pale, her halves held together by Saizou's cradling arms.

There was no one left alive to interrogate or question. They left the bodies where they found them and took the weapons, leaving a feast for the jungle behind them.

Saizou left more.

He gave them no more orders that night. He only sat at the edge of the camp, the firelight flickering across his unblinking eyes and expressionless, haggard face.

And when Shi opened his eyes and saw the blackness of the storage unit and the thick cable knit of Fumiyo's sweater, he pushed a single word out of his dry throat into the stale air.

"Captain."

# THIRTY-THREE

*I CAN'T MOVE.*

Saizou tried to take a deep breath, to remember where he was. He was no longer on the battlefield. There were no screams, no one was dying. Shi was nearby.

No.

Shi wasn't nearby. And there was no sound at all. He blinked rapidly, trying to force his body to move faster, to wake up, to think clearer. *Wake up. Wake up. Move.*

But he couldn't move. He couldn't see, he couldn't hear, and for a brief moment his only thought was, *I've been buried alive.*

It was a tactic he had seen before, although never used. A tactic meant to instill fear in the hearts of anyone who watched, and to let that fear loosen their tongues...except there was nobody else to watch, nobody else to be afraid. Was there? No.

He was somewhere in the palace. He was not entombed anywhere; he was too valuable.

He tried to take another deep breath, and this time his

lungs expanded, allowing in a rush of air and overwhelming relief, and again, his thoughts drifted to Shi.

He was here for Shi. A poison was pumping through Shi's blood, killing him, while Saizou was trapped here in total darkness. He had to find a way out, he had to find another way to save—

Noise—movement. Someone was coming, a door was opening somewhere.

Again Saizou tried to move, but it was as if his muscles had been removed, or the part of his brain that gave orders had been tied down. He had no control over himself.

He closed his eyes, his ability to breathe now threatening to overpower him as he panted, trying to slow it down. *Don't hyperventilate. You don't know where you are. You aren't dead. As long as you're alive, you can find a way out. Listen to me, you idiot, you can still find a way out. Think. Wait.*

A door opened. Saizou tensed, listening as people—two, by the sound of their footsteps—entered the room. One was taller, lighter than the other, but both were confident. People with military training of some kind. Guards, probably.

Guards wouldn't have any reason to be here unless they were leading the way for the Prince-Regent. As soon as he had the thought, Saizou heard another set of footsteps enter the room, followed by two more. The first had to be the Prince-Regent; the scent of jasmine and sandalwood was too strong to hail anyone else. As for the other two, he wasn't sure. One of them was probably the muzzled assassin. The other was much smaller...

It probably didn't matter.

"Saizou Akita."

Saizou opened his eyes again, blinking, but his vision was

met with nothing but yawning darkness. All he could do was breathe and listen.

"How soon until he's functioning?" was the Prince-Regent's first question.

"It shouldn't be long now, Your Radiance," an unfamiliar voice responded.

"That's not specific enough."

"Less than fifteen minutes by my estimation, Your Radiance."

"Amazing. He's not even tied down but look at him. Wait, he can't see me, can he?"

"No, Your Radiance."

"Absolutely amazing."

The Prince-Regent moved closer, his voice louder the next time he spoke. He was less than three feet away, Saizou guessed, when the Prince-Regent said, "That pain in your left side is thanks to my beautiful Kiko. I call her the Crane for the way she strikes at lesser animals, spearing them like a crane spears a fish. Of course, most cranes aren't equipped with neurotoxin-coated bills, either. I can't remember the name of it, but this beautiful toxin renders you immobile. It cuts off your eyesight, but don't worry, you'll get that back. You'll be able to move soon." A pause. "If I don't have Kiko stab you again."

"I'd be more than happy," said a female voice.

Saizou focused on regulating his heartbeat, on keeping his pulse steady and his breathing even.

"Not yet," said the Prince-Regent. His voice was even closer now.

Something touched Saizou's neck. A hand, he realized with a flash of unpleasant surprise.

"Right now, your body is little more than a sarcophagus for your mind," the Prince-Regent continued, his voice quiet as his hand slid down like Saizou's throat, as soft and cold as a snake's belly. "It's a sarcophagus I'm very keen on excavating. Imagine excavating a living, breathing human being." A single syllable of laughter. "I may be the first."

A shiver swept unbidden across Saizou's skin. He prayed the Prince-Regent would fail to notice it.

Saizou felt the hand on his neck pause and cursed his body for giving him away. There were too many sensations to focus on: the helplessness of paralysis, his blindness, the knowledge that someone he loathed, someone who wanted him dead, was in full control.

He breathed out slowly. Was there light entering his vision, or was it his imagination? Did he even want to see his surroundings?

Someone touched his eyelid, and he wanted to flinch. He wanted to jerk away, but he could do nothing. "The toxin is wearing off, Your Radiance," said the voice from before. "I suggest restraining him now."

"Put him in the box," said the Prince-Regent. To someone else, he added, "I want you to oversee his transport personally. Kiko! Come on, darling, there's something I want you to see."

Their footsteps left the room, followed by two more pairs, the two guards. The only people remaining in the room besides himself were the apparent medic and the person who had been ordered to oversee Saizou's move.

There were less people cluttering up the space now, and Saizou heard the faint buzz of the Prince-Regent's Hand breathing through his apparatus.

Saizou blinked. He could do that, at least; although now the pain in his side was sharper, more poignant. He would take that pain a thousand times over before he would take another dose of that cursed toxin.

"Strap him down," said Kirikizu's voice. His filtered voice was not quite monotone.

Saizou felt hard, cold restraints lock around his wrists and ankles, and his heart picked up speed as another restraint locked around his neck.

*Breathe. You're being moved. It won't last long. One. Two. Three. In. One. Two. Three. Out.*

Saizou shut his eyes and watched the pattern of lights blossom across the inside of his eyelids. It was brighter with his eyes shut than it was when they were open.

He realized he was on a stretcher with wheels, like those found in hospitals. Someone began to push him out of the room; he heard Kirikizu following close behind. He was pushed for a steady three minutes, and Saizou counted the turns. *Right turn. Straight for six seconds. Left turn. Straight for three seconds. Right for eight seconds.*

They stopped after the twelfth left turn. The air was heavier here, full of the sweet, spiced scents of cinnamon, honey, jasmine, and sandalwood. The smell was accompanied by the sound of running water.

Saizou opened his eyes and found the darkness had withdrawn even more; he could see a kind of reddish light and a dark figure poised over him. The figure released his restraints and dragged him from the wheeled stretcher.

He was set down—on the floor? He couldn't make out any walls, only the red light. Then he heard someone pushing the stretcher out.

Now the only remaining sound was the hum of Kirikizu breathing through his muzzle.

Saizou automatically tried to lift his hands and rub his eyes. His body had not yet returned the ability to move his limbs, but he felt a brief flicker of relief as his hand twitched in response to his attempt.

Kirikizu's footsteps came closer before stopping again, perhaps six feet away. Maybe eight; Saizou clenched his jaw. *Wait. You can do nothing until you regain control of yourself. Panicking helps nothing, worry profits nothing. Live now. Fight later.*

"Less than a week since your...frankly spectacular exit from these very walls," said Kirikizu. His voice was almost idly curious, but not quite. There was too much calculation behind his tone. He was attempting to mask the true depths of his interest. "And yet here you are. Again. For what?"

Saizou tested his voice. A faint sound scratched free, and he twisted the sound into the only weak rebuttal he could think of. "Your mother?"

The Prince-Regent's Hand chuckled then, deep and bemused. "Is that the best you could come up with?"

Saizou shut his eyes again, weary with the effort of keeping them open. Then he nodded, a faint gesture, only once. It took less effort than he anticipated. That was something.

If the assassin thought Saizou was pathetic, he had the good grace not to say so. Instead, after a moment of prolonged silence, he remarked, "Your friend. You care about him."

Saizou wanted to say *I can't talk, you moron, and you know it. Stop trying to make conversation and leave me alone.* Instead, lacking the ability to speak a full sentence, he said, "Yes." *That's what you do with a friend. You care about them. And Shi is a better friend to me than I am to him.*

"Your caring makes you sloppy."

God was testing him, Saizou decided. All he wanted was to be left alone, to regain his senses and physical functions in peace and quiet. Yet here was the Prince-Regent's Hand, who, of all people, apparently wanted to keep talking.

"Done...worse," Saizou said, his voice scratchy and feeble in his ears. His voice was the least of his worries.

"Hm," said Kirikizu. It was an amused noise, but not a laugh. "Your friend will die knowing you were captured. Knowing you are currently trapped in the Prince-Regent's private chambers for whatever painful amusements he devises. He has quite an imagination. You have nothing to look forward to."

Saizou found he could curl his fingers palm-ward, into fists. Shi would not die. They had not survived the jungles of China and the atrocities of war to be felled here, by something as simple as a bite.

His face must have registered more expression than he thought because Kirikizu said, "I'm not attempting to rile you." His purring, robotic voice lacked spite, Saizou noted with surprise. He would have thought the Prince-Regent would only surround himself with those equally as vile. Maybe the Hand was less vile than the head. Kirikizu continued. "You are too old to be drawn into the fold. He will probably offer you a deal."

Saizou could not fully laugh yet, but a whispered, one-syllable *ha* escaped him easily enough.

"The offer will seem preferable to the position you will be in when he makes it."

*The Prince-Regent can go screw himself,* thought Saizou, but he did not try to voice his opinion. If he gave Kirikizu enough silence, perhaps he would leave him alone.

He did not need to wait any longer; apparently done with his odd remarks, Kirikizu's blurred form turned and shrank in the red haze, his footsteps fading. There was the sound of a door closing, and Saizou had no company but the heady, spiced air and the sound of running water.

———

OTTER RACED down the stairs with Lieutenant Takuan close on her heels. "I brought—" She stumbled at the bottom of the stairs, distracted by the sight of the cell door left wide open. *The prisoner has escaped.* She swallowed the lump in her throat and raced through the door.

Winter was still chained to the wall, his head hanging. He looked like he was asleep. No one had escaped; Kirikizu had simply left.

She raced over to Haka, his hands, feet, and torso still bound to the chair. His skin was a sickly, ashen shade of grey, but the only signs of torture were his torn shirt and the tiny pinpricks in his stomach and his neck, each sporting a bright dot of blood.

"How is he?"

Otter looked over her shoulder at Takuan, who was leaning around the cell, his eyes bright with anger. His hair was unkempt, his uniform jacket unbuttoned over his white shirt. She had dragged him out of his bed.

"I don't know. Commander?" Otter felt for a pulse but stopped when she saw Haka's chest rise and fall. He was breathing. "He's breathing. Haka? Haka, hey, can you hear me?" She put a hand on either side of his head and tilted it back. His eyes were ringed with red, his face streaked with the tracks of dry tears—but he was alive. He was breathing, and he was alive.

"Get his cot ready," said Otter, untying the ropes around

Haka's legs. "And water, get a bowl of water, and some bandages."

"Right." Takuan turned to go but paused. "Did Kirikizu leave?"

"It looks like it. I really don't care," Otter snapped. "Just please get the things ready and then get back down here and help me carry him upstairs."

Takuan dashed out of the cell, and Otter finished working Haka free of the restraints. She kept glancing at his face, searching for signs that he was about to wake up. He remained as limp as a rag doll, his skin devoid of any healthy color. He might as well have been a corpse.

Every ounce of sympathy Otter felt for the Prince-Regent's Hand was shoved to the back of her mind as she pushed Haka's lank, inky hair out of his face, over his shoulders. "Haka, please, open your eyes. It's Otter. Kirikizu is gone." The lump in her throat swelled twice as large as she studied him. "You jackass."

His face twitched; a movement so slight she stared at him for several long seconds, wondering if she had imagined it. "Hey, are you awake?" She tapped the side of his face. "Haka?"

His muscles spasmed once, then twice, jerking his body forward. Otter gripped his shoulders, pushing him back, keeping him from falling out of the chair. He went still, then, like his inner machinery had finished recalibrating.

Except he wasn't an android or a cyborg; he was a flesh-and-blood human being, and nobody deserved to feel that much pain.

Nobody deserved to feel the pain he had been in since she had met him.

She lifted her right hand and brushed his cheek. "Haka?" she asked, her voice even softer than she intended. "Please wake up. It's me, Otter. I'm here, okay? Come on. Open your eyes."

Haka obeyed, opening his eyes just enough that Otter saw slivers of his dark, brown-black irises. Then, like it was too much work, his eyes drifted shut again and he slumped forward.

Takuan burst back into the cell and hurried over to the chair. "You get his legs, I'll get his arms," he ordered, and proceeded to lift Haka's torso out of the chair before Otter even had time to grab his ankles.

It was a difficult process. Halfway up the stairs, Takuan grunted, "He's a lot heavier than he looks."

"Yep," Otter grunted.

They got him to his cot, setting him down as gingerly as they could. Takuan took a step back and pointed toward the bowl of water on the floor. A cloth was draped over the rim. "I think he needs a doctor."

"I'll take care of him," said Otter quickly, shooting Takuan a glare, although she knew the man didn't deserve it. The thought of anyone else looking over Haka in this position...he would hate it. He would hate it down to his bones, and besides, he was her responsibility.

*Not really,* whispered a voice in the back of her mind.

*Shut up,* she whispered back. Aloud, she said, "I've got this. Get him some painkillers."

"Right. I'm going to call Mayumi and have her bring some things over," Takuan added, exiting the room without bothering to close the door.

Otter dipped the cloth in water and wrung it out, then studied the tiny hole in Haka's stomach. There wasn't much blood. In fact, as Otter rinsed the blood away, the wound all but disappeared. If she hadn't known where it was, she might never have seen it.

Kirikizu was good at what he did, and at the very least, he hadn't torn Haka's fingernails or molars out.

*So why aren't you waking up?*

Carefully, she lifted his right eyelid with her thumb. She meant to study the response of his pupil when exposed to light, but she forgot that intention when she realized that his eyes were not pale and glazed over like a blind man's.

He wasn't just suffering from torture—he was suffering a withdrawal. He'd gone too long without stardust.

She half-rose to her feet, meaning to find his supply and bring a dose back, but she hesitated. *What if...* She licked her lips and glanced from his desk to his face and back to his desk. The drug was a fatal habit, and she was no fool. She knew it allowed the Prince-Regent to keep Haka under his thumb. The Prince-Regent held the promise of new shipments over Haka's head, and conversely, threatened to withhold them.

This was the longest she'd ever known Haka to go without stardust. She could wait a bit longer, then give him just a little. Not quite cold turkey.

But almost.

She knelt back on the hard ground and pressed a quick kiss to his forehead, damp with sweat. "I'm sorry," she whispered, and placed the wet cloth against his neck, rinsing away the faint traces of blood. "It's for your own good."

# THIRTY-FOUR

ANOTHER LATE NIGHT. That's what the boys would think. Hiro chewed on the tip of a pen, his sharpened teeth leaving small indentations in the plastic. Late nights weren't unusual for him. He had carefully cultivated the reputation of a workaholic in order to disguise his real activity, which ironically made the cover somewhat real.

He glanced toward the door. Most of the boys would have gone by now, except Kido and Yuu; they were his right-hand men, and like their boss, they lived at the docks. If he needed something delivered or someone nosy killed, they did the job without asking questions, and got paid extra for their trouble.

The blue light of Hiro's computer screen flickered, and the speaker switched on unbidden. "How's my favorite reptile?" asked Riza.

"How's the safe house coming?" Hiro retorted, removing the pen from his mouth.

"I found the perfect location. It should be wonderfully safe for a few days at least."

"Fine. Just tell me where it is."

"Like I'm that sloppy. I'll guide you there."

Hiro snorted. "After all we've been through, you don't trust me?" He clicked the pen against his knee and tossed it onto the desk. "Will the safe house be ready tonight?"

"Oh. About that; I'm afraid we're going to have to tweak the schedule."

Hiro straightened, his eyes narrowing at the screen. "What?"

"Needs must. Just a minor change, nothing big," Riza replied coolly. "But you're going to have to move the packages this morning, not tonight."

Hiro glanced at the door across the room. "Hilarious."

"It's funny because it's true."

"You cannot," he growled, "expect me to—"

"Careful with your next words, sweetie. Remember who you work for."

Hiro smiled. It was the expression he put on when he felt like ripping someone's throat out with his teeth. His smile often proved more intimidating than his threats, but it was also a self-imposed restraint of sorts. It reminded him to think. He smiled until he felt the flare of anger cooling down.

Then he cleared his throat, collected his thoughts, and said, "You want me to move four fugitives across the city in broad daylight."

"If I could get my hands on narrow daylight, I would. As it is, the best I can give you is a cloudy forecast with a seventy percent chance of rain."

Hiro laughed breathlessly and rubbed his forehead. "Damn you."

"Besides," Riza continued casually, "you'll only have to transport three fugitives."

He leaned forward. "What?"

"Saizou Akita's currently a prisoner inside the palace. Some grandiose plan to get an antidote for his injured friend who's probably dying."

"What the hell was he thinking?" Hiro hissed, gripping the edge of the table with both hands until it cut into his skin.

"I think," said Riza, "he was trying to be noble. Looks a lot like stupidity so often, doesn't it?"

"Akita," said Hiro, "is an idiot. I can't finish this. It's too much of a risk." Hiro stood up, pushing the chair back from the table. He picked up his handgun from the desk and tucked it into the back of his pants. "I'm taking care of it."

"Yes, you are," Riza agreed, "but in a way that doesn't involve three murders."

"You should dump the conscience where you left your brain." Hiro hit the *off* key, shutting down the computer and Riza's voice at the same time. He strode out of his office, shutting the door softly behind him.

He walked past the lounge. The television was on, and Kido was watching some idiotic game show while Yuu sat at the table, engrossed in a game of solitaire.

He heard Kido say, "You want a beer?" and heard no response from Yuu, who rarely spoke anyway. Advantageous for this line of work, Hiro thought as he slipped out the front door and strode toward the docks.

The sun was just beginning to rise, but Riza's forecast looked accurate: a thin haze of gray cloud smothered the dawn. Hiro reached into his pocket and pulled out a silencer cap, then drew his gun with his other hand and fitted the cap over the muzzle.

Saizou's friends were going to pay for his bad decisions. He had left Hiro with no other viable option.

Some hero.

———

OSCAR SLEIMANN WAS A BIOENGINEER, not a custom toymaker. But that's what he was doing, or rather, that's what he had already done. He had taken the ingredients left over from the Prince-Regent's frankly horrifying dog-man-creature and added his own twist to it, at the Prince-Regent's specifications.

He hated that it was so easy. He'd barely had to do anything. Whoever had created the last monstrosity had done a decent job; all he'd had to do was upgrade what was already there.

He glanced at the timer. In six more hours, this little science project would be over and, in the unlikely event that the Prince-Regent kept his word, Oscar would be on a plane headed back to England where he could forget the last several days.

Maybe he could even write an autobiography about his experience.

"Nobody would ever believe this, mate." He sighed aloud, adjusting his elbow-high plastic gloves. He leaned against the table, trying not to look at the incubator.

It was an interesting setup, rather like a walk-in freezer. White, sterile, and humid; the inside was kept at the exact temperature of a healthy womb. Once he had assembled the stew of ingredients, all he had to do was leave it to simmer and grow.

The door opened, and he spun around, shocked to see the Prince-Regent, dressed in a black silk jumpsuit and dripping with gold finery, stride into the room like he owned the place. Which he did, Oscar reminded himself quickly, aiming a lazy, half-hearted bow in the Prince-Regent's direction. The bow, as unenthusiastic as it was, was cut short when a woman followed the Prince-Regent into the lab.

Her face was whitened by makeup, her eyebrows as thin and sharp as pincers. A gleaming array of sharp sticks fanned out of her coiled hair, and she wore an interesting combination of trousers under a short kimono-style robe made of some kind of shiny, blue-black latex.

Oscar could hardly help noticing that she was beautiful, but beauty was fleeting, and she had silver blades on her fingers.

"Excuse me," Oscar barked, glaring at the woman but softening the glare into a scowl when he looked at the Prince-Regent. "What exactly is she doing here?"

"I'm going to show her my project." The Prince-Regent smiled at Oscar like a benign demigod deigning to favor a mortal with his presence.

It was the last straw.

"*Your* project?" Oscar scoffed. "That's rich, considering the only work you've done was order me to put the bloody thing together."

The woman gasped. "Let me kill him," she snapped, stalking around the edge of a silver table, her taloned hands poised to strike.

The Prince-Regent's soft voice stopped the woman in mid-stride. "Oh, leave him alone."

"Why?" she demanded, refusing to lower her poised hands.

Oscar glared at her as the Prince-Regent continued. "Kiko. He's a very famous English scientist. Doctor, meet my Left Hand. You can call her the Crane, although I doubt you'll be meeting her again." He gestured politely, like a good host introducing two party guests.

Kiko folded her arms, the blades over her hands retracting.

"You shouldn't let him speak to you like that," she said, but her words were directed toward the Prince-Regent.

"You're distracted." The Prince-Regent came up behind Kiko and put a hand on her shoulder, gently turning her around toward the incubator. "You're supposed to be paying attention to this."

"It looks like an oven."

"It's the incubator," said Oscar, barely refraining from adding, *bitch*.

Kiko stared at the Prince-Regent. "You didn't!"

"No, he didn't," Oscar muttered. "I did, but what thanks do I get? None. Not even an ounce of acknowledgement. Bloody wan—"

"Doctor, please don't make me regret being kind to you," said the Prince-Regent sternly.

"Oh, please do," said Kiko, smiling viciously.

"Sorry," said Oscar unapologetically. He tore his latex gloves off. There was no reason to do so except frustration, and everything around him was too fragile to hit or throw. "When can I leave? It's not like I'll need to babysit the thing once it's done."

The Prince-Regent stared directly at Oscar this time. Then he smiled oddly.

Oscar frowned, his pulse spiking. "No."

"I'm afraid you're wrong. You *will* need to babysit the thing once it's done," said the Prince-Regent, tucking a lock of hair behind his hear.

Oscar couldn't stop himself. "Absolutely bloody not."

The Prince-Regent stepped around Kiko and strode toward Oscar, stopping when he was three feet away. His posture was graceful and relaxed, but there was a black shadow behind his makeup-enhanced features that made

Oscar want to curl in on himself, like a leaf shriveling in the heat of the sun.

"Doctor," said the Prince-Regent, and his pleasant voice hid a thousand unspoken threats. "I would consider it a personal favor if you oversaw the care and training of this creature until such time as I see fit to release it."

Oscar laughed and shook his head until he felt dizzy. "You wanted your very own human-hybrid-freak; I made you one. This whole—all this nonsense, is—it's—" Oscar stammered, caught on his own baffled indignation. "It's bollocks."

The Prince-Regent blinked rapidly, as taken aback as if he had been slapped. Then his lips twitched, and his smile grew and became a laugh. It was not a practiced, silvery laugh meant for polite company; it was a full, hearty sound. Genuine.

Then the Prince-Regent turned and strode back toward the incubator, ordering Kiko side with a wave of his hand. "Well, we'd all better hope the creature is ready," he said, and pulled the incubator door open.

Oscar barely had time to register what the Prince-Regent had done. Pale wisps of hot air and hormone gas spilled out of the black, square mouth of the incubator. "What the *bloody hell!*" Oscar was across the room in three bounds, staring at the open door, at the readings on the computer. "It's six hours too soon! You've probably killed him, I hope you know that!"

"Oh no," said the Prince-Regent.

Oscar raced over and reached in, gripping the handle of the box inside. It was a small box, four feet long, a foot and a half wide, designed to grow something partway. Inside, it was like an aquarium, filled with gray liquid swirling around the body inside. There was no smell to the cocktail of growth hormones, artificial embryonic fluid, and nutrients—just moist heat.

"Do you even realize what you've done?" Oscar demanded,

bending over the keyboard and furiously typing one command after another into the system. "Once you open that thing, you stop the process! You can't just start it all over again. This is an incredibly delicate system, not a game!"

"I know that," said the Prince-Regent.

Oscar straightened and stared at the man, equal parts aghast and furious. "That is unbelievable. You're willing to risk all this work because what, your prisoner—excuse me, bioengineer—said something you didn't like?"

"If it dies, you die," said the Prince-Regent, as calm and collected as if he were sitting on his throne. He turned his back to Oscar and said, "Come, Kiko."

Then, just like that, they were gone, leaving Oscar with nothing but a premature life form and an alarm yowling faintly from the wall, letting him know the birthing process had been sabotaged.

Oscar hit the *drain* button on the incubator lid. He could hardly contain his anxiety as he watched the liquid drain around the subject, leaving its body coated in a thick sheen that would need washed off.

The incubator beeped twice to say *drain complete*.

He threw the lid off the incubator and let it tumble to the ground with a bang, expensive equipment be hanged. He reached into the box and began doing everything he could, which did not feel like enough.

"Come on, love, come onnnn," sang Oscar under his breath. The thing had grown rapidly, he realized with a start; it would have outgrown the box in less than six hours. Could it have been a backhanded blessing that the Prince-Regent was such a petty bastard? "Come on, you. Rise and shine. Open your eyes. Do something. Breathe."

The subject did nothing. There was no sign of life, except

the reading from the incubator lid assuring him the subject had been alive fifteen seconds ago.

Oscar swore and began to clear the gelatinous liquid away from the creature's mouth and nose. *Come on, breathe. I need you to breathe or it's both our necks, kiddo.* "We don't have time for this," Oscar announced briskly. He put one hand around the creature's back and the other under its legs and lifted it from the incubating box.

He carried the creature to the nearest table and knocked every beaker, syringe, and piece of equipment onto the floor before setting the creature down as gingerly as possible.

"Oxygen, oxygen, oxygen," chanted Oscar, turning in a half-circle until he saw what he was looking for. He grabbed the mask and the tank and carted them over to the table. He placed the mask over the creature's face and turned the oxygen supply on, then stepped back.

"Come on, mate, you have to help me out here," he coaxed. He could feel the sweat dripping from his forehead and down his neck as he studied the deathly body stretched out on the steel table. "If you die, I die, and I'm being perfectly honest when I say my life is probably worth a bit more than yours. I've been around longer. I'm practically famous. You're..." His voice trailed off.

Beautifully, miraculously, the oxygen mask dulled with a cloud of fog.

The subject was breathing.

"Igor," he whispered to the empty room, "it's alive."

———

GLASS CRUNCHED under the weight of Kirikizu's foot as he stepped into the Poisoner's dwelling. Yellow tape still stretched around the perimeter, but it was only a formality, to keep any of the more curious guards from getting the bright idea of waltzing into the house and contaminating the scene.

Kirikizu walked over shards of glass and pottery, studying the floor. It was covered in dark soil from the various pots of poisonous plants, which had been removed already—along with, as he understood it, two halves of a Chinese pit viper.

"Go see what you can find," the Prince-Regent had told him, and so here he was, searching. The situation seemed obvious.

Saizou had come looking for an antidote to the poison killing his friend, he had attacked One-Eye, the Dog had attacked Saizou, and the Crane had arrived to finish the skirmish.

Still, being thorough never hurt anything. Kirikizu moved around the damaged room, stepping over the fallen shelf, now splintered into six or seven pieces.

He kicked a large piece of blue pottery aside, but crouched down to pick it up again. He turned it over in his hand, studying the way the scaled pattern swept through a gradient pattern of deep royal blue to a lighter shade, like a robin's egg.

It was a shame, for something so beautiful and useful to be broken like that. He tossed it back down and watched it shatter into four more pieces. The fourth piece spun in a wild circle and came to rest near a curiously-shaped mound in the spilled dirt.

Kirikizu swiped at the spot with two fingers and felt a strange, metallic curve. He lifted the object and blew the dirt away.

It was an earring or ear cuff of some sort. He turned it over, bemused. Strange; Saizou didn't seem like the kind of man to wear jewelry. He had larger concerns than his appearance.

He tilted his head. There, where the cuff hooked over the inner ear, was a small strip of different texture from the rest.

Slowly, Kirikizu placed the ear cuff around his right ear and tapped it with a finger. He said nothing, but he heard a faint click on the other side, like a phone being lifted. He remained silent. There was another click, and then nothing but dead air.

Kirikizu looked at the floor and smiled.

# THIRTY-FIVE

KIRIKIZU DUCKED under a swatch of yellow caution tape and nodded at the guard by the front door. "It's clear for cleanup."

"*Hai,* sir. The Prince-Regent requested that you bring your report directly to him."

Kirikizu halted and thought of the ear cuff tucked inside his belt. "Don't tell me the Prince-Regent's orders. I know them."

If the guard was surprised at the snap, his impassive helmet failed to show it. "*Hai,* sir," he repeated, and lifted a hand, motioning at the guard stationed at the other end of the building. "It's clear for cleanup!"

Kirikizu strode away from the house. He saw One-Eye exiting the infirmary, a bandage wrapped around his throat.

"You," Kirikizu called, changing his trajectory and heading toward the poisoner instead.

"What do you want?" One-Eye asked, sullen, as Kirikizu approached.

"The Prince-Regent wants to know how the Dog is faring."

One-Eye shrugged, but the way he pressed his lips together

told Kirikizu he was more concerned for the Dog than he let on. "He'll live. He's taken a few beatings this week."

"What poison did you give him?"

One-Eye frowned. "Poison?"

"The Dog."

"First of all, it isn't poison," One-Eye snipped. "It's venom. Secondly, don't say 'I gave it to him' like I tried to kill him. Building up an immunity is a long and difficult process, and do you realize what a breakthrough it is to make a living subject venomous without killing them?"

"Answer the question before I finish strangling you myself."

One-Eye folded his arms and continued frowning, but said, "It's a tetrodotoxin from the *Takifugu* fish, combined with ammonia."

Kirikizu tilted his head. "I thought there was no cure for *Takifugu* venom."

"Well, aren't you the smart one," One-Eye retorted with a snide expression. "There isn't one, hence the balance of ammonia. There's a binding solution for that. The ratio of tetrodotoxin to ammonia is one to five, so the paralysis takes a while to set in. It gives enough time for the cure to be administered within forty-eight hours."

Kirikizu remained silent for a long moment. If he pursued this conversation, his next question could easily raise enough suspicion for One-Eye to relay it to the Prince-Regent. If that happened, Kirikizu doubted even he could allay the Prince-Regent's suspicions. He also had no desire to kill One-Eye.

"Can I go now?" asked One-Eye. There was a nervous edge to his voice, as if he realized there might be more to the conversation than he previously thought. "Or do you have more fascinating questions? Because I obviously have all day."

Kirikizu's mouth twitched. He almost wished he'd had the

boy's attitude when he was younger. Instead of asking outright where One-Eye kept the antidote to the Dog's venom, he said, "We'll be moving your residence to a more secure location within the palace until Saizou Akita's compatriots have been found. Take inventory and label everything you want moved."

One-Eye's mouth fell open. "Move everything? Into the palace? That's a terrible idea."

"Then you can tell the Prince-Regent your opinion. Because obviously he has all day," said Kirikizu, and brushed past the indignant poisoner.

———

AS SOON AS his sight returned, Saizou was able to see the glass box trapping him on all sides. When he stood up, it reached a foot or so over his head, so he guessed it was about seven feet tall and twelve feet wide. He remembered a faint hissing sound as he was put inside the cage, and figured instead of a door, the front half of the box probably lifted up. There were small, round speakers embedded in each wall. He could hear the water rushing from the fountain in the center of the large chamber.

Red lanterns hung from the tall ceiling at irregular intervals, their chains dangling at similarly irregular lengths. An enormous bed surrounded by a sheer black canopy was positioned on the far side of the room, while the fountain made a grand statement on the other.

It felt more like an indoor courtyard than a bedroom.

The arched double-doors opened, and the Prince-Regent strode in. The Crane wasn't with him; that was something. Better one enemy than two.

Saizou sat back down and draped his arms over his knees,

watching as the Prince-Regent sashayed toward the cage. "I have to say, you're the only person I know with a human terrarium in their room."

"Do you like it? Occasionally I keep two or three humans in there at once." He crouched in front of the cage and tilted his head, then lifted a sharp fingernail to tap the glass. He smiled.

Saizou leaned the back of his head against the wall. "Just do it."

"Do what?"

"Whatever it is you're planning on doing. Interrogation, torture. Get it over with."

"I'd rather wait." The Prince-Regent tucked his legs underneath him and leaned forward. "I hear interrogation would yield very few results from you. Guerilla fighters are taught to withstand their own methods, are they not?"

Saizou sighed. He didn't have time for this.

Shi didn't have time for this.

"I don't really feel like having a conversation with you," he said bluntly. "I'm not in a talkative mood."

"Aw." The Prince-Regent clicked his tongue. "I can think of much worse things to do with you than hold a pleasant conversation."

"Ah," said Saizou. "I'm sorry. I didn't realize it was pleasant."

"Your spirits don't seem dampened by your situation," the Prince-Regent remarked. "I'm impressed."

Saizou rubbed his eyes with the heel of his hand. His vision had returned, but bouts of blurriness continued to sweep across it at regular intervals. "Thanks."

The Prince-Regent laughed. "I don't dislike you, you know. In fact, I've found you very entertaining."

Saizou levelled a tired, irritated glare at the Prince-Regent. "Really."

The Prince-Regent nodded, his eyebrows arching as he said, "I could get a great deal of use from you."

"If you're thinking about trying to hire me, you can just forget it." Saizou licked his dry lips, trying not to think about Shi. He could be dead by now.

No. He wouldn't be. He was too stubborn. But stubbornness could only hold out for so long...he had to get that antidote. He had to.

"I anticipated that answer," said the Prince-Regent easily. "Of course you would refuse a job offer, if only on principle. Besides, you have several criminal friends you've dragged into your escapade. We can't forget about them."

*Dragged into your escapade.* The words cut Saizou deeper than he expected. He knew the Prince-Regent was trying to wind him up; it was the oldest tactic in the metaphorical book, and it came as no surprise. And yet, as Saizou looked into the Prince-Regent's serpentine gaze, he found himself wishing for physical torture over the prolonged conversation.

"Oh!" The Prince-Regent straightened his shoulders as if he had just remembered something important. "I forgot. I had some interesting information dug up on Shi."

Saizou lifted his head, staring at the man on the other side of the glass. "Leave him alone."

"He's not here. What would I do to him?" The Prince-Regent lifted his ring-encrusted hands and looked around the room. "I may not have shared the horrors of war with him, but I'm confident I know enough about him to beat you in a quiz."

*He wants to quiz me about Shi?* Saizou let out a deep breath. The Prince-Regent's mind was a bag of cats, and he belonged in an asylum—but he was here, in lavish surroundings, with all of Japan at his fingertips. *Show me the justice in that.*

"Is it true you'd never experienced any combat before you were given an officer's commission?" The Prince-Regent's voice broke into Saizou's clouded thoughts. "It happened to many sons in many privileged families, of course, but most of them never came home. Lack of experience, it seems, is deadly on the battlefield. What set you apart, do you think?"

"I don't see how it matters," Saizou muttered, lifting his knees and folding his arms across them. If he was going to endure more of this conversation, he might as well be comfortable.

"Your ruler is asking you a question."

"My ruler," said Saizou softly, "is spearheading an army in China to keep us safe while his baby brother destroys the nation he left behind like an angry child throwing a fit."

Slowly, the Prince-Regent exhaled and leaned back, his palms pressed flat to the smooth stone floor. "'Power tends to corrupt, and absolute power corrupts absolutely.' An English historian, Lord Acton, said that in the nineteenth century."

"I've heard it," said Saizou.

"Then perhaps you've heard another saying of his." The Prince-Regent closed his eyes and in a silken, almost shuddering voice, said, "'Great men are almost always bad men.'" He opened his eyes. "Greatness and goodness don't need to walk hand in hand. History rarely remembers the deeds of good men. However, it holds corrupt men with great power up to the light and watches them shine. Every mass slaughter in history is romanticized. Cruel leaders are hailed as geniuses."

"That's how you want history to remember you?" Saizou loathed meeting the Prince-Regent's gaze, but he kept it, unwavering. "A grim reaper with a diamond scythe?"

A distant look entered the Prince-Regent's eyes. "'The greatest names are coupled with the greatest crimes'. Another lesson from Lord Acton."

"You know, I learned about Lord Acton in grade school," said Saizou. "He wasn't just a historian, he was a moralist. He condemned the great, cruel men you prize so greatly."

"Nobody's perfect." The Prince-Regent shrugged one bare shoulder. "Do you know of stardust?"

"It's a drug," said Saizou. "One of your Shinsengumi commanders seems pretty hopped up on the stuff."

"He's not the only one. Stardust is one leash with which I keep many key people in hand. There is great value in learning to control people with their own desires. 'The strong man with the dagger is followed by the weak man with the sponge.'"

"Just like you," said Saizou in a low voice, "so controlled by your lust and bloodthirst that you let them jerk you around like a tame house pet. Let me ask you something, while we're here." He leaned forward. "Without that weak man with the sponge, where would you be?"

The Prince-Regent's face hardened, but he did not draw away or back down. Instead, he leaned closer, his breath fogging the glass. "It's a useless question. Where strong men are in short supply, weak men multiply like insects. When they use up a sponge, I will give them another. That's my advantage."

"Just answer the question," said Saizou, brushing past the deflection. "Call it curiosity."

"You want me to say I would be nowhere."

"I want you to answer the question," Saizou repeated.

The Prince-Regent's lip curled, somewhere between a smile and a snarl. "I would be in exactly the same place."

"Yes," said Saizou. "And you would have drowned long ago.

No ruler is autonomous. Fire can't exist without something to burn."

"Then it's a good thing I have this nation at my disposal."

"You will, until you've reduced it to ash and have nothing left to burn but yourself."

The Prince-Regent's fingers curled into a fist, and he opened his mouth to reply, but a knock on the door interrupted him and a muffled, robotic voice said, "Prince-Regent?"

With a dirty glare in Saizou's direction, the Prince-Regent rose to his feet. "Come in."

Kirikizu pushed the doors open and strode into the room. His eyes went from Saizou to the Prince-Regent, and Saizou wondered how many times Kirikizu had entered this bedchamber and seen someone trapped in the glass cage.

The Prince-Regent snapped his fingers, rings clinking. "You have a report for me?"

"Yes, Your High—"

"No." The Prince-Regent held up a finger. He turned his head to look at Saizou and said, "Call me *my lord*."

Saizou broke his gaze away from the Prince-Regent's and looked instead at Kirikizu, unsure what was happening. It felt significant, although he did not know why.

Kirikizu was watching the Prince-Regent, his eyes a fraction wider than they had been before, although his posture gave away no surprise. A second passed; then he bowed his head a few inches and acquiesced. "Yes, my lord."

"I want you to wait a moment before giving me your report."

There was a single moment of silence. "Yes, my lord."

"Now come here."

It was bizarre to watch. Saizou saw Kirikizu's face go blank, any visible thoughts stripped immediately away as he walked toward the Prince-Regent and stopped maybe two feet away.

The Prince-Regent smiled and walked around behind Kirikizu, placing his hands on his shoulders. "Kneel."

Saizou straightened, his pulse quickening as his discomfort grew. Whatever was happening, the blank look on Kirikizu's face confirmed that it was nothing good. "Hey."

The Prince-Regent gave Saizou a coy expression as Kirikizu sank to his knees. There was no hesitation in the assassin's movements, but where the lines of his body had been graceful and lithe before, they stiffened as his knees met the floor.

"Now." The Prince-Regent raked his fingernails through Kirikizu's thick, dark hair and continued to look at Saizou. "Tell me what you found, in detail."

Saizou saw Kirikizu begin to glance back toward the Prince-Regent, but he stopped himself. "There isn't much to tell."

"You let me worry about that. Continue. In detail."

Saizou got to his feet and stepped closer to the glass. The Prince-Regent was making a statement, that much was clear. "I get it," he snapped. "You're powerful. You don't need to prove it to me."

"That is for me to decide, I think," the Prince-Regent replied archly.

Kirikizu went on. "The furniture in the workspace had been knocked over. Most of it was broken or damaged in some way."

The Prince-Regent slid his fingers down Kirikizu's neck, under the folds of his shirt. "How many pieces of furniture remained intact?"

"Two. One shelf and a smaller table, under the window."

"Good. Remove your shirt and continue."

There it was—a flash of...something almost like fear, almost like rage. It passed over Kirikizu's face as quickly as a bolt of lightning across a roiling sky as he unbuckled the leather straps across his midriff and pulled the garment over his head.

The Prince-Regent took the shirt and tossed it onto the floor, looking at Saizou all the while. He was putting on a show for Saizou's benefit, and Saizou was painfully, agonizingly aware of it.

"Stop."

"No," said the Prince-Regent. "I answer to no one. You see?" He bent down behind Kirikizu and ran his hands slowly over his bare shoulders, down his chest. "I said continue," he said, a sharp edge in his voice at Kirikizu's silence.

"That's all. I said there wasn't much to report," said Kirikizu. As the Prince-Regent's tongue met Kirikizu's neck, Saizou saw him flinch.

"Enough." The word felt lost in Saizou's throat, but he knew he had said it. He repeated the word again, louder. "Enough!"

The Prince-Regent licked a slow line up Kirikizu's throat, onto the muzzle wrapped around his face. Without looking over he said, "It pains you to watch this, doesn't it?"

Saizou swallowed and glanced away from Kirikizu. He was lithe and strong and, according to Riza, as deadly as they came. "How can you sit there?" he demanded, clenching his hands into fists. "Why don't you do something?"

"Silly Saizou doesn't know," said the Prince-Regent in a singsong voice as his hands continued to roam. "He doesn't understand. What are you, Kirikizu, my flower?"

The answer came too quickly, too practiced. "Yours," said Kirikizu quietly, staring at the floor.

Saizou felt his heart pounding hard enough to make him sick.

"See, Saizou." The Prince-Regent's smile was suddenly the vilest thing Saizou had ever seen. "You have very noble thoughts, but they're misguided. People without power are restrained, caged by lack of ability or resources. And yet good, decent men like yourself...frankly, they kind of disgust me. They settle for so little."

"I would rather settle for little than abuse anyone underneath me," said Saizou, grinding the words between his teeth. "You have no right."

"Abuse? No right?" For the first time, the Prince-Regent sounded genuinely surprised. "I have every right. I just told you. Kirikizu is mine, to use however I want. You don't abuse a gun by firing it." He lifted his hand to Kirikizu's chin and tilted his gently head to the side. "Tell him."

"I am yours, my lord."

The Prince-Regent's eyes gleamed. "To use however I want?"

"Yes."

Saizou felt his mind slipping, shaken with rage. His stomach churned with the knowledge that he was about to witness a rape not fifteen feet away and there was nothing he could do to prevent it. "I said that's enough!" He slammed his fist against the glass once, twice, until his knuckles split and bled.

"Are you trying to tell me what to do?" The Prince-Regent's eyebrows both rose, then plunged back down as his face turned into a grimace. "I hate it when people do that, Akita. I was in a pleasant mood before you did that." He snapped his fingers. "Remove the rest of your clothes, Kirikizu."

Saizou stepped away from the glass, his hands lifted,

unsure of what to do with them or how to react. His stomach twisted like a pit of snakes, and his heart was beating hard enough to make him dizzy. "I've seen enough. I get it. You're powerful. Stop."

"No," said the Prince-Regent. .

Saizou felt his rage boiling into a scream, but just then —*thank God, thank God*—the doors opened and the Crane rushed into the room, her shoes clicking rapidly on the floor.

She took in the entire scene with a brief, scathing glance before saying in an urgent voice, "Mamushi, you need to come see this."

The Prince-Regent's face paled in anger at the interruption, but he straightened, as though he knew the Crane would not interrupt him without a good reason. "What is it?"

"They don't need to know. Come with me." She turned and hastily exited the room.

The Prince-Regent spun on his heel and smiled at Saizou: a sharp, crocodile grin. "Maybe we'll finish later," he said, before turning and following the Crane out of the bedchamber.

Saizou leaned his forehead against the glass and slid to his knees, mirroring the position Kirikizu was still in. "Hey," he said, his voice strangely hoarse in his ears. "You." Gently, he rapped his knuckles on the glass, leaving smears of blood. "Assassin." No, that felt wrong. The man had a name. "Kirikizu."

Kirikizu's deep sigh trembled through his muzzle. Slowly, as if standing was painful and he was too tired, he got to his feet. He did not even cast a glance at Saizou as he turned and walked over to his shirt, discarded on the floor.

As he picked it up, Saizou said, "The Prince-Regent doesn't own you. You're not his property. Just because he says something doesn't make it true."

"You don't understand, Akita." Kirikizu's voice sounded heavy, even through the muzzle, as he pulled his shirt over his head and re-buckled the straps across his stomach with practiced fingers.

"I know I don't," said Saizou, but Kirikizu's resignation was a knife-edge under his skin, and he couldn't let go. "Explain it to me. Why do you stay? Why do you put up with that treatment?"

"It's none of your concern, Akita."

"None of yours either, or so it seems." Saizou shifted his jaw, angry with an anger that surprised him. "You must be content, otherwise someone with your skills and abilities wouldn't still be here. I didn't mean to question."

Kirikizu angled a dark look at Saizou and adjusted his belt. "I have nothing to say to you."

"And what if the Prince-Regent comes back to finish, like he said?" Saizou demanded. "Will you still have nothing to say?"

"No," said Kirikizu. "I will have nothing to say."

"I don't want to see that happen."

"Then close your eyes," snapped Kirikizu. It was the loudest Saizou had ever heard him speak, and it shocked him into silence long enough for Kirikizu to say, quieter this time, "You don't seem to understand reality. Words don't change anything. Life is what it is, and the sooner you accept that, the more at peace you will be."

"You aren't at peace," Saizou growled, hitting the glass with the side of his fist one more time. "And words might not change anything, but your actions could."

Kirikizu turned his back on Saizou and strode toward the doors. "Your friend will die soon."

Numbness washed over Saizou, stilling him as he processed the out-of-place statement. But Kirikizu did not stop there.

Glancing over his shoulder at the glass cage, he said, "There is an antidote, but I wouldn't hold my breath. I don't foresee him getting it in time."

Then Kirikizu left, shutting the doors behind him, and leaving Saizou to wonder whether he had really heard a note of regret in Kirikizu's voice.

Saizou swallowed a sudden sob and shut his eyes before cracking the back of his head against the glass once, twice, three times. *Shi, you will not die. You will not.*

"Saizou, step back."

Saizou opened his eyes at the sound of the familiar female voice. He leaped to his feet and turned, searching the room. "Tsuki?"

"No time," she said in a commanding, disembodied voice. "We're freeing you."

# THIRTY-SIX

"FIFTY HOURS," Oscar muttered, checking on the creature's vital signs. "Fifty bloody hours, and not a wink of sleep. That's catastrophe in the making. It's also very much NOT ALLOWED IN LEGITIMATE WORKPLACES," he shouted at the door.

The EKG beeped, and Oscar walked around the table and studied the readings on the computer screen. The creature's heartbeat was regular—a good, steady pulse. It was much better than he expected. "That's great," he said, frowning in bewilderment as he glanced back at the table. "Perfect, actually."

A multilayered, full-body scan had also shown a perfect reading: vitals were healthy and well-grown, everything working as it should. There were a few readings he didn't quite understand, but given the thing had been grown from a soup, that was hardly surprising.

The only element left to concern him now was the creature's brain. He rubbed his hands over his face, his vision watering with exhaustion and overthinking. The incubator had finished preparing the creature's body an hour before the

Prince-Regent had waltzed in and flung the door open, but the body wasn't the part that took the longest. The brain had to be incubated and grown and finished far longer than the rest of the body. And instead of six hours, it got one.

One bloody hour.

"You're going to be a real charmer, you are," Oscar told the creature. For all he knew, the only thing that had really sunk into the creature's brain was the program the Prince-Regent had specifically ordered to fit inside it.

The Japanese had too much time on their hands, Oscar had decided, as the Prince-Regent handed him a vial of pink liquid filled with programmed, microscopic nano particles. Those had been fed into the brain quickly enough, but that was it. Oscar didn't even know what the particles were, only that he'd been assured they would work.

Wonderfully reassuring.

"Don't see what could go wrong," Oscar said, turning off the EKG and pulling the various wires off the creature's body.

The thing was, he didn't know how long he should let the creature remain unconscious. Should he give him some adrenaline and wake him up, or would that be too dangerous? Should he let him sleep and awaken naturally, or was he possibly in some kind of coma?

He studied the creature, lying motionless on the table, his hands palms-up at his sides. He was small. Oscar got out a measuring tape. Five feet four inches. Well, whatever the Prince-Regent wanted with him was his business.

All factors considered, the creature was physically about thirty years old, but he had a very delicate face, somehow youthful. His face would have been round, if not for the deeply angled cheekbones. Oscar tilted the creature's head, studying it upside-down. A few odd markings had appeared on the creature's skin, its tangled black hair was shot through with streaks of white, and streaks of inky black ran down its neck and sides. He lifted an eyelid and almost jumped; the eye didn't resemble a human's so much as cat's, the pupil shrinking to a fine line as light touched it.

Oscar frowned, leaning closer to look at a small, almost imperceptible ridge on the creature's forehead. "What is that?" he mused aloud, placing his thumbs on either side of it. He pulled gently, and this time he did jump back.

The thing had a bloody third eye on its forehead.

He cleared his throat and glanced at the camera that watched him. He tapped the creature on the forehead above the third eye. "Wake up, would you? I can't go to sleep and leave you here. The last thing I want to do—" he stifled a huge yawn "—is pump you full of morphine." He paused. "Then again, they say growing kids need sleep." He scratched the back of his head and didn't bother to stifle the next enormous yawn.

"Fine," he said, shaking his head. "I'm going to lie down right here." He pointed at the cot pushed up against the wall. "You need anything and you just wake me up, all right? All right. Good."

As he collapsed onto the cot and tucked his arm under his head, Oscar felt his thoughts running together, growing blurry until only one thought remained: *Just forty winks. Just forty...*

———

"SNAP OUT OF IT, Saizou. You can't see us, but we're here."

"We?" Saizou turned, following the sound of Tsuki's voice. This wasn't real; it couldn't be real. He had lost it completely.

"Kiba's here, too. Now turn around and face the back wall. Cover your face."

Saizou obeyed, facing the back wall and lifting his arms around his head. There was a loud crackling sound, as if lightning had struck the glass cage. There was a split second of silence before another sound followed, fainter, like ice breaking underfoot, and the front wall of the cage shattered.

Saizou turned, staring at the mess and then beyond it at the seemingly empty room. He couldn't bring himself to believe that his mind wasn't simply conjuring an illusion born of sheer desperation, but then he saw glass scatter across the floor and something touched his arm. He jumped, and a gruff, clipped voice said, "Come with us."

He recognized that voice; the Shadow. Kiba had come with Tsuki. "What is this?" he demanded, stepping back, reaching for a gun he didn't have.

"Listen, Saizou, I'll explain everything as soon as we're out of the palace walls, but for now, you need to put this on and come with us."

Saizou began to ask, "Put what on?" but he didn't have time —something grabbed hold of his hand and slid a bracelet around his wrist. It was made of simple red beads, but as soon as it was on, he could see Tsuki standing in front of him, flushed and impatient.

Kiba stood beyond the line of broken glass with something that looked like a foot-long baton in his hand. "Hurry," he said, barely sparing Saizou a glance. "Out the window."

Tsuki took Saizou's hand, and he felt a strange, indescribable sensation hit him like longing, or the shock of waking from a dream.

He began to run but stopped himself after three strides. "No. Wait."

Tsuki stared at him, aghast. "We don't have *time* for this."

"The Prince-Regent's Hand." Saizou glanced at Kiba,

whose expression might as well have been carved from stone. "I'm not leaving without him."

Kiba's eyebrows arched simultaneously. "We're not here to negotiate with you, punk. Come or stay."

"You got in here. I'll ask how later," said Saizou, hardly able to believe what he was saying. "But if you have the means to do that, then you have the means to find him. Or just give them to me and I'll go get him myself, but I can't leave him here."

"Are you insane?" Tsuki cried, whirling to stare at Kiba, as if he held the answer to Saizou's behavior.

Kiba pressed his lips together. His eyes narrowed into dark, glittering crescents, and he said, "I'll find him. Take Saizou and get out."

"There's an antidote," Saizou pressed, shaking his head. "I have to find that first."

"An antidote for *what?*" Tsuki's face held more frustration than Saizou had ever seen, but he couldn't think about her, not in this situation.

"Shi was poisoned. One-Eye has the antidote somewhere. Shi needs it within the next ten hours or he'll die. I don't have time to argue about it."

Kiba shot Tsuki a dark look as if to say *I told you this was a terrible idea.* "We don't have time."

"I didn't ask for a rescue party," Saizou exploded, stepping away from Tsuki. He pressed his palms against his thighs and took a deep breath, attempting to calm his spinning head. "Get out. I'll find a way out of the palace without you." He lifted his head and felt his expression soften when he looked at Tsuki. "Thank you for coming."

"Oh, I don't think so," Tsuki snapped. "There's no way I'm leaving you here. Not after we went to all this trouble."

"Take him," barked Kiba, gesturing toward the window with a strong sweep of his arm. "I'll get both."

"You don't know where they are," Tsuki began, but Kiba slipped out of the doors and shut them behind him with a hollow bang.

Tsuki stared at Saizou. "You really have a way of doing the unexpected, you know that?"

Saizou said nothing and crossed over to the window instead, unlocking and opening it. He glanced outside, then backed in. "One guard about ten yards to the right. I'll handle him."

"I'm the invisible one," said Tsuki, and leaped lightly out the window.

It was surreal, watching Tsuki race toward the guard without the guard noticing. He simply stood, oblivious, until Tsuki attacked him, leaping onto his shoulders and bringing him down as if he were nothing more than an obstacle in her way. She stamped her boot onto his head, and Saizou heard the snap from his vantage point.

He jumped out the window after her. "Where—"

"Follow me," she said, and ran in the other direction.

———

VIRGO NUDGED SHIMO'S ARM. They were still camped out at the top of the ridge, a third of a mile away from the docks. They had taken turns sleeping while the other kept watch. Now, for the first time in hours, something was happening. "Hey. Wake up."

Shimo groaned softly and sat up, unfolding his red alligator-skin jacket from where he had been using it as a pillow. "What?"

"Look." Virgo nodded toward the docks, specifically the storage unit holding the fugitives.

Shimo reached up and lifted his binoculars off the seat of his Scorpia. Virgo grinned. He supposed it was the competitive streak that came with being thirteen minutes younger than Shimo, but he enjoyed holding his advantage over his twin's head. Virgo's eyes were an unnatural silver with clearer vision than was naturally possible, according to the first optometrist he'd ever been to. He could see perfectly well in any light.

Shimo had a very different talent. He squinted to see as far as the storage unit, even with the binoculars. Instead he lifted his head, his nostrils flaring delicately as he breathed in the wind and frowned. "Is that the boss?"

"Hiro, I think. That's definitely him. Nobody else is that pale, not even gaijin."

"He's not going to feed them," said Shimo. "He doesn't have food with him."

"Maybe he's moving them," Virgo suggested, tilting his head. "Oh. Crap."

"What's 'crap'?"

"If you don't already know—"

"Besides what comes out of your mouth."

Virgo pointed. "He has a gun with a silencing cap."

Shimo jumped to his feet, shrugging his jacket on and cinching it at the waist. "Let's go."

"He's drawing. No time," said Virgo. He lifted his rifle to his shoulder, watched the red dot land on Hiro's back, and fired.

# THIRTY-SEVEN

KIBA HAD LONG AGO LEARNED the key to inner stillness. Patience, his father had often told him, was a virtue one could not afford to lack, and stillness was achieved only after patience. As the book said, one must be quick to listen, but slow to wrath.

The key to stillness was to view every aggravation as a moral challenge. If an aggravation succeeded in angering him, a petty enemy had won a victory. Petty enemies should never be allowed to win. It was a humiliation far above an average battle —in an average battle, the enemy was an equal, a worthy opponent.

So when Saizou foolishly claimed he would not leave without the Prince-Regent's Hand—a lethal assassin infamous from one end of Japan to the other—as well as an antidote for his injured friend, Kiba took a deep breath and thought *stillness. You are a stone washed smooth by the rushing water around you.*

As Rumi said, if you were irritated by every rub, how would you be polished? And no rub was as irritating to Kiba as Saizou.

Kiba ground his teeth as he raced down the hall, toward the front of the palace. Nix was providing a distraction, and no doubt the Prince-Regent's hand would be nearby. Tsuki had suggested the kitsune rescue Saizou while she and Kiba created a distraction, but Nix pointed out that he could cloak them both without getting himself injured. If she and Kiba provided a distraction, they were vulnerable to arrows, blades, and whatever artillery was available to the Prince-Regent's guards.

Kiba glanced down at the electric baton in his hand. He flicked his thumb across the pad, lowering the charge. He might be invisible to most in his current state, but there was no guarantee he could capture the Prince-Regent's Hand without harming him if he used a blade. He would have to forego the use of swords. Electricity was not a form of combat he was particularly well-versed in, but he supposed, as he rounded the corner, there was a first time for everything.

———

KIRIKIZU RAN down the front steps, his swords drawn. The Prince-Regent's face was aghast as Kiko stood in front of him, staring at the chaos. Soldiers ran in every direction, their swords and reizaa-naginatas whipping through the air as they tried to hit...what?

The form was unclear and muted, like a drop of ink in a glass of water. It was a humanoid shape, but it passed through the gauntlet of whirling blades with ease, darting in and out of reach with leaping, slinking movements.

For one split moment, Kirikizu thought he saw something inside the smear of colors, but too quickly the form faded once again into a cloud of gray, lit through with orange, a blur of smoke and flame.

"Get the Prince-Regent inside," Kirikizu shouted at Kiko. He could hardly believe she was just standing here while the Prince-Regent was vulnerable and unprotected—it showed a severe lack of competence. "Now!"

A black scowl passed over Kiko's face, and she pointed toward the mayhem. "You'd better catch him, or else," she snapped, and took the Prince-Regent's arm, pulling him back up the stairs. He whirled about and followed her, his steps carrying him past Kiko in his rush to get away.

Kirikizu strode across the hard-packed dirt, cold clouds of dust kicked up in the frenzy. He sheathed his left sword and drew a shuriken from the same pouch in which rested the ear cuff he had found at the crime scene.

He didn't want to waste a sword by throwing it through an intangible shape, but perhaps he could secure the creature's attention. He threw the shuriken at the head of the figure. It passed harmlessly through, but the whirl of gray and orange spun like a tornado and faced Kirikizu, seeming to loom larger than it had before.

Kirikizu drew his left sword again and was struck with a sensation like wind, like a tropical storm slamming into a coastline.

He leaned back like a tree bending in the wind, letting most of the force pass over him. Then he spun, righting himself, and cut at the figure's legs with both swords. The figure dodged nimbly around it with inhuman speed. Kirikizu was fast. Faster than anyone else he knew, yet he felt slow by comparison.

The figure whipped around him, and Kirikizu realized what bothered him about the dematerialized form.

It had not seriously injured anyone.

As Kirikizu jumped high and twisted, slicing through the air, he realized the Thing's movements seemed playful. It was like a dog nipping mischievously at a stranger's heels. Like it wanted to play.

There was no reason for its behavior, no reason for it to want to risk 'playing' inside the palace walls.

Unless...

Kirikizu turned and ran up the stairs, pushing his way through the stream of guards jogging out of the palace, prepared to provide reinforcement. It would do no good, but Kirikizu had no time to tell them—the creature was either idiotic or a distraction, and he doubted a creature with supernatural abilities would behave stupidly without a reason.

He raced down the long hall, past the dozen looming pillars usually guarded by a soldier each, more for looks than anything else.

He rounded the corner, angling for the Prince-Regent's bedchamber and the prisoner within, but something stopped him. A sound?

He glanced over his shoulder. If it was a sound, it did not repeat itself, but his skin crawled with the sense that something was watching, waiting to pounce.

Kirikizu twirled out of the way as something sizzled past his head, crackling through the air. The assailant couldn't be the same one outside the palace steps—he could still hear the commotion, even from this far inside the palace.

If that creature was the distraction, then this assailant was the infiltrator.

He turned, creating an X in the air with both blades, protecting his torso as he listened for another sound. He heard it, something faint, like a breath—and lashed out, cutting a slice across the air with his left sword while slicing his right sword in the opposite direction.

Blood splattered onto the wall by his head. His opponent could bleed, then, unlike the creature outside.

Good.

He sliced his swords through the air again, flicking more blood off the blades onto the floor, and spun. He could sense the person there, feel their energy shift as he turned. He struck again, felt something touch him—

Brilliant white light flashed across his vision like an electrical storm, and then darkness.

————

THE PRESSURE of the bullet knocked Hiro forward, slamming him into the door of the storage unit. The pain caught up several seconds later as his mind still reeled from the shock of the attack.

Hiro turned, grinding his teeth against the burning pain lodged in his back like a lit match. He lifted his gun with his left hand, his right shoulder in too much pain to use, and fired. He saw headlights in the distance—two sets. He fired twice before reaching down and hauling the door of the storage unit open. Whoever was on the ridge had a rifle, perhaps two of them—handguns didn't shoot that far, and he couldn't shoot back until they were closer.

"You three," he demanded, gesturing toward the open with his gun. "Out."

Shotgun was already standing. "What's going on? Is someone shooting at us?"

"This unit isn't bulletproof," Hiro barked. "Out, now!"

Shotgun turned and looked at the back of the unit where Fumiyo clutched Shi's arm. "I don't think he can move."

Hiro pointed his pistol at Shotgun. "Pick him up!"

Shotgun's eyes widened, but one look at the end of Hiro's gun and he crouched, gathering Shi in his arms. To Fumiyo, he said, "I know you don't like me, but—"

Fumiyo darted past Shotgun, toward Hiro.

"Right," said Shotgun. "Good." He nodded toward Hiro. "Where do we go?"

Hiro pointed toward the dock. "Get in the water, stay out of sight."

"What about you?" Fumiyo blurted as he turned, watching the pair of approaching headlights cut through the gray dawn. "Oh—you're sh—"

"I know! Go with him before I shoot you myself," Hiro snapped. He moved quickly around the side of the unit and crouched down. He hadn't heard a gunshot; they had high-quality silencers, as did he. It made for a very quiet gunfight—he doubted Kido or Yuu would hear anything, and nobody else was scheduled to show up until midmorning.

There were two of them, and they had good aim and professional gear: mercenaries, probably. Who hired them didn't matter; once someone was trying to kill you, that was it. He would survive now and ask questions later. Yuu could get the information out of whichever attacker Hiro let live.

———

VIRGO AND SHIMO slowed down within three hundred yards of the storage unit. "Blood," said Virgo. "I hit him."

"You didn't kill him."

"He's a yakuza boss. You really think he hasn't been shot before?" Virgo rested his rifle over his shoulder. "Smell anything?"

"Water." Shimo nodded toward the ocean, lapping at the docks. "We're too close to it now."

Virgo nodded and dismounted the Scorpia. "You stay here. I'll rat him out and send him your way."

"Right." Shimo unhooked his electric crossbow from its position on the rear of his seat. "Hurry up. I haven't eaten in six hours."

"Gotcha." Virgo nodded one more time at his twin and broke into a lope. He reached the splatter of blood on the asphalt and turned in a wide circle, probing the shadows surrounding the various storage units, stacked like a child's alphabet blocks. That's what they reminded him of: the toys he and Shimo had used as kids. He'd have to remember to tell Shimo that.

"Hey," he called, eyeing the alley created between two larger units. Nothing. "Come out, come out, and make my job easier." He cocked his head, listening, but heard nothing. Not the scuff of a shoe, not the bang of an elbow against a metal wall. This guy was slippery.

"I do this kind of thing for a living," he continued, his voice echoing between the units as he walked in front of them, ready to jump or drop at the first sound. "You push paper and give orders, right? I've got the upper hand. I'm curious, though," he went on. "You kept those fugitives safe all night. Why the sudden decision to blow them away? It wasn't the Prince-Regent, otherwise this place'd be crawling with palace samurai. Oh—wait."

Virgo stopped walking and lifted his rifle to his shoulder. "You realized Akita was missing. I'll bet that's what it was. All of a sudden, three unled fugitives became kinda risky, so wanting to kill them makes sense. You don't need to worry about them; we're not here to kill them. Just you."

———

HIRO CROUCHED low atop the storage unit and watched the bounty hunter stroll cautiously past. Well, now he knew they were here to kill him specifically. That simplified the situation. He crept toward the edge of the unit, and as soon as the other man disappeared, he sprang from one roof to the next.

The calculation was simple: there were two bounty hunters. One was quite a distance away—if they were a team, they would work together as one. No doubt this bounty hunter would attempt to herd him toward the other, if he couldn't kill him alone.

All he had to do was break them up.

He guessed the distance to be roughly three hundred yards between him and the other bounty hunter. His handgun wasn't a sniper rifle, but it was custom-made. He lifted it with his left hand, dropped his right shoulder to minimize the pain in his back, and fired.

## THIRTY-EIGHT

"YOU'D BETTER HAVE an exit plan beyond jumping out the window," said Saizou, his back pressed flat against the wall.

"Nix will be here any second. That's the exit plan." Several strands of hair had fallen out of the confines of their ponytail and were clinging to Tsuki's damp forehead.

"If takes much longer, we can't wait for him."

"You'll be seen the second you go around that corner," she pointed out. "Just be patient for a minute."

"That's rich, coming from you."

She laughed a little. "That's fair."

Saizou held up his wrist, indicating the bracelet of red beads encircling it. "What is this?"

"Nix is keeping me and Kiba cloaked. He said he can't expend the energy to provide a distraction and cloak three people, so that's the best he can do."

"Who is this Nix person?"

"He's—" she began, but Kiba raced around the corner, moving at an impressive rate considering the long body slung over his shoulder.

"Back gate!" he barked. "Now!"

Tsuki grabbed Saizou's arm and pulled, but he was already following Kiba's orders.

A sound split the dawn—a sound somehow made of mist-wreathed mountains, of helpless screams and lonely wolves howling at the moon.

Tsuki looked back, distress crossing her face. Saizou saw her body language change, thinking, angling back. "Nix—"

This time, Saizou twisted her hold on him and clamped his hand around her wrist, turning the tables and pulling her behind him. "No time."

"You don't understa—"

"You! Put your hands behind your heads and get on your knees, now!"

Saizou let go of Tsuki's wrist and turned to see a tall, white-armored samurai flanking them, his reizaa-naginata glowing like a demon's eyes in the gray light.

"What the hell?" The samurai angled his head, and Saizou glanced at Tsuki, then Kiba—with the body of the Prince-Regent's Hand draped over his shoulder.

"Can he see that?" asked Saizou suddenly.

Tsuki nodded, her eyes wide, her stance widening, ready to fight. "He can't see Kiba or myself."

"Shut up!" the samurai barked, obviously still staring at Kirikizu's limp form. "Drop—uh, get on the ground! On your knees! Now!"

"I'll handle him," Tsuki said in a low voice. "You do what he says."

Saizou lifted his hands and placed them on the back of his head, then slowly sank to his knees.

"What is that?" the samurai demanded, his scowling mask nodding toward Kirikizu. "How are you doing that?"

Saizou shrugged. "He's following me home."

The samurai began to stride forward, towards Kiba, who remained where he was.

As he passed her, Tsuki gripped the staff of the reizaa-naginata and wrenched it to the side, twisting her body so the surprised samurai spun, thrown down by his own weight.

Tsuki lifted the weapon and plunged the glowing end through the samurai's helmet. She pulled it back out and dropped it. "We need to hurry!"

Saizou began to run again. They rounded the corner of the last outbuilding, and the back gates now loomed in sight. They were firmly shut, and without the code to open them, they would remain that way.

"Your friend going to fix this, too?" asked Saizou, glancing both ways. They were far too exposed, far too open. The palace samurai would descend on them like a swarm of ants any second. Twenty seconds. They had twenty seconds at best.

The sound of thunder rumbled low through the air. Saizou would have paid no particular attention if the sound had not increased, growing louder and deeper until it shook the ground.

It stopped as quickly as it began, but a crack was now visible in the gates ahead.

How much could this friend of theirs do?

They reached the opening, and Kiba nodded at Tsuki, holding Kirikizu's unconscious body securely over his shoulder. "Go."

A brief movement flashed across the space between the gates. Saizou jumped forward, pushing Tsuki to the ground as a black reizaa-naginata sliced through the opening. Saizou felt the heat of the laser blade on his face, felt pressure knock him backwards as a black-clad palace samurai pushed his way through the space.

The newcomer twirled the staff over his head and around his body in a whirlwind of laser-blades, forcing Saizou back as he prepared to strike, to cut Saizou in half.

A figure materialized just behind the samurai and whistled, sharp and clear as a bell.

The samurai spun, but his reizaa-naginata cut through the figure's torso with no resistance, as if the figure was only a trick of the light.

Stunned, the samurai faltered, and Saizou tackled the samurai from behind, knocking him to the ground.

That was the thing about these suits of armor, Saizou thought as he wrestled the reizaa-naginata from the samurai's grasp—they were all well and good while you were on your feet, but once you were knocked down, they were cumbersome. They trapped you.

He let go of the staff and instead gripped each side of the samurai's helmet and wrenched it back and to the side. He felt the bone break in his hands like a thick, dry stick. He picked up the weapon, now limp in the dead samurai's hands, and stood.

He shook his head, his vision spinning. No, not spinning—gone, black. The heat from the reizaa-naginata must have burned his face—he reached up and felt near his eye. He brought his hand back down, his fingers coated in a sticky, bloody substance.

*What—?*

A figure materialized in front of Saizou—or did he just walk around his right side? Saizou shook his head again, as if trying to rid himself of a buzzing fly.

"Hey, friend," said the copper-haired newcomer, "so sorry about this."

The ground rose to meet Saizou, but he never felt himself hit it.

———

HIRO SAW the bounty hunter slide off the seat of his vehicle. He lowered his gun and jumped to the ground. One less assailant to worry about. The closer one was loud; if this was how he approached everyone he hunted, the fact of his existence was surprising.

Hiro decided to let the bounty hunter know where he was. He bent down and picked up a broken chunk of asphalt, the size of a beach pebble. He tossed it once, then chucked it over the roof of the nearest cargo box.

He heard it rattle along the top of the unit before coming to a stop and waited, listening.

Nothing.

So the bounty hunter *could* be quiet, then. Hiro took a gamble and turned to the left, pointing his gun down the narrow alley between two units. Something flashed between them, darting to the right, and Hiro ducked around the far corner, firing two silent shots at the bounty hunter. One shot went just over his assailant's head, the other clipped his ear.

He was fast. It was too bad he was a bounty hunter. Perhaps he could persuade him to join the Tokyo yakuza and put his skills to better, more reliable use?—but that would require a conversation he did not have time for.

Hiro decided to switch tactics. He raised his voice and called, "I shot your partner."

No sound, no movement responded to his statement. Hiro crept along the front of another unit and peered around the corner, every nerve on edge in case he needed to dodge or duck.

Then there was sound—footsteps, running back toward the vehicles.

*Gotcha.* Hiro took off, racing silently in pursuit of the

bounty hunter's footsteps. He heard several muffled shots, but they went wild, passing him by several feet on either side.

Suddenly the clouds overhead, already thinning and ragged in several places, drifted apart. The bright sunlight hit Hiro like the blast of heat from an open oven; he threw his arm over his eyes, squinting against the flash of light, hissing as the heat seared his skin.

He turned back and raced into the shadow of the nearest cargo box. He crouched, his hands clenched into fists, his teeth grinding against the pain. He was not prepared to be outside this long. Shooting three fugitives and lighting them on fire would have taken ten minutes at most. He should have been back inside before the sun burned away the cloud cover.

In his mind, he swore again and again, cursing his own lack of preparedness. He shaded his eyes with a hand and looked at the sky—there was a chance the cloud cover would return long enough for him to go inside, grab his sunglasses and a jacket, and head back out. If not, he would have to alert Yuu and Kido to his situation.

He heard a purring engine roar to life as the bounty hunter took off. He had nailed one of them in the chest; it might not have killed him, but they wouldn't be on his tail for a long while. Unless the healthy one decided to pull a revenge mission, which bounty hunters weren't likely to do unless they got paid.

In fact, if he could justify dredging up the money, Hiro could probably pay the bounty hunter to leave him alone—but he was getting ahead of himself. He growled and turned his face toward the wall, drawing as deeply into the unit's shade as he could.

For now, he would wait.

———

OTTER DID NOT BOTHER to stifle the barrage of huge yawns that assailed her as she shuffled down the hall toward Haka's office, a cup of coffee in each hand. If he was awake, he would want one. It might appease his wrath when he realized what she'd done.

She pushed the door open, and her yawns ceased immediately when she saw the cot was empty, the blanket draped in a pile on the floor. "Commander?" She turned around, but he wasn't at the desk, either.

She frowned and took a sip of her own coffee before continuing down the hall to the shower room. Her hands occupied, she banged her forehead lightly against the door instead of knocking traditionally. "Hey, Commander, are you in there?"

"Yes," was the thin response from somewhere inside the room. A puzzled note entered his voice. "Why did you knock?"

"My hands are full."

"With what?"

"Coffee cups." Otter bent down and set Haka's cup on the floor and opened the door. She picked the cup back up and walked in, her head swinging left, then right. He was sitting on the floor with his back to the wide, glass door of the shower.

Otter swallowed the rush of fear—*does he know already? How bad is his withdrawal? Did I do the right thing? Is he furious at me? Am I killing him?*—and quelled it with sympathy. "I hate to break it to you, Commander, but that's not how you take a shower."

He opened his eyes with apparently monumental effort. "I'm not up to your sass right now."

That was a first. Otter walked over to him and settled down on her knees. "Can I do anything to help?"

"No sarcastic remark." He let out a deep sigh. "Amazing."

"Here." She set his cup of coffee down, then lifted his hand and wrapped his fingers around it. "There you go. It's strong, too. It ate the spoon." She chewed her lip, watching his haggard face and trying not to let her concern show through. "How do you feel?"

He pressed his lips together and shut his eyes again.

"Stupid question?" she asked.

Noiselessly, he lifted his right hand, his middle finger pointed toward the ceiling.

"My bad."

He lifted the cup of coffee. Otter glanced away when she noticed the ripples trembling across the surface of the beverage. He was shaking so much she was afraid the cup might spill over, yet he hadn't mentioned the drugs. Yet.

Maybe it was her lucky day.

He swallowed the hot coffee like it was cold water before crumbling the Styrofoam and letting the crumpled cup fall to the floor.

"Can I do anything to help?"

"You can put them back where you got them."

Otter swallowed hard and opened her eyes wider to compensate for the horrible look of suspicion she knew had appeared on her face. "Put what back where?"

"You know damn well what. Stop it. I'm not in the mood."

Otter licked her lips and leaned back—not out of his reach, but the slight lengthening in distance between them made her feel better. "I didn't—"

"Don't." His voice was cold, colder than Otter had ever heard it. It sank into her bones like frostbite, numbing her from the inside out. "I know you," he continued. "You thought, 'why not hide them while he's unconscious?' I appreciate the thought, but put them back."

He was trying to control his temper. He really was trying, and it twisted Otter's gut. "Why can't you just yell at me for hiding them?" she snapped.

"Otter."

"I'm not putting them back. Here." She plopped her half-full cup of coffee down next to his left hand. "Drink that, too."

She moved to stand up but fell back in surprise as he knocked the cup against the wall, splashing steaming coffee across the floor. "Put the stardust where you found it before I fire you."

"You can't fire me, and you know it," she retorted, her heart pounding against her ribcage like a thing that wanted out. "I'm trying to help you; you have to understand—"

"I don't care!" He lunged to his feet with surprising speed, given how clumsy his movements were, still clogged with pain and sleep and haze. "Give it back to me! You have no right—"

"I don't need a right! I care about you, you stupid, stupid piece of *trash*; you'd be so much *better*…" Tears clogged Otter's throat and blurred her vision, and she wished to God she had clocked out for the day instead of hanging around waiting for him to wake up.

"It's none of your business what I do!" Haka's voice rose, but it was as though the effort it took to shout was too much. He sagged against the shower door, pitiful and pathetic and so, so in need of help.

"Sorry." Otter's whisper was so quiet she could barely hear herself. "I'm sorry. I can't give it back."

He was so tired. He'd been through so much; it hurt her like a punch to the heart when he simply looked at her and asked in a hoarse, weary voice, "Why?"

This was a horrible place to confess. In a bathroom after a night of torture and withdrawal—truly, she couldn't think of a worse place. But she didn't consider it; she only blurted, "I love you!"

Then she turned and fled from the room without bothering to shut the door. She pulled open the door to the dungeon and raced down the stairs. She'd had enough of humanity. She needed her monsters.

## THIRTY-NINE

WINTER HEARD the girl dashing down the stairs at a pace only those very familiar with the steps could maintain. She sounded upset, but not until she rounded the corner, striding purposefully past his cell, did he see her face, tear-streaked and reddened.

Without turning to look at him, she said, "Your brother is an idiot."

Winter responded, not so much out of curiosity as from habit. "What did he do now?"

Otter halted and turned, a startled expression crossing her face, like she hadn't actually expected him to reply to her statement. She hesitated, and Winter could see the questions crossing her face. Should she talk to him? He was a prisoner, after all.

"I don't have anything to do but listen," he said gently, rotating his shoulders as far as he could to relieve the tension in his neck. "How is he?"

"Haka," she said, fully facing the cell and folding her arms over her chest, "is a mess. I mean it. Literal, figurative, metaphorical—you name a way, it's a mess."

It was a polite understatement.

"Is he in pain?"

"I said he was a mess everywhere. Yeah, he's in pain. He was tortured, and you know, I'd love to be next to him, helping and all, but I kind of hid his drugs while he was out cold and he's not happy with me."

The amount of feeling in her voice surprised Winter. He loved Haka, if only because they were blood and it was as natural to love him as it was to love the blood flowing through his own veins. However, this girl clearly loved Haka with a different kind of emotion in spite of all he was, and all he did.

"Is he all right?"

Otter dug the heel of her hand into her left eye, then her right. She looked up, blinking rapidly, and shrugged. "No? I don't know. He's furious at me. And you know, he gave me a chance to give them back, too. A couple chances, actually. But like—what kind of person would I be if I just gave them back? But I don't know which is better. Actually, no, I do know, I just...I don't know. It's hard."

Winter's mind spun with Otter's words and implications, so he settled on voicing the first question that came to mind. "You kept the drugs, correct?"

She rolled her eyes, and her voice took on an insulted tone. "Duh. It's not like I'm yanking him off the drugs cold turkey. Geez. I don't want to kill him."

Winter nodded. Smart girl. "Good."

"Hey," said Otter suddenly, frowning. "You don't seem too upset, if you don't mind my saying."

"What don't I mind?"

"Any of this. The whole torture thing—oh, I mean you're

worried and all, but you don't seem terribly upset to be chained up in a dungeon. Kirikizu'll probably be back to finish you off at some point, you know."

"I know."

Her frown deepened. She uncrossed her arms and wrapped her hands around the bars of the cell. "No offense, but you're weird."

He felt himself smile a little, for the first time in his memory. "I know."

"Hey, is it true? You don't feel any pain? I heard Kirikizu mention it. That's why he tortured Haka instead, right?"

"That's right."

"I've never heard of that before. Does it have a name?"

"Congenital analgesia."

"That's intense. You've never felt pain?"

"Not physical."

"So I could set you on fire and you wouldn't feel anything?"

"I imagine my eyes would sting," said Winter. Her questions amused him. She was open and friendly and inquisitive—a stark contrast to Haka. Perhaps she was good for him.

Otter snorted, but her face softened as she said, "He never mentioned you. Not once."

"I'm not surprised. We did not part well."

"When was the last time you saw him?"

He didn't want to tell her how he had kept track of his little brother at every possible moment, how he had watched from a distance as Haka clawed his way through life and finally landed a respectable position. Winter had been so proud of him, despite the drugs. Despite everything, until the Prince-Regent's rule began to demand more and more illegal activity from the Shinsengumi. Until Haka bowed under the imperial thumb.

Winter sighed. "I was eighteen."

"How old was Haka?"

"Twelve."

Otter cocked her head to one side. Her eyes widened as she did the math, and she cried, "Are you telling me you haven't spoken to him in twenty years?"

Twenty years. It *had* been that long... "Yes."

"I've gathered you have issues." Otter held up both her hands. "I get that. But that might be the most hardcore estrangement I've ever heard of, and I've heard of some whoppers. Do you have any other siblings I don't know about?"

"You needn't worry. Our parents only had two children."

"Whew." Otter dramatically wiped her hand across her forehead but dropped it as the levity faded. "What happened?"

Winter knew what she meant. She wanted to know why they had broken apart, why it had been twenty years since he had spoken to his little brother. The only thing was, he preferred not to discuss it. He had pondered it enough as it was. "I'm sorry. That's none of your business."

"He's my business," she snapped, but leaned her forehead against the bars and sighed. "But I get it."

Winter regarded her with something almost like warmth for a long moment. Then he said, "He is not a violent person."

"Who, Haka?" She lifted her head. "I know that."

"However," he continued with a pointed look, "stardust is a popular drug among mercenaries and the like. I've seen it used many times. Consequently, I've seen what happens to strong men when it is taken from them."

Otter swallowed visibly. "So I should give it back?"

"No. You should be careful."

Slowly, she nodded, backing away from the bars. "I will."

Winter closed his eyes and let his shoulders sag again. Once the Prince-Regent's Hand came back, sore muscles would be the least of his concerns. He almost hoped they would be his last. Almost.

Every time the urge to end his life reared its head again, chewing through his reason and his faith, reminders came in small forms. Forms like Otter, who had not given him a reason to live, but reminded him that they existed. They reminded him that kind people existed, that good things happened in a world populated by sinners and failures. That every now and then, a green shoot pushed up through the hard, frozen ground.

He was not one of them, those signs of life, of goodness; but as he leaned his head back against the wall, a thought fluttered through his mind like a butterfly born on a wild breeze. *If I get out of here, I must find Fumiyo.*

———

THE PRINCE-REGENT SAT on the edge of his bed, his arms wrapped around himself as if for warmth. His head was bowed, his back stiff, and Kiko was almost afraid to approach him. She brushed away the gauze curtain surrounding the bed and sat on the edge opposite. "My prince?"

"They took him."

"Who, my prince?"

"Kirikizu. They took him. They actually stole him from me." The Prince-Regent turned, his face drawn and pale with fury. "How dare they?"

"I don't know," said Kiko, torn. She wanted to comfort Mamushi, but she hardly wished to help find Kirikizu and bring him back. If she handled the situation gingerly, it could prove the best opportunity she'd had yet. She shifted across the middle of the bed and wrapped an arm around the Prince-Regent's shoulders.

"Who knows what they want with him?" The Prince-Regent leaned into her embrace, welcoming her touch. Kiko felt her heart perform a strange kind of slow, exotic dance. Did the Prince-Regent know what it felt like? Could he hear it? Did his heart dance like this when he took Kirikizu in his arms?

The thought made Kiko's blood boil. She pressed a kiss against Mamushi's hair. "I don't know, my prince. We're trying to track them now, but we've found nothing helpful."

He gripped her arm with iron fingers. "They have to find him. You have to find him."

"I promise to do my best, but..." She let her sentence trail off diplomatically, leaving everything else to his imagination. *What if he is never found? What if he is dead when we do? What if...?*

"If they touch him," the Prince-Regent growled, his breath hot against her collarbone, "I will sever them into a thousand pieces and feed them to the Dog. I swear I will."

"Yes, my prince," Kiko soothed, looking over his head at the empty, broken glass cage. "Of course."

# FORTY

*"...DIDN'T HAVE TIME."*

*"I understand. Nobody would have, but...that's his friend. His good friend, from what I can tell. How are we going to..."*

*A deep sigh. "I'll tell him."*

*"No—no. I'll tell him. He might take it better coming from me."*

*"Or it may taint his opinion of you."*

*"You've done enough. At least let me handle this."*

Saizou listened to Tsuki and Kiba converse, his mind too foggy, too thick to put any pieces together. They were unhappy. He didn't know where he was. He couldn't move. Shi—no. Shi would not be here, just like the last time he'd woken up. He would regain his ability to move soon—he didn't want Tsuki to know about his sleep paralysis, but he absolutely did not want Kiba to know about it. He would keep his eyes shut and feign sleep until his motion returned.

*Blood rained from the black sky. The storm swelled around him—*

No. His sleep had been dreamless. *It's a reflex. A habit.*

"Not to interrupt or anything, but what the hey, I'll be the one to break the tough news to the guy." That voice was the unfamiliar one—the intangible, form-shifting creature. Nick? Nix? Nix.

*Tough news. Didn't have time...his good friend.*

*Me. My good friend?*

Shi.

*Shi.* Saizou curled his fingers toward his palms, forming half-fists; he didn't have the muscle range to clench them farther yet. Shi...the antidote. Kiba had seized Kirikizu but had failed to get the antidote for Shi.

Saizou had sent Kiba after both; Kiba had chosen one over the other. Saizou opened his eyes and found he could sit up. "What are you saying?" His voice was scratchy and rough, but his mind was clear enough now.

He was in a dingy square box of a place; a single-room apartment. He was on the bed, and Kirikizu was tightly bound and leaning against the far wall, his eyes shut. For a brief moment, Saizou wondered if he, too, was feigning his sleep, but it looked real. His body was too limp to be pretending.

Kiba straddled a chair, leaning back, his hands behind his head. Two bloody gashes carved a large X across his torso. Tsuki was in front of him with a sponge in her hand, an open first aid kit on the floor.

"Feeling better?" A hand on his shoulder made Saizou jump, but he wasn't ready for movement of that caliber. He bent forward, squeezing his eyes shut at the sudden clenching of his muscles when his brain told them to do something they could not.

"Whoah," said Nix, stepping around the other side of the cot. "You're a little jumpy, aren'cha?"

Saizou lifted his gaze to Tsuki's face. He said nothing, but he knew in his state, his expressions were too unguarded, too easy to read.

Tsuki pressed a hand against Kiba's shoulder, then walked over and crouched in front of Saizou. She pressed her hand against one of his. "I'm so sorry, Saizou. Truly."

"It's my fault," said Saizou flatly. He almost pulled his hand away but could not bring himself to. "I shouldn't have bothered with Kirikizu. I should have just asked for the antidote." The words tasted bitter and cold in his mouth, but he spat them out with no regret. He didn't have room for it. Shi was going to die, and because of a last-minute decision, it would be Saizou who killed him.

———

*"I SHOULDN'T HAVE BOTHERED with Kirikizu. I should have just asked for the antidote."*

The words pushed through Kirikizu's subconscious as he began to wake up, a fraction at a time. He assessed his situation by sound before opening his eyes—small room, wooden floor, plaster wall. Four voices: Saizou and three he did not recognize.

For reasons he couldn't fathom, Saizou's words stung, like vinegar sprinkled on an open wound he hadn't noticed until now. They hurt. They implied something that Kirikizu understood, but which confused him greatly.

Saizou's words indicated that he had 'bothered with' Kirikizu, that for some strange reason he could not grasp, Saizou had wanted Kirikizu brought here.

Saizou had a plan, no doubt something to use against the Prince-Regent. Kirikizu had to escape, and escape would be easy enough if he could remove his muzzle. He could kill everyone in the room before they had time to make a move against him—but he was tied, and he could tell the knots were not sloppy or loose. It would take time to free himself.

He opened his eyes and took in his dingy surroundings. Saizou sat on a cot to his right, and a foreigner—no, he wasn't a foreigner; he was Japanese, with a head of orange hair. Kirikizu recognized the other two. He knew Lady Tsuki and her bodyguard; he had seen them at the Imperial Ball.

"Well, look who's up!" said the orange-haired man, pointing at Kirikizu.

Kirikizu watched Saizou, who gazed back at him for a long, heavy moment before he stood and crossed over to the rusty sink sticking out of the side of the wall. He turned the faucet on, and water gurgled out at erratic intervals—brown with dirt at first, then clear after another moment. He splashed his face, smearing the black kohl around his good eye until, with his dark eyes and pale skin, he looked more wraith than man.

"What do we do with him?" This question came from Tsuki's bodyguard. Through the fog in his mind, Kirikizu wondered how Kiba had rendered himself invisible during their fight. He knew it had to be Kiba, from the gashes on his chest.

*It would be in your best interests to let me go.*

That was what Kirikizu wanted to say; those were the words he began to speak. But as soon as he said, "It would be—" an instant reaction cut him off halfway.

Everyone in the room cried out in pain and doubled over. Tsuki collapsed to the floor, blood streaming from her nose, while Kiba kicked his chair back and covered her ears. Saizou and the orange-haired man also covered their ears, but the screaming did not stop for a full eight seconds.

Silence fell again, and Kirikizu stared at the blood trickling from eyes and ears, at the ashen pallor that had swept over everyone's skin.

The orange-haired man recovered himself faster than anyone else. "Oh-kayyy," he said, and snapped his fingers. "That was *not* fun. Ow. I didn't enjoy that at all."

"What was that?" Saizou gasped, rising unsteadily to his feet. He reached out and pressed his hand against the wall for balance. Again, louder, he demanded, "What was that?" and winced at his own voice.

Kirikizu's mind raced.

His muzzle was electric. When Kiba electrocuted him, it must have shorted the filter, damaged something inside. Had he finished his sentence, he might have killed everyone in the room.

But he did not finish his sentence.

He regarded everyone in silence as they gathered and stared at him like visitors at a zoo exhibit, like he was something they had never seen before.

And they never had.

"I have less than no idea what that was," said the orange-haired man, scratching his ear, "but why hasn't it happened before?"

Kiba's gaze dropped to Kirikizu's mask. "I electrocuted him. The mask must have filtered his voice somehow."

"Nobody's voice has the ability to do that," said Saizou. He reached up to drag his sleeve across his eyes, but paused when the tip of his sleeve touched the gauze patch over his right eye. He hesitated.

"It's been bandaged," said Tsuki softly. "It's bleeding underneath. Sit down. I'll take care of it."

"Hold on a teensy-weensy second," said the orange-haired man, holding up both hands. "I personally think we ought to do something about..." He pointed toward Kirikizu. "You know. His adorable 'I can probably kill you all with my voice' thing."

Kiba reached down, his face barely registering a wince, and drew a knife from his boot. "I'll handle it."

Saizou stepped toward Kirikizu. "I won't allow it."

Kirikizu tilted his head. Why was he so valuable to Saizou? Were they turning him in for ransom—exchange for their freedom, perhaps? It was risky, but there was a good chance the Prince-Regent would actually agree.

"That's not what I meant, dear fellows," said the orange-haired man, sounding both incredulous and bemused. "I meant gag him."

Saizou's posture relaxed.

"Good idea," said Tsuki. "He obviously doesn't want to kill us, or he would have kept talking."

"And we, like idiots, would have just stayed where we were and let him," grunted Kiba.

Kirikizu glanced at Tsuki now. She wasn't wrong, but hearing the words said aloud, 'he doesn't want to kill us,' well... it was odd. He had not fully realized it himself until then. It made him uneasy. He was an assassin. Killing people was his job. Not that he enjoyed it, like Kiko did, but still and all...

It should be easy by now.

It should be habit. Muscle memory.

But if it were easy, he would have finished his sentence and let them fall to the ground with their brains bleeding out their ears.

"Everybody OUT!" The orange-haired man clapped his hands together and made shooing motions toward the door.

"Nix," said Tsuki with a hint of reproach in her voice. "You bled just like we did. If he decides to speak—"

"Precious girl, if he decides to say another diddly-darn

word, two things will happen." Nix held up a finger. "I will hurt like a bitch, but it takes more than a siren's song to kill this fox. Secondly, I'll make him wish he hadn't." A wide, narrow-eyed smile took over his face, like a confident parent reassuring a child there was no monster under the bed. "Now, out. Go, go, go, go," he cooed as everyone filed out of the door and stood on the stairwell outside.

Kirikizu caught a glimpse of gray skies and crumbling buildings before Nix shut the door behind them and turned around, clasping his hands behind his back.

"Now," he said, and his voice sounded quite different—deeper, less playful. "Let's see what we have here."

# FORTY-ONE

TWENTY MINUTES PASSED before the clouds were thick
enough to shield Hiro from the sun's rays. He jumped to his
feet and ran back to the main office. He slipped through the
front door, inwardly continuing a string of curses levelled at his
own lack of foresight.

"Boss?" Kido walked around the corner, his eyebrows
arching when he took in the sight of Hiro, panting and leaning
against the front door. "You okay there?"

"What?" Yuu walked around the corner behind Kido. He
glanced at Hiro before saying, "Forgot his sunglasses" and
walking back into the lounge.

Kido blinked. "Is that it?"

Hiro stormed past, into the lounge. He had left his jacket
here somewhere—ah. He lifted it off the arm of the couch and
shrugged it on, biting back a hiss as he pulled the hood up with
one hand. He couldn't remember where he'd put his sunglasses,
so instead, he picked up a pair from the card table—probably
Yuu's—and shoved them onto his face.

Yuu kicked the door of the mini-fridge shut and popped

open a can of orange soda. He glanced at the sunglasses on his boss's face before shrugging and settling down in front of the television and switching the channel from comedy to sports.

"That's choreographed, you know," said Hiro, eyeing the two wrestlers on-screen as they danced on opposite ends of the ring.

Yuu shot him a dirty look. "It's performance art."

"Boss, are you going back out?" Kido leaned against the wall, his hands in his pockets. He looked—not suspicious, Hiro noticed, but concerned.

"Yes." He walked out the door without another word.

———

AS THEY STOOD outside the door, waiting to hear Kirikizu's voice and experience the excruciating, mind-numbing pain again, Saizou reached up and touched the corner of the bandage. He was trying not to think about it; whatever had happened to him seemed near-irrelevant in the current situation. He lowered his hand and shoved it into his pocket.

"Does it hurt?"

He glanced at Tsuki, who had moved closer, her back pressed against the rusty iron railing. Behind her, the stairs plunged down four stories to the street, empty save for a few trash cans and a bicycle.

"No."

"Good. The painkillers should last up to six hours."

Saizou glanced at Kiba. Tsuki followed his gaze and said archly, "He didn't want any."

"His injury is worse than mine," Kiba grunted. He lifted his hands as if to cross his arms, but thought better of his wound. He placed his hands on his hips instead.

Saizou looked at the ground and sighed. It was all the reaction he had energy for. Quietly, he asked, "How bad is it?"

"How bad is what?" asked Tsuki, feigning ignorance.

Saizou lifted his head. "It must be bad if you're stalling with stupid questions."

Kiba snorted. "The black samurai's reizaa-naginata cut through your eye. You'll probably be blind."

"Great!" Tsuki spun to glare at Kiba. "I was going to break it to him gently."

"He's a soldier. He doesn't need coddled."

*Probably be blind.*

*Blind.*

*Soldier.*

What good was a blind soldier? Next to none. The sudden, crushing realization that he was now handicapped, that he was now half-blind, that his right side would always be vulnerable, that he would need to be twice as vigilant, twice as alert and suspicious—he couldn't stand.

He walked noiselessly past Tsuki and Kiba and sat on the stairwell, his right side—his vulnerable, open, weak side—pressed against the wall. He felt numb.

Shi would die.

He would live on until his new handicap got him killed.

In the span of a few hours, it was like every battle worth fighting for had turned its back on him and melted into the shadows. If they still existed, he couldn't see them.

He swallowed the massive lump in his throat and felt it splinter into a dozen shards. *God, what is it about me? I never wanted to hurt anyone, but it became my lot in life. I never wanted to tear people apart or throw those I love into the path of a danger I created, but I can't seem to stop. And now this? You kill my best friend—my only friend, and you leave me blinded.*

He breathed out. Anger pulsed through his veins with every beat of his heart, pounding in his ears. *This is a joke to you, right? I'll show you a joke. I'll give you exactly what you give me. Nothing.*

The door opened, and Saizou turned, glancing up as Nix stepped halfway onto the landing, an odd expression on his face.

"So, here's a funny thing," said the kitsune. "I decided to search him while I was in there, since we hadn't before—"

"We were busy," Tsuki muttered.

"Tsk, dear, let's not interrupt," said Nix, and then continued, "I found this odd article. Amid about thirteen thousand various deadly weapons, I might add." He held up a small glass vial with a black lid, sealed with red wax. "Being a curious individual, I asked him what it was."

"He spoke to you without hurting you?" Tsuki questioned, glancing down at Saizou, who did not look at her.

"Er, no, he didn't actually answer me. I gather he can't do that. Hence the muzzle-filter-mask-whatchamacallit. My point is—does anyone want to know what this is, or should I just take my story back inside?" Nix demanded, sounding wounded.

Tsuki sighed and gestured for him to continue. "Finish your story."

"Thank you." Nix raised the vial with a flourish. "As I was saying, I noticed the vial had a label. It says, rather pointedly, *Dog Antidote*. I thought our new invalid down there might be interested." He pointed toward Saizou, who was already jogging up the stairs.

He snatched the vial from Nix, who made no effort to get the vial back. Saizou's vision was blurry, even in his good eye, but Nix was right. *Dog Antidote* was spelled out across the tiny label in neat, miniscule characters.

Saizou curled his fingers around the vial and felt hot, stinging tears pressing against both eyes, bandage or no bandage. He turned and began to jog back down the stairs, but Tsuki's voice stopped him.

"You can't just go give it to him! What if it's poison?"

"Then Shi will die either way," said Saizou, without turning around.

"Wait!" She raced down the stairs after him and caught his arm before he reached the second landing.

Reluctantly, he turned to face her. "I want to come with you," she said. "You and your companions could come back here. It's safe for now."

"We already have a contact with a safe house," said Saizou, roughly jerking his arm from her grasp.

"Saizou Akita," she said sharply, "don't you dare treat me like the enemy after the trouble we went through to save you."

"You also told me not to fight for my domain," he snarled, "and like an idiot, I listened to you."

"I didn't force you to listen to me! I gave you the facts, and you listened to them. You made up your own mind."

"That's what you wanted."

"Of course it's what I wanted!" She looked away from him. "The people of your domain don't deserve to be casualties in a war you don't need to fight."

Before he realized it, Saizou's hand had curled into a fist and he was swinging a punch and his fist collided with the brick wall, cracking his knuckles open farther. Blood smeared the wall as he lowered his hand. "I know what I've done," he rasped, wondering if he would need to hit the wall again to keep from hitting something important.

Some*one* important.

Tsuki's expression was hard, harder even than the brick he

touched, but she reached out and ran a surprisingly gentle finger across his cheek, under his eye. "Blood," she said, by way of explanation, but her touch lingered longer than necessary.

The moment stretched, but it did not grow thin with every second as most silences did. Instead, it seemed to swell, like a boiling storm cloud growing larger and darker. But this cloud released no rain, and no words.

Tsuki removed her hand and sighed. She glanced away from Saizou, and in a voice so low and sharp he barely made out the words, she said, "I'm sorry, too."

"What?" he asked, in case he had misheard.

"I said I'm sorry. Not as sorry as you are, but...I am sorry. You don't need to believe me. I wish...it seemed like the lesser of two evils. I don't think...I don't think I was wrong. But I had no right to ask you to do what you did."

"The lesser of two evils," Saizou repeated softly. He uncurled his fingers and pressed his palm flat against the wall. "The longer I'm here, the more I think that's the problem."

Tsuki lifted an eyebrow. "What?"

"Every action, everything I've tried to do, has been the lesser of two evils." Saizou lowered his hand, but pressed his forehead against the wall instead. It was cool; he hadn't realized how warm he was until now. "It doesn't feel right."

"Wartime." Tsuki shrugged. "It asks hard things of us. Sometimes being the hero of one story means being the villain of another."

"I..." Saizou's mind raced, turning her statement over, attempting to quickly read it from all sides before he responded. "I don't agree with you."

"What do you mean?"

He pushed away from the wall and faced her. He was beyond tired. He felt threadbare with exhaustion, and all he wanted was to create a world that could protect itself for an hour while he slept. "A hero is a hero, no matter what story they're in. I'm not saying I am one. I know I'm not." He rubbed the back of his neck, gathering his thoughts, trying to fit them into words. "But good and evil aren't interchangeable. One doesn't become the other because the circumstances change."

Tsuki shifted her jaw, thinking. Abruptly, she said, "Let me ask you a question."

"Quickly. I only have a few hours," he said, nodding toward the street.

"It's quick," she assured him. "And I'll help you find your friend." He nodded, and she continued. "There's a train track. There is a bridge ahead, but the track over it is broken, and the conductor isn't aware of the situation. The train, full of passengers, is speeding toward the broken bridge. If they crash, they will die."

Saizou watched her closely, wondering what she was getting at.

"There's another bridge over the track," she went on. "And two men are on it. One of the men is hugely obese. The other man notices that if he pushed the obese man down onto the track, the train would hit him, and the crash would be minor. Most likely nobody would die. What should he do? Should he push the obese man over the bridge onto the track, even if the fall would surely kill him? Or should he let the train continue across the broken bridge, which would surely kill the passengers?"

Saizou shook his head. It was a weighty question. Pushing the man off the bridge would be murder, but standing by and watching innocent people die—which was worse? "You know I've killed people."

She nodded. "I know. This has nothing to do with self-defense, but the defense of others."

"Killing in wartime—it's..."

"Different. I know. It's a simple question, Saizou."

"What do you believe?" he asked, and met her gaze, unblinking. "Tell me. How would you answer this question?"

She hesitated, and Saizou wondered if she had considered her own question. "I don't know," she admitted, shaking her head slightly. "I was curious as to your answer."

"I have my answer," he said. "I would jump onto the track and hope I could wave the train down."

"And if you couldn't? The other man's body would be large enough to stop the train before it hit the broken track. What if you couldn't flag it down in time?"

"Then I would know I had done everything I could without harming anyone else," said Saizou softly. "If you're coming, come. I'm not waiting." He turned and hurried down the stairs, the antidote deep in his pocket.

———

"MR. KARIDURO?"

Virgo lifted his head from his hands. A nurse stood a few feet away, looking at the various tired forms sitting in the waiting room.

"That's me," he said, jumping to his feet. His heart throbbed painfully in the side of his neck, and he swallowed, trying to prepare for the worst. He had done this at least half a dozen times before—no, more than that. A dozen. Each time was infinitely harder than the last.

"You're the brother of Shimo Kariduro, yes?" she asked.

"Yeah." He swallowed hard, the motion scraping down his throat like an unchewed bite. "Is he all right? How bad is it?"

"Come with me, please." Her smile seemed genuine, but there was a crease in her forehead that belied it. He followed her out of the waiting room and around the corner. As they approached the front desk, the nurse slowed down and turned to face him again. "The bullet cracked his breastbone, but the heart wasn't injured. He's out of the operating theater and resting comfortably now."

Overwhelmed with dizziness, Virgo bent his knees and crouched, his arms over his head. He was all right. Shimo was all right.

"Sir?"

"I'm fine." He waved her concern away and straightened again, but immediately leaned over, his palms pressing against his thighs. "Almost fine," he amended.

"Mr. Kariduro...you are aware of your brother's condition, yes?"

His brother's condition. *Condition* was such a vague, ambiguous word for it, Virgo thought. It made it sound so open, so hopeful. There were treatments for conditions. "I am," he said, and hardened his voice as he met the nurse's gaze. "Shimo isn't."

Her eyes widened. "He doesn't...legally, he ought to be made aware—"

"Legally, you ought to keep your mouth shut before I rip you a new one," Virgo growled, aware of the sudden change in his attitude. It had intimidated nurses before, and this time was no different.

She paled and took a step back, blinking rapidly. "I don't think you understand how sick—"

"I understand perfectly how sick he is," Virgo snapped,

striding toward her. She continued to back up until she hit the front desk. He leaned against the desk, imprisoning her with his arms on either side. Lowering his voice, he said in softer tones, "I know. I'm saving up for the operation."

"Sir, he's—he's not even on a waiting list," she stammered. "He needs to be on several waiting lists, in fact, and he's not signed up for one transplant."

"He doesn't need to be," said Virgo firmly.

"Mr. Kariduro—"

Virgo stepped back and lifted his arms, turning in a circle, a rock star before an empty theater. "I'm his donor, all right?" he snapped. "He has me. He doesn't need a waiting list."

The frightened, nervous look on her face faded to something sadder. "What was his condition the last time you checked?"

"Stage two."

She swallowed visibly.

Virgo's pulse quickened again. "Why? What is it?"

"He's progressed far enough—he's almost at stage three. Stage four is when..."

"He needs the operations. I know." Virgo nodded and reached out, absently patting the nurse's shoulder. "How long do we have?"

"He'll need the operation within six months, at the longest. I recommend coming in for a checkup in three." She must have seen an expression he didn't feel through his numbness, because she added quietly, "I won't tell him. I'll leave that to you."

"Thank you." He nodded again, rubbing his bare arms. Suddenly, he was cold. He was never cold. "Which room is he in?"

She pointed down the hall. "Fourteen."

He thanked her half-heartedly and walked down the hall. It may as well have been a mile-long stretch until he found himself staring at the number 14 on the door to his left. It was several more seconds before he gathered up the courage to go in.

Shimo's nurses had taken good care of him: a white blanket was pulled up to his shoulders and someone had given him a thorough wash, cleaning away the blood and dirt previously coating him. Nurses always loved Shimo for his politeness. He was so soft-spoken and never put anyone out, never asked for anything.

He looked very different with his hair damp and straight to his shoulders and his face free of its usual makeup. He looked older.

"Hey, bro." Virgo flicked his brother's forehead, ever so lightly. Judging by the IV in his arm, drugs would keep him under for a while. "So, guess what? The nurse said the bullet wound won't keep you down. I think I scared her." He laughed a little. "Anyway, you'll be fine. It's not like you've never been in a hospital before, right? The last injury was worse than this one."

Shimo continued to breathe evenly, in and out, in and out. That was the important thing. "Keep doing what you're doing," Virgo said aloud, nudging Shimo's hand. "As long as you keep breathing, we'll be fine."

He pulled up the chair from the corner and sat down, propping his feet up on the edge of the hospital bed. "If I'm still asleep," he told his sleeping twin, "yell at me when you wake up, huh? Thanks."

# FORTY-TWO

HIRO STRODE down the dock and stopped at the end. "Come out," he ordered, kicking his boot against one of the posts.

Shotgun immediately splashed over the side with all the grace of a beached whale. Hiro raised an eyebrow, but as he reached down to assist the soaked man up, he saw Shotgun was attempting to hoist an unconscious Shi up as well.

"I have him." Hiro grabbed Shi's shirt and hauled him over the side, then checked for a pulse. "He's ali—"

Hiro was stunned by a blow to the side of the head that sent him reeling. His sunglasses clattered to the dock as he gripped one of the posts, his vision sparking like an electric current. He reached up and shaded his eyes so he could stare in wrathful astonishment at Shotgun, who stood three feet away, his hands still in fists, poised to swing like a waterlogged boxer waiting for someone to announce *ten*.

"You want another one?" Shotgun snarled. The joking light was completely gone from his face, and Hiro realized he had possibly misjudged him.

"Listen, kid," Hiro began, but Shotgun snatched up the sunglasses and held them in a way that threatened to crush them.

"You listen," Shotgun interrupted, but Hiro didn't let him get any further.

He drew his gun from the back of his belt and cocked it, then aimed for Shi's body. "Shut up or I turn him into dead man."

Shotgun froze, and from under the dock came a muffled shriek. Hiro glanced at the water. "Get the girl up and give me those sunglasses."

For a moment, he thought Shotgun might toss the sunglasses into the water, in which case Hiro was fully prepared to shoot him in the elbow and cripple him for life. Instead, Shotgun shook his mane of cherry-red hair, spraying water like a bird dog, and tossed the sunglasses at Hiro's feet.

Hiro picked them up and settled them on his nose as Shotgun hoisted Fumiyo up over the edge. She wrestled her way out of his grasp before he could set her down, and she thudded to the dock by Shi, where she perched over him and scowled at Hiro.

"It's not my fault, honey," said Hiro, unaffected. He motioned toward Shotgun. "Your friend Saizou got himself captured at the palace, and I doubt he'll be back any time soon. I'm moving you to the safe house now."

Shotgun's mouth fell open. "Does Riza know?"

"She's the one who told me. Use your comlink and ask her yourself, if the water didn't ruin it completely."

Shotgun reached into his pocket. A frown crossed his face, and he reached into his other pocket, but his hand came up empty. "It must have fallen out."

Hiro grunted. "Trust it is, then."

"That's a bad joke, right? You were ready to shoot us and dump our bodies in the water half an hour ago—"

"And I could do it again," Hiro interrupted coldly, pointing the muzzle of his gun at the gray sky. "I could do it any time I wanted, in fact. So pick him up, drag the girl if you have to, and follow me before my boys wonder what's taking me so long."

———

*LIGHT. Light?*

*Air. Smells funny.*

*Where? Where—table.*

*White.*

He sat up slowly, staring at his surroundings, trying to make sense of them. He felt a strange sense of...newness, like he had never opened his eyes before, never seen anything before. And yet he knew the names of things. He could see the wall and knew it to be a wall. *Wall. Door. Table.*

He moved his focus closer, to himself. He held his hand up in front of his face and moved his fingers, curious and a little frightened. *Five.* Five fingers, and they were his. The hand was his. This body was his...

Wasn't it?

Why did it feel so strange? He slid off the table, but the moment his feet hit the ground, he collapsed. He collapsed, but he caught himself before his knees hit the floor, and he remained, crouched, a strange pounding in his ears. Was that him? He glanced at the door. Things came through doors.

Was something going to come through that door?

Cold. The skin that covered him was cold—no, it didn't cover him. They were the same thing, him and his skin. Weren't they?

He rubbed his eyes and crept closer to the door. He didn't know what he wanted. Did he want to go out the door and see what was beyond?

No. No, he wanted to go back where it was dark and warm and safe. This was too much. The air, the smells, the floor, too many feelings, too much to consider.

Something tapped the other side of the door. The creature froze, staring at the silver metal, waiting. The door moved. It opened, and something came in. It had two legs, like him, and two arms and a head, but no face.

Suddenly, he felt rage. He was angry for a reason he couldn't name. He was furious. He wanted the other creature gone, and not just gone, but destroyed. Torn apart. Ripped to pieces.

Kill it. *Kill it.*

The creature waited until the figure was inside the room, waited until it had cut off its own escape.

Then he attacked, and it was the most natural thing in the world.

*Good,* thought the creature, and suddenly he was warm again, warm and red and sticky. *This is good.*

———

OSCAR NEARLY ROLLED off the cot in his sleep, and the sensation of half-falling startled him awake. He sat up abruptly, blinking and wondering where in the blazes he was.

Something was off, but he couldn't put his finger on it. He yawned and stretched, trying to clear the cobwebs from his brain. Ah, right. He was at the palace. In the lab, more precisely. Lab—

The creature.

He jumped to his feet, staring at the table. The *empty* table. And what was that red stuff on the floor? *Good heavens, it escaped and knocked something over...*

Oscar rounded the corner and gaped in horror at the sight in front of him. A white-armored samurai, probably come to deliver a message, or maybe even just check in on the prisoner and his science project, lay in scattered chunks on the floor.

Oscar covered his mouth and crouched down, trying to find a way to work the helmet off the severed head. *How did this happen? How is this even possible?* His mind raced, but above all was the hope that this samurai wasn't the kind baby-faced man who had arrested him in the first place. The world needed more decent people; it just wouldn't be fair—

The helmet popped off, and Oscar slumped forward with relief. He didn't recognize this guard. He had never seen him before.

Oscar wiped his face with his sleeve and dropped the helmet. Blood pooled beneath his sneakers; it splashed across the door and the walls. Whatever had torn this man apart...

No. Calling it 'whatever' was an excuse. He knew.

The creature had done this; he knew. There was no doubt.

He got to his feet and stared at the door. It was open by several inches, leading out into the hallway, to places Oscar hadn't been allowed since they had marched him to the lab and locked him in. He could escape now, but the thought was ridiculous. How far would he get?

How far had the creature gotten?

"What have I done?" asked Oscar of the empty room. "What the *hell* have I done?" He wondered whether he should push an alarm, but he didn't know where any alarms were. He could always start a fire and trigger the fire alarm, but that seemed a bit drastic.

Or...well. He backed away from the shredded corpse. How had the creature managed that? How had it...

He crouched down again. There was no sign of a weapon, unless the creature had snatched one of the various tools lying around and made a run for it, which was entirely possible.

Ugh, the smell was really something. Oscar straightened and grabbed a surgical mask from the plastic container on the nearest table. He positioned it over his mouth and nose, then folded his arms, rehearsing what he would tell the Prince-Regent.

"Yes," he said, glancing at the door, "it's a bit awkward, but you see, the thing you had me create decided it was a murderous hellbeast. No, that won't work." He scratched the back of his head. "I'm terribly sorry," he tried again. "I don't know what got into it. No, I wasn't awake, I was asleep. Yes, the creature was asleep, too, but it would seem it has an extraordinary metabolism and it woke up anyway. Oh, you're going to kill me? Fine, go right ahead."

Oscar sank back down onto the cot. "I'm dead," he finished. "No matter how this turns out, I'm bloody dead."

"Bloody dead," said a soft, rasping voice.

Oscar clutched his chest and fell back against the wall. "Who's there?"

Then he saw it.

A dark shape pressed between the ceiling and the top of the incubator. A pair of pale eyes gleamed at him from the shadows.

Oscar stared. "How did you get up there?"

"Bloody dead," said the creature again. It reached one pale hand out and pointed toward the death scene near the door. "Bloody dead."

"Yes," snapped Oscar, his astonishment temporarily overwhelming his horror. "Bloody dead. Look what you've done. This is not what we discussed—not that we really discussed anything, but honestly, this is terribly bad behavior considering you've been alive all of...not very long." Before he quite realized what he was doing, he pointed at the floor and demanded, "Get your arse down here."

The creature whimpered and withdrew his hand, backing farther against the wall.

"Now," said Oscar.

The creature's whimper sharpened into a brief growl, but he reluctantly dropped to the ground. Oscar stared as the creature landed nimbly on all fours, as agile as a cat.

"Right," said Oscar, raking his hands through his hair again. If this creature had slaughtered the guard like a rabid butcher, who was to say it wouldn't do the same to him? He needed to find a weapon, a way to defend himself...well, the dead guard had a sword. He could use that.

He inched toward the guard, keeping his eyes on the creature. The creature tilted his head, watching Oscar with wide, unblinking eyes as he reached the corpse and bent down, feeling for the sword. Oscar was hardly squeamish, and the blood didn't bother him nearly as much as the thought of the Prince-Regent walking in and seeing the mess.

Oscar finally felt the samurai's leg of armor, then the sword. He drew it from its scabbard and took it with both bloodied hands. He had no idea how to use it, but of course, the creature wouldn't know that. Oscar cleared his throat and kicked the door shut.

The creature hadn't moved; he simply remained crouched by the incubator, blood matting his hair, streaking his face, rendering him as something from a horror film. A gory, naked abomination that was—*well, not entirely my fault,* thought Oscar, *but I definitely had a part in it.*

And yet...well.

It was alive and breathing and surprisingly coordinated. "You aren't supposed to have ideas yet," Oscar told it. "You have the barest concepts imprinted in that head of yours." He gestured toward the dead samurai. "So where the hell did those ideas come from, eh? Where?"

When the creature did not respond, Oscar licked his lips and tried to think. It wasn't attacking him—then again, he wasn't exactly the most intimidating figure, he knew that perfectly well. He probably looked ridiculous, holding a sword like this.

"Right," said Oscar. "I don't have a name for you yet, so I'm just going to call you *Creature* for now, all right? I'm Oscar." He patted his own chest. "Oscar. Yes?"

Slowly, Creature nodded. "Oscar."

"Right! Ha!" Oscar realized he was grinning, which was probably in bad taste under the circumstances. Still, Creature could speak! He could move shockingly well! And he could understand what Oscar told him! "You're a bloody miracle, Creature. A bloody miracle. Do you know what a miracle is?"

Creature hunched his shoulders and tilted his head farther to the side, a picture of confusion.

"A miracle is...something terribly excellent. I don't really believe in them for the most part, but, well, here you are." Oscar approached Creature and cautiously held out his right hand. After all, there were people who interacted with wild animals on a daily basis and survived, and Oscar had practically given birth to a sentient one.

"Come on," he coaxed, clicking his tongue. Something told

him that it might be the wrong approach, but it was the only one he could think of. "Come on, I won't hurt you. I made you."

Gingerly, like a stray cat approaching a stranger, Creature rose to his feet and stepped warily toward Oscar. He reached his own hand out and allowed his fingertips to brush Oscar's.

Oscar felt a strange thrill at the touch, and he wondered if this was how fathers felt, holding a brand-new baby for the first time. Even if most babies weren't quite so...violent.

"There's a good boy," whispered Oscar, slowly lowering himself to one knee so he could look Creature in the eye. *Boy.* Well, man: a delicate man with a child's mind and, apparently, all the bloodthirst of a mercenary army. "Good Creature," he said, for lack of a better term.

A cautious smile touched Creature's face. "Good Oscar," he said.

"Well," said Oscar, "I don't know about that. I do, however, know you need a bath and some clothes." He glanced again at the dead samurai and sighed. "I suppose it's time to call room service."

"Bloody dead," agreed Creature.

# FORTY-THREE

*The Imperial Palace, twenty-one years ago*

"MAMUSHI? PRINCELING, WHERE ARE YOU?"

Mamushi ducked behind the chess table and crouched, peering around the gilded, golden legs at the door. How his mother the Empress would scold if she knew he was hiding from his uncle. It was time for his lessons, but he didn't feel like learning. Not today.

He saw the lower half of the Prince walk into the room and pause. His voice was disgruntled when he said, "Mamushi, this is no way for a royal to behave. Especially not the second in place for the throne."

That wasn't quite true, Mamushi countered mentally, scowling. It may not be the proper way to behave, but it was certainly a way.

"I can see you, you know."

Mamushi groaned softly and stood up, gathering his robe around him like a cloak. He only needed to wear the robe during political lessons, which was a good thing. Royal clothes were heavy and boring and too bright, like his mother's garden of obnoxious flowers. Except nobody required the flowers to wear those petals—he could strip the petals off a flower when the color annoyed him, but he couldn't remove his robes until lessons were over.

"It's not fair," he muttered, kicking the leg of the chess table. His toe throbbed, and he immediately regretted the action.

The Prince clasped his hands behind his back and sighed. "Did that help?"

"Yes," Mamushi lied in defiance.

The Prince lifted an eyebrow. "Your stubbornness never fails to amaze me. Kick the table all you like; at the end of the day, you'll be doing lessons in spite of yourself, and with a sore foot, no less."

Mamushi leaned his elbows on the top of the chess table, knocking over two pawns and a rook. He didn't care. It was a stupid, boring game, and he was losing the last time he looked. "I don't feel like learning."

"Well, it's a good thing the planets don't orbit around you, then."

"My nurse says they do," Mamushi sniffed.

His uncle chuckled and seated himself at the other end of the table, where his half of the board still sat. He had all his pieces left, save a bishop Mamushi had been able to sneak away from him during the last session.

"Your nurse is paid to be kind to you," said the Prince, tapping the head of a pawn. "She is one of these. She has no will of her own and no mind of her own. She says what is expected of her and she does what she is told. Do you understand?"

"You're saying she lies and the world doesn't revolve

around me," Mamushi sighed. He refused to sit down, but he eyed the pawn under his uncle's finger. "If she's a pawn, what am I?"

The Prince smiled and lifted his hand from the board, gesturing toward the scattered pieces. "What do you think you are?"

Mamushi eyed the chess pieces and found himself carefully picking up those he had knocked over before. He placed them back where they had been, his eyes drifting over the rooks, the knights, the bishops, and finally the king and queen.

He glanced at his uncle. This response was risky—he would either be reprimanded and told he was as arrogant as his father, or the Prince would laugh and applaud him for his bold choice.

Mamushi was about to point toward the king piece, when suddenly he stopped. Tilting his head, he looked at the grander scale of the unfolding game, with the sudden realization that the pieces were just that—pieces in a game, to be moved about as he desired.

Slowly, he seated himself on his stool, arranging his robes for minimal discomfort. He lifted his chin.

"Well?" his uncle prompted, his eyes glimmering with curiosity. "Do you know what you are?"

"I just told you," said Mamushi, folding his hands in his lap.

The Prince leaned back in his chair and crossed one leg over the other, rubbing his chin with a finger. There was something like amusement on his face—amusement, but harder. Colder.

The previous year, for his seventh birthday, Mamushi had received a caged snake from his favorite playmate, Kiko. Delighted, he had stared at the glass for hours, watching the snake slither slowly about the bottom of the enclosure, every so often sliding up the glass to stare at the roof, as though assessing the weaknesses of the box.

The snake had decided to sleep, worn out from its attempts at plotting, which bored Mamushi. Wanting the snake to wake up and be interesting again, Mamushi had tapped the cage. The moment his finger touched the glass, the snake struck, and Mamushi had jumped back, astonished. It was the first time all day he had considered the reptile dangerous, and he began to consider what would happen if the snake happened to escape. All night he dreamed that the snake had somehow gotten out and was waiting under the bed to strike his heel the moment he awoke. The next day, he had ordered his nurse to remove the cage and burn the snake.

His uncle reminded him, in this moment, of himself on his seventh birthday.

Mamushi's swell of pride deflated as quickly as it had grown, and he remembered the horrible hissing and writhing of the blackened snake as it fell out of the brazier, charred and dying.

Quickly, he reached forward and set his finger on the crown of the king piece. "I'm the king."

Almost before the last word left his mouth, the Prince was laughing, a loud, harsh sound that Mamushi had never enjoyed hearing. His mother sometimes told him he had the same laugh, so he tried his hardest to soften the sound of his voice. His uncle was clever—far cleverer than he was, but that did not mean Mamushi had to like him.

"Do you know," said the Prince, leaning forward, tears of laughter still gleaming in the corners of his eyes, "I do believe you may grow up to be more dangerous than your namesake."

Mamushi's fear mounted, brushing cold across his skin.

*Mamushi.* Viper. Did his uncle perhaps know about the snake? Did he know where Mamushi's thoughts had been?

He gripped the folds of his robe in his fists and swallowed his fear. It wasn't royal—and fear, his uncle had often told him, was the enemy of respect.

"A viper," he said clearly, glad his uncle couldn't see his hands, "is only dangerous when threatened."

The Prince nodded, his eyes falling to the chessboard, but he clicked his tongue softly against his teeth. "That isn't strictly true." He moved his knight forward in an L-shape, casually lifting another of Mamushi's pawns from the board. "Tell me where you were wrong."

"Is this a lesson in politics or a lesson in ethics?" Mamushi wanted to know.

"Think of it as a lesson in life," said his uncle, waving a hand toward the board. "Move. Answer."

Mamushi frowned and studied his pieces. He had three pawns, a bishop, a king, and a queen left. It was hardly enough to contend with his uncle's nearly full army, but numbers didn't necessarily win battles.

"Answer," said his uncle, his tone sharper than before.

"I don't know," Mamushi snapped. "I wasn't wrong." He moved a pawn forward, blocking the knight the Prince had just moved.

"That was a bad move." The prince brushed past the pawn with his rook and placed it three rows down from Mamushi's king piece. "Check. The answer," he continued, as if the *check* were nothing, "is that you were wrong because a viper is not dangerous when threatened. A viper is dangerous when it *feels* threatened. Whether a thing is an actual threat is of no consequence. A viper would strike at a falling leaf, if the leaf fell close enough."

Mamushi ground his teeth in anger. His uncle was right, of course, and the answer was obvious. He narrowed his eyes and stared at the board, unwilling to meet the Prince's gaze. It would be condescending just now, and above all things, Mamushi hated condescension.

He was a child, but he was a royal child. He might never be the Sun, like his brother, but he was still in the sky. He still shone. "Fine," he said, and moved his queen in front of his king. If his uncle attempted to remove his queen from the board, he would simply remove said assassin with the king. "I undo your check."

He lifted his gaze, expecting to see a look of disappointment on his uncle's face, but rather than disappointment, he met incredulity.

"'Fine'?" The Prince arched an eyebrow. "How is that 'fine'?"

"I blocked your move."

"Come now, nephew. We both know your 'fine' was in response to the question, not the move."

Mamushi hissed like a feral cat and said, scowling, "I said *fine* because no matter what I say, you'll always find some fault with it. None of my other teachers are this difficult."

"None of the other teachers have the authority to reprimand you," said the Prince. "I am placed in the fortuitous position of being family, as well as your teacher, and I can reprimand you however I wish."

Mamushi sank lower on his stool. Suddenly, he wished his robes were larger, large enough to swallow him up and hide him until the Prince gave up and stopped looking. "I'm sorry."

"Sorry means nothing," said the Prince. He uncrossed his legs and pushed his chair back from the table. "Nobody remembers 'sorry,' and do you know why?"

Another question. Another question to which he could provide another wrong answer. Another wrong answer to which his uncle could provide a punishment. Perhaps if he played along... "Why, Uncle?" he asked, hoping to present himself the picture of meekness and teachability.

"I am not your rhetoric teacher," said the Prince passively. "Nor am I in the habit of answering my own questions. You tell me."

Mamushi knew if he got this answer wrong, he was in trouble. He squinted at the chessboard. It was easier than looking at the Prince's face. "Because actions speak louder than words?"

"Are you really going to throw me a generic answer like that?" the Prince asked. "I'm disappointed. I thought you were cleverer."

"I *am* cleverer than that," said Mamushi. His uncle's tone of voice was fanning Mamushi's spark of irritation into a blaze. "But you ask me stupid questions instead of telling me the answer, when you know it and I don't."

"So impatient," the Prince sighed. He locked his fingers together and rested his arms behind his head. "Try again."

Mamushi blinked, bewildered. "You aren't going to punish me?"

"I am, but I'd prefer to hear an answer directly from you, rather than a pithy saying you got off a bumper sticker or some nonsense."

Mamushi's heart sank. There was no point in trying to wriggle out of it now. He cleared his throat and leaned his elbows on the chess table, pondering. *Nobody remembers 'sorry.'* But why not? It was a tepid word, but that was hardly the answer his uncle was looking for. If politics were grand, bloody tapestries, then words made up the threads. He supposed that rendered his 'actions speak louder than words' remark a moot point. He rubbed his forehead.

"Do you give up?" asked the Prince.

Mamushi groaned. "Am I allowed to?"

"I'll already have to punish you. I've made up my mind, so you can give up now if you wish."

"Whatever." Mamushi folded his arms, dropping any semblance of royalty in his pouting pose. "I give up."

The Prince nodded, as if he had expected that answer. "Suppose your father made a terrible mistake and executed an innocent man. What then?"

"I imagine he would cover up the man's innocence and continue to label him as guilty, to save Imperial face," said Mamushi, shrugging.

The Prince grinned unexpectedly. "You're probably correct. What wouldn't he do?"

"Well, if he covered up the man's innocence, he wouldn't say 'sorry', that's for sure."

"Do you think he would say 'sorry' even if he proclaimed the man's innocence to the public?" his uncle pressed.

"No."

"No. Because 'sorry' is a whisper in a hurricane. It is a particle of dust floating in front of you. It has no strength; it holds no weight. 'Sorry' holds no weight because it is weak." As the words sank in, the Prince unclasped his hands and placed them on his knees. "And weakness is the unforgiveable sin."

Mamushi frowned, and the Prince asked, "What? You have something to say?"

"I'm just...wondering," said Mamushi, formulating his question as carefully as he knew how, "what if someone is weak by nature?"

"What if they are?" His uncle shrugged. "It's the way of

things. Some people are weaker than others, which is why the strong survive."

"Then I wonder why you bother teaching me at all," Mamushi sulked. "Not only am I a child, I'm not a very strong one."

"Not physically," the Prince agreed, "but a strong mind has nothing to do with the strength of a body. That being said, it is the nature of the world for strength to overcome weakness, and those who mimic the actions of the strong provide the perfect illusion."

Mamushi's mind spun with this newfound idea. "You mean they can trick people into thinking they're stronger than they are?"

The Prince nodded. "That's exactly what I mean. By mimicking the nature of something better, we become better ourselves."

Mamushi felt like cupping the information carefully in his hands so none of it spilled over or trickled out. He wanted to consider this. "Should I consider this a political lesson," he inquired, "or an ethical one?"

"We're done with lessons for today," said the Prince, waving his hand as if physically dismissing the question. "I'm afraid now we come to your punishment."

Ah, yes. The punishment. Mamushi hated this part. A perfect lesson was very rare, and anything less than perfect was not permitted—not by his uncle. Then again, thought Mamushi as he studied his uncle's impeccable robe, impeccable braids, impeccable everything—imperfection was a form of weakness, too. No wonder the Prince despised it so much.

Mamushi was imperfect and weak, so it was perfectly logical for someone stronger and less flawed to treat him however he liked. Mamushi sighed and bowed his head, his hands clasped in front of him. "What punishment today?"

Just because it was logical didn't mean he had to like it. In fact, it terrified him, but the gods forbid he ever showed terror in front of his uncle. The punishment would no doubt be much worse, then.

The Prince sighed. "Recite the names of the major *kami*." Mamushi lifted his gaze. That was it? A recitation? Then the Prince's gaze dropped to Mamushi's robe. "And undress."

Not for the first time, Mamushi swallowed his fear of the Prince, along with his hope that someone would walk in and save him. They never did. They knew better. As he took off the hated robe, wishing he had a dozen more underneath it, he began. "Amaterasu, Sarutahiko, Ame no Uzume, Inari, Izanagi..."

*Present Day*

"MAMUSHI! MY PRINCE?"

Mamushi rolled over, away from the sudden touch that startled him awake. Sunlight streamed through the drawn curtains. Was it morning? No, it hadn't been night.

"It's only me." Kiko sat down on the edge of the bed and placed a hand on his arm. "I came to see how you were."

"Why did you wake me?" Mamushi snapped, pulling his arm away from her touch.

A wounded expression crossed her face. He did not fail to notice it, but he did not mention it. She deserved to feel wounded. "You were reciting the names of *kami* in your sleep. I thought you might be having a nightmare."

"Is there any word on the fugitives?"

Kiko sighed. "No, my prince. Not yet. It's only been a few hours since they escaped. It's a bit early to be hoping for anything—"

"Don't tell me that!" Mamushi slid off the bed and crossed over to the window. The glass from the shattered cage had been cleared away, although telltale scratches marred the tiled floor. "I expect more from you. I need my Hand back."

"If I may point out," said Kiko softly from the bed, "you still have one."

Mamushi scoffed and pushed the curtains aside, blinking rapidly in the sudden blaze of light. He lifted a hand to shade his face and gazed across the palace mile, toward the gates. "What's the name of Saizou's domain?"

"Akita Domain, although I believe it's soon to be re-christened as Shigure domain."

"He thinks he can escape from inside my palace." Mamushi pressed his palms against the glass, his golden nails scraping the surface. "Thinks he can take *my* property."

"As soon as he is recaptured, I'd like to oversee his torment personally." Kiko rose to her feet, a small, pleased smile on her face. Clicking her tongue, she said lightly, "Maybe I'll cut out his tongue first."

Mamushi straightened, his gaze drifting in the direction of Akita Domain. Tongues... "I like that idea," he murmured, tapping one finger against the window. *Tap-tap-tap.* "I like it very much."

"I'm glad you do, my Prince. It will be my pleasure."

Mamushi turned from the window. "Cut them all out."

Kiko pursed her lips. "I...he only has one."

Mamushi pointed toward the window. "Akita Domain." He stepped toward her, softening his voice with every word. "Announce it to everyone. Let them hear it in China, for all I care—every hour, some poor soul in Saizou's precious domain will lose a tongue until he returns Kirikizu to me and turns himself in."

Kiko's eyes narrowed as her smile stretched wider. "When should I start?"

He placed a hand on either of her shoulders and pressed a kiss to her forehead. "Now," he whispered.

Kiko fairly ran from the room, and Mamushi stared at the floor, filled with quiet, patient rage. *Now we will see, Saizou Akita. Now we will see how weak I can make you.*

# FORTY-FOUR

AFTER THE WAR broke out and most forms of electronic communication became illegal, news came to Akita Domain via messenger. On normal days, said news was printed in gold ink on black paper, and on normal days, it beckoned Matahachi to the palace to prevent the Prince-Regent from making the effort of an unnecessary journey.

So when one of the house guards strode into the kitchen where Matahachi was waiting for the coffee to brew and announced that the Crane was waiting outside the front door, Matahachi felt understandably taken aback.

"Did she say why?" he demanded, his mind turning over every thought, wondering why the Prince-Regent had sent his Left Hand, wondering whether Lady Tsuki and her complicit bodyguard had finally been caught. They had, after all, failed to return that night.

"She did not say, my lord." The guard bowed politely from the waist, but there was an undisguised look of fear and surprise on his face.

Matahachi carefully kept his face from mirroring those emotions and said coolly, "Let her in, of course."

The guard turned and strode quickly from the kitchen, while Matahachi followed. The Crane at Akita Domain? There were various reasons for her presence: all unprecedented, none of them good.

The guard reached for the front door, but Matahachi interrupted him. "No, wait. I will let her in."

"Yes, my lord." The guard backed away, looking as if he had just been ordered off the front lines.

Which, Matahachi knew, he probably had. He opened the door himself and stepped onto the front stoop. The Crane stood with her hands at her sides, half a dozen silver daggers fanning from the dark, coiled hair on her head.

While he had always kept a polite distance from the woman in order to avoid a possible demise by her infamous hand, it was not hard for Matahachi to envision one or more of those daggers piercing his throat should he say the wrong thing.

He settled a welcoming smile on his face and bowed low— not as low as he bowed for the Prince-Regent, but lower than he bowed for most. They were tricky things, bows. He straightened, gesturing toward the room behind him. "What an honor. Please, come inside."

She stalked past him and spun when she noticed the house guard still standing in the living room. "You." She jerked her chin toward the door. "Out."

He bowed rapidly once, then twice, and made a hasty exit.

Matahachi ignored her breach of protocol and shut the door. "Is there something I can do for the Prince-Regent?"

She glanced around the room with a critical eye. "He needs to borrow your domain."

The Prince-Regent had asked many unreasonable things of

Matahachi over the past five years, but Matahachi had been fully prepared to meet the Prince-Regent's demands, however strange, in exchange for this domain.

And now he was being asked to lend it, like an article of clothing? Matahachi narrowed his eyes, but carefully held his smile in place. "What an interesting way of putting it. I'm afraid something may have been lost in translation."

The Crane grinned, quick and unpleasant. "Oh, I meant what I said. Well...maybe not," she amended, running her finger across a vintage copy of Musashi's *A Book of Five Rings*. It was not Matahachi's. In fact, very few of the items in the house were his.

The home had been well-stocked when he arrived, and he had felt little need to change it although he knew that was not the whole reason. Somewhere in the back of his mind, he held the restless fear that Saizou Akita would return and somehow wrestle the domain back, out of Matahachi's possession. Changing things would have only made it more difficult.

Still, Matahachi watched the Crane study the books with a sense of unease. She was too unpredictable, too temperamental. She might choose to tear a book from the shelf and fling it to the floor at any moment, for no reason other than to watch the spine crack.

"No," said the Crane again, after a tense moment of silence. "My prince doesn't actually want the domain itself, just the people in it."

Matahachi pinched the bridge of his nose and sighed. "Your presence is an honor, but I neither want to hear, nor have time for, your word-games. Say what you mean and be clear."

Her eyes widened, and she drew *A Book of Five Rings* from the shelf. She leafed through the dry pages with so little care that Matahachi barely restrained himself from plucking it away from her. "I could cut your face open for talking to me that way, pretty man."

Matahachi pressed his lips together. "The people of this domain are my responsibility. I have every right to know why the Prince-Regent requires use of them. Is it for labor?"

The Crane did not lift her gaze from the dry pages of the book. Aloud, she read, "'When the enemy makes a quick attack, you must attack strongly and calmly, aim for his weak point as he draws near, and strongly defeat him. Or, if the enemy attacks nimbly, you must observe his movements and, with your body rather floating, join in with his movement as he draws near. Move quickly and cut him strongly. This is *Tai Tai No Sen*.'"

She was pulling at his patience, seeing how far it would stretch before it snapped. Matahachi kept silent. The Crane finally sighed and snapped the book shut before placing it back where it belonged.

She cocked her head to the side, still studying her surroundings rather than Matahachi, and said, "You remember Saizou Akita? I believe he still technically holds the title to this domain."

"Technically, yes," Matahachi began, but the Crane cut him off, adding, "He's run off with Kirikizu."

Matahachi blinked. He knew better than to react to the interruption, but that was not what confused him. "Run off...?"

"Not in the lover's sense," the Crane laughed. "I don't actually believe Kirikizu swings that way, if you know what I mean. That's the Prince-Regent's doing. No, we had Saizou in the palace, in the Prince-Regent's cage, but he escaped and took the Prince-Regent's Hand with him."

Matahachi's lips twitched. "He escaped?"

"He had help," the Crane snapped. The words may as well

have been acid in her mouth for all the violence with which she spat them out. "The Prince-Regent has decided to tug on our deposed lord Akita's heartstrings."

"And he views this domain as the instrument on which to play?" Matahachi glanced out the window, at the stretch of manicured lawn, and beyond that, the long, gravel pathway.

"You have a very pretty way with words," said the Crane, leaning her back against the shelf and folding her arms. She smiled. "You're very pretty all around, aren't you? Although, it would seem, not attractive enough to tempt your very own lady Tsuki."

Matahachi bristled at the implication. The Crane knew how to wield her words with vicious accuracy, but he maintained his passive expression, carefully groomed through years of experience. "The lady Tsuki is not my property," he replied.

"That's not what I heard, and I hear many, many things." The Crane tapped the side of her head with a sharp fingernail. "I hear she lives under your roof and leeches off your generosity but refuses to behave in a befitting way. Of course, I also hear she spends more time with that bodyguard of hers than any proper woman should."

Matahachi released a long breath through his nose and allowed his shoulders to relax. "She is her own person. I do not own her as a person owns a dog."

"No," the Crane agreed, a teasing light in her strange, blue-black eyes. "You don't own much, it seems." She straightened and crossed halfway to him before adding, "The Prince-Regent has a dispatch of one hundred palace samurai currently surrounding your domain. The captain will choose one poor, unfortunate villager to be made an example of every hour."

Now was the time, Matahachi decided, to let his civility slip. "The people of this domain are under my authority."

"Yes," she cooed. "And you are under the Prince-Regent's authority. He told me to tell you these words: 'if he kicks up a fuss, make it two villagers an hour. If he insists again, make it three.'" She smiled and strode past him, her shoulder barely brushing his. "He also said you would be rewarded for your cooperation."

"And if Saizou Akita fails to turn himself or Kirikizu in to the Prince-Regent?"

The Crane glanced over her shoulder. "What difference would it make?" She opened the door and strode out. Beyond her, Matahachi saw half a dozen palace samurai coming down the road toward the house on four-wheeled vehicles suited for rough terrain and running people down.

Matahachi licked his lips and stood in the doorway, watching the Crane make her way down the road to meet the oncoming soldiers. Perhaps it was time to remove a card from his sleeve.

———

LIEUTENANT TAKUAN BURST into Haka's office with a breathless, "Commander! Commander, you need to get out here."

Haka clutched his head with both hands, his heart racing at the sudden noise. He needed stardust back, but it was nowhere to be found. All drawers, boxes, and filing cabinets were devoid of the stuff, and Otter—Otter was not willing to divulge their location. Not yet. He would need to wring it out of her or petition the Prince-Regent for more, but how long would that take?

Longer than he had, he was sure—

"Commander!" Takuan snapped his fingers in the air, a foot from Haka's face. "Commander, this is important."

"What?" Haka snapped, kicking his chair back so hard it slammed into the wall and left a small dent. "What's important?"

Takuan's face wore an expression somewhere between fear and irritation. "There's an imperial officer outside, with half a dozen retainers."

Haka clenched his hands into fists, hoping to hide the intense trembling from the lieutenant. "What of them? What do they want?"

"The officer," said Takuan, concern cutting a line between his eyes. "He's a cyborg, Commander."

Haka's eyes widened. *A cyborg? What in the name of all kami is an imperial cyborg doing—*

"He says he's the new commander," said Takuan, gesturing toward the door. "He's here to take over the precinct."

# FORTY-FIVE

BASKING in the pale glow of her computer screens, Riza chewed on the tip of her pen. The time had come to make a decision. She had too many players running around the game board wherever they pleased, making their own decisions and wreaking havoc. It was galling. And not only galling, it threw a wrench in every plan she had. Her beautiful machine couldn't continue to work if the pieces kept jumping ship.

To expect that everything would continue smoothly while her contacts scurried around like deranged sewer-rats—it was too much.

She tossed the pen onto the desk and pushed her chair back. If Hiro had done his job—that is, if he was currently hauling the fugitives to the safe house rather than turning them into a bonfire, all she had to do was meet him there and explain things in a more personable way. Mono a mono.

"Except mono a mono is hardly your modus operandi, is it?" she asked her faint reflection, staring back at her from the computer screen like a pale-blue half-ghost. "You're better than this. You keep better tabs on your white mice than this. No, you don't," she added aloud. "Let's face it, this particular round hasn't gone so well. You should pack everything up and move. But you can't do that. Everything is *here*. And where else would you go, I'd like to ask? Granted, you can find anywhere to settle down, but where are you going to find enough room to house all this beautiful equipment?"

*It isn't yours.*

"I know it isn't mine," she snapped, folding her arms. A peaceful smile settled over her face, and she kicked back in her chair. "But let the losers weep; the finder has snitched all she can keep. Well, not *all*. But it's a good lot of stuff, you have to admit."

*I don't have to admit anything to you.*

Riza rolled her eyes. "Fine. Be that way. I'm staying here. What do I want for dinner?" She straightened and opened a new tab, scrolling down the menu of a noodle house nearby. "Noodles don't sound brilliant. Sushi. Sushi sounds brilliant; I'll order some sushi."

*You go right ahead and do that. I just hope the lovely reptile hasn't killed your fugitives to save his own scaly skin. Oh, and I also hope that Saizou's doing well, after his second spectacular escape from the palace.*

"I didn't engineer that one. Don't talk to me about it. I don't care."

*So petty. You can't orchestrate everything, you know.*

"Well, I should. Things go so much better when I'm in charge of it all."

*That's what YOU think. But don't mind me! Go ahead, eat your sushi. I'm sure everyone will survive just fine without you. Oh, and Shotgun. Poor Shotgun, poor kid. He's going to miss us.*

Riza frowned and tapped her index finger rapidly against

her forehead. "That's not fair. It's not my fault if he gets attached to me."

*No, you're right. You really shouldn't have expected it. It wouldn't be ordinary to attach yourself to the first person who contacted you after everyone you loved was brutally murdered. Honestly, that would just be weird.*

"Give it a rest." Riza shook her head violently and rose to her feet. "Geez."

*I'm going to pretend I didn't hear you say that.*

"You have no room to talk. Literally zero room."

*About what?*

"Caring. Feelings. Attachments. Coding. Puppies. Tall, red-haired extroverts. You name it, you have no room to talk."

The voice scoffed loudly. *If this job tugs your threadbare heartstrings too much, why don't we just parade ourselves back to our last job? If you call being harnessed in a straightjacket a job. I don't, usually, but I can't really speak for the both of us. As you said, I have no room. Although, I would like to put forward the theory that we have even less room when straightjackets are involved.*

Riza gazed fondly at the dark room around her. It wasn't large, by any means, but it was big enough for three tables, six computers, eight monitors, four keyboards, and a coffee table. There was a small, triangular, grimy bathroom on the other side of the door, just behind the third computer display.

It wasn't the most charming of places, but the Wi-Fi was really something.

*You can always come back for your junk. Just take the essentials.*

"There's actually no point," said Riza suddenly. "There's no point going anywhere until somebody contacts me. I'd be sticking my neck out for absolutely no reason. What am I supposed to do, hang around the safe house and hope some-body shows, while all my stuff is just sitting here, defenseless? No. No, that's a stupid idea."

When there was no response, she cocked her head to one side and frowned. "Go ahead, shut up now. See if I care."

*This is me, with no room to talk. I don't care what happens to us. Do whatever you want.*

"Oh, fried octopus on a stick."

*Ah, a new expletive. I like it. Very colorful.*

"I told you to shut up," Riza snapped. She stalked over to the nearest desk and reached underneath it, withdrawing a spacious black duffel bag. She ripped a handful of cords from the wall and watched as two of her monitors went black.

*Don't tell me you're actually doing that whole 'sticking your neck out' thing.*

"Oh, now you sound like you think it's a stupid idea."

*I think it's a moronic idea, and I think if the pretty lizard man was smart enough to shoot the fugitives and get rid of the evidence, then he's smart enough to go to the safe house and lure you in so he can shoot us, too.*

Riza rolled up the nearest wireless keyboard and tucked it into the corner of the duffel bag. This was routine: every deci-sion she made, the voice would take the opposite stance, advo-cating point A one second and switching to point B the next. "Well, congratulations, you changed my mind the last time. You got one chance, and that was it. For the next twenty-four hours, I'm totally immune to your drivel."

———

NIX CROUCHED in front of Kirikizu, watching him from the corner of his eye as he removed another small item from his pocket. He had found it going through the assassin's things. It looked like an ear cuff, but there was definitely something odd about it.

He held it up between his thumb and forefinger and said, "You just don't strike me as an accessory kind of fellow. Unless you count the frankly *ludicrous* amount of weapons, which I honestly do not."

The assassin, of course, said nothing. Nix had quieted him with three generous strips of duct-tape.

"It's very irritating, you know," said Nix, tossing the ear cuff into the air and catching it in his palm again. "I have so many questions to ask you, but if you answered, well, let's just say I don't love the idea of going through that again." He gave an exaggerated shudder.

Kirikizu sighed and glanced toward the window, and Nix followed his gaze. "Oh, them? They took off to God-knows-where. It's just you and me, baby, letting the kids run around doing whatever kids do these days. You know what I'm most curious about," he said suddenly, sliding the ear cuff over his pinky finger and smiling, "it's these." He tapped his lips. "Some very interesting scars you have there."

The assassin leaned his head back against the wall and closed his eyes.

"Ah, yes, the universal sign for 'I'm not interested in this conversation.' I respect that, I really do, but I'm also bored. I haven't been bored in absolute ages, and I refuse to let it continue."

As if on cue, he heard a faint sound, like the buzzing of a distant bee, coming from the object. He lifted an eyebrow and tapped it with a finger. It continued to buzz. Curious, Nix hooked the cuff around his ear.

"Hello? Yes? My goodness," he said immediately as a voice threatened to deafen him, "indoor voices, *please!*"

The previously unintelligible voice went silent, and then a woman said in a firm, aggravated tone, "And how about now?"

"Oh, that's *much* better, I thank you."

"You aren't Saizou."

Nix turned in a lazy circle. "One point for the mystery woman who can clearly tell differences in cadence and pitch. I am impressed, madame."

"Ha. I'm going to call you Smart-Aleck."

"Oh, exciting! I haven't had a nickname in ages. Except the name I currently go by."

"And what," said the other voice, even more annoyed than before, "would that name be?"

"Ah-ah, I asked yours first. Fair is fair."

"Riza," said the voice.

Nix gasped loudly and pressed a hand to his heart. "Do I have the honor of speaking to *the* Riza? You know I've wanted to talk to you for a few hours now, just to ask, have you ever considered being a professional dog walker? Your ability to hold so many leashes at once, it's...it is *truly* a gift. I would really consider putting it to better use."

"All right, Smart-Aleck, I don't actually care what your name is so just give the cuff to Saizou."

"Much easier said than done."

"Why?"

There was a new note in her voice, something urgent. Nix stretched out on his back and squinted at the ceiling. There was a face in the plaster above if he stared hard enough. "Something about a cure for a dying army pal. But don't ask me! I'm not really in the loop here. I'm just in it for revenge."

"Stop him!"

"That's the plan."

"Saizou! Stop Saizou, you idiot!"

Nix's smile faded to a thin line. "What did you just call me?"

"I called you an idiot. I know exactly where you are; you got this from the Prince-Regent's Hand, right? And you're in a dump on the corner of Ichi and Yama—"

Nix slowly sat up. "Well, well, well," he said coldly, "you're becoming more interesting by the second, dear."

"If Saizou goes back to the docks, he's heading into a trap. Their last contact changed his mind and decided not to help. You need to give this ear cuff to Saizou so I can give him the new address."

Nix glanced at Kirikizu. "You did mention knowing I have an assassin tied up and gagged in this room, yes?"

"I assumed he was there with you, since he was the last one to pick up the cuff. Drag him along with you or leave him, this is more important."

Nix huffed. "I'll tell you what."

"I don't have time for crazy demands."

"Cra—what! Crazy demands?" Nix stared at Kirikizu and rotated his finger around his head, rolling his eyes. Kirikizu sighed and shut his eyes again, but Nix was too engrossed in his conversation with Riza to particularly care. "All I want is a teeny, tiny favor."

"Spill."

"Do you know of anyone who would fix an electronic muzzle-slash-mask device thingamabob without asking too many questions?" He glanced at the broken thing on the floor. "Because we very much require that."

# FORTY-SIX

MURASAKI SQUARE WAS nothing like Saizou remembered. Once it had been known as the culture district: a unique blend of different cultural flavors selling various ethnic food, clothing, herbs, or toys. It was a hub of exchange. Now, the hand-painted signs were gone, replaced by neon lights in purple, green, red, and blue, garishly advertising whatever wares were inside. Booking clubs, hostess bars, love hotels. Everywhere Saizou turned, he saw evidence that the once-thriving Murasaki Square had become a red-light district.

"I told you this was quicker," said Tsuki, striding ahead of him, her hands in her pockets.

It had been quicker, but he almost wished he had not seen it. The gray sky made the neon seem that much brighter, that much harsher.

Tsuki glanced over her shoulder and slowed her fast pace down to fall alongside him. "What's wrong?"

Saizou looked down at the pavement and shook his head. Trying to sound as indifferent as he could, he said, "It's not how I remember it."

"Is anything? You were away for over five years. Things change over time."

"This isn't change," said Saizou, unable to mask the bitter edge in his voice. "This is entropy."

Tsuki's expression grew sympathetic, but it was the kind of sympathy generated by an insider for a stranger. Saizou felt a brief moment of anger toward it, but the anger died as quickly as it flared. He may have been fighting a war of blood and violence in Liaoyang, but Tsuki had stayed behind and watched the world she knew crumble to pieces around her. The change would have been slow and painful, a creeping cancer rather than the sharp gut-punch Saizou felt.

He wasn't sure which was worse.

He took a deep breath, inhaling the city-scent of sweet smoke and frying seafood. There was another smell—hazy, thick, and acrid. Opium. Who knew how many dens were hidden behind the storefronts or how many of these hostess bars were merely facades for human trafficking rings? The thought twisted his stomach.

It felt as though he had been fighting to wake up from a nightmare, only to discover upon awakening that reality was the greater of two evils.

"I know it's not the easiest shortcut to maneuver, but if you want to get to the docks within the next two hours and not draw attention, this is the way to go. Just keep your head down."

———

THE MOMENT OTTER heard the commotion outside the front of the precinct, she left Violet and Hibiscus in the courtyard and raced around front and ducked into the foyer through the office door. She expected to see a band of drunks being dragged in for disorderly conduct or possibly the mailman.

She did not expect to see a seven-foot cyborg standing by the reception desk, flanked by four palace samurai bearing the Prince-Regent's symbol: a black sun rising over a purple mountain.

Three Shinsengumi officers stood near the bulletin board, closer together than she had ever seen them. Intimidation, she thought, bringing people together since the Stone Age.

"Hey," she called, walking around behind the reception desk and wondering where on earth Lieutenant Takuan had gone. She lowered her voice and adopted the most professional posture she could. "Can I help you?"

The palace samurai to the right of the cyborg stepped forward, leaning halfway over the edge of the desk. "Where is the current commander?"

Otter stretched to her full miniscule height and snipped, "Who wants to know?"

The samurai lifted the front of his mask, revealing a scowling face. "Get your commander, girl."

"You will not speak to her in that manner while I'm still commander of this precinct!"

Otter froze in astonishment at the sound of Haka's voice, stronger and harsher than she had ever heard it before.

"Finally." The samurai turned and faced Haka and Lieutenant Takuan, who emerged from the hall and stopped at the other end of the reception desk.

Haka looked awful, Otter noted; worse than usual, which was saying something. But his posture was straight, and his shaded eyes gleamed with a fierce light as he took in the sight of four samurai and a cyborg and said, "It's for your own safety. She handles the mutts. You aren't much of a problem, I don't think. Otter," he said abruptly, "is he a problem?"

Otter gaped at Haka. Was he trying to goad the cyborg, or had he temporarily lost his mind as a result of his withdrawal? Otter decided she didn't care either way.

She liked it.

"I don't know, Commander; he sure doesn't look like one," she drawled, leaning both elbows on the desk. "Looks like your one-eight-hundred dial-a-samurai to me."

At her response, all four samurai drew their katanas and surrounded the cyborg on each side. It was a pretty comical sight, since the cyborg was a good head and shoulders taller than all four of them.

"Geez, guys," she said, strolling around the desk, "it's sarcasm, not a bomb threat."

"How dare you speak that way to Lord Nobunaga." The samurai who seemed to be in charge of the small party extended his sword toward Otter. "I could have your head for your insolence."

Otter wrinkled her nose. "Did you really just say *insolence?* It's the twenty-second century, mister. Get with the times."

"Lord Nobunaga?" Takuan's voice cut through the rising tension, polite and calming. "I don't believe I've ever heard of him before."

"Now you have." The samurai lowered his sword several inches, but Otter felt that if she opened her mouth one more time, she might never speak again. "He'll be Commander Nobunaga to you Shinsengumi."

Otter glanced at the cyborg. The florescent lights overhead gleamed off his black, faceless mask, providing a distorted reflection of the foyer. Otter lifted her hand as subtly as she could and waved, watching the stretched version of herself wave back.

The cyborg turned his head a fraction, and Otter dropped her hand immediately. She felt the hair on the back of her neck prickle as she realized he was looking directly at her, somewhere behind the smooth, expressionless visor.

"He's taking over the precinct?" One of the officers by the bulletin board stepped forward, glancing from the samurai to Haka and back again. "I mean—you're taking over the precinct?"

"Commander," snapped the samurai. "The Prince-Regent handpicked him personally to straighten out this cesspool of a station. Insubordination and failure to comply with the new regime will result in you being out of a job. Disobeying orders will get you behind bars. Are we clear?"

"Yes, Commander," the officer barked, embellishing his response with a stiff salute. The other two followed suit, casting glances at Haka, then at anything but him.

Otter clenched her hands into fists. She knew Haka was hardly adored, but she also knew complaints were rarely filed against him. He went easy on his precinct and rarely stirred up trouble, but from the sound of it, Nobunaga was about to provide a very harsh change to the usual routine.

The idea made her see red. "Are you saying *Commander* Haka is fired?"

"Yes," the samurai began, a sneer twisting his mouth with obvious enjoyment. He had no chance to finish his sentence.

The cyborg tilted his faceless head back, and in a surprisingly soft, clear voice, intoned, "Commander Haka will be demoted to lieutenant. He will remain at the precinct and serve his civic duty for now."

It was impossible to give the voice an age, but it sounded so reasonable that Otter was unsettled. She folded her arms across her chest like a shield and took a step back, closer to Haka and Takuan.

"*Hai*, Lord Nobunaga." The samurai reached up and pulled his visor back over his face—probably to hide a pout, Otter guessed.

The lean, long-limbed cyborg stepped past the samurai and bowed from the waist toward Haka, extending a mechanical arm so lithe and well-designed that Otter found herself momentarily dazzled by the craftsmanship.

"I hope," said Nobunaga, "you and I will be able to work together in harmony. For the safety of the citizens and this beautiful city."

Otter frowned. "What does a cyborg know about harmony? Or beauty, for that matter."

Haka groaned, just loud enough for Otter to hear. His voice was strained and thin, as if the show of strength earlier had drained him completely. "She doesn't know when to shut up," he said tiredly. "Otter?"

"I'll shut up," she said, automatically extending an arm to steady him, although he was not to the point of wavering yet. "Also, I'd like to offer a sincere apology for my sass. From the bottom of my heart—which you...well, I don't know if you understand that or not, but I do apologize."

"Basement," snapped Haka, shoving her hand away and pushing her toward the dungeon door. "Now. Take care of your mutants."

"Fine." Otter stalked down the hall with the distinctly uncomfortable feeling that she was standing on a rooftop, watching a storm approach. Except this storm rumbled in the distance, carried on the wings of a soft breeze, not the raging maelstrom she expected.

"It's coming," she muttered, yanking the door open and stalking down the stairs. "It's coming."

## FORTY-SEVEN

OSCAR HAD Creature sitting on the floor dressed in a white lab coat when the Prince-Regent strode into the lab and nearly tripped over the corpse in front of the door.

"Oh, don't mind that," said Oscar, rising to his feet. He pointed at Creature and said in a lower voice, "You stay there." Louder, he added, "Bit difficult to move, that one, and I didn't really feel like getting blood everywhere."

The Prince-Regent lifted his eyes slowly from the corpse and met Oscar's gaze. Oscar felt an abrupt chill, like an unexpected gust of winter wind in an otherwise autumnal landscape.

"Where is it?" the Prince-Regent asked. He showed no signs of shock, only displeasure, probably at the close brush with falling on his face. He looked as though someone unpleasant had brushed against him as he passed and he had graciously refused to punish them so long as they did not repeat the offense.

"Where is it?" Oscar repeated. He glanced at the body and

back at the Prince-Regent. "You know he—how did you know who did it?"

"Doctor," said the Prince-Regent, stepping over the body, "you are many things, but capable of this mess, you are not. At least not without significant help. You create life. Death is not in your nature."

"Well, it *wasn't*," said Oscar scathingly, glancing at Creature. "It is, however, most definitely in someone else's. Currently. At the present time."

Creature was still sitting patiently where he had been instructed to stay, but he glanced under the table in the Prince-Regent's direction before giving Oscar a quizzical expression. Oscar shook his head as subtly as possible, but the Prince-Regent must have noticed it, because he said, "Is it there? Show it to me."

Oscar suppressed a groan. "I would stay back," he warned.

"Is he already showing violent tendencies, then?"

"Might I," said Oscar in disbelief, "draw your attention back to the dismembered corpse you nearly fell over just now? What the hell was in that cocktail you had me give him?"

"Let's call it a Bloody Mary," said the Prince-Regent, flipping his hair over his shoulder and striding around the nearest table.

"That's one hell of a Bloody Mary," said Oscar. He patted Creature's shoulder. "Stand up."

"No, don't bother," said the Prince-Regent. He approached Creature carefully; at least he didn't rush. Oscar didn't want to think about the consequences should Creature get it into his head to kill the Prince-Regent. The Prince-Regent lowered himself to one knee two feet away from Creature and crooned, "Let me have a look at you."

"Your Highness," said Oscar, hoping to get the Prince-

Regent's attention with the honorific. "I really would stay back. As far as I know, the...er, guard over there didn't provoke Creature."

"Creature. Is that what you've chosen to call it? A bit bland, isn't it?" The Prince-Regent glanced at Oscar, ignoring the warnings completely.

*Well,* thought Oscar, *if he has a death wish, that's entirely his fault. It's not like anyone will miss him when he's gone. Except maybe the Crane woman. Heavens.*

"Instruct him never to harm me."

Oscar stared at the Prince-Regent. "I beg your pardon?"

The Prince-Regent did not move his gaze from Creature, but Creature was looking at Oscar in total bewilderment. "I'm not really sure he'll listen to me," Oscar began, but the Prince-Regent interrupted him.

"You are still alive," he pointed out. "You are its creator. Given enough time, I have no doubt it will imprint on you."

"I—well." Oscar cleared his throat. "I hardly think—"

"Order him," said the Prince-Regent slowly, "never to harm me."

Creature's expression darkened, but his eyes did not leave Oscar's face. "I don't like him."

Oscar sighed. "You are never to harm him, do you understand?"

"Why?"

Oscar bent down to deliver a more effective glare. "Now, listen here, you're too young to be questioning everything I say. You are not to hurt the Prince-Regent, do you understand me?"

Creature curled his lip. "No."

*I am not cut out for this. I've never disciplined anything but myself. I've never even trained a dog.* Oscar scratched his head —Creature had not killed him yet, but that didn't mean Creature would listen to everything he said. And the Prince-Regent was two feet away from it, this small, brand-new killing machine...

"You will obey what I say," said Oscar sternly, employing the only effective tool he remembered from his own childhood. "Or *else.*"

Creature's expression became a blank slate as he tried to understand whether or not Oscar's words held a threat.

Oscar watched him closely, hoping against hope that the vague parental phrase had sunk through Creature's skull. Then again, he might be too new to be susceptible to the idea of consequences...

Finally, Creature drew his sharp eyebrows together and twisted his mouth in displeasure, but he leaned his back against the wall and folded his hands in his lap, an exaggerated picture of forbearance.

*Mum, I owe you a very expensive gift and a kiss on the cheek.* "Good boy," said Oscar, enormously relieved.

Creature frowned in confusion at the word *boy*, but if he had any existential questions about himself, he did not give them voice. Instead, he watched the Prince-Regent, who smiled at Oscar and said, "Well done. It does listen to you. When I have commands for it, you will pass them on to it."

"I'm still in the dark as to why you wanted Creature in the first place," Oscar admitted, scanning the Prince-Regent's face for any signs of an answer to the hinted question.

"I'll let you know in due time," said the Prince-Regent softly. He cupped Creature's chin in his hand, turning its face toward him.

Creature moved as if to jerk his head away, but the Prince-Regent gripped him harder and snapped, "Be still. Doctor, tell it to be still."

Oscar did not want to tell Creature to be still. In fact, he was astonished at the strength of his own desire to tell Creature to *get away from that man,* but there was nothing he could do except say, "Creature, he wants to meet you. Don't move."

"It's lovely." The Prince-Regent smoothed his fingers down the curve of Creature's cheek. "Exquisite."

"Yes, and also rather dangerous," said Oscar, frowning. "It's not a marble statue in a museum, you know. It could bite."

As if to prove Oscar's point, Creature bared his teeth in a terrifying parody of a smile.

The Prince-Regent's eyes narrowed, and he removed his hand from Creature's face. "I expect you to teach it better behavior in the upcoming weeks."

"Give it a little credit," said Oscar. "It's only been alive for a few hours. All things taken into consideration, I'd say it's doing rather well." He caught the scowl darkening the Prince-Regent's face and hastily added, "Of course, however, intensive behavioral training is required. Of course."

Creature shot him a baleful look, to which Oscar replied, "You don't even know what I'm talking about. Don't look at me that way."

The Prince-Regent hooked a finger around the collar of Creature's hastily-buttoned lab coat and pulled it aside. "These markings," he asked, with a hint of displeasure in his voice. "Will they heal?"

*Oh, for pity's sake.* "If you wanted him to enter a beauty contest, you should've mentioned," said Oscar. "Personally, I think he looks amazing, given what I had to work with. The very fact he's not ripping you to pieces right now is incredible, so I'll thank you not to criticize my handiwork just yet. Hail the Sun."

"I don't appreciate your sarcasm, Doctor." The Prince-

Regent looked Creature up and down, his gaze lingering longer than it had to.

Oscar frowned. "He'll get x-rays later."

"He needs better clothes."

"Ha! I even agree with you. Can't very well run around and do whatever the hell he's supposed to in a lab coat," Oscar said. "Not to mention it's too big."

The Prince-Regent rose to his feet. "I'll send a seamstress to take his measurements once you are both moved into your new quarters."

"New quarters? Whoopee," said Oscar, eyeing the Prince-Regent, wishing he would back farther away from Creature. It was rather like watching a reptile circle around a baby chick, except the baby chick could take the predator down in three seconds had Oscar not ordered him to leave the reptile alone.

"Doctor Sleimann," said the Prince-Regent, his face stiff, too controlled, "I have shown you more leniency than anyone before, because I judged you would be the best for your task. That being said, there is always someone second-best who could replace you if necessary. Please don't forget I could take your new creation away from you."

Never had Oscar wanted to punch the Prince-Regent in the face as much as he did right then, but more was at stake now. He glanced at Creature, who was intently focused on his own hands and did not seem to be paying attention.

Oscar cleared his throat and bowed again, clasping hand over fist. "I'm sorry," he said, and he half-meant it, if only for Creature's sake. It wasn't *his* fault he'd been brought into the world. "I'll do my best to show you proper respect." *Not the respect you deserve, mind. It'll be a performance. An Oscar-worthy performance, you could say. Heh.*

The Prince-Regent smiled, a barely-there expression that

lifted the corner of his mouth in such an unbearably condescending manner that Oscar almost threw his apology out the
window and slugged him anyway.

"Guards!" The Prince-Regent glanced at the door, which
opened immediately. Two palace samurai stepped through and
stood at the ready.

A faint growl came from Creature. "No," hissed Oscar,
with vehement shake of his head. He seemed to have a tenuous
sort of control over Creature, but he was afraid the presence of
the samurai might be asking more of the Creature than he
could give.

"Your Highness," barked the samurai in unison.

"Clear that body away." The Prince-Regent gestured in the
direction of the corpse. "We'll be moving Doctor Sleimann and
the experiment to the resident suite."

*Resident suite.* Fancy name for a different kind of prison
cell. Oscar scratched the back of his head and watched Creature for any signs of aggression. Creature stood up, his back still
pressed against the wall. A low growl still emanated from his
throat, but he made no move to attack anyone.

*The Prince-Regent is watching,* Oscar wanted to say—if
Creature attacked anyone else while the Prince-Regent
observed, things could go very badly. Creature could be taken
away within the first few hours of birth, of all things. *Please
behave. Please behave.*

"*Hai,* Your Highness." The samurai bowed and bent to lift
the body of their fellow guard, and that's when Creature
struck.

Before Oscar could grab him, Creature sprang forward,
launching himself over the table and landing on the taller
samurai's back with precision and ferocity. His arms were

around the man's neck, his fingers clawing at the helmet as he pried it free in less than three seconds.

The second samurai jumped back and drew his katana, but the Prince-Regent stopped him.

"Put it back." He held out a hand, his eyes focused with burning intensity as the Creature raked his fingernails into the screaming samurai's exposed face. "I want to watch."

Oscar stared at the Prince-Regent, aghast. "Watch? He killed one already and you want him to—"

"Be quiet," the Prince-Regent snapped.

Oscar licked his lips and folded his arms. If he tried to interfere, the Prince-Regent could have his head. He watched, unable to look away, as everyone stood by and let Creature tear down the samurai, which he did. He tore out mouthfuls of flesh with his teeth, he dug out eyes, and finally—mercifully—he snapped the samurai's neck so hard bone punched through flesh.

The samurai crumpled to the floor.

"And now there are two," muttered Oscar, raking his fingers through his hair.

Creature crouched down, his white lab coat stained a deep, brilliant red. He was soaked in blood again: his face, his hair, his hands. He was horrifying.

"I've already given you one bath today," Oscar groaned. He turned to the Prince-Regent and demanded, "What was the point of that? What was the bloody point?"

The Prince-Regent was not looking at him; he was fixated on Creature with an almost feverish light in his eyes. "He's perfect." He blinked once, twice, and said with a bit more realism, "Or he will be, once he's matured."

"Matured? We don't even know how long that will take. If he grows perfectly, and I mean *perfectly*, with no hitches whatsoever, he might behave like a fifteen-year-old within a year. He might. To catch up to a thirty-year-old body? That's going to take some time."

The Prince-Regent tucked a strand of hair behind his ear and said coolly, "You have two weeks." He snapped his fingers at the remaining samurai and said, "Out. Servants will clear this up."

Oscar stared as the Prince-Regent and the guard exited the lab, shutting the door and leaving the smell of blood behind them.

# FORTY-EIGHT

RIZA GLANCED at her packed bag. She had to get a message to Saizou before he reached the docks and was shot by Hiro. She really needed to have a word with that reptile. The sheer gall—well, now wasn't the time. She tucked a strand of hair behind her ear, adjusted her headphones, and cracked her knuckles. They popped like fireworks, and she put her fingers to the keyboard.

According to Nix, Tsuki Shimabukuru and her bodyguard had accompanied Saizou when he left. Riza realized she was one of the few people aware of Tsuki's underground activities, and for the first time, that knowledge was helpful. Tsuki had been in this part of the city before, which meant she probably knew shortcuts. If she knew shortcuts, then she would take Saizou through the nearest one, straight to the docks, and save time.

If they had left between twenty and forty minutes ago, they should be in Murasaki Square. It took all of fifteen seconds to pry her way into the Shinsengumi Traffic Database, and from there, she began to scour through Murasaki's CCTV streams.

There weren't as many cameras in red-light districts; nobody cared enough to keep them running, and many were deliberately taken down as part of the 'live and let live' agreement between the current government and those dealing in illegal black-market activities.

Riza reduced the CCTV streams to thumbnails so she could watch more of them at a time. She leaned back and watched the center of the screen, unfocusing her eyes just enough that her subconscious would alert her when Saizou, Tsuki, or the bodyguard appeared on any of the cameras.

After ten seconds that seemed more like minutes, she saw Saizou—but it was not the view she'd expected. He wasn't ducking through some alley, he was running across a rooftop with Tsuki and Kiba close behind him.

Riza shook her head. "You found a shortcut through the shortcut," she said aloud, removing the last ball of gum from the bowl on the desk. "Nice work, but I hope you realize that just made my work harder. I don't appreciate that. You're a stinker."

She couldn't just use any sign in town, then. She had to find a billboard, something Saizou would definitely see from a rooftop before he was out of the square.

She searched for all electronic billboards in the nearby area. She considered doing a sky-search and looking for signs of UFOs—it would be way easier to just beam Saizou up and plop him down at the correct place—but UFOs were infamously good at cloaking themselves, and she didn't have the time.

Billboards. Billboards. Bill—ha! It took her half a minute to take over the billboard and switch the message running across it in bright blue, neon letters. She cracked her knuckles again and began to type up a message that would catch Saizou's attention.

———

SAIZOU TURNED, scanning for the shortest route to the docks. Murasaki Square ended in roughly three blocks, and after that was a large stretch of abandoned outer buildings and concrete. Beyond those, he could see the vague forms of two ships in drydock, half-hidden behind the veil of ocean mist and haze rising from Murasaki.

"The air's bad today." Tsuki tugged her thin turtleneck up over her mouth and nose. "They must be cooking up more cocktails."

"Drugs?" Saizou glanced over his shoulder.

She nodded. "You name it, someone here probably makes it. Usually behind ramen stores. You go into half these places and ask for a salad, it's usually code for drugs."

"Not that you would know," said Kiba.

"Of course not." Tsuki's smile was visible behind the folds of the turtleneck, now acting as a filter. The smile froze, then shifted into an expression of incredulity. "Saizou, look to the right."

He turned his head, unable to see out of his bandaged right eye. He nearly asked Tsuki what he was looking for, but the words caught in his mouth. Rising up behind an apartment building was a billboard. Flashing across it in neon blue letters were the words, *YOU THREE. DANGER. PAY PHONE BELOW. WAIT FOR CALL.*

"That can't be aimed at us," said Tsuki, her voice filled with bewilderment.

"It doesn't sound like an advertisement," Kiba pointed out. He crossed over to the edge of the building and looked down toward the sidewalk. "There is a pay phone."

"I don't have time." Saizou began to calculate how far he needed to jump to the next rooftop when Tsuki said, "Look again."

Saizou frowned and turned. This time, indisputably, the billboard read *LISTEN TO RIZA. GET YOUR ASS TO THE PAY PHONE.*

"Pretty sure she's talking to you," said Tsuki. "Let's find a way down."

Saizou frowned and reached into his pocket. The ear cuff was gone—he hadn't given it a thought since the palace. He shook his head and climbed quickly down the service ladder, keeping his back to as much of the passing crowd as possible while he made his way to the pay phone. He entered the booth and rapped his knuckles against the rusty phone.

It probably hadn't been used in years, but Riza might be the only one who could make it work if she really had sent the message. He would give her thirty seconds to call, and then he was gone. He'd wasted enough time as it was.

The phone rang, a rusty, grating noise. He snatched the receiver from the hook on the first ring and put it to his ear. "What?"

"You were just going to ignore my message, weren't you? Do you realize the day I've had?" Her voice was deep and distorted, no doubt using a filter to keep her from being recognized, should the conversation reach a third party.

"I don't care about your day. Shi's dying."

"The docks aren't safe anymore. You need to go to the martial arts gym in the Chiyoshi district. It caught the brunt of a homemade bomb a couple years back, and nobody uses it anymore; it's the current safe house."

"What do you mean the docks aren't safe anymore?" Saizou demanded, gripping the receiver until his knuckles turned white. "What about Shi?"

"They...will...meet you there."

The answer was sloppy and unconvincing. Saizou felt his

blood run cold. "Try answering my question again before I hang up and go to the docks anyway."

Riza cleared her throat. "Hiro heard about your capture."

"He heard, or you told him?"

"It doesn't matter," she said, brushing his question aside. "He decided to take the situation into his own hands, and I think he may have shot everyone to save himself."

The words knocked against Saizou's skull but refused to penetrate. "What do you mean?" he asked, then again, louder. "What do you mean?"

"Is your head as thick as your police record? I'm saying Hiro killed your friends and the docks are no longer safe. You need to get to the gym and wait for me. I'm coming there in person. This entire thing has gone to hell, and I need to salvage what I can."

Saizou's grip on the phone loosened as his remaining vision blurred and the sounds outside the phone booth faded to white noise. He barely felt himself drop the phone, barely heard it catch on the line and slam against the wall of the booth.

"He's coming to the gym, if he goes through with the next part of the plan."

The voice was tinny, far-away, unimportant. Saizou slid down the wall, staring at the broken sidewalk beyond his boots, at the blur of people walking past, oblivious and uncaring. They were not part of his world. His world had shrunk down to the size of a single fact: Shi was dead.

It entailed so much. Too much.

A moment ago, Shi was dying. There was a chance. Now that chance was gone, along with Shi. Killed not in a Liaoyang jungle, not under orders, but shot in a city that was not his, for a cause that was not his, because his friend had failed him.

Saizou clutched his chest and tried to breathe. He tried, but his lungs were gone, replaced by paper that crumpled and tore at the first attempt. He tried to see, but there was nothing to see, and everything faded to a dull gray.

"Saizou?" The voice pushed through the dull throbbing in his head, as if he was drowning and someone was calling from above. "Saizou, what happened? What's wrong?"

Hands gripped his jacket and tried to pull him up. He felt the pressure of his jacket against his shoulders, felt the shift as he stood.

"Saizou!" The voice snapped through the throbbing, louder this time. The hands that had pulled him to his feet now struck his face. He caught the wrist—slender, female—Tsuki's wrist—and stared into her face.

"Shi," he said, then swallowed; his voice was too dry, he couldn't hear it. Tsuki should know. She and Kiba could return before their absence was questioned. He began to say Shi's name again, but the word faded in his mouth. He couldn't speak it. "Get back before Matahachi knows you're missing."

"No, Saizou. Tell us what happened."

Only then did Saizou notice Kiba standing behind Tsuki to her right, just inside his blind spot.

He released Tsuki's wrist, pushing her hand away with the same motion. "Go home."

"Saizou!" His name was a slap, but he could feel nothing. Tsuki glanced at the dangling phone, then back at Saizou. She picked up the receiver; she spoke into it.

Saizou sagged against the wall, trying to bring himself into the present moment, where he could take action. Where he could get Tsuki back to safety, where he could...

It startled him to realize there was nothing after that goal. Nothing to accomplish. Shi was dead, and the thought was too much. The hole was too much—how could there be such a black, empty space where, just moments before, the space was full?

He hadn't noticed how big it was. What sense did it make, that something could rip him in half so casually? That Riza...

Riza.

He turned, reaching for the receiver, but Tsuki was lowering it from her ear, staring at Saizou with such overwhelming shock and pity in her eyes that he looked away and snatched the receiver from her.

"You." His breathing was heavy, his heartbeat heavier, drumming inside his skull with such violence that it nearly drowned out his own voice. "I'm coming to the safe house."

"Good," Riza began, but he ignored the rest of what she had to say. He didn't want to hear it. He didn't care. He pushed past Tsuki and Kiba and strode down the sidewalk, oblivious as his shoulder bumped against passers-by. Chiyoshi was in the opposite direction.

He would head back. He would wait at the gym, and when Hiro arrived, he would kill him.

## FORTY-NINE

RITA SHUT down her computers and picked up her bag. She'd told Saizou that Hiro was coming to the gym; that should be enough bait to get him there, and then hopefully she could keep any more of her chess pieces from dying.

Chess pieces she could get anywhere. But highly skilled, highly motivated chess pieces? Those were limited edition, and if they didn't stop killing each other and mucking up the game, she was going to lose, and big time.

She stood at the door and sighed before reaching into her duffel bag and withdrawing a small, oval grenade. She pressed the indentation on the top, threw it inside, and shut the door before racing down the stairwell.

————

MATAHACHI STOOD on the roof of his house—for it *was* his house: the papers were signed, the documents officiated—and watched the samurai place four antigravity discs on the ground. On top of the discs, they set an eight-by-eight square of material. It was too distant for Matahachi to make out exactly what the material was, and the samurai stepped back, raising the platform six feet above the ground. They assembled four floating stairs in a similar manner: the killing platform had to be high enough for a gathered crowd to witness whatever spectacle took place atop it.

Down the long gravel drive spilled the sounds of questions and protests, the faint noise growing louder as the people drew nearer. The rest of the samurai were herding people in like cattle, directing them toward the platform.

Matahachi could see the Crane watching from her position at the front of the house. He imagined a cruel smile cutting her face as she watched the villagers—his villagers—poked and prodded around the platform.

Matahachi looked down at his watch. It was four minutes until high noon, when the event would begin. He had to make up his mind. He was in limbo, standing with a foot on either side as the chasm beneath him widened, threatening his balance. Tsuki and her bodyguard were with Saizou Akita. He knew their exact location as of ten minutes ago. His drone still followed them; it would not be hard to find them again, to turn their location in to the Prince-Regent.

And yet if he did that, Tsuki would never forgive him. Tsuki herself might be punished, even if he could manage to provide her with a lenient punishment over death. He was responsible for her, in the Prince-Regent's eyes. She would get them both into trouble, and she would hate him for Saizou's sake.

Matahachi reached into the folds of his robe and withdrew the object. He had kept it pressed against his skin for years, since the moment he had come by it. It was too valuable, too precious to leave anywhere but on his person, and yet he had never used it. A kitsune's tail could be used only once by a mortal human, and with varying results. He knew his literature, he knew his folklore, and he knew the stories to be true—

And now he knew the kitsune was closer than he thought. Possibly, he had returned to take his tail back. Possibly, he had forgotten the favor Matahachi had done him.

The tail was not its true form, not once it left the kitsune's possession. Instead, it became a black twig, as if coated with gleaming matte paint. To use it, one only had to snap the twig with force and direct the power toward your wish.

A scream interrupted his thoughts, followed by more screams, mingled with desperate, begging cries. The samurai atop the platform had motioned to one of his nearby comrades, who forced a villager up the stairs at swordpoint, the tip of his blade glowing red. The samurai unhooked a smaller blade from his belt. This was not a razor blade; it was simply metal, sharp and thirsty.

The villager was an old man Matahachi recognized as one of the village elders. Did they know they had chosen a respected member of the domain? Probably, he thought; the Crane would choose someone who had the most potential to shake the rest of the villagers. She would stir up as much fear as she could, by whatever method. She enjoyed it too much.

The breeze carried the people's cries clearly to Matahachi's ears as one samurai held the old man down and the samurai with the knife poised over the victim's face.

Someone cried, "Stop!" and for a moment, Matahachi held his breath, wondering if someone had come to interrupt the proceedings. It was a short-lived moment. The Crane strode forward and jogged up the stairs, motioning for the samurai with the knife to give his weapon to her. She took it from him, and he left the platform, leaving her with the knife and a smile crueler than the one Matahachi had seen before.

He watched, unblinking, as the Crane placed the knife in the man's open mouth and sliced. The blade must have been well-sharpened, for it took only one motion to sever the man's tongue from his mouth. The villager's screams became sobs, and fear became hysteria as their elder collapsed choking on the platform, blood spewing from his mouth in an endless stream.

The Crane coolly kicked him off the platform. The pale sunlight glinted off the silver blades in her hair as she turned her head and looked up at Matahachi. He could see her red smile clearer now, and he knew she was no longer daring him to act.

She believed he would not, and she gloated over that fact.

Matahachi turned and walked away from the roof's edge.

———

TSUKI RACED up the stairs to Nix's apartment. She had made a promise in exchange for one from Kiba: she would bring Nix and Kirikizu to the gym and they would figure out where to go from there, while Kiba would follow Saizou and keep him out of trouble as long as possible. Tsuki had the utmost faith in Kiba, but she did not know Saizou's temperament—he was so different from the young man she had said goodbye to five years ago. It put her on edge.

She knew he had to feel the same way about her, and she wanted there to be time; time to study Saizou, to figure him out again, time for her to reveal herself for who she was now and hope he still held a spark of interest. But the Saizou who had stared her down in the phone booth was not a Saizou she had ever confronted before—the empty rage, the blank expression. She remembered his shaking hand gripping her wrist, and although she did not want to admit it, she had been afraid, just for a moment, that he would snap it completely, before he came to his senses.Kiba had sensed it as well, which is why Tsuki was the one going back to get Nix, instead of Kiba. He had firmly told her he would rather remain with Saizou than leave her behind with him.

*"In his current state, he is unpredictable. You saw the footage of his escape from the palace. He's unstable. Were he to act foolishly and you attempted to intervene, he might not even recognize you. You can't count on anything where he's concerned, not now. You go back, get the fox, have him bring the assassin to the gym. We'll meet you there."*

Tsuki pounded against the door. "Nix! Nix, it's Tsuki, open up!"

The door swung open, and Nix stepped aside to let her in. "What's the rush, doll? And why are you back here? Aren't you supposed to be saving a friend of a friend or something?"

She glanced at Kirikizu, who did not appear to have moved even an inch since she left. She turned to Nix. "Saizou's contact got ahold of him. She says the yakuza boss they were depending on shot Shi and the other two fugitives at the docks."

Nix gasped and planted both hands on his hips, the picture of utter indignance. "Well, this is a flaw in the plan."

"Yes. We have to meet them at the gym."

"Excuse me for failing to see why."

"Saizou is headed to the gym because the yakuza boss is also headed there, to meet up with the contact." Tsuki attempted to portray more patience than she felt. "Saizou wants to kill him. Do you understand?"

Nix raised both eyebrows and simultaneously narrowed his

eyes. Then he smiled quickly and said, "Oh, sweet revenge. And so quickly, too, my goodness. To think, an hour ago he was rushing off to save his best friend. Will we be taking this delightful person?" He gestured to Kirikizu.

"We have to. We can't leave him here." Tsuki gave Nix a brief *this conversation is over* smile. "I just announced our destination."

For a moment, Nix was silent, his eyes darting left and right as if reading his response as he mentally wrote it. Then he said brightly, "Oh, well, I suppose we'll have to kill him."

"Grab anything you want to take," said Tsuki, opening the cabinet over the two-burner stove.

"Am I to take that as a yes, we are indeed killing him, or a no, we can't do that?"

"The latter. Do you have anything but ramen?"

Nix flicked a firefly off his shoulder. "No," he said. "However, there does happen to be a convenience store two blocks down the street, if you'd care to stock up on supplies."

"We'll have to, since apparently nobody thinks about practical items like food anymore." Tsuki turned around and pointed toward Kirikizu. "Get him."

Nix lifted both hands. "Yes, madame empress."

She shot him a dark look, and he slunk over to Kirikizu and stood studying him. "How to carry him, that's the question. Over my back like the proverbial potato sack? In both arms bridal-style?"

"Nix, I don't care if you're a thousand years old." Tsuki slammed the cabinet door shut. "If you don't take this seriousl—"

She never finished her threat. An odd look passed over Nix's face, and he drew his eyebrows together, as if something strange had just taken place and Tsuki had missed it completely.

"What?" she began, but Nix suddenly coughed and bent over, his breathing strangled as he choked.

"What is it?" Tsuki crossed the room in three strides and gripped his arm. "What's happening?"

He shook his head and straightened, and Tsuki thought the event had passed, but he suddenly dropped to his hands and knees. It sounded like each breath tore a new hole somewhere inside him. Tsuki fully expected to see him start bleeding somewhere or to begin foaming at the mouth.

What came from his mouth was neither blood nor foam, but black mist. It began as a single curl, like smoke from dying embers, but the mist grew heavier and thicker, pouring from his mouth billow after billow until Tsuki could hardly see through the haze of it.

Nix rolled onto his back, his face twisted with pain. When he opened his eyes, they were holes of burning black, as if his eyes had been stolen away without replacement. He snarled, and just for a moment, Tsuki caught a glimpse of the fox—an elongated snout and razor-sharp teeth, ears pinned flat against his head.

Then he howled, and she recognized the sound from the palace; the sound of wolves and screams and wind, and she felt the same frozen shiver wreath her like a deep-winter frost. She braced herself, but it wasn't enough. The sudden blast of cold wind knocked her off her feet and threw her across the room.

Her head cracked against the wall, and she fell to the floor, unconscious.

# FIFTY

IF THERE WAS one thing the Empire did well, it was take over other operations with unsettling efficiency. Haka and Takuan watched as Nobunaga assumed the position of commander with ease and called a lineup. He listened to everyone state their full name and rank. He did not reassign anyone except Haka, but he was quick to set everyone to work. Nobunaga's samurai brought in several boxes and began to unpack new technology—the computer setup was torn out completely and replaced with technology that had been updated at least three times since their last installment.

"Oh, look. All that funding we've been putting in requests for. It's here," said Takuan under his breath, shaking his head in disbelief.

Haka said nothing; he watched, unmoving, as the old computers were carried out in boxes by the samurai. Nobunaga stood on the other side of the room, next to the door. It was impossible to tell whether he, too, was watching the old supplies be carried out or whether his gaze went farther, to Haka and Takuan. For all Haka knew, the cyborg's smooth, faceless exterior might allow a full panoramic view of everything.

"Are you all right?"

Haka glanced at Takuan. "Yeah."

"I call bull. You could barely stand up twenty minutes ago."

His throat was parched, his head felt hollowed-out and empty, his skin felt like it was barely holding together, and if he moved from his position, he legitimately feared he would collapse. Haka did not mention any of this and, instead, opted for another truthful answer. "How I feel is an improvement on how I felt twenty minutes ago. That damn girl hid the stardust."

"That damn girl is doing you a favor." Takuan unfolded his arms and abruptly called, "Hey, wait a second—you, in the office!"

Haka glanced at the open office door and saw a samurai pulling books off the shelves an armful at a time and depositing them gracelessly in a cardboard box.

The samurai gave Takuan a dirty look and dropped the next load in the box.

"Of all the—immature—honestly, this is unacceptable." Takuan stepped away from the wall and raised his hand. "Commander Nobunaga!"

The cyborg's head moved a fraction of an inch. "Lieutenant Takuan."

Takuan sighed, as if realizing that his upcoming action would give him the appearance of a three-year-old. He pointed into the office and said, "One of your samurai is cleaning out the office in an extremely careless manner."

Nobunaga strode forward and turned to gaze into the office. "Eguchi."

He did not raise his voice to speak the word, but the

samurai snapped to attention and turned, bowing from the waist. "Commander."

"Please vacate the office. Lieutenant Takuan will see to clearing out the office. Please vacate the space and allow him to work."

Takuan unleashed a relieved breath. "Thank you, Commander."

Nobunaga faced Takuan and nodded a fraction of an inch. "Have it ready in twenty minutes," he said, before turning and ducking out the front door.

"Well," said Takuan after a moment, as the samurai stalked past him without so much as a glance, "at least the new commander is reasonable."

Haka gave Takuan a dark look. "You just volunteered yourself for cleaning duty."

Takuan stretched his arms in preparation. "You need to go find Otter and ask for a dose, Commander."

"I'm not commander," Haka snapped. His head spun with the effort, and he closed his eyes, groaning softly at his own miserable existence. Right now, the idea of drowning himself in a bathtub was preferable to the idea of trudging down the dungeon stairs in search of Otter so he could ask nicely for another dose of a drug she was pulling him off of, please and thank you.

"You're commander to me. Nobunaga is just a temporary fixture." Takuan gripped Haka's shoulder firmly for a moment before saying, "He's attempting to take over as smoothly as possible, but I wonder what this means for the prisoner."

*Winter.* Haka opened his eyes. If Nobunaga was switching the regime as thoroughly as it seemed, Winter's fate would no longer be uncertain—he would either be found innocent and free to leave, or he would be found guilty and dealt with.

He took a step forward, and the world spun. Before he could even reach out and catch his balance, Takuan caught his arm and pulled him up. "I'll get you down there, Commander," he said in a low voice, casting a glance at the front door.

"You've only got twenty minutes to pack the whole office," Haka grunted.

Takuan grinned. "I've moved three times in the last six years. I'm a certified packing expert. I'll get you downstairs and pack every item in that office with time to spare."

Haka fought to suppress a coughing fit as Takuan draped Haka's arm over his shoulder and started toward the dungeon door. They reached the door—Takuan was not as tall as Haka, but he was strong and solid, and Haka was almost irked at how easy he was to move around.

"I'll make it down the stairs." Haka gave Takuan a pathetic shove toward the office. "Get to work."

"I said you're still my commander," said Takuan, straight-faced, "but I regret to inform you that the right to boss me around has gone out. In with the new."

"Well," said Haka after a brief moment, "all good things must end, I guess."

"Exactly that, Commander."

Haka grudgingly allowed Takuan to help him down the stairs before he told Takuan he could make it from there. Takuan gave him a smile that attempted to hide his concern before he jogged back up the stairs.

As soon as the door shut at the top of the stairs, Haka sank to the ground, pressing his forehead against the cold stone. It had been bearable up there for five, maybe ten minutes. He thought it might not be too bad. It might be all right.

Now sweat dripped from his hands and he wanted to vomit.

"You look pathetic."

Haka knew Winter's voice. He knew he looked pathetic. He *was* pathetic. Never had he felt it more keenly than now, and he wanted to take Winter's chains and fling them against his teeth. He could laugh at him and spit blood at the same time.

"What goes on upstairs?"

Haka barely managed to lift himself onto his hands and knees. Keeping his gaze fixed on the floor seemed the best remedy for his nausea, so he did not bother to look up. "The precinct has a new commander. Nobunaga. A cyborg."

Chains rattled; perhaps Winter was leaning forward.

Haka said, "I doubt he'll find you innocent."

"I don't suppose he will."

Haka's nails scraped against the stone as he curled his fingers into fists. "Why do you always have to be so damn *resigned*? Are you content to await your death in chains without even trying to free yourself?"

"What else should I do? Tell me," said Winter coldly, "whether rattling my shackles and shouting for freedom would help."

Haka slowly straightened then, and he fought through his blurry, swimming vision to see what was visible of his brother from this corner. "I never thought I would see this. I didn't think you were capable."

Winter snorted softly. "Of what?"

"Giving up."

"I haven't given up."

Haka groaned as another wave of nausea threatened to knock him back to the floor out of sheer weakness. "Then what are you doing now?" he demanded, reaching up with a shaking hand to wipe the sweat from his forehead before it stung his eyes. "Is this you not giving up?"

"Giving up and acceptance of one's fate are hardly the same thing."

"Oh, right. Right." Haka sneered. "Of course. You always have a pithy answer for everything." He knew from arguing with Otter that *always* and *everything* were poor words to throw into a heated conversation, but he couldn't be bothered to care. In this case, they were true. "You have an awfully pious view of yourself for someone who..." He cleared his throat.

"Who what? Left you?"

Haka squeezed his eyes shut and took a deep breath. "No."

"That's what you think I did, isn't it?"

"Shut up."

"You think I left you alone after twelve years of acting as your shield."

"Shut up!" Haka flung the words at Winter with all the strength he possessed. It wasn't much, but it was enough to make Winter turn his head and look at him, one eye visible around the corner of the cell.

"You shouldn't begin arguments you don't want to finish," said Winter softly, but a swift look of regret passed over his face, so brief it was almost imperceptible, and Haka wondered if he had imagined it. "I'm sorry."

Haka ground his teeth until pain shot into his skull. He eyed Winter with caution, mistrustful of his brother's words. "You're sorry," he repeated, the statement twisting into an accusation. "You're *sorry*."

"You don't believe me," said Winter. "I did not expect you to."

"Twenty years." Fueled by a sudden burst of righteous

anger, Haka staggered to his feet. "Twenty years and we never spoke. You never even thought to show your face."

"I—" Winter began, but Haka cut him off and snapped, "I'm sure you watched from a distance, whenever you were around. I know you. But I know you never cared enough to step down off your throne and mingle with someone like me."

He strode over to the bars and gripped them, not out of fervor, but to keep himself upright. Winter stared back at him, his face gaunt from lack of food, his eyes sunken just enough to make the unusual blue of his eyes glitter, like stars in a dark, faraway sky.

"Were you there when he died?" Haka asked, the words falling brittle in the silence.

Winter held his gaze, and slowly, he nodded. "I was there."

Haka rested his forehead against the cell bars. Slowly, he let out a deep, relieving breath, hoping it would at least help his spinning head slow down.

"Did you regret it?"

Haka lifted his head a fraction. "Regret what?"

"Killing him."

"You think I killed him?" Haka asked softly. "Why?"

"Because of all the men I have killed, he deserved it most. And I never had the strength to do it."

"I didn't kill him." Haka smiled, exhausted, weary, and finished. Finished with all of it. "I let him die."

"That's the same thing."

"Not quite."

"If you have the power to save someone's life and you withhold that power, it's the same as killing them." Winter shook his head gently. Quietly, almost under his breath, he added, "Although, if you are right, I suppose that makes you the better man. I would have severed his head."

"You delayed too long."

"I did. I will not apologize twice today." Winter met Haka's gaze, and true to his word, he did not apologize. But regret shadowed his face, and Haka understood.

He understood, and he did not want to. "Spare me your sympathy now," he snapped. "There's no point. You'll wait here until the new precinct commander orders your execution. Don't try to cleanse yourself now."

For the first time in his life, Haka saw his brother's frozen exterior crack, just enough. For half a moment, it was there—in the lips parted as if to speak, in the eyebrows drawn together as if in pain. For half a moment, he saw a heart still alive, not quite as petrified as he had thought.

Winter then did something that shocked Haka even more than letting his mask slip—Winter broke his gaze and lowered it to the floor, his shoulders sagging in something like defeat.

Perhaps it *was* defeat.

Haka turned away from the bars, disgusted. With himself for wishing he could hate Winter half as much as he wanted, disgusted for the ruin he had created. For the abyss he had opened between them. And disgusted for the uncertainty, after all these years, of exactly how he'd done it.

As he stumbled down the hall, fighting the urge to just lie down and pass out, he cursed Winter every way he knew. And then he cursed himself, because Father had always been right, even now, as his bones lay rotting in the silt, wherever the rushing water had carried him.

Haka was a failure. He was a disappointment. And he was just like the man he had let die.

———

OTTER LOOKED DOWN at the syringe of stardust in her hand as Haka walked past the cell. She stroked Lotus's flank and remained silent until Haka had passed out of view. She hadn't meant to listen in on the brothers' conversation, but it became hard not to eavesdrop when their voices echoed. She scratched Lotus under her rose-pink crocodile jaw and slipped out of the cell, locking it carefully behind her.

Quietly, she followed Haka to the other end of the dungeon. There, he stood in the doorway to the courtyard, his palms pressed against either side of the doorframe. Otter licked her lips and cleared her throat. "Um...here."

He glanced over his shoulder, and Otter wanted to cry. Each time she saw him, he looked worse. He was made of ash and sweat now, and she had done it to him. She blinked rapidly and swallowed her tears, holding out the syringe. "Here."

He eyed it as if it was a viper waiting to strike for several seconds before reaching out and wrenching it from her hand. He didn't bother to roll up his sleeve; he simply jabbed the needle into the inside of his arm, underneath his elbow. He sagged against the wall with a groan, his hand slipping from the syringe, letting it clatter to the ground.

Otter stepped back. "Are you...is that better?"

He lifted his head, and she saw his now-pale eyes gleaming through the long strands of his lank hair. He ran his fingers through it and straightened, kicking the empty syringe aside. Without a word, he walked through the door into the courtyard and around the corner, out of sight.

Otter crouched down and picked up the syringe. "Litter-bug," she muttered. She gripped it until she thought it might break and shuffled back down the hall. "I'm always picking up after you. Do it yourself sometime. Geez." She kicked the bars of an empty cell and listened to them rattle.

She felt like crying but wasn't entirely sure why. She buried her face in her sleeve and let slip a muffled sob, determined to let that be the end of it.

"You heard."

She turned around, already prepared to glare at Winter, but she couldn't bring herself to complete the expression. He had always looked so stalwart before, so untouchable. Now he looked raw. Raw and weary.

She took a few steps forward and stopped halfway to his cell. "Hard not to," she admitted. "Did...he—did Haka really kill someone?"

"That depends," said Winter. He sounded tired.

"On what?"

"A technicality."

Otter tilted her head. "How does that work?"

"Suppose you see someone fall into a river." Winter did not lift his head. Otter wasn't surprised; he didn't look as if he had the effort in him. "They can't swim. If you do nothing to help, they will drown. What would you do?"

"I'd try to help," said Otter truthfully, but a sinking feeling in her stomach made her ask in a low voice, "Haka let someone drown?"

"Our father."

Otter's jaw fell slack. "He killed your *father*?"

"He stood by and watched him die," said Winter.

"You saw it happen?"

"News comes to those who listen. I knew when I heard of it."

Otter sank to the floor and sat, cross-legged, staring into the cell. Her mind spinning, she sputtered, "But—I mean —why?"

"Our father..." Winter sighed deeply and leaned his head

back, the weight of his head grown too heavy for his neck. "Was a father in name only. He did not raise us well."

For the first time, Otter noticed the web of scars starting at Winter's throat and trailing down, hidden by his shirt. "Did he do that to you? Your dad?"

"Do what?" Winter looked at her with genuine curiosity.

"Your...the scars." She gestured toward her own throat.

"Ah." Winter blinked once. "I suppose, but indirectly."

Otter leaned back on her palms. "Are you always this vague?"

His smile was a pale ghost, flitting across his mouth and gone. "It keeps me from the opposite," he said, raising a handful of questions in Otter's mind, but she did not have time to ask them for he answered her previous question with, "Dog fights."

Otter's eyes widened at the horrific implication of his answer. "You were put in dog fights?"

"I suppose he felt justified by the fact I felt no pain." Winter lowered his eyelids, as if too tired to keep them completely open.

That was a lie, Otter thought suddenly. Winter felt pain. He was a wound in human form, a wound that refused to scar. Instead, it scabbed over, and every time it caught on something, it began to bleed again. She remained quiet, hoping he would continue.

He sounded resigned when he said, "Dogs terrify Haka. Most animals do, for that reason. He cared for me after the fights, although I felt nothing."

"He never talks about himself, really. Especially not his childhood," said Otter. She felt as though someone had reached inside her chest and begun to squeeze her heart until she could hardly breathe. "I guess I wouldn't, either. Why..." She shook her head, deciding against the question.

Winter made a sound somewhere between a scoff and a grunt. "I doubt I have much time left to answer questions. Now is the time."

"You don't mind? They're not exactly impersonal."

He shook his head tiredly. "I don't mind."

Otter leaned forward, resting her elbows on her knees. "Why did you leave? Or did you?"

He flinched like she had struck him, and Otter instantly regretted the question. "Sorry. Never mind that one."

"I..." He cleared his throat. "I did leave."

Otter blinked. "You did? I didn't actually—you don't seem like the type."

Winter's jaw clenched, and he was silent for a long moment before answering, "Our father was addicted to stardust. He was rarely sober. One day before a fight Haka thought I would lose, he took stardust for the first time and let the dog out of its cage, hoping to spare me. It attacked him instead."

Otter swallowed a gasp and managed a more controlled, "Yikes."

Winter's mouth twitched again, but it was half-hearted. Worn out. "I killed the dog, but it ruined the fight. Haka was in bad shape. I thought he had been too foolish. I was angry. I had shielded him from our father ever since our mother left, and I felt as if Haka had flung that protection in my face. I hated him for it. I thought...if he wanted to take things into his own hands, fine. There was no need for me to waste any more of my life."

Otter blinked rapidly, attempting to squeeze back tears. She was afraid that crying would make him stop talking, and she couldn't let that happen. Not yet. "From what I've heard, I gather you became a mercenary or something."

"That's a story for another time." He let out a long, slow

breath and let his eyes shut completely. "I should never have left him. It's too late now, I suppose."

Otter rose quietly to her feet. "I guess I'll talk to you later."

He did not respond, and she guessed she had worn him out. He had fallen asleep.

She turned toward the stairs and trudged up them. "Execute him, huh, Mister Cyborg?'" she hissed, pausing before opening the door. "I don't think so. Not until he and Haka get some dang *closure*. You just try and execute him," she announced again. "I'd like to see you try."

# FIFTY-ONE

FLOOR. Wooden floor.

Tsuki blinked twice, dragging herself out of the black fog that threatened to pull her back in. She pushed herself into a sitting position, moving gingerly as she felt each part of her, praying nothing was broken. She didn't have time for broken bones. They had to get to Saizou.

Saizou.

Wait.

She turned around, searching the empty room. "Nix?" She climbed to her feet and raced unsteadily to the door, gripping it for support. Her head and back throbbed, but at least her spine was intact. "Nix!"

She heard footsteps thudding up the stairwell, and she stepped back, drawing the knife from the back of her belt and waiting behind the door.

Nix burst into the room, his breath ragged. "Tsuki? Tsuk—whoah." He turned and noticed her, lifting his hands immediately. "It's just me, love."

"Where is Kirikizu?" she demanded, lowering the knife and glancing past Nix, out the door.

"That," began Nix, squinting one eye, "is a very good question. A very good question, and if you happen to discover his whereabouts, I, personally, would be thrilled to know the answer."

"You let him escape?" Tsuki kicked the door. It slammed shut, rattling the doorframe and half the rickety room along with it.

"I wouldn't exactly say I let him," said Nix with a grimace. "Where exactly were you, miss, the entire time?"

"I was unconscious on the floor, where your seizure put me," she said, trying not to snap at him.

"Precisely. There were circumstances beyond your control. And I'm sorry, but I didn't exactly ask for that moment of horrendous agony, thank you very much." Nix shook himself and turned back toward the door. He leaned one hand against it, and for the first time Tsuki noticed the black blood creeping through the veins visible in his arms.

"That had better be a kitsune thing," she said flatly. "Because if it isn't, we need to go to the hospital."

"You're in luck! It's a kitsune thing," Nix retorted.

"Are you going to tell me what exactly happened?"

He pulled the door open. "Your friend Matahachi has apparently just wasted roughly a century of my life," he said, his words practically tripping over each other as he spat them out. "It's a thing I don't appreciate. I don't appreciate it at all, and when I see him, I hope you're all right if I rip his throat out with my teeth."

A flash of fear and bewilderment burnt through Tsuki like bonfire, rippling through her and fading again. "We'll see when the time comes," she said in clipped tones. "For now we need to catch up with Saizou and Kiba. There's no point in going after Kirikizu."

"I tried," said Nix. "He moves faster than I gave him credit for. Although with a broken muzzle, his life may become awkward. Or," he continued, flinging his arm out in a wild gesture, "he has thrown off all shackles of inhibition and plans to yell at anyone who gets in his way upon his return, effectively killing—"

"I don't have time for this." Tsuki stepped under his arm and out the door. "We have to get to Saizou before he does something he'll hate."

————

HIRO PEERED AROUND THE CORNER. The street was empty; the only people populating this part of Chiyoshi were either homeless or drunks, and there was nothing here for them to gain except an uninterrupted night's sleep. He lifted a hand and motioned to Shotgun. "Stay close."

"How much farther?" Shotgun grunted. Shi was slung over his shoulder; Hiro glanced back at regular intervals, but Shi had yet to open his eyes. Fumiyo hurried behind Shotgun. She had not said a word since they left the docks.

Kido and Yuu were probably searching for him by now. They would have found the bullet casings by the storage units and put things together. Most likely they thought him either dead or taken hostage; and as one of those options had happened before, they would not begin to truly worry for twenty-four hours. They would search, but the search would not become a real concern until a full day and night had passed with no word from their boss.

"Not far." Hiro jogged across the street, his boots kicking up dust from the cracked concrete.

The sound of a motor caught his attention, and he turned, reaching out and pulling Fumiyo onto the sidewalk as a drone buzzed around the corner and flew down the center of the street, fifteen feet off the ground. It slowed down to a near-halt, and Hiro frowned.

He looked down at Fumiyo, who stared at the drone with a glare on her face, as if its presence personally offended her. Shotgun ducked as far behind the corner of the empty shop as possible, but he gave Hiro a wide-eyed look that asked, *What do we do now?*

Hiro lifted a small stone off the ground and eyed the drone. It was roughly twenty-five feet away; if he made it look in the opposite direction for three seconds, he could get the fugitives into the shop and out the back.

He drew his arm back and threw the rock in an arc over the drone. The stone clattered against the wall of the building on the other side of the street. Immediately, the drone turned and sailed toward the sound. Hiro turned and ducked through the shattered shop window behind him, then turned to pull Fumiyo through and assist with Shi.

"Go through the back," he whispered, pointing toward the broken *EXIT* sign. It looked like it had once been a clothing store: the floor was strewn with broken hangers and clothing racks, and here and there, a discarded, moth-eaten article of clothing.

Fumiyo was the first to move, ducking low and scurrying toward the back door. Shotgun followed close behind. Hiro turned and watched the drone on the other side of the street, circling around the stone. He saw a flash of blue light as the drone snapped a photograph of the stone, and then the drone rose back into the air and turned, the front facing the shop window.

That was the trouble with imperial drones. They were clever enough to know that rocks didn't throw themselves.

Hiro drew his gun from his belt and lifted it, aiming it toward the drone as the machine flew toward the shop window, searching for the source of the projectile. He glanced over his shoulder at Shotgun and Fumiyo, who had reached the door and now held it half-open, waiting.

"Get out and shut the door," Hiro ordered. "Wait for me."

They asked no questions. Shotgun nudged Fumiyo out the door and followed, keeping Shi's head clear of the door as it swung shut with a faint creak.

Hiro waited as the drone approached. It was cautious; Hiro knew the inside of the shop was too dark to see from the outside. It would scan the interior with sensors first, but he needed to make sure it didn't follow them.

Silently, he cursed Saizou Akita for kicking the hornet's nest and stirring up trouble. You had to play the game and keep your cards close to your vest in this climate. Charging headlong into problems like an enraged bull was foolish and caused things like unexpected drone patrols in dead areas.

If he shot the drone, a report would be sent back to its home precinct. There was a chance that if he remained where he was, the drone wouldn't see him and would simply carry on with its assignment.

The drone turned and flew closer. Hiro sighed. He had to risk the report. He pulled the trigger once, twice, three times. The drone dodged each bullet, flying ever closer, but just as it flew through the opening in the shop window, a fourth bullet ripped through it front to back. The drone dropped to the ground, a mess of flashing sparks.

There was no point in crushing it or attempting to get rid of it; the report would already be sent. Hiro tucked his gun back into his belt and jogged out the back door. The others were still there, thankfully.

Shotgun asked, "Did you shoot it?"

"I did." Hiro moved swiftly past them, down the alley. "It's this way. Hurry up."

"Wait!"

Hiro turned and saw Shotgun lowering Shi to the ground. "What is it?"

"I don't think he's breathing. I can't feel it." Shotgun leaned Shi's back against the wall and was nearly bowled over by Fumiyo, who squatted next to Shi and gripped a fistful of his jacket.

Hiro strode back over and bent down. He lifted Shi's wrist, waiting for a pulse, good or bad. Nothing.

"Is he dead?" Shotgun stepped back, his mouth opening in horror as he stared from Hiro to Shi, then Fumiyo. "He's not, is he?"

"Back off," Hiro ordered. Shotgun stepped even farther back, and Hiro bared his teeth at Fumiyo, who also moved back. Hiro put an arm under Shi's neck and set him down on the ground. Hiro drew his gun from his belt, but his movement was interrupted by a harsh "Don't" from Fumiyo.

He glanced at her and pointedly released the magazine into his left hand. She did not relax; she looked at the chamber, where she knew another bullet waited. Hiro removed a bullet from the magazine and held it next to Shi's mouth, waiting.

It took longer than he hoped before fog appeared on the metal casing.

Hiro straightened and reloaded the gun. "Pick him up," he

ordered, barely sparing Shotgun a glance. "We need to get him to the safe house."

"How is he?" Fumiyo let go of Shi so Shotgun could throw him back over his shoulder, but she stepped around Shotgun and narrowed her eyes at Hiro.

Hiro did not tuck his gun back into his belt; he kept it in hand. "He'll be dead weight in half an hour," he declared, and strode ahead, leading the way without bothering to tell them to keep up.

# FIFTY-TWO

*LIAOYANG, China.*

IN THE TWELVE months following its formation, the White Cobra squad became equivalent to a curse word for the Chinese army. Where White Cobra went, rumors followed: they were evil spirits conjured by a dark priest in the Japanese army, they were old gods reincarnated to take revenge for their country.

The unit shifted over the first three months. Lieutenant Shota and Kyung-Ho were transferred to another province, and another man—a half-Korean named Takuya Takamori—was assigned to White Cobra in their place.

After three months, when White Cobra's test run was over and they were given an official go-ahead, Captain Akita had each member of the unit give themselves a callsign. Should they be captured, their callsign was the only piece of information they were allowed to give up to their captors. Their real identities would remain a secret. Their callsigns became their identity; their real names forgotten as they replaced who they had been who they were now. Captain Akita's callsign was Tsuchigumo.

While he allowed them each to pick their callsign, the remaining seven men in the unit ended up naming one another, usually as a joke that stuck and refused to go away. Shi had remembered them all by assigning them brief mental descriptions.

Kamen Rider's real name was Satoh Sakaguchi. He was twenty-seven, and he smiled often.

Mustang's real name was Ibuki Mitsudaira. He was thirty-five, a stoic but efficient transfer from a disbanded guerilla unit.

Legolas's real name was Takuya Takamori. He was twenty-nine, keen-eyed and quick-witted.

Izanagi's real name was Kazuya Satsuki. He was thirty-six, a Staff Sergeant who had chosen to join White Cobra rather than receive a promotion.

Iron Man's real name was Choi Seok-Hoon. He was thirty-two, a tight-lipped South Korean in charge of the technological equipment.

Shi's callsign was Gaksital, a joking gift from Kamen Rider, who stated Shi's personality reminded him of the mythic hero. Having never heard of the "mythic hero" before, Shi had no idea what he was talking about, but the name stuck.

This was White Cobra unit—seven men with no names and no identities, going where the General ordered them, striking quickly and quietly. There was no friction among them, aside from casual jesting or the occasional argument over which actress was prettier.

Saizou had chosen them well. After the incident with the governor and his envoy, Shi paid close attention to Saizou, now known only as *Captain* or *Tsuchigumo*. Real names were not to be used until White Cobra unit was disbanded.

There were two ways to tell the character of a man, Shi thought, two surefire ways. The first was to study the people surrounding the man. The second was to study the way that man treated his inferiors and subordinates.

Saizou did not fail him, on either count. He treated everyone with equal measure and a fair hand, rare things, in Shi's experience. Shi also felt, with a strange certainty, that he could trust the character of every man in White Cobra unit. Each day was an exercise in trust, and every day, Shi found himself without cause for doubt.

On a rainy day in July, White Cobra unit was ordered to move seventeen miles into the jungle and wait within a half-mile radius for a caravan of ammunition being smuggled from Wensheng to Liaoyang. White Cobra unit would wait near the Taizihe border and overtake the smuggling operation when they came through at the predicted time.

Kamen Rider chose the place of ambush when they arrived at seven forty-six P.M. It was a good spot; the hidden road was a quarter-mile away to the south, the Taizihe border a mile to the west. There was plenty of coverage, enough to reduce the rain above the trees to a light mist, although the constant dripping was enough to make Legolas remark, "I heard stories about Chinese water torture."

"I don't think this is what they meant," said Shi, setting his pack on the ground.

Tsuchigumo set his pack against the base of a tree. "I'm going to secure the southern and eastern parameters," he said. He rarely raised his voice, but he rarely needed to. He never said anything unnecessary, so when he did speak, the men listened. "Mustang, you secure the western and northern parameters."

"Yes, Captain," barked Mustang, rising to his feet.

"The rest of you," said Tsuchigumo, "rest up. Stay quiet. No fire."

"Yes, Captain," they responded in unison.

"Captain," said Shi, rising to his feet, "I request to take your place. It's more important to the unit that you remain alert and efficient. You've had less rest than we have."

Tsuchigumo clicked his tongue—something he did, Shi noticed, before making a statement of any kind. It was like he did all his thinking as he made that sound, and that was all the time he needed. "I'm touched by your concern, Gaksital, but it isn't necessary. You all need rest as much as I do. We have until tomorrow night, so take it easy. I'll get some rest tomorrow morning."

Shi frowned, but nodded. "Yes, Captain."

Tsuchigumo nodded and turned, walking into the darkness as Mustang walked past the men in the other direction.

If Tsuchigumo had one failing as a leader, mused Shi, it was his inability to delegate. Not that he was incapable—he could do it, and well—but he rarely took advantage of the privileges a leader had. When he could rest, he worked alongside his men.

It made Shi want to knock him out with a rock. *There are limits to being helpful, Captain, and if you ask me you should lie down and take a damn nap.*

He crouched down, deciding not to concern himself about it. The captain might be quietly overzealous, but he wasn't stupid. If he needed rest, he would take it. Shi leaned his back against a damp tree trunk and tugged his cap down over his eyes.

He dozed off, listening to the casually antagonistic banter between Legolas, Izanagi, and Kamen Rider while Iron Man, too, settled down nearby to do as the captain had ordered and rest up.

Shi awoke with the sound of a question—"What do you mean, he isn't back yet?"

Shi shook his head, flinging away the last vestiges of sleep, and rose to his feet. He saw who asked the question—Mustang was looking sharply at Legolas, who lifted his hands in defense and said, "He should have checked in twenty minutes ago, but he didn't."

"He should have stayed with the group," said Mustang, his hands in fists. He looked at Shi. "Gaksital and Izanagi, come with me. We'll find the captain. Kamen Rider, Legolas; stay with the equipment."

"Yes, sir."

Out of habit, Shi checked to make sure he was still weaponized; a handgun in its holster, a knife in his belt. Then he nodded toward Mustang. "Ready."

"Move out." Mustang turned, the moonlight casting mottled patches of shadow across his back as he strode away from the checkpoint.

Not for the first time, Shi wished regulations allowed the White Cobra unit to carry two-way radios. Unfortunately, the Chinese army was known to employ drones over dense areas, with the specific purpose of searching for radio signals or electronic transmissions. To maintain total secrecy, they must also maintain total radio silence.

Before he joined the army, Shi had never needed to use technology. He never needed to—it was a farm, and anything technological was taken care of by another family. He had only to look after the animals. He saw the news when he went into the city for business reasons. He occasionally used a payphone.

He missed that.

He missed home.

*No,* he reminded himself, stepping around a thick tangle of underbrush. *Don't think about what isn't there. Stay focused. Find the captain.*

He was far enough away now that he could no longer hear the others. Izanagi and Mustang were silent in their searching; only the faint rustle of leaves farther away let Shi know they were there, unless it was a wild animal on the prowl. Fortunately, aside from the occasional cat or snake, there was little sizeable wildlife in this jungle.

*Where are you, Captain?* Tsuchigumo would not have delayed his return without a good reason. He would know it would raise concern. It broke protocol. It was sloppy, and the captain was anything but sloppy.

Shi searched for sixteen minutes, according to his watch, before he ducked through a tall grove of bamboo and finally found his quarry.

Tsuchigumo stood with a vine-covered slope to his left casting him mostly in shadow. If not for the occasional patches of moonlight, Shi would have missed him completely.

"Captain!" Shi broke into a jog forward, but Tsuchigumo held up a hand.

"Hold," the captain ordered.

Shi halted. "What is it, sir?"

Tsuchigumo turned his head and said in a controlled, even voice, "There is an IED under my right foot."

Shi stared back. "This area was cleared. How could there be a minefield?"

"I don't care how," said Saizou. "We'll worry about *how* later. Go back, alert the men. This area has to be inspected."

Shi swallowed before saluting. "Yes, Captain."

He turned and strode back the way he'd come, careful not to rush too quickly lest he misstep. Halfway back to camp, Mustang emerged from the trees to his left.

"Did you find the captain?" Mustang asked tensely.

"Yes," said Shi, pointing in the direction he'd come. "About two hundred meters behind me."

"Why isn't he with you? Is he injured?"

"Not yet," said Shi, picking up the pace again. Mustang strode alongside him as Shi continued, "We need Iron Man to get his equipment and come back with me. The captain is standing on an unidentified IED."

Mustang's expression went from concerned to unreadable. "Go stay with the captain. Secure the area. I'll get the unit and bring them back."

"Those aren't my orders."

"If the captain takes issue with the counter-command, he can take it up with me."

Shi nodded, agreeing not because he had been ordered, but because it was a command he wanted to follow. "Yes," he barked, spinning on his heel and heading back toward the minefield.

He entered the area again with caution, crouching on one knee and drawing his knife from his belt. He inserted the knife into the ground and lifted the blade. It struck nothing but dirt. He placed his knee where the knife had been and once again inserted the blade into the ground. Slowly, foot by foot, he made a clear path toward the captain.

Tsuchigumo did not speak to him until he was within ten

feet of him. Then, in a near-growl, he asked, "Do you think you can disobey my order just because I can't move?"

Shi straightened and saluted. "Yes, Captain."

Tsuchigumo blinked, and a rare smile softened his sharp features, just for a moment. "You will be punished for insubordination," he said as soon as the smile disappeared. "I'll see to it."

"Yes, Captain," Shi repeated. "Mustang is bringing the rest of the unit here to secure the perimeter and identify the mine."

Saizou nodded. He glanced at the ground by his feet, drawing his eyebrows together as he studied the grass. "This area should have been clear."

"Perhaps there was an unrecorded battle fought here," said Shi, crouching again to continue working a path toward the captain. "In places like this, small battles often go unnoticed, I'm told."

"Kamen Rider was supposed to clear the area."

Shi progressed another foot forward, brushing aside grass and weeds with his fingers. "Anyone can make a mistake."

"A mistake like this will strip him of his rank."

Shi bit his tongue and inserted the tip of his knife into the ground again. "I'm not finding any more mines. Perhaps his detector missed only one."

Tsuchigumo glanced at him, deliberating, but just then, the tip of Shi's knife struck something hard, and Shi froze. It could easily be a rock, he thought as he dug carefully around the point of collision. His hopes fell as he saw not the rough, gray surface of a rock, but the dull, metallic green of another mine.

"I can't see what you just found," said Tsuchigumo, "but from the look on your face, I doubt it's a rock."

"It's another IED," said Shi reluctantly. He had no warning flags, and it was night—it would be difficult to remember where it was. The flags would be with Iron Man. Shi sighed and remained crouched near the mine. A gust of wind rattled through the trees, spraying rainwater across Shi's face. "I used to like rain," he muttered.

Tsuchigumo smiled again. "Had enough of it?"

"Rain used to be useful. Crops needed it." Shi rested his elbows on his knees. "Here it lowers visibility and just gets in the way."

"Mmm," said Tsuchigumo in a low voice, as if to himself. "I've always liked it."

Shi lifted his head and realized it was the first personal fact Tsuchigumo had ever mentioned about himself. Everything else Shi knew about him was either hearsay or information passed on by another soldier. "Still like it?" he asked, half-joking.

"Now I have to agree with you, I'm afraid. Unfortunately, your punishment still stands."

"Yes, Captain." Shi turned his full attention on Tsuchigumo. "Speaking of standing, how are you holding up?"

"Don't concern yourself, Gaksital. The fact I'm wishing I had let you go in my place doesn't negate your awaiting punishment."

Shi smiled grimly. "Yes, Captain."

A loud bird whistle pierced the humid silence. Shi rose to his feet and answered the call. After a moment, Mustang appeared with the rest of the unit following close behind.

Iron Man removed a flashlight from the case in his hand and switched it on, shining the beam low across the ground. "Is this the trail?"

"That's it," said Shi.

"All right," Mustang instructed, stepping back and

gesturing for Iron Man to go first. "Single file. Move slowly. Let Iron Man inspect the IED first."

"There's another here where I'm standing," said Shi. "Did you bring the flags?"

Iron Man gestured toward Legolas. "He has them."

Legolas removed the pack from his back and drew a red six-inch flag from it. "Here." He passed it along to Iron Man, who took it in hand and stepped carefully along the path Shi had cleared. He crouched by Shi's boots and stabbed the flag into the ground several inches away from the IED.

"I'll deal with that one later," he said briefly, continuing on toward the captain.

"Is the captain all right?"

Shi turned in the direction of Kamen Rider's voice. "He's fine."

"I'll patrol," Kamen Rider called back.

"Keep your voice down," Mustang snapped. "Go carefully. We don't know how far the minefield goes."

"Yes, sir," said Kamen Rider. He hefted his rifle and stepped back into the forest. The shadows engulfed him, and he disappeared.

Iron Man placed his flashlight in his mouth and crouched in front of Captain Tsuchigumo. Gingerly, he brushed away the grass and dirt around the captain's right foot, then removed the flashlight from his mouth and shone it closely around the base of the IED.

After a moment, he nodded, put the flashlight between his teeth again, and opened the black case. It took several minutes with a small brush before the IED was fully exposed beneath the captain's boot. Iron Man leaned back on his heels and scratched the back of his neck, his eyes trained on the explosive.

"Well?" asked Mustang.

Iron Man took the flashlight in hand and shook his head. "It's not manufactured anywhere. It's spare parts and gunpowder. Made by mercenaries, I'd say."

"That shouldn't be a problem," said Mustang.

"It shouldn't be," said Iron Man, "but it is. There's a wire at the base of it, running deeper into the ground." He shone the light, highlighting the visible inch of black wire.

"What does that mean?" Izanagi demanded. "It's connected to something?"

"More than one, I would guess. It looks like a network. If I had to guess, I'd say it's connected to that"—he pointed toward the other mine Shi had uncovered—"and possibly more. Setting off one will trigger the rest."

"And we don't know where they are," said Legolas, voicing what no one else would.

"Right."

"What steps need taken?" Tsuchigumo's voice remained even and calm, but his eyes darted across the ground as if he could see the explosives buried underneath.

Iron Man glanced up. After a moment, he said, "I'll study the other IED. I'll come up with something."

"Whatever you come up with, make sure it happens before two A.M. tomorrow night," said the captain. He did not smile, but the bleak humor lifted the mood, and with a salute, Iron Man went to work on the other IED.

Kamen Rider returned to check in, then set out again with Izanagi.

Shi took out his knife and began to search for more mines, moving back and forth in a wide, methodic circle around the captain. It was hard, slow work in the dark with only a single flashlight. Legolas put in the request to use more, but the captain denied the request, stating that one light was already bad enough.

Some time later, Shi glanced at his watch. He rose to his feet and looked back at Tsuchigumo, who stood unwavering atop the IED. Shi re-tied his ponytail and crossed over to Iron Man as inconspicuously as possible.

The sheen of sweat on Iron Man's face contrasted with the harsh, blue glow of the flashlight and made him look on the verge of death. He wiped his forehead with his sleeve and glanced up as Shi crouched on the other side of the cleared mine.

He did not ask what Shi wanted; he waited for him to speak as he flipped through the X-ray camera in his hands, studying small photographs of the IED from every angle.

"The captain's been standing for three hours," said Shi in a low voice.

Iron Man set his jaw and looked at Shi. "So?"

"How much longer is this going to take?"

Iron Man's set expression became a glare. "I'm working the fastest I can. Do you realize how delicate this is? If I do something wrong, the captain isn't the only one who blows up."

"How many do you estimate there are?"

"Have you found any more?"

"One." Shi jerked his thumb in the direction of the other IED he had discovered, roughly twenty feet behind Tsuchigumo. "That makes three."

"That we know of," said Iron Man darkly.

Shi returned his glare. "How much longer do you estimate?"

"Longer if you don't get off my back," Iron Man snapped. Almost immediately, frustration washed over his features and he rubbed his hand over his face, like he could force the tension away.

Shi patted Iron Man's shoulder and stood. "I know," he said quietly.

Iron Man nodded and set the camera down, taking a pair of pliers from the toolbox. "I can't hurry too fast," he said after a moment, "but I'll move as quickly as I can."

Shi was never able to reply. Izanagi's voice rang out—"Gunfire!" just as the rounds of automatic fire shattered the silence.

Weapons were drawn, and Izanagi raced through the grove of bamboo trees shouting, "I call eight, maybe nine mercenaries over that ridge!"

"They're twenty-six hours early," cried Legolas, staring.

"Where is Kamen Rider?" Captain Tsuchigumo's voice snapped the men to attention.

Izanagi shook his head. "I don't know, sir."

The captain did not hesitate. "Get undercover," he called. "Spread out in pairs. Gaksital, go with Iron Man. Izanagi, go with Legolas. Mustang, find Kamen Rider."

Mustang stepped forward and saluted. Then he said, "Respectfully, Captain, we refuse."

Shi and the rest of the unit snapped into line behind Mustang, raising their hands in a simultaneous salute.

"I gave you a direct command." Tsuchigumo lowered his head, staring Mustang down with an intensity that would have turned a lesser man to ash.

"Respectfully, sir, you can strip my rank later," said Mustang, and lifted his right hand, gesturing clockwise. "Fan out! Surround the captain!"

"Yes, sir!" The answers resounded as Shi and the rest of the men spread out in a circle around Tsuchigumo. It was the only time Shi had purposefully placed his back to the captain. It was the only time any of them had.

Shi heard the sound of the captain drawing his gun. "I have sixteen rounds in this gun," he said calmly. Shi did not turn around; he kept his eyes on the ridge to the left. "I'll use ten on the mercenaries. One of you will have to shoot the two remaining."

"The six bullets left in the chamber, sir?" asked Legolas.

"One for each of us," said Mustang.

With one voice, the men enthusiastically responded, "Yes, sir!"

The sound of gunfire grew closer.

"They're testing to see exactly where we are," said Legolas.

Iron Man glanced over his shoulder at Shi. "If they hit one of the mines, we all go up."

"I order you to leave." There was no room in the captain's voice for questions, but nobody asked any.

"I will take full responsibility, sir." Shi heard Mustang's voice, although he did not turn around to look at him. "Once this is over, please don't punish the men. Men?"

"Yes, sir!"

"Stand your ground and do not move."

"Yes, sir!"

Everything fell silent as the echoes of gunfire died away.

"Are they gone?" Legolas asked finally, his voice a tentative half-whisper.

"Don't bet on it," said Izanagi in a low voice.

As if to illustrate his point, two more shots rang out, punctuated by a strangled cry abruptly silenced.

Shi stiffened. "That was Kamen Rider."

"What happened to him?" Legolas stared at Shi, then back at Tsuchigumo. "Captain?"

"Legolas, Izanagi, find Kamen Rider's location," Tsuchigumo ordered.

Shi glanced at Mustang, who nodded toward Legolas and Izanagi.

"Yes, sir," they responded, saluting quickly before running through the cleared path and disappearing into the trees.

An uneasy feeling swept up Shi's spine as he watched the ridge, waiting for any motion, for a silhouette to appear and tell him where to shoot. "This doesn't feel right."

"I know," said Mustang in a low voice. "Stay focused."

More gunfire cracked through the air, closer this time—just beyond the ridge, close enough that Shi ducked instinctively. One by one, figures appeared on the ridge, forming a half-circle around the minefield.

"If it isn't the infamous White Cobra unit," said a loud voice, carrying through the humid night air. "You don't look so dangerous now."

"Sir," said Mustang in a tense voice. "Orders?"

Tsuchigumo said, "Hold your fire."

"What's the matter?" the figure called, his Japanese accent rough, but understandable. "You boys having a bad day? Because I know three people having a worse day than you. Oh —here's one of them right now. Or at least part of him, I guess." The black silhouette lifted his arm and threw something down. His aim was good, and his arm was strong; the object landed less than ten feet away from the unit gathered around Tsuchigumo.

"It's a hand," said Iron Man stiffly.

"Whose?" Mustang demanded.

"I don't know. I—I think it's Izanagi's," said Iron Man.

Shi caught a glimpse of the silver band on the right index finger. "It is."

A snarl broke from Mustang. "Those bastards," he hissed, lifting his rifle. "Captain?"

Tsuchigumo raised his voice. How he managed to sound calm, Shi did not know. "I want to see my men."

The silhouette laughed. "Oh, you do, do you? Pardon me for saying it, but you're not in much of a position to be making demands."

"You want us alive, or we would be dead," Tsuchigumo answered, his voice tight and controlled.

"That's not strictly true," said the other man. "Close. We really only need one of you alive, and currently, we have three. The rest of you are just cannon fodder. Inglorious, maybe, but sadly true."

Slowly, Iron Man lowered his left hand from his gun and reached into his pocket.

"What are you doing?" Mustang demanded in a low voice.

Iron Man did not turn his head. "Grenade."

"Can you throw far enough to reach him?"

"Remember the last time I did three hundred and fifteen pushups, beating you by fifteen?"

Tsuchigumo asked, "How much impact?"

Iron Man hesitated. "It may knock us over."

Shi looked back at the captain, then at Iron Man.

"Throw it," said Tsuchigumo.

"Yes, sir." Iron Man switched the grenade to his right hand, lowered his rifle, and pitched the grenade as far as he could. It sailed across the minefield, and Shi did not watch it land.

He turned and ran toward Tsuchigumo, locking his arms around the captain's waist as the explosion went off, rocking the ground.

Iron Man and Mustang crouched as Shi pushed against Tsuchigumo, using his weight as a counter-balance.

"We'll handle it here," said Tsuchigumo even before the blast cleared. "Go find the other men. If you find a situation, do not engage. Give me a situation report before you proceed. Do you understand?"

Mustang and Iron Man saluted and responded in unison. "Yes, sir!"

Shi looked at Tsuchigumo as Mustang and Iron Man raced in different directions, one to each side. Tsuchigumo's face was grave.

"Sir," said Shi, glancing up at the ridge, still engulfed in smoke and dirt, "Izanagi said there were ten men up there. The grenade may have taken out one or two. We're still sitting ducks."

"They want me alive," said Tsuchigumo. "And I have the feeling the one at the heart of it will circle back around."

Shi glanced away from the scope of his rifle. "Sir?"

Tsuchigumo continued to hold his gun steady, his eyes darting from the ridge to the left to the ridge in front of them. "Someone betrayed us."

The uneasiness that had tormented Shi grew stronger, sharper. He knew the captain was right. "Who do you think it was?"

"I don't know. That's why I sent the others away. I need a moment to think."

"You don't think it was one of them?" Shi asked, incredulous. He didn't want to believe it was possible, that any of his comrades was capable of turning the rest over to the Chinese army.

"Not Mustang. Not Iron Man. Not..." Tsuchigumo wiped his forehead with his sleeve, and only then did Shi remember that he had been standing still for hours, and not only that, but standing still with one foot on a mine that would kill him if he moved. "Not Izanagi," Tsuchigumo continued, half under his breath.

"Why do you think it wasn't me?" Shi asked, unhooking his canteen from his belt and handing it over to Tsuchigumo. "Or do you?"

"Keep your friends close," said Tsuchigumo, taking a long swallow of water. He handed the canteen back to Shi with a grateful nod and said, "I don't suspect you."

Shi peered back through the scope of his rifle. "Why not?"

"I trust you."

"That's not a very good reason, Captain."

"Call it instinct," said Tsuchigumo.

Shi tightened his grip on the rifle. "What makes you think they want you alive? Their leader said they only needed one of us, and it looks like they have Kamen Rider, Legolas, and Izanagi."

"There's no reason for them to wait around for us like this otherwise."

"Then why aren't they coming down?"

"My guess is that they're getting the schematics of the minefield from the mole."

Shi licked his lips. "Kamen Rider."

"I think so." The words were flat and without emotion, but Tsuchigumo's fingers curled more tightly around his gun, his knuckles white with the effort of restraint.

Shi looked at him for a long moment. "We could be wrong."

Tsuchigumo shook his head. "He chose the location. He left on patrol first. His cry made me send out two of my men to find him, and they haven't come back. It was him."

The sound of running footsteps made Shi and Tsuchigumo shift their focus to the grove of trees on the right, but Mustang hissed, "Don't shoot, it's me!"

"Where's Iron Man?" Tsuchigumo wanted to know.

"Here, Captain," said Iron Man, making his way carefully down the ridge to the left. They gathered around Tsuchigumo and Mustang said, "They're not far. Maybe three hundred yards north."

"Report on the others," said Tsuchigumo.

Mustang said, "Izanagi, Legolas, and Kamen Rider are bound to a tree with ropes and gagged."

Iron Man knelt down and picked the severed hand off the ground. "This is Izanagi's," he said quietly. "I don't understand why they're playing around like this. Why not just blow up the minefield and kill us all, if they put it here?"

"They want the captain alive," said Mustang, watching Tsuchigumo closely. "Their leader was bluffing."

"I don't think he was their leader," said Iron Man.

Tsuchigumo turned his head. "Then who was it?"

"I don't know, but there was a man with the hostages. He wore a mask, but they referred to him as Gengxin. He seemed to be in charge."

"Have they sustained any damage?" asked Tsuchigumo.

Iron Man nodded. "Yes, sir. The reason the grenade blast was so powerful? There were two men behind the spokesman, and one of them had a grenade vest. Our grenade set that off and killed all three of them."

"So there are only seven of them now," said Mustang.

Iron Man shook his head. "Six, I think. We've pissed them off, but they don't seem too upset about it."

"They wouldn't be," said Tsuchigumo, studying the ground. "They're mercenaries. They expect this."

Mustang glanced from Shi to Tsuchigumo, then at Iron Man before saying, "What is it?"

"What?" Shi kept his rifle trained on the ridge, but he

looked at Mustang as the other man tucked a thumb into his belt and said, "The mood isn't right. It's not a funeral for us yet."

Iron Man said nothing, but one look at Shi's face and he nodded slowly and lowered his head. "We were betrayed," he mumbled.

Mustang's face became a passive mask. "Who?"

"Oh—" Iron Man looked up and swallowed, then held up Izanagi's hand. "It was Legolas."

"What?" Tsuchigumo looked at Iron Man, startled.

Iron Man's eyes widened slightly as he held up Izanagi's hand. Between the thumb and forefinger was a deep, crude cut in the shape of an *L*. "It has to be."

"He cut that into his hand? Did they tell him they were going to cut it off and throw it down?" Mustang took the hand from Iron Man and studied it.

"It looks like it was done with the opposing hand," Iron Man pointed out.

"Don't you think they would have noticed it before they threw it down?" Shi asked skeptically.

"It doesn't seem likely," said Mustang.

"It was Kamen Rider." Tsuchigumo leaned back on his left foot. He looked tired, but Shi knew it wasn't only physical exhaustion—one of his men, one of his comrades, had betrayed them, and now he had to decide what to do about it.

It sounded so practical, broken down like that. They didn't have time to deal with emotions now.

"Captain," said Mustang, his voice strangely soft, "are you sure?"

"I'm sure," said Tsuchigumo.

Nobody asked, *And if you're not?* They glanced at one another and nodded.

"Orders, sir?" asked Mustang, clearing his throat.

Tsuchigumo took a deep breath. "Did you get positions on the mercenaries?"

"The one called Gengxin and two others are guarding the hostages," said Iron Man.

"The other three are keeping communication via two-way radios," said Mustang. "I don't know their positions, but they aren't far. They're probably circling."

"I don't like it," said Iron Man.

Shi scanned the tree line. "They haven't killed us yet."

"That's what I don't like." Iron Man's frown was deep, his eyes narrowed. "We're in a kill zone. They should have taken us out by now."

Tsuchigumo pushed his right hand through his hair. "They could have shot us by now, but if we fall, there's a chance we could trigger another explosion. They don't know where the mines are yet, and it's possible they're receiving orders via radio we don't know about."

Shi shook his head, trying to wrap his mind around Kamen Rider's betrayal. It was well-planned—he had discovered the land mines, he had brought them there. He had trapped them in a kill box and led mercenaries right to them, but his cleverness hadn't anticipated the kill box being the only thing keeping them alive.

Those were the facts.

Right now, facts were all they could afford to face.

"Describe the mercenaries to me," said Tsuchigumo, looking at Mustang. "What's their bearing?"

"They aren't a professional guerilla unit," Mustang responded immediately. "I'd say ex-military. They've done this before, but the explosion made them back off. They aren't particularly loyal, and I don't think they're all Chinese, either.

I'd say it's a mixed-group of ex-military mercenaries out for money and nothing else."

"That explains why they haven't rushed us," said Iron Man, nodding once. "They're willing to wait us out."

A grim smile cut Tsuchigumo's face. "We have the advantage."

Shi turned to face the captain. "Sir?"

"We have two men in their camp," said Tsuchigumo. "We need to use them. Mustang, how many knives do you have?"

Mustang hesitated for a split second, mentally counting. "Five, sir."

"How many won't gleam in moonlight?"

"Three, sir."

Tsuchigumo switched his focus to Iron Man. "You've already proved your aim is good. Mustang, give him two of your knives. Provide a subtle distraction they won't question. Iron Man, you throw Izanagi and Legolas each a knife. They'll be able to take it from there."

Iron Man nodded and turned to receive the two knives that Mustang removed from inside his jacket. Then he knelt down and took the first black knife, set it flat on the ground, and began to inscribe something on the blade with the tip of the other knife. It took about thirty seconds before he straightened, and scratched into the blade were the words *K. R. = danger.*

"Short notice," was his only remark as he tucked the knives into the front of his belt and looked at Mustang. "Distraction ready?"

Mustang's half-smile was tired but set. "I do a pretty mean howler monkey imitation."

Shi grinned. "I guess beggars can't be choosers."

Mustang raised an eyebrow. "Do you have a better idea?"

"Even if I did, I probably wouldn't tell you. I'm looking forward to your method."

There was something strained and urgent in the exchanged humor, as if everyone knew how important it was to make a joke or two for the sake of morale and was doing it out of duty. It was something Shi had noticed with surprise during his first few weeks of enlistment—the way a soldier would joke about any available subject and his comrades would laugh, whether the joke was lame or not.

Shi recalled an instance soon after he was placed in guerilla training—one of the men had made a disparaging remark about another soldier's manhood, causing everyone, including the soldier in question, to erupt in laughter that Shi didn't understand.

The man Shi now knew as Mustang had noticed Shi's lack of reaction and clapped a hand on his shoulder. "Doesn't look like training," he had said, "but it is."

"I fail to see how that's training," Shi had said.

Mustang had smiled at Shi's confusion and replied, "If you can't take it from your comrades, you sure as hell won't be able to take it from the enemy. If you're captured, you better know how to handle a little humiliation."

Possible capture, Shi had come to realize, wasn't the only reason to crack a joke. Sometimes, it could be the only thing standing between a broken spirit and a whole one.

It was too bad, he thought, that he didn't have a great sense of humor.

"Mustang," said Tsuchigumo, "you said they're using two-way radios."

"Yes, sir."

"Get one."

Mustang saluted. "Yes, sir. As soon as I finish howling."

Iron Man saluted as well, and together he and Mustang turned and jogged into the darkness, where Shi envisioned them circling up the quarter-mile over the ridge to their captive comrades.

"It's a good thing Izanagi is left-handed," said Shi. He wanted to crouch, as if crouching would help him avoid the gunfire he felt was inevitable. That they had lasted this long in the open was surreal. There had to be something else at play here, a factor he wasn't aware of.

Tsuchigumo leaned forward, pressing his palms against his knees for a moment before straightening again.

"Are you all right, Captain?"

Tsuchigumo said, "Stiff."

Shi knew it was only a half-truth—after all, prisoner-of-war camps often used standing without rest as a form of torture, and by all reports, it was shockingly effective. The human body was made to either move or sit, not stand for extended periods of time. "I'd say a hot oil massage is in order, Captain."

"I appreciate the offer," said Tsuchigumo, grinning a little, "but the others might take it the wrong way."

Shi rolled his eyes, although his remark had been received with the humor he'd intended. "I meant after we get back to civilization."

A sudden sound screeched through the night—a howler monkey, so convincing that for a moment, Shi stared at the trees, searching for a sign of the animal.

"He wasn't kidding," said Tsuchigumo. "He does do a mean imitation."

The animal sounds died, fading into the syrupy air. Shi rotated his head and relaxed his shoulders, lifting his rifle again. "No offense, Captain, but as far as dates go, you're pretty boring."

"Is that what this is?"

"It's the closest thing I've come to."

"You need to get out more," was Tsuchigumo's helpful reply. "I hear not all dates are this life-threatening. Some even get to walk around."

"City superstition," said Shi, looking above the scope. "I don't believe it for a second."

Somewhere over the ridge came the sound of a gunshot. Shi looked back at Tsuchigumo. "Captain?"

Tsuchigumo jerked his head. "Go."

"Yes, sir." Shi lowered his rifle and, glancing to reassure himself that his captain had a gun, broke into a silent run. He ducked under the tree branches and around grasping bushes, avoiding loose rocks and tangled vines as he headed up the hill in the direction of the mercenary camp.

He nearly ran into Mustang, who emerged from the shadows in front of him, a hand outstretched as if to warn him away.

"What—" Shi began, but Mustang interrupted him.

"Legolas is down," he said. "Go find Iron M—"

The sound of another gunshot made Mustang whirl around as Shi lifted his rifle and moved alongside Mustang in the direction of the sound.

Izanagi stumbled around a thick, twisted tree trunk, his remaining hand pressed against his stomach. Mustang ran forward and caught the other man just as he began to pitch forward and draped one of his arms around his shoulders. To Shi, he said, "Go, we're right behind you."

Shi backed up, but said, "I'll cover you."

Kamen Rider was nowhere to be seen. *Legolas down. Izanagi badly injured. Kamen Rider...* Shi shook his head and stepped aside, letting Mustang and Izanagi pass. They did not question him, but that wasn't what disturbed Shi. There were no mercenary shouts, no cries wondering where the prisoners had gone, no angry noise.

"Move it," Shi hissed.

They obliged; Izanagi's strides lengthened, and Mustang adjusted his step to keep up with him. Shi wished for a movement, a sign of life—something to shoot at. It would reassure him. He hated mercenaries—their lack of loyalty relaxed them, made them patient.

They reached Tsuchigumo, and Shi's heart skipped a relieved beat when he saw the captain was still standing—even if it was irrational, given that he would have heard the explosion had Tsuchigumo fallen.

*Where is Iron Man?*

Shi swallowed his fear. Focusing on unnecessary questions detracted from the present, where his focus was needed.

"What happened?" Tsuchigumo demanded as Mustang lowered Izanagi to the ground several feet in front of him.

"I think Kamen Rider shot him, sir," said Mustang, unbuttoning his jacket. He shrugged it off and pressed it against the bleeding wound in Izanagi's side.

Izanagi blinked rapidly and stared at the sky, his gaze half-focused. "Don't give him so much credit," he breathed, his voice strained. "I shot myself."

"If you were in a hurry to die, you could have just told me," Mustang snapped. "I'd have done the honors. I'm sorry, Captain," he added, unable to bring himself to look Tsuchigumo in the eyes. "I didn't get the radio."

"Don't shoot," said a nearby voice. Iron Man pushed his way through the trees and made his way carefully across the path Shi had cleared. In his right hand was a two-way radio. "I got it. What happened?"

"Kamen Rider was never tied up," said Mustang, relief visible only in his eyes when he saw the radio. "I thought he was, but that was a farce, too. He didn't even call for assistance when he saw Izanagi and Legolas escaping." He swallowed hard and brought his gaze to Tsuchigumo's. "He shot Legolas in the back, Captain."

Shi wondered if Tsuchigumo's face went a shade paler or if it was only the moonlight passing over it. He felt his own simmering blood begin to boil, and he clenched his right hand into a fist so tight he hoped his fingernails cut into his palm.

"Is Legolas dead?" asked Tsuchigumo, his voice slightly fainter than before.

"Yes, Captain." Mustang blinked and looked down at Izanagi. "And what do you mean you shot yourself?"

"He's shorter than I am," said Izanagi. "I figured pulling my gun on him wouldn't work, so I just pulled it on myself."

"You shot him through your body?" Shi stared at the man bleeding on the ground.

"I didn't invent the idea. Pretty sure it's been done before," said Izanagi, with a wheezing laugh that ended in a grimace.

"Don't laugh," growled Mustang. "You'll bleed faster. Orders, Captain?"

Tsuchigumo took the two-way radio from Iron Man. "What frequency are they using?"

"I think three," said Iron Man, "but I'm not sure we need it. I overheard someone on the other end talking to Gengxin. More of this makes sense now." He hesitated, but only for a second. "Apparently the belief that we're inhuman spirits is popular among the Chinese commoners and they wanted us taken alive and killed in public to disprove the idea."

"I was crippled for superstition?" Izanagi asked. "I'm wounded." He winked, the expression barely visible. "Get it?"

"Shut up," hissed Mustang, but there was too much concern flooding his face to make the command stick.

"Did you kill Kamen Rider?" asked Shi quietly.

"Don't think so," said Izanagi. He groaned through gritted teeth as Mustang applied more pressure to the bleeding wound. "Hurt him, but last time I saw him, he was heading off in the other direction."

"Good," said Shi grimly.

Nobody asked what he meant—they knew. Death by gunshot was too quick. It didn't hold the weight of his betrayal.

"They aren't attacking," said Iron Man, eyeing the ridge.

"They don't have to. They know where we are," said Mustang.

"We need to lure them down," said Tsuchigumo.

All heads turned toward him.

"Captain?" Shi took a half-step closer.

Tsuchigumo straightened his shoulders and gestured toward his right foot. "You said this will trigger the rest of them if it goes off, yes?"

"Yes, sir," said Iron Man, adopting a passive expression. It didn't take a genius to figure out where Tsuchigumo's plan was headed.

"No, sir," said Mustang. He lifted Izanagi's remaining hand and pressed it over the jacket, then tugged his shirt over his head. He wrapped it around the meaty stump of Izanagi's wrist and secured it with a knot, eliciting another moan from Izanagi.

"Excuse me?" Tsuchigumo turned his black, glittering gaze toward Mustang.

The other man rose to his feet and saluted. "I said, no, sir!"

"Your loyalty is noted," said Tsuchigumo, adding in a softer voice, "and it is appreciated. But I can't stand here much longer as it is, and I need you to get the men out." Mustang moved as if to refuse again, but Tsuchigumo cut him off. "That's an *order*, Mustang."

"With all due respect, Captain, how are we going to lure the mercenaries down here when they know about the mines?" asked Shi, turning to face Tsuchigumo.

"We don't need to lure them all the way," said Tsuchigumo. "Iron Man, how many grenades do we have left?"

"Fourteen," said Iron Man quietly.

Tsuchigumo nodded. "You two," he said, nodding toward Iron Man and Mustang, "plant them around the basin of the minefield as soon as the light is gone. Don't be seen."

Shi tilted his head up and looked at the moon overhead. The light was beginning to fade as clouds slowly enveloped it, threatening to plunge the jungle into total darkness.

"Shi," said Tsuchigumo.

Shi turned. "Yes, sir."

"Keep pressure on Izanagi's wound."

"For heaven's sake," muttered Izanagi, "I still have one hand. I can keep pressure on it myself."

Mustang flicked Izanagi on the forehead, hard, with two fingers. "It doesn't want to stop bleeding. I'm going to plug the hole."

"Great," said Izanagi. His breathing was shallow, and in the quickly-fading moonlight, his pallor was that of a ghost. Shi tried to imagine the pain he must be in and failed completely. Mustang took out one of his remaining knives and tore a strip from his shirt. He lifted Izanagi's jacket and shirt, then glanced at the man's face.

"Don't coddle me," Izanagi grunted. "Just do it."

Shi watched as Mustang stuffed the piece of cloth into the bullet wound, eliciting a sharp growl from Izanagi, like a wounded animal.

"I said not to coddle me," he panted, "I didn't say make the hole twice as big."

"Shove it," said Mustang, "I was careful."

And with those words, the clouds covered the moon completely.

"Now," said Tsuchigumo. Mustang and Shi traded place as Mustang lifted his pack and followed Iron Man away from the captain and their injured comrade.

"Wish I could help," said Izanagi.

Shi pressed down on the other soldier's injuries with both hands. "Don't apologize for getting shot."

"I'm not apologizing. Hell, it wasn't *my* fault."

"Yes, it was," said Shi.

"I was being heroic. Stuff it up yours."

Tsuchigumo laughed. Shi looked over at him, amazed at the sound. He'd never heard it before. After a moment, Tsuchigumo noticed Shi staring at him and asked, "What?"

"I didn't think you were capable of that sound."

"Who cares," grunted Izanagi. "YOLO, right?"

Shi blinked and pressed down harder on the other man's injury. "YOLO?"

"Westerners. They say it when they're about to do something stupid," Izanagi explained, panting. "Or brave. I don't know why."

"In English, it stands for 'you only live once,'" said Tsuchigumo, almost offhandedly.

"No, you don't." Izanagi smiled. Shi could barely see it in the darkness, a wry twist of the lips that looked strangely peaceful given the situation. "I'm going to come back as a powerful ghost and scare Gaksital here spitless."

"I grew up in a daimyo where ghosts were as common as cattle," scoffed Shi. "It would take more than your half-assed attempts to frighten me." He felt too much blood under his hands and wondered whether the bullet was just an inch too far to the left. If Izanagi hadn't calculated the shot correctly.

"Captain." Mustang ran up, followed closely by Iron Man. They both saluted, and Mustang said, "The grenades are set."

"Good." Tsuchigumo nodded toward Izanagi and Shi. "Take them with you. Get far enough away that the blast won't injure anyone. Mustang, when it's over, I want you to come back and search for survivors. If you find anyone injured and still alive, interrogate them. Kill anyone else."

"And if you're still alive? Should we kill you too?" There was an underlying strain beneath his joke.

Tsuchigumo looked down at his boot, planted above the IED. "I don't think I will be, but if I am, by all means come get me before I pass away."

Something shifted inside Shi then. Something cracked, and through the newfound opening sprang a determination born of the refusal to let his captain die like this. The man wasn't even thirty yet. The man held a daimyo. He had a girlfriend back home. He had too much to live for, and Shi had only Tsuchigumo.

Izanagi reached up and grabbed a fistful of Shi's jacket, pulling his face closer. "You listen to me, you scrawny little punk," he whispered. His voice sounded too wet, like he was drowning on dry land, and Shi pressed harder against Izanagi's injury. Izanagi groaned and released Shi's jacket to slap his face lightly. "Stop that."

"You're going to bleed out if I don't," Shi hissed.

"It doesn't...it doesn't matter." Izanagi coughed suddenly, his body convulsing in pain at the sudden, sharp movement. Shi felt hot blood splatter across his face and put a hand under Izanagi's shoulders, rolling him to the side. Izanagi spat out a mouthful of blood, and then another, until the ground beside him was soaked.

"What's happening?" Mustang's voice demanded. "Gaksital!"

"I'm fine," Izanagi managed, then looked at Shi. The clouds over the moon thinned, releasing just enough light to reflect the sheen in Izanagi's hard eyes. "The captain trusts you, and I've seen the way you stick next to him. Keep doing that. If he makes it out of this, if anyone does, you stay right next to him, do you hear me?"

Shi nodded before he fully realized what he was doing, before it had all sunk in. He had no plans to leave the captain, but he saw no way out of this. Not unless some god somewhere provided a miracle, which he doubted. He and the captain had committed too many sins for the gods to bother with them.

"I haven't got all day, Gaksital."

"I got it," said Shi, swallowing. His voice fading to a whisper he repeated, "I got it."

"Good. Now we can get on with this war—" the end of Izanagi's sentence never came. He began to cough again, his body wracking so violently that Shi was thrown off before Mustang and Iron Man could get there. Izanagi coughed and coughed, his breathing more strained with each sound, until he wasn't breathing at all; there were only spasms and blood and then a strangled, unfinished silence.

As Mustang crouched over Izanagi, no one spoke. Then Mustang said, "Looks like he got out of here faster than we did."

Iron Man put his hands on his hips and turned away, while Shi got to his feet and looked at Tsuchigumo. His face was frozen, but there were no tears in his eyes, no sign of soft mourning. There was only sharp, cold anger.

"I'll bring him," Mustang began, but Tsuchigumo interrupted.

"Leave him. He'll slow you down."

"Sir—"

"That's an order, Mustang," said Tsuchigumo. He did not snarl, he did not growl, but he might as well have for the way it silenced Mustang.

Mustang stood up and saluted, as if he had to complete the gesture before he could obey, like it was a physical restraint from insubordination. "I'll retrieve his tags when we get back to base and send them to his family."

A gunshot rang out over their heads, then another, and then they were crouching again, praying they didn't feel the sudden pressure of a bullet puncturing their bodies.

The mercenaries' patience was running out. They didn't have much longer to wait, Shi thought; as soon as this round of gunfire stopped—

He heard a sound like a boxer's fist meeting an opponent, and there was a soft groan from Tsuchigumo. Shi lifted his head, disregarding the guns still firing, and saw Tsuchigumo bending over, both hands pressed against his thigh.

"Stay low," the captain shouted, raising his voice to be heard over the gunfire. "Go now. They're on the ridge. It's now or never."

Mustang and Iron Man glanced at each other and nodded. "Yes, sir," they said, saluting. Then they were running, running away and disappearing through the grove of whispering bamboo. Tsuchigumo turned his dark eyes on Shi. "Go with them."

"No, sir." Shi lifted his hand to salute, but paused halfway. Then he lowered it. "I've already made up my mind."

"There's nothing you can do." There was a note of desperation in Tsuchigumo's voice. His calm exterior was eroding, revealing the urgency, the hint of fear, underneath. "Please go, Gaksital."

"No, Captain."

Tsuchigumo wavered, planted his left foot farther behind him. He was leaning forward, his straight posture sinking into something weaker. Shi realized the pain from the bullet in his thigh must have set in, and he strode forward.

"Shi—" Tsuchigumo lifted his head and held out the hand that was not pressed over his wound. "Get out of here."

Shi paused at Tsuchigumo's use of his real name. He had been faithful in referring to his men only by their callsigns. This was the first time he had slipped since assigning them, and it was a jolt.

He did not pause for long; he broke into action and braced himself behind Tsuchigumo again just as the other man stumbled, his injured leg refusing to hold him upright any farther. He wrapped his arms around Tsuchigumo's waist and pushed his weight forward, keeping his captain's boot planted firmly on the mine.

"You're..." Tsuchigumo sagged, and Shi grunted at the sudden increase in weight. "You're going to die."

"Let's not get ahead of ourselves," said Shi, straining. Tsuchigumo was larger than he was, taller and heavier, and Shi had no kind of plan at all, except he couldn't bring himself to leave his captain as bait alone on a battlefield to be blown up.

The clouds parted then, drowning the jungle in moonlight.

A faint shout was heard from the ridge, and one after another, silhouettes appeared. Their words were unintelligible, but Shi guessed they were now seeing that half their quarry was missing.

Two mercenaries began to run across the ridge into the

trees, in the direction of Mustang and Iron Man, while the rest descended the hill, their guns raised, making their ways toward Tsuchigumo and Shi.

"Too late to run now," Shi pointed out, in case his captain felt the need to suggest he run again. "They'd gun me down."

"I'm about to blow you up, and you're worried about a bullet?"

"Just tell me when."

All the mercenaries were in the trap now, picking their way carefully around the mines Kamen Rider had told them of.

"This could be considered suicide," said Tsuchigumo in a strained voice.

"You're not dying alone. They're in position."

"Now," said Tsuchigumo.

Shi planted his right foot by Tsuchigumo's and turned, hauling Tsuchigumo's weight to the side. He landed on top of him, covering his captain in a slim attempt to keep him from worse injury.

"Stay where you are!"

"Don't move!"

"Put your hands up!"

The cries from the mercenaries were muffled; Shi's left ear was pressed against Tsuchigumo's back, his arm covering the other ear, but one thing he knew—the mine hadn't exploded.

"Don't tell me you were standing on a dud the whole time just to be dramatic, Captain," he muttered, glancing over his shoulder. A warning gunshot rang out, and he heard the bullet hiss over his head.

"Well," grunted Tsuchigumo, "not intentionally."

"Stay down! Put your hands up," a mercenary shouted. Amid the shouting, Shi realized he did not hear Kamen Rider.

Shi lifted his hands as well as he could and said in Tsuchigumo's ear, "Give me your handgun."

Shifting his shoulder, Tsuchigumo reached around his left side, making the gun visible. Shi pretended to fall a little, off-balance, and grabbed the gun as he did so. "They're getting closer," he said quietly. "When they're close enough, I'll shoot at the mine and hope something catches. At least that way we all blow up instead of getting captured."

"If it doesn't set off the mine, you'll be full of holes," Tsuchigumo pointed out.

"If it does set off the mine, I'll be full of holes," said Shi, grinning a little in spite of himself.

"You two! Stand up slowly! Keep your hands above your head."

Deftly, so the mercenaries wouldn't see the motion, Tsuchigumo slid the handgun up Shi's sleeve as far as it would go before Shi stood up, his hands placed on the back of his head. He glanced at his captain as he pushed himself up, his wary expression masking the pain in his leg.

They stood, their hands behind their head, as the mercenaries approached, eyeing the ground like it might open up and swallow them.

Shi took a step forward.

"Stop," demanded the nearest mercenary.

Shi stopped. That step had been far enough; his body now blocked Tsuchigumo's. Kamen Rider wasn't here, neither was the one called Gengxin. The traitor and the squad leader—Iron Man and Mustang could handle them, if they were found.

It was now or never.

Shi swiftly lowered his arm, sending the gun into his palm, and fired at the flattened grass where Tsuchigumo had stood for hours. The mercenaries, momentarily bewildered at his seemingly aimless shooting, did not react quickly enough. They began to fire at him only just as the fifth bullet caught the IED, trigging the mechanism that had failed before.

It was the heat, thought Shi, that he hadn't expected—he should have expected it, he supposed. Explosions were hot. But the overwhelming wall of it stood out most prominently in his mind as he was blown backwards, turning just in time to catch Tsuchigumo's sleeve and pull him to the ground just a yard from where they had landed before.

Heat was still the one thing on his mind as the view of singed grass surrounding him faded to a darkening red, then black.

———

THE HEAT WAS STILL THERE, but the light was different. Shi blinked slowly, every blink an effort. His vision cleared, and he saw a tent. He recognized the gray-green color of it, the thick canvas. He blinked again. So he wasn't dead. Something was across his face. He reached up to push it away and realized it was a bandage; he brushed his cheek, and realized the bandage wound around the center of his face, around the back of his head. This brought his arm into view—it, too, was bandaged thoroughly.

He carefully sat up, eyeing the rest of himself. His right arm and his face seemed to have taken the worst of it, although he had a few gauze patches scattered across his torso—his shoulder, his chest, and one across a tear in the thigh of his pants.

He studied the bedroll, gathering his wits and mustering the energy to stand up. He had to find the captain. He had to make sure he was the one who had brought him here, had to know he was alive.

The tent flap was pushed aside before Shi stood, and Tsuchigumo met Shi's stare with one of wide-eyed, equal shock, as if he had not expected the other man to be awake yet.

"Captain," said Shi—it was the only sound he could make, that word. Something was wrong, terribly wrong, and it wasn't the bandages on Saizou's legs or the way he limped like a cripple, leaning on a stripped piece of bamboo. "Where...did Mustang—"

"Mustang is dead." He held a knife, Shi noticed—his hunting knife; one side for gutting, the other for skinning. It was coated in red. "Iron Man came back for us just in time for the fireworks. He's dead, too."

Shi swallowed. He would process it later. For now, he would store the information in a safe place until he knew the full situation. "Kamen Rider?"

With a flick of his wrist, Tsuchigumo cleared the blade of the blood that coated it. "Lie down. We're on our own until we're well enough to get back to base."

"Where," repeated Shi, "is Kamen Rider?"

"He'll be dead soon enough," said Tsuchigumo. "If you get up, I'll kill you." It was a teasing phrase, but there was no humor in his tone. It was a direct order, and a threat. As Tsuchigumo turned, having assessed Shi, he said nothing else and left the tent.

Shi watched the flap, listening. Waiting for something he wasn't sure of.

Tsuchigumo's...no. Saizou's eyes. There was nothing behind them; they might as well have been glass marbles shoved in empty sockets, and Shi wanted to stand up, wanted to walk out and see for himself, demand what was happening.

He tried to get up, but his legs refused to cooperate. Pain seared under ever bandage; he stood halfway up and fell, clutching at his face. What could have injured that? Why did it hurt so much?

He reached up again—his expressions, the muscle movement. His face burned. It was wrong; he couldn't breathe right. Saizou needed him. He had to get up. He had to get up.

He couldn't stay down.

*I have to get up. I have to*....

## FIFTY-THREE

HIRO PUSHED OPEN the back door of the gym, gun in hand. He paused, listening. Silence. He flicked the light switch on. A single, naked bulb hanging in the middle of the room shed dim light on the dusty surroundings: two rows of lockers stood on either side of the hallway, some open, some shut, some falling off their hinges.

"In," said Hiro, stepping aside and ushering Fumiyo in before Shotgun, bearing the unconscious Shi. Hiro did not want to use the word *lifeless*, but it was how Shi looked—limp, pale, without signs of visible breath.

"Never been in a gym before," Shotgun remarked, keeping his voice low. He glanced at the floor and wrinkled his nose at the dirt. He hefted Shi in his arms and did not set him down.

Hiro glanced at Shotgun, whose clearly defined muscles formed clear impressions under his drying jacket.

Shotgun saw the look and said, "I make my own gym, man."

Fumiyo stared at Shi's face, unblinking. "Is he dead?"

Shotgun lifted his left arm and bent his ear toward Shi's mouth. "Nnn...wait." A frown flitted across his face, and for a moment, Hiro sighed, thinking this really had been for nothing and he should go through with it and shoot the remaining two fugitives. Then he could get out of here and smooth over any suspicions.

"No," said Shotgun suddenly, "he's breathing. Barely, though. It's not good."

Hiro blinked. "I'll say one thing for him," he remarked, moving past Shotgun and glancing once more at Shi, "he doesn't give up easily."

"Where do you think you're going?" Shotgun demanded as Hiro strode down the hallway toward the door at the other end.

Hiro only said, "Stay here," before stepping through and shutting it behind him. He lowered his gun, but kept his finger alongside the trigger as he moved down the wider hallway—the office was just across from him, and he pushed the door open, peering inside. It was completely empty and stripped of whatever technology it had once held. Somebody looking for cash had come through and cleaned it out, no doubt.

He left the door open and continued down the hall. It was almost too dark to see, but he spent more time in darkness than light, and he could make out enough to find his way around. He discovered the cafeteria, wide and empty and strewn with knocked-over chairs and a buffet line sporting years-old food. It didn't even smell anymore.

He left the cafeteria and found another door with the sign POOL written in kanji and English. He pushed it open. The roof here was glass—dirty glass, but with enough clear spots to let some weak sunlight filter through. The pool had not been covered; everyone had left the gym in a hurry after the bombing a few years ago, and it seemed nobody had ever returned. The pool was still full of water, but it had long since turned green.

"Not exactly the place to go skinny-dipping," said a husky,

female voice, and Hiro spun as fast as he could, setting his teeth against the pain of the bullet in his back. There was nothing behind him except the open door, and the turned again, moving his finger to the trigger.

"The acoustics in here," the female voice continued, "are perfect for yodeling."

"Riza," snapped Hiro, his voice carrying across the stagnant water. "I'm not in the mood for games. Get over here."

"Look up, precious," said Riza, and Hiro clenched his jaw in annoyance. The one time he hadn't bothered...

The overhang above the door had just enough room for Riza to perch, but as he looked up she somersaulted down with all the grace of a gymnast and landed in front of him. "That," she said, "was exceptionally sloppy of you."

He took a half-step back, providing more space between the woman and the gun in his hand. Knowing Riza, there was a good chance she'd been waiting there for a while, just so she could get the drop on him. "They're in the back," was all he said, lowering the gun. He did not move his finger away from the trigger.

Riza's sharp smile grew wider, and she sidled up to him, grasping his wrist and lifting his hand and the gun in a smooth motion. "It's good to see you," she told him. "Did you bring this just for me?"

"Maybe," he said. He had meant it to be vague and show his lack of interest, but he realized it could be misconstrued as coy. If anyone was going to misconstrue something to their own advantage, it was Riza.

She clicked her tongue twice. "Maybe, hmm? Does this mean you *are* in the mood for games? I know a few fun ones."

Hiro sighed through his nose and did not turn his head to

look at her. "I don't think Saizou's companion is going to make it. He's still alive, but not for long."

"Are you trying to change the subject?"

"I'm stating a fact."

"You're no fun sometimes." She tapped the gun with a long, aquamarine fingernail and lowered her hand. "Saizou's not here yet, which is annoying."

Hiro raised an eyebrow. "Annoying?"

"I told him to be here as soon as possible."

"Of course. Somebody's not going along with your perfect plan. Amazing."

Riza stepped in front of him and clasped her hands behind his neck. "Stop looking at me like I'm a poisonous snake. That's your department."

Hiro snorted and reached up with his left hand, unclasping her hands. "Stop changing the subject."

"I can't even touch you, huh?" She frowned and placed her hands on her hips, her long ponytail swinging as she tilted her head and said, "We're not divorced, you know."

"Neither," he said in clipped tones, "are we together. You saw to that."

Her eyes darkened. "Watch it," she warned in a venomous tone. "Give me your gun."

"And why would I do that?"

"So I can see if three bullets are missing from the magazine."

Hiro turned away from her, tucking the gun back into his belt. "They're in the locker room."

"The bullets?"

"The fugitives."

"You didn't shoot them?"

"No, Riza, I didn't shoot them."

Silence stretched long and thin. Then Riza said, "I honestly thought you would have."

"That's what people do, isn't it?" said Hiro scathingly. "Change over time."

"Don't use that tone with me," Riza snapped. "It's not like we haven't been working together for the last year. I still know you."

"Well, maybe that's your problem, then." Hiro lifted a hand, as if he could physically swat Riza's presence from the room. "Maybe we never really knew each other at all."

"Do my eyes deceive me," said Riza suddenly, adopting an altogether sterner tone, "or are you shot again?"

*Again*, as if she had been there for every time. "I hesitate to remind you—"

"No, you don't," she interrupted.

"—that you've only witnessed me get shot once," finished Hiro, turning back to face her. He had nearly forgotten about the bullet lodged back there; the pain was only surface-level, but now that Riza had pointed it out, he found himself extremely conscious of it. He tried not to hold himself too stiffly. "*Again* hardly seems like an appropriate term for you to use."

"Kido and Yuu gave me a list," she retorted. "This makes eight, unless you've been shot in the last twelve months."

"We have more pressing matters at hand than the number of times I've been shot." Hiro moved to step around Riza, but she placed her hand firmly in the center of his chest.

With a wide smile, she cooed, "That was a hilarious sentence, dear, but I already know you're a tough guy. You don't need to walk around with a bullet lodged in your back just to show off."

"I'm not showing off," he began, but she lifted her free hand and pressed a finger against his lips, effectively shushing him.

"Saizou isn't here yet, and I can't do anything about Shi Matsumoto dying in the locker room," she said practically. "Let me deal with it before you get an infection and die a slow, painful death."

Hiro could find no argument.

———

THIS HAD to be the place.

Saizou crossed the street and gripped the front door, but a hand grabbed his wrist, wrapping around it with iron fingers.

Grinding the words through clenched teeth, Saizou said, "Let go."

"Tsuki sent me to do more than keep an eye on you."

Saizou lifted his head and stared Kiba in the face. He hated him. He did not hate him for his closeness to Tsuki, he did not hate him for any of the reasons he had toyed with at earlier times. He hated him because the man was in his way. "Following me is one thing," said Saizou, gripping Kiba's forearm with his free hand. "This is another. Let. Go."

"I can't, in all good conscience, let you kill a possible ally," said Kiba. "You could be shooting yourself in the foot."

Saizou felt his mouth twitch even as his eyes began to burn with rage. The burning sensation increased the pain in his right eye, blurring his vision, and his rage boiled hotter than before. He released Kiba's forearm and spun instead, kicking the man squarely in his injured chest.

Kiba growled and lunged for Saizou, but Saizou was faster, shoving the unlocked doors open and running inside. His footsteps echoed through the abandoned foyer, the empty reception area.

Saizou wanted to bellow Hiro's name, to make sure the snake knew he was coming, to prepare him. He wanted to, but he did not. He trod quietly and strode down hallways as silent as an avenging ghost, his heart strangely still. Maybe it was already dead.

"You have no weapon."

He stopped at the end of the third hallway. He did not turn around. "I don't need one," he said simply. Quietly.

"I doubt your friend would want you to throw away your life because his ended." Kiba's voice was not raised, but it carried. Saizou heard his footsteps approaching and began to judge the distance with each one. *Thirty feet. Twenty-eight feet. Twenty-six...twenty-five feet.* "Tsuki will be disappointed in you. You are letting her down."

Saizou dropped his gaze to the floor. Swiftly, he bent down and lifted a shard of dusty glass, twice the length of his hand, sharp enough to cut his palm as he held it. Letting people down was the one thing he was good at anymore. He had failed Shi. He had let him die while the cure sat in his pocket. He had valued the life of a stranger too much.

"I might as well have killed Shi with my own hands," he said, his voice strangely thin and tired in his ears. Tired, but set. He would not change his mind. "You're the only person Tsuki has left," he continued, swallowing. For a moment he felt almost soft. Almost. "Keep her safe."

"She can keep herself safe. You're the one who needs help."

Saizou turned around, facing Kiba. The other man was barely more than a silhouette, paused twenty feet away. "Revenge is many things," Kiba continued, "but it is rarely noble or selfless. I don't think you're an exception."

"You know nothing about me," said Saizou, taking a step forward. "Don't talk like you do."

"I know nothing about you? I spent years watching you. I know you nearly as well as I know Tsuki, and I've spent half my life with her. Killing the person you think responsible for the death of a friend who was already dying won't help you. It will hurt you more than it hurts the man you seek to injure."

Saizou realized he was allowing Kiba to wrap him up in conversation, to stall for time. He stopped walking and shook his head once before spinning on his heel and breaking into a jog, away from Kiba, toward the gangster who had shot his friend.

With Kiba behind him, he didn't have time to stalk Hiro the way he wanted, to surprise him and cut his throat before Hiro knew what hit him.

"Hiro!"

Saizou's scream sounded quiet and far away, so he screamed again, as loudly as he could, scraping his throat raw. "*Hiro!*"

"I'm right here, Akita." Hiro rounded the corner ahead and stood still, his hands at his sides. He was shirtless, revealing a deep, blood-red pattern of scales winding from the backs of his hands and up, encircling almost every inch of his torso. He cracked his knuckles and said evenly, "You seem upset."

The red scales on Hiro's paper-white skin blurred together in Saizou's vision, spilling off Hiro's body, dripping into the floor. The red swallowed everything whole. It was all Saizou saw.Everything was red, and it was all he remembered.

# FIFTY-FOUR

"WHAT WAS THAT?"

"I didn't hear anything."

"I heard something."

"So?"

"So go see what it was, you big oaf!"

"Watch your mouth, shrimp."

"I can't leave him. Go see what it was."

"I'm getting real tired of you trynna boss me around."

"If you weren't so thick, it wouldn't be so easy."

"Hey!"

"Hey."

"Don't *hey* back at me, I *hey'd* you first!"

"No, you twit, he just moved."

"Shi! Shi, are you okay?"

*Shi. That's my name. I moved. Did I move?* He tried to open his eyes and found only the barest sliver of light there. He wondered if it was dark, wherever he was. *Where am I? Who's shouting? Gods, I wish they'd stop.*

"Is he awake or isn't he?"

Then the speaker was attempting to pry his eyelids open, and had he been able, Shi would have shoved them backwards. Blinding light flooded his vision, and he curled his fingers into a fist, unable to cringe.

"Yo, yo, yo, his hand's in a fist."

"What?"

"I think you're blinding him."

Darkness returned immediately, and Shi gave a mental groan. Waking up shouldn't be this difficult.

"There it was again!" said the male voice, still fuzzy and vague.

"Wha—"

"There! See?"

This time, even Shi heard it. A distant sound, like a strong wind blowing through a keyhole. No, wait, no...it wasn't wind. It was a voice. A scream.

It wasn't a familiar scream, but the next sound—a wild, shredding cry—that was familiar.

*Tsuchigumo.*

"I'm gonna go check it out."

"You can't leave; we don't know what's going on!"

"Riza's screaming, okay? That's a pretty big deal!"

Shi was not interested in Riza. "Get me...up."

The female voice—Fumiyo, he remembered now, Fumiyo and Shotgun—stammered, "Did he just—he did, right? Shi! Shi, are you awake?"

Shi opened his eyes. He felt as though the small motion drained every ounce of energy he had, but he looked past Fumiyo at Shotgun. "Get me up," he repeated, forcing the words past his clenched teeth.

Shotgun knelt next to him, leaning so close that Shi squinted and drew back as far as his strength would allow. It wasn't far, and Fumiyo placed her palm on Shotgun's shoulder and shoved him back with surprising force. "Give him room to breathe!"

"You're like, on death's door, man," Shotgun told Shi, ignoring Fumiyo but backing up a few inches. "You should just stay here."

"No," snapped Shi. "Get me up. Now."

"What *for?*" Fumiyo cried, casting a desperate glance over her shoulder.

"Riza's screaming again," said Shotgun.

"If you want her to...live," said Shi, each word draining what faint energy he had, "take me—take me out there. Right now."

Shotgun did not hesitate any longer. He scooped Shi up in his arms as if the man weighed no more than a bullet casing as Fumiyo said, "It's dangerous out there!"

"He's a soldier," Shotgun reminded her. "I'm sure he knows what he's doing."

"He's half-dead!"

"I'm taking him."

"Oh my gosh, Shotgun, you can't just—"

"Fumiyo." Shi did not shout the word, but it dropped like a boulder into still water and silenced the girl.

Shotgun jogged out of the locker room and down the hall. "Just follow the screams," he said aloud, although Shi could tell the younger man was talking to himself. "Good plan. What the heck is going on out there?"

"Tsuchigumo," hissed Shi, shutting his eyes briefly against the flash of hot pain in his shoulder.

"What's that?"

Shi shook his head once, unable to say anything else. They took several turns down various hallways and backtracked once before they rounded a corner and came to a stop.

"Riza!" Shotgun bellowed.

———

*"CAPTAIN!"*

The word swept through Saizou's consciousness like a gunshot, ricocheting off the walls of his mind and pushing a fragment of his attention outward. He blinked once, but it did nothing to clear the red out of his remaining eye. Everything was red; his hands, the walls, the man in front of him.

"Tsuchigumo!"

Saizou turned to face the voice behind him. *Tsuchigumo. Is that my name?* He repeated the question out loud, staring at the masked figure in front of him. The figure...masked figure. A man in a mask, who caught his hand as it flew towards his face. Saizou didn't remember throwing the punch, and the hand catching his fist was weak, but as his arm lowered, Saizou registered the mask, and the face he knew was behind it.

"What's my name?"

The voice was blurry—blurry, yet calming somehow. Saizou searched his mind. He knew who it was, and it was significant. What was this man's name?

"Captain, what is my name?"

A baby was crying. Saizou reached up, wiping blood from his eye. A baby...

"Shi?" He lifted both hands—not in rage, but in a sudden, broken attempt to grip something solid, to keep him from floating away.

"I'm here," said the bulldog voice. Shi. It was Shi, and he was solid, flesh and blood, under Saizou's hands. Then lightning struck the back of his head, and there was a white flash and then...black.

———

THE PALACE WAS DARK, save for the lines of red light around the walls, illuminating everything in a hellish glow. Kirikizu approached the front gates, his broken muzzle held in one hand. The samurai in front of the gates raised their reizaa-naginata and took a single step forward. "State your name."

Kirikizu stepped into the light and waited for recognition. For a moment, there was only silence, and he knew it was not because his identity was a mystery any longer. Very few people save the Prince-Regent had seen him without his muzzle. Even through their scowling oni masks, even in the dim red light, it would be hard to miss what the muzzle daily hid.

"Hand," said the samurai on the right, his bow stiff in his semi-automated armor.

The other samurai caught on and followed suit, bowing before pressing against his earpiece. "Open the gates."

The gates opened, and Kirikizu strode past the samurai, their gazes hidden as they turned their oni-masked faces, watching him pass through the gates. He heard them shut behind him and paused, though he was not sure why.

He tapped a finger against his muzzle and continued forward, avoiding the samurai. He preferred to get inside without an entourage or anyone alerted to his presence—the less commotion, the better. It had been a long day, and the day was not yet over—at least, not for him. He still had not figured out how to explain his absence to the Prince-Regent.

No doubt Kiko would use this situation to her advantage,

attempting to undermine Kirikizu's competency in the Prince-Regent's eyes, but he would deal with that later. It would not be the first time she had attempted to knock him aside, and it would not be the last.

He paused, guessing the Prince-Regent would be in his chambers. There was a good chance Kiko was with him. Kirikizu made his way to the roof of the House of the Sun, where the Prince-Regent resided, and slinked through a window in the upper casement. The drop into the hall was a good fifteen feet, but he landed softly and without jarring, used to longer falls.

Kirikizu straightened and walked down the dark hallway, his feet soundless on the stone floor. The two guards in front of the Prince-Regent's chamber straightened in shock when they saw him, but they stepped aside and let him in without a word of protest.

The Prince-Regent was not asleep. He sat on a cushion on the floor, staring unfocused at the game of chess in front of him, his face angled away from Kirikizu. A fire crackled like a group of spectators in the fireplace, casting flickering shadows across the Prince-Regent and his opponent, Kiko. She leaned on one hand, her eyes half-shut.

The Prince-Regent ran the tip of his finger around the top of his queen piece, over and over, in hypnotic circles.

Had Kiko been the only person present, Kirikizu would have simply cleared his throat and allowed the sharp pain to stab through Kiko's head, alerting her of his presence. But injuring the Prince-Regent was a fatal offense, and he did not wish to startle him.

"What is a game worth without this piece?"

Kirikizu glanced at the Prince-Regent, inside the firelight's glow. He held up the queen and Kiko straightened, eyeing it like it was a dead rat.

"Mamushi," she said in a voice still soft but sharpened by a day of patience stretched thin, "you can keep playing long after the queen is gone. I'm sure Kirikizu will be back."

"Don't condescend to me; you know I hate it."

She sighed. "I apologize, my Prince, but I hate seeing you like this. And over someone who failed his duty, no less."

"We do not know if he failed his duty," said the Prince-Regent in a low voice. "He was taken from me. He did not leave of his own volition."

"But he has not yet returned. A man of Kirikizu's skill would surely have freed himself by now, if he wanted to."

Kiko wasted no time, Kirikizu noticed, narrowing his eyes.

With a sudden cry, like a feral forest animal, the Prince-Regent threw the queen piece across the room. It struck the wall and clattered to the ground, no more than six feet from Kirikizu. He bent down and picked it up with his free hand, his muzzle still held in the other.

The Prince-Regent rose, but he was not as quick as Kiko. She was in front of the Prince-Regent before he was halfway to his feet, her claws out. "Who is it?"

Kirikizu took three steps forward into the ring of firelight and dropped to one knee, bowing his head.

The Prince-Regent pushed Kiko out of the way and knelt in front of Kirikizu, who held up the queen piece. The Prince-Regent plucked the piece from Kirikizu's grip and tossed it behind him, sliding his fingers through Kirikizu's and pressing his face into the assassin's neck.Kirikizu glanced up at Kiko. Her eyes glowed orange, reflecting the flames in the fireplace, and she merely stood to the side, where the Prince-Regent had pushed her out of the way.

The Prince-Regent lifted his free hand and pushed Kirik-izu's hair back. "Why do you not speak?"

Kirikizu lifted the muzzle in his left hand before he lifted his head.

Kiko burst into laughter. "Oh, gods, it's still awful."

Kirikizu tightened his grip on the muzzle but swallowed his emotion, burying it down until he had time to break it down and breathe it out. The Prince-Regent wore an expression torn between relief and disgust. He hated disfigurement of any kind.

The Prince-Regent hooked his index finger around the muzzle and took it, giving it a critical look before tossing it to Kiko. "Have it fixed."

She stiffened, but bowed after a tense moment. "And if it cannot be fixed?"

"A new one will be made."

"Yes, my Prince." She bowed once more before turning on her heel and stalking from the room, letting the doors slam shut behind her.

The Prince-Regent turned back to Kirikizu and lifted his hand, placing it over the other man's mouth, covering the scars. "That's better," he said softly, and leaned forward, pressing a kiss against the back of his own hand. "When your muzzle is back, you must tell me everything that happened. I expect a full report."

Kirikizu nodded once, even as he wondered what he would say. Saizou Akita had ordered him abducted from the palace by Lady Tsuki's bodyguard and a kitsune, and for reasons unbe-knownst to Kirikizu? Most likely it was to hurt the Prince-Regent...but the Prince-Regent would have retaliated during his absence, and Saizou Akita did not seem a big enough fool to let that happen intentionally.

He wondered, briefly, whether Saizou Akita had managed to get his friend the cure before it was too late.

"Have you been away from me for so long that you cannot focus on me, even when I'm here?"

The Kirikizu blinked and focused on the Prince-Regent again. He smiled and reached up, encircling the Prince-Regent's wrist with his hand and pulling it gently away from his mouth. The Prince-Regent shuddered faintly at the sight of Kirikizu's mouth, but he allowed Kirikizu to lower his hand.

The Prince-Regent studied him for a long moment before saying, "Wash up. Use my bath. You will sleep with me tonight. It might be some time before I want you out of my sight."

# FIFTY-FIVE

MOONLIGHT FILTERED through the half-open curtains, casting a pale beam across the bed. Kirikizu watched the silhouette of a bird flit past, its presence betrayed by the shadow it cast across the glass.

He glanced over at the Prince-Regent, sound asleep. His right arm draped across Kirikizu's stomach, and in his hand he held the end of a sash. The sash trailed up over Kirikizu's shoulder, where the Prince-Regent had knotted it around his mouth in the absence of a muzzle.

Carefully, so as not to wake the Prince-Regent, Kirikizu reached up and tugged the sash down around his neck, twisting it until his fingers found the knot. He was used to a variety of knots and had it undone in seconds; he set it carefully on the mattress and slid his fingers under the Prince-Regent's wrist, gently lifting his arm off his stomach.

The Prince-Regent did not move, and Kirikizu let out a faint breath before pushing himself up and looking back at the moonlight shining through the window. He leaned over the edge of the bed and picked the silk robe he'd worn earlier off the floor, shrugging it on before easing off the bed and crossing the room.

He turned the latch and pushed the window open. Only a handful of stars were visible in the sky, and the late-autumn air was enough to send a shiver across his exposed skin, but he felt breathing come easier.

*Has it always been this stifling here?* He reached a hand out the window, letting the cold breeze caress his hand. For a moment, he considered reaching back, searching the last fifteen years, taking a long, hard look at what he had felt and experienced since the Prince-Regent took him in.

He thought about it, but only for a moment. He took a deep breath and pulled the window shut. He paused, listening to his heartbeat drumming as if he'd done something dangerous, something life-threatening.

He heard a rustle of blankets and took a deep breath, letting it out slowly, returning his heartbeat to steady intervals.

He felt the soft, smothering velvet of the sash drape across his neck again, and the Prince-Regent's voice said softly in his ear, "Put it back on."

Kirikizu reached up, but as his fingers brushed the fabric, he hesitated. He had gained control over his vocal impulses long ago, out of necessity. When he chose to remain silent, nothing, not pleasure, anger, pain, or fear, could make him speak. Most of the time he lacked the desire to speak anyway; he kept his thoughts to himself and spoke when spoken to.

There was only one real reason to wear the muzzle, and it was to keep from offending the Prince-Regent with the appearance of his mouth. With the scars that were not his fault, the scars he could not remove. That was the only reason he wore that stifling machine, day in and day out.

"Kirikizu, flower," said the Prince-Regent, and his sharp

fingernails dug into Kirikizu's shoulder, "put the sash on, and come back to bed."

*I don't want to.*

It was a brief, almost childish thought, and it struck Kirikizu as an odd reaction to a simple request. No, not a request. A command, a direct order—cover your mouth, lie with me. Two direct orders.

Kirikizu clenched his jaw as he lifted the sash and tied it securely around his mouth. As he turned and followed the Prince-Regent, he clenched his hands again and again as that same, single phrase echoed in his head.

*I don't want to.*

————

THE CEILING CAME INTO FOCUS, and Saizou blinked. Something blocked his right eye. He reached up to move his hair out of his eye, and then his fingers brushed a bandage.

*The black samurai's reizaa-naginata cut through your eye. You'll probably be blind.* Kiba's words cut through his memory and he moved to sit up, but he could not.

He breathed, fighting his automatic panic, angry at himself for the first time in months for having this problem. *You should be past this now. Damn it, Saizou, you should be over—*

"I'm here, captain." The figure appeared over him—a blur, at first, until it cleared into Shi. His lips were pale beneath his mask, his skin ashen, but he appeared to be standing on his own. He was awake. He was talking. "You'll feel better in a minute."

Then Saizou remembered to breathe, his mind racing. *You're here? You're alive?* "How..." His voice was barely audible; he cleared his throat and blinked again.

"Neither of us are dead. Not sure how yet."

Saizou felt his muscles twitch and realized he was now able to move. He pushed himself up while Shi watched him, unblinking. "The antidote..." he began, but his confusion halted his sentence.

"It was in your pocket. Fumiyo found it. It's the reason I'm standing instead of vomiting on the floor."

"You're in a good mood," said Saizou offhandedly, attempting to collect his thoughts, to find something that made sense, something worth saying.

"Not dying usually puts me in a good mood."

Saizou reached up to rub something sticky away from his eye and saw blood on his hand, half-dried. Unable to look away from his raised hand, he asked hoarsely, "Did I kill somebody?"

"No."

"Did I hurt anyone?"

"Yep."

Saizou looked up, and Shi sighed. He sat down next to Saizou, and only then did Saizou realize he was on a stack of dusty punching bags in a large, empty basketball court. Right— it was a gym, although why the punching bags were in the basketball court was beyond him.

He cleared his throat. "Who did I...how badly?"

Shi hesitated. "Everybody has a few more scars. Including you, captain. You attacked the wrong people."

Saizou looked down at himself and saw bandages around his thigh, around his shoulder. There was a gauze patch on his left side. "Apparently." He shifted uncomfortably, recognizing the tension in the air and despising it. He opened his mouth to speak, but Shi got there first.

"We need to talk about Tsuchigumo."

A cold knot twisted in Saizou's stomach. "I don't have anything to say."

"That's not like you."

Saizou straightened, focusing on his pain. "I don't want to talk about it."

"Yeah, well, you haven't wanted to talk about it since Liaoyang."

"For a reason, Shi. Drop it."

Shi stood up again. His breathing grew heavier; he pushed his fingers through his damp hair. "No. No, we need to talk about it, you know why? Because you just about tore two of our only allies to shreds. You can't keep ignoring this...this part of you. It's a problem now. We're not in Liaoyang anymore, captain."

"I know we're not!" Saizou stood up and looked down at Shi, his blood surging through his veins so hard he thought his heartbeat might punch through his chest. "Do you think I don't? Do you think I don't know that? I didn't ask for this."

Shi did not meet Saizou's eyes. He folded his arms across his chest, staring straight ahead, his gaze unfocused. "I know you didn't."

"Then stop pushing me."

"What, you're going to handle it on your own? Because I haven't seen much of that so far."

"What," snarled Saizou, "is your problem?"

"You." Shi lifted his head and snapped, "You're my problem. And you know what? I don't mind. Lots of worse problems out there. You're my problem because I've seen the good and the bad of you and I love you anyway, and damned if I don't know anyone else who would put up with you like I have, but you still do this."

The words were not unlike Shi, but they were the kind of

words he used in cases of emergency, when he needed to trade in a sword for a missile. Saizou knew he had better take stock of them, so he forced himself to swallow the rest of his tirade temporarily and instead ask, "So why do you?"

"Why do I what? Put up with you?"

Saizou nodded once, wishing he hadn't stood up. It was harder to look at Shi's eyes this way. "You think I don't know you hated me when I first took command?"

"Hate's a strong word, captain."

"Are you saying you didn't?"

A brief half-smile curved Shi's mouth. "No. It wasn't just me, though, give the rest of the men some credit. We all hated you."

Saizou scratched the back of his neck and sighed. "So what happened?"

The humor faded from Shi's face, and he unfolded his arms, tucking his hands into his back pockets and tilting his chin up. "Sit down and I'll tell you."

Saizou snorted. "Why should I have to—"

"You stood up so you could look down at me. I'm not talking to you this way. Sit down."

Saizou's empty protest faded in his throat, and he sat back down, his throbbing leg injury grateful for the reprieve. He rested his hands on his knees and cleared his throat. "What were you saying?"

"First of all, if you ever do that to me again, I'll sincerely make you regret it." The phrase, which could have been teasing in any other situation, was deadly serious.

Saizou nodded, surprised at the amount of shame he felt over a split-second impulse. "Got it."

"You sure?"

"Yes. I've got it."

"Good. And it was the baby."

*Baby.* "I'm sorry?"

"The reason I stopped hating you. The baby."

"I thought you warmed up to me before that."

"No, I just kept to myself. There's a difference. Interrupt me one more time and I'm ruining your other eye."

Saizou clenched his teeth together and simply nodded, withholding the angry response he wanted to give Shi.

Shi took a spread-legged stance and folded his arms again, looking directly into Saizou's eyes until Saizou wanted to look away. He did not, however; he kept his gaze steady and waited for the other man to speak again.

After a long moment, Shi let out a breath and said, "I don't think I'd really seen you until that night in Liaoyang, with the convoy. I'd seen a spoiled, over-educated rich boy whose daddy got him a commission. Why you went from that to the captain of a guerilla unit, I'll never know. But that night with the baby, you had two choices. You could have left her there to die, slow and painful, or you could kill her quick and save her hours a grown man couldn't handle."

He fell silent for long enough that Saizou said, "So?"

The single syllable was hoarse and broken, and Shi responded, "You did it yourself. That's when I stopped hating you. For selfish reasons, I guess," he added, glancing up at the ceiling. "I was just glad I didn't have to do it."

Saizou laughed then, and Shi said nothing until the sound subsided. Saizou shook his head as his laughter turned to something like a sob, and he felt tears burning his face underneath the bandage. "A murdered baby? That's what made you trust me?"

"No," snapped Shi. "Your ability to carry a scar you could have given me instead. That's what made me trust you. That's what made me trust Tsuchigumo for years. But, captain, we need to figure something out. Tsuchigumo can't help us now. What saved our lives in Liaoyang endangers civilians here."

"It doesn't happen often," said Saizou quietly, staring at the view of the floor between his knees.

"It's happened twice since we arrived in Tokyo, if not more while I was out cold."

*Since we arrived in Tokyo.* That was...how long was it? He tried to put the days together, to come up with a number. Whether it was three days or two weeks, it made no difference to him; it felt too short. Far too short.

"I have a point," said Shi.

Saizou hated the next words he spoke. "I don't know what to do about it."

"There we go."

Saizou frowned. "What's that supposed to mean?"

"You just admitted you don't know everything. Big step for you."

"Hilarious," Saizou grunted, but he felt the hint of a smile form on his face. "You seem to be on a roll today. Any bright ideas?"

"Yeah. Figure out all the facts before you go nuts."

"What?"

"You thought I was dead. I wasn't."

Saizou ran both hands through his hair and groaned softly into the crook of his arm. "Sorry."

"Not as sorry as I was," said Shi casually, adding, "and probably not as sorry as Hiro and Riza are. Too late to do anything about that, but you're going to have to earn their trust after this."

Saizou shifted his jaw and thought for a moment. The air felt open; either of them could speak and carry on the conversation, or it could end here. "I..." Saizou cleared his throat. "I did it to prove myself. That's why I accepted the guerilla assignment when General Isao suggested it." His eyes still burned, but he blinked rapidly and said, "I knew what everyone thought of me. Everyone kept telling me I had nothing to prove."

A few seconds passed, and Shi sat back down next to Saizou. "That's what you get for being a stubborn bastard, captain."

Saizou laughed again, but this time, the sound was a little less broken. "That's what I get."

Shi nudged his shoulder. "So are you going to get an eye patch like the Prince-Regent's poisoner?"

Saizou snorted. "Not likely."

"Matching's hardly a cardinal sin. Maybe you can spark a trend."

"I want to spark a rebellion, not a trend."

Shi eyed Saizou gravely. "Captain," he said without a trace of humor, "you should embroider that on a pillow."

"Never been very good at embroidering," said Saizou thoughtfully. "Maybe I'll just get it airbrushed on a tee shirt."

Shi bowed his head and made a choking sound. Saizou grinned in spite of himself, and before he was quite aware of it, they were both laughing. Saizou moved to lean back on both palms and winced as the motion stretched his fresh injuries.

"Careful," said Shi. "You'll probably get beat up again when you apologize to Hiro and Riza."

The thought of facing the allies he had attacked made Saizou wish he had taken longer to awaken from unconsciousness. "Right."

Shi stood up, and Saizou followed suit, staring down at his boots for a moment. He lifted his head as Shi said, "Hey."

"What?" asked Saizou tiredly.

Shi tapped the side of his mask, his eyes so shadowed they were nearly invisible. "I've never viewed you as a friend."

Saizou took a step back, startled by the statement. "What?"

"You have never been my friend. You have been my captain." Shi hesitated, then reached out and patted Saizou's arm, a warm gesture for all the uncharacteristic intimacy of it. "Now you're my brother."

Saizou stared at Shi in silence as Shi nodded to himself once and turned to leave.

With a long-legged stride, Saizou reached him and wrapped his arms around Shi, regardless of his own injuries.

Stiff with surprise, Shi made no move to return the embrace for a moment, and Saizou was equally surprised when, after several long seconds, Shi clasped Saizou tightly and then let go, half-pushing him away.

"All right," he grunted. "That's enough."

Saizou grinned. "Brother, is it?"

"Don't overdo it. Most brothers don't hug except on holidays. You wouldn't know, being an only child, but that's the way of it."

"Right," said Saizou, adopting a solemn expression. "I'll remember that."

"Please do," said Shi, but as he turned away again, Saizou caught the hint of a smile on the other man's face.

# FIFTY-SIX

WINTER HEARD the footsteps coming down the steps, but he did not look up until an unfamiliar voice said, "Winter Mizushima, yes?"

"Yes." He lifted his head and regarded the imposing robot outside the cell with mild surprise. "Who are you?"

"Nobunaga." The robot looked back down at the tablet in his hand, lifting a finger to swipe something on the screen. "Unfortunately, I had to change the schedule to make room for incoming prisoners. Your execution has been moved to dawn."

"Tomorrow?" It was the first Winter had heard of an execution, although he had expected nothing less.

Nobunaga regarded him with an air of patience, despite his lack of a face. "Yes. Tomorrow."

"You're a robot."

There was no sigh, no holier-than-thou response. "Cyborg," said Nobunaga, "actually."

"I've never seen a cyborg like you."

"No, I doubt you would have."

"Prototype?"

After a moment, Nobunaga responded in a clipped, even voice, "Similar."

There was only one reason why a high-quality experimental cyborg would be at the precinct. He bore the stamp of the Empire across his left forearm. He was here to take over.

Winter briefly wondered what Haka had done, before shaking his head. His brother had ruined his own career. It was no problem of Winter's—and apparently, unless he came up with an excellent plan before dawn, it never would be.

"Are you comfortable with a firing squad, or would you prefer decapitation?" Nobunaga lifted his head, his finger poised over the tablet.

Options, thought Winter. How progressive. "Decapitation."

Nobunaga nodded, as if he had expected that response. "Very well. Winter Mizushima, decapitation at dawn." He turned to walk away, but Winter said, "I don't suppose I get a last request."

The cyborg turned around, a puzzled air surrounding him. "A last request? Is that typical?" Almost instantly, he answered his own question. "It is not typical. I'm sorry."

Winter shrugged, the motion stretching his cramped muscles. He had been chained to the wall for about a day now, he guessed, not that it would matter soon. Not unless he came up with something.

"Would you like to speak to your brother, Haka Mizushima?"

The question was so polite that, for a moment, Winter only stared, unblinking, at Nobunaga, unsure whether he had imagined it. "I would," he said as soon as his tongue loosened.

"I will send him to you," said Nobunaga. Then he turned

and strode back up the stairs, his fluid motions making no noise. He might as well have been a ghost.

Winter stared at the floor and tried to let his reality sink in. In just a few hours, he would die. And after death...would heaven open to him? He clenched his hands into fists, his heart suddenly racing as his mind took him on a bloody time-lapse through the last two decades.

*I have not done it right.* The thought shot through his mind, a scream that echoed against his skull and refused to fade. *I have not done it right. I have not done a single right thing. I have done it all wrong, and tomorrow morning, I will have to face my maker. I will be tried and found guilty. I have not done it right.*

He knew, from all his extensive reading, that his train of thought was on the wrong track. He knew that was not how it worked—he had begged forgiveness, night after night, day after day, until it seemed routine. He had shut himself off, he had helped whoever staggered across his path, and he had tried to set things right, but some things could not be set right. Setting things right was not the point of it all, he knew it. He had read it, been taught it, thought he believed it.

But now...

*I'm not ready.* A hollow panic settled in his chest. *I'm not ready.*

More footsteps sounded, and Winter shook his head, attempting to clear the fear from his head, like cobwebs he could sweep aside with a wave of his hand. They stubbornly clung to him, refusing to leave, and he took a deep breath. He would ignore them.

Haka walked slowly to the cell and stopped a foot away from the bars, his hands in his pockets. His uniform looked as if it hadn't been pressed in a week, and his long ponytail was as untidy as the rest of him—but his eyes were not coated with an unnatural pale film, and despite his ashen pallor, his air was sharp and watchful.

"What," he said, framing the word as a demand and not a question.

"I assume you heard."

"And I assume you mean your execution at dawn." Haka hitched a shoulder in a half-shrug. "What of it?"

Winter smiled. "Do you think I would ask to see you without death impending?"

"No. What do you want?"

*What do you want?* Winter took another deep breath, the same black, hollow panic rising inside him like a tsunami of empty fear. He licked his lips, hoping that fear—unnatural, uncomfortable—didn't show. "I want...I would like to beg your forgiveness."

Haka drew his eyebrows together, his eyes narrowing in mistrust. "Really. For what?"

Of course, his brother would not make this easy. He would make it as difficult as possible—*and perhaps,* Winter thought, *I deserve it.* It was unnerving, how quickly a death sentence could rearrange one's thoughts and feelings, flipping them upside down, giving cause for examination with no time for completion.

When Winter did not answer, Haka scoffed, "Are you expecting me to fill in a blank somewhere? Should I start with the recent episode of torture or go back farther? Although if we did that, we would have over twenty years of literally nothing. So tell me, what exactly have you done that begs my forgiveness?"

"Everything." Winter allowed his gaze to settle directly on his brother's face. He watched Haka stare back, defiant, for several seconds before glancing at the ceiling. "You feel wronged. You feel I have mistreated you."

Haka laughed. "I don't feel mistreated by you, Winter." He spat the name out like a curse. "But how would you know what I feel? You left me alone with a drunken bastard to fend for myself when all I'd done was try to save you, to help you for once in the miserable life I'd spent hiding behind you."

"I protected you!" Winter felt his spine stiffen, as straight as the wall behind him. "You did not hide."

"Sure, you protected me," Haka agreed, strangely calm. "Until I returned the favor. Did you like having somebody to take care of? Somebody to take blows for? Did I ruin that for you?"

"That's not how—"

"That's how it felt!" Haka's voice snapped, loud enough to elicit a low growl from a mutt farther down the hall. Haka glanced in that direction, a sudden watchfulness coming over him, and he lowered his voice. "But you wouldn't know. You've never known how to feel, and that was always my problem. Your God split us into two halves—you didn't feel a damn thing, and I felt too much. That wasn't very fair of him, was it?"

"I am sorry," Winter interrupted. He didn't mean to speak, but the words left him before he realized it. "I'm sorry for leaving you."

Haka blinked then, going silent. He rubbed his forehead with the side of his fist. He smiled again, his face twisted as if in sudden pain.

"Are you all right?"

Haka lowered his hand from his face and stared at Winter as if he'd spoken an alien language, and Winter realized in a single moment that he hadn't asked that question in over twenty years.

He had wondered it every day, but never asked.

"I have headaches," said Haka, shrugging.

"Is that why you take stardust?" Winter meant to ask the question fairly, to better discern the reasoning behind his brother's addiction. He did not expect the flash of white-hot anger on Haka's face, did not expect the snarled reply, "I have headaches because after you left, the man who called himself our father decided to beat my face in every night. Since, obviously, he couldn't throw you in with the dogs and bet on you anymore. I'd taken away his source of income. I take stardust because it…" The rage in his voice faded, and suddenly, he looked tired. Too tired, too thin, too pale.

"Anyway," he continued, waving a hand, "I'm off stardust currently."

He said it with such nonchalance that it took a moment for the phrase to sink in. "Off?" Winter repeated. Haka was always high. Every time he saw him. Off?

"Don't get too excited about it." Haka cracked his knuckles. "It's temporary."

"That is your choice."

"Save the preaching." Haka's lip curled in a sneer. "Forty-eight hours and I'm already tired of you."

"I am not…" Winter paused. "I am not trying to preach."

Haka turned around, about to walk away. A strange panic seized Winter, and he raised his voice to a half-cry. "Wait!"

Haka paused before turning back around, slowly, as if he might bolt any second. "What?"

"If I'm to die in the morning, this…" Winter cleared his throat. He had rarely felt so unsure of himself, and he loathed it. Death was almost preferable over uncertainty. "This is not how I wish to leave you."

"Too bad," said Haka, his voice hard. "You should've said that a long time ago."

———

THE PRINCE-REGENT WAS UNUSUALLY quiet the next morning. The sun remained cloaked in a dark sky, the moon only just beginning to fade from view. He awoke at this time every day, punctual and without any trace of exhaustion. Kirikizu awoke at the same time, out of habit, and watched as the Prince-Regent splashed his face with cold water from the embossed basin near the window.

*Something must be troubling him.*

The Prince-Regent glanced at Kirikizu before breezing past him into the bathroom. Kirikizu remained sitting on the bed, wondering what had gotten into the Prince-Regent. When the other man walked out of sight, Kirikizu reached up and inserted his index finger between the sash and his mouth, giving himself some breathing room.

His thoughts drifted back to Saizou Akita. *Why do you stay? Why do you put up with that treatment?* The other man had asked him those questions, simple, naive questions. He recalled his answers, recalled telling Akita that his words would change nothing.

*Your actions could.*

Kirikizu lowered his hand, winding the end of the sash around his knuckles like a boxer preparing for a fight. He wanted to curse Saizou Akita, curse him for thinking anything could change, for making him doubt himself. For making him wonder. Most of all, he wanted to curse him for taking him away from the palace, for dragging him out of the shadows into...into what? Was it light? Or was it just different? Different didn't equal better, and he certainly hadn't experienced much. A kidnapping.

Someone determined to free him—at the risk of another's life, apparently.

But free him from what? Freedom implied captivity. From Akita's point of view, Kirikizu was a captive.

From Kirikizu's point of view... He rubbed his hands over his face and leaned forward, staring at the ornamental rug on the floor. *Am I free or a captive? What am I?*

He wanted to curse Saizou Akita, but he did not. He wasn't sure why.

Someone knocked on the door, and Kirikizu lifted his head as the Prince-Regent strode out of the bathroom, a towel around his waist. "Who is it?"

"Kiko, my prince," said the muffled female voice.

"Come." The Prince-Regent sat down on the edge of the bed alongside Kirikizu and placed a gold-plated brush in his hand. Kirikizu took the item and pulled the Prince-Regent's hair away from his face and began to brush, listening as Kiko entered, but refusing to raise his eyes.

"Nice sash," she remarked, reaching across the corner of the bed and giving the end of it a tug that snapped Kirikizu's head to the side.

"Kiko," warned the Prince-Regent.

The Crane grinned. Kirikizu rotated his shoulders and continued to draw the brush down the Prince-Regent's silken hair. He did not allow himself to envision what it would be like to put a stop to Kiko's behavior, to see her demoted, thrown out of the palace. Killed, even, bleeding scarlet on the ground, thrown from a rooftop. He shook his head once and focused on the brushstrokes.

He couldn't afford to envision things like that, to open a box like Pandora. He had kept the lid shut for too long—he could wait.

*I can wait. Saizou Akita be hanged.*

Kiko bowed toward the Prince-Regent. "The captain stationed at Akita Domain asks whether or not he should continue cutting out tongues."

"Has Saizou Akita turned himself in?"

"He has not."

The Prince-Regent sighed, sounding nearly regretful as he responded, "Then, of course he should continue. It's being televised?"

"It is. I'm wondering whether or not Saizou Akita has seen it yet. It's possible he's isolated, and it has not yet reached his attention."

"The longer it carries on, the heavier his guilt when he finds out." The Prince-Regent smiled and leaned his head back. "Continue."

"Oh. Right. Kirikizu's muzzle should be ready by noon." She grinned. "Although, personally, I like this look better."

Kirikizu closed his eyes briefly, gripping a fistful of the Prince-Regent's hair until the Prince-Regent turned his head just enough to give Kirikizu an angled look. Kirikizu relaxed his grip and continued brushing. He refused to rise to Kiko's taunting remark.

"He's unable to speak this way," said the Prince-Regent.

"Exactly," said Kiko.

The Prince-Regent laughed, and Kiko joined him.

Kirikizu pressed his teeth together, clenching his jaw until it ached. *You're used to it,* he reminded himself. *You're used to it. You're used to this. You should expect nothing else.*

*You're used to this.*

"Kirikizu, flower," said the Prince-Regent.

Kirikizu kept his jaw clenched and glanced up. The Prince-Regent turned, leaning back on one hand so he could better see the assassin. The Prince-Regent made a *closer* gesture with a finger, and Kirikizu leaned forward, breathing through his nose, fighting the odd, unsteady rage swelling inside him

The Prince-Regent pulled the sash down around Kirikizu's neck and lifted his jaw, studying his mouth with something between pity and loathing on his face. "It's a shame," he remarked, lifting his free hand and covering Kirikizu's mouth with it as he had the night before. "Everything else is so perfect."

Kiko snorted softly and glanced at the door, her hands on her hips.

Kirikizu closed his eyes, swallowing everything he felt. It was too much; it was too dangerous. He had to fight these feelings back. He had to retain control over himself—or regain it. *Do I really need to regain it? Just endure it for a little longer.*

*A little longer?* The voice sprang unbidden to his mind, questioning his own thoughts. *What makes you think 'a little longer' will get you anywhere? You'll always be here. Nothing is going to change.*

*Your actions could.*

"I've just had a fun idea," said the Prince-Regent.

Kirikizu opened his eyes and tried not to stiffen.

"Oh?" Kiko raised an eyebrow and glanced at Kirikizu. "How fun?" she asked, with an air that said, *Tossing you out a thirty-story window would be a blast, let's go find one.*

"I have a new pet," said the Prince-Regent, tucking his hair behind his ear and rising from the bed. "A very dangerous and bloodthirsty pet who needs a firm hand." He smiled at Kirikizu. "You may be just the person to keep an eye on it."

Kirikizu blinked, confused. He had two jobs: please the

Prince-Regent and kill whomever he was ordered to kill. This suggestion fell within neither parameter, and he cast a quizzical look at the Prince-Regent.

"I know it's hardly usual," said the other man, "but that shouldn't matter. It's an order."

Kirikizu bowed his head, accepting the order even as his mind raced. Was this a demotion? Was he being tossed aside? Was there an ulterior motive behind the strange command?

"Go get dressed," said the Prince-Regent. "Come back here when you're ready to meet your new charge."

Kirikizu stood and bowed before walking past the Prince-Regent and Kiko, ignoring them both, attempting to make sense of this job.

———

AS THE DOOR shut behind Kirikizu, Kiko turned to Mamushi and folded her arms over her chest. "He's a babysitter now?" she asked, unable to contain the entirety of her glee.

"Don't gloat too much." Mamushi patted her cheek. "There is a reason for everything."

"And the reason for this is...?"

A sharp smile curved his mouth. "Kirikizu has many talents, the least of which is his ability to remain unattached to things."

"I don't understand," Kiko admitted. She didn't want to discuss Kirikizu's talents. Those talents had blocked her path every step of the way for longer than she cared to remember.

"He was away from the palace." Mamushi fingered the ends of his hair absentmindedly. "I'm concerned about that. It may have given him a taste of life away from me."

"So you're making him a nanny?"

"That's one way to look at it." Mamushi shrugged his shoulders and smiled again. "Another way would be to see it as me giving him something else to which he can attach himself."

Kiko's eyes widened. "You're—"

"Chains come in many forms. Some people need more than others. It's a relief that you don't need any," said Mamushi, touching her chin with a finger. "Thank you for that." He turned and disappeared back into the bathroom while Kiko stood, reeling.

"You're welcome," she said in a hushed voice, staring at the space recently vacated by Mamushi. "Of course you're welcome."

# FIFTY-SEVEN

"OW! You're doing that on purpose." Hiro lifted his hand an inch away from Riza's skin. "It's antibiotic cream, Riz. This is so it doesn't hurt even more later." She slid her gaze to the side, away from him, and muttered, "Don't use that baby-talk tone with me. I'm not a kitten." "That's certain." Hiro dabbed the cream onto Riza's face. In his rage, Saizou had torn two long, shallow gashes across her face and down across her collarbones and chest. "I can't believe you trust that man."

"What man?" She lifted her eyebrows, then winced. "You mean Saizou?"

"That's the one."

"I never said I trusted him. I never said that!"

"You sent him to me. Is this why?" He gestured up and down, indicating her injuries. "You hoped I'd piss him off and he'd go rabid on me?"

"First of all," said Riza, rolling her eyes, "don't act like an eleven-year-old. I'm not that petty."

"You're the expert on behaving like an eleven-year-old," he replied under his breath.

Riza ignored his response and continued. "Secondly, that's not why I sent him there, and you know it."

"No? Then why did you? He doesn't seem like the most stable guy on the planet."

"Oh, I see." She leaned back, away from his hand. "Well, if you're looking for stability, no wonder you ditched me."

Hiro reached behind her head, grabbing a fistful of her ponytail and bringing her face closer again. "Seems like you have the order of things wrong, doll. I didn't ditch you. If I recall correctly, you ditched me."

"You let me ditch you," she snapped, planting her hands on her thighs and attempting to duck her head to the right. "Same difference."

"Stop moving," he snapped. "And it's not the same difference."

"Oh, yeah? Well, to my mind, not coming after me was the same thing as letting me go."

"Hold still," Hiro commanded. She attempted to jerk away again, her face a stubborn mask, and he gripped her head harder. "Hold still," he repeated in a deeper voice, forcing her to look him in the eyes.

She ceased struggling, and he relaxed his grip on her hair before blowing gently across the bloody gashes curving over her nose from eyebrow to chin.

Her eyes drifted shut, and she smiled. "That's nice," she said, with unexpected enthusiasm. "How does it look?"

"It's oozing," he said, glancing at her face before blowing across the injuries again.

Her lip curled. "Oozing? Like a snail or what?"

"Like a wound."

"You should be a doctor."

"Stop talking while I stitch your face. I don't want to hit your mouth and sew it shut by accident."

"Aww, babe." She pushed her lower lip out, batting her eyelashes. "You wouldn't really do that, would you?"

He stifled an inward groan. "Don't push me." He reached down, opening the first aid kit and removing the curved needle.

"Yikes," said Riza, grinning. Hiro sighed, and Riza said, "Don't sigh at me like that."

"You're grinning at a surgical needle."

"What, I can't grin at sharp objects?" She ran the tip of her finger down the side of his face. "I married one, right? Can I grin at you?"

"There's nothing to numb the pain, so it'll hurt." He straightened and threaded the needle on the first try. He was used to sewing himself up, and other people weren't that different. At least, not usually.

This time, however, the victim was the woman he loved, injured at the hands of a man he had harbored on her behalf. It was a puzzle, and one he wasn't sure he cared enough about to let live.

"Babe," said Riza, "you've got that look on your face."

"What look?" He pinched the eyebrow-side of the gash shut and tucked the needle through her skin, pulling it out the other side.

"Like you want to murder the nice fugitive."

"He's not a nice fugitive. He's a rampaging, bloodthirsty fugitive."

"No, he's nice. I have definitive proof. I've watched him since he made a fuss at the palace a week ago."

"If I recall what I saw on television, he was on a bloodthirsty rampage then, too."

Riza snorted. "Imperial guards. Who cares about them, anyway?"

"Their families might."

"Their families should have persuaded them not to work for the Prince-Regent. Ow!" She narrowed her eyes at him as he pulled another stitch through. "You did that on purpose, too."

"No," sighed Hiro, "I didn't."

"Your bedside manner is atrocious."

"You aren't in bed. I don't need a bedside manner."

"I could be in bed." She winked at him. "Your in-bed manners make up for a lot."

He opened his mouth to respond, but she lifted a hand, grimacing as she touched the bandage over his right ear. "I can't believe he took half your ear off."

"I can't believe you were yelling 'get him, Saizou' while he did," Hiro responded, angling her chin up.

"I was caught up in the moment," she explained. "Besides, I got in front of you the next time, didn't I?"

Hiro bared his teeth. "I don't appreciate that," he replied, tugging the thread slightly harder than necessary.

Riza yelped, then kicked him hard in the shin. "That one really was intentional, don't tell me it wasn't. If you're sore about your missing ear, don't be. It'll just make you look even more interesting."

"It's not *missing*," he said tightly, "it's only half-gone, and I'm not sore about it."

"Mmm-hmm, well. You're sore about something, that's for sure."

He said nothing, only closed the last stitch several minutes later and tied the thread off. "Remove your shirt."

Riza pressed her lips together and grabbed the hem of her

shirt, but pulled in a sharp breath. "I can't lift my arms quite yet." She gave him a beguiling smile but said, "Sorry. Just cut it off."

Hiro reached into his boot and pulled out a knife. "Don't move," he instructed, inserting the knife between her skin and the shirt, pulling through the fabric like he was cutting rope. He began to pull the fabric away, but hesitated when it stuck to the blood drying from her injuries.

"Oh, just rip it off. Like a band-aid," she said cheerfully.

Hiro shut his eyes briefly and shook his head once. Sometimes, he wasn't entirely convinced Riza was real. More likely she was a figment of his imagination, some kind of coping mechanism for something. Maybe she was a psychological trauma personified, the manifestation of a serious problem.

But gods, he loved her. *Damned if I do, damned if I don't.*

He put the knife between his teeth, took hold of each side of her shirt, and ripped them apart. Her wounds began to bleed again, and he pushed the bloody fabric down around her elbows before picking a half-empty water bottle off the floor and rinsing the wounds off.

"You look sexy with a knife in your mouth," she told him.

He recognized her attempt to lighten the mood and removed the knife, setting it on his thigh as he pulled a two-foot length of thread from the first aid kit. "I only *look* sexy, is that right?"

"Sweet thing, you are the sexiest creature I've ever laid eyes on. Or laid anything on, come to think of it. But sometimes you look sexier than other times."

"You're saying there's been a time I didn't look particularly sexy?" He removed the bottle of wound-sealant and spritzed it across the long, clean cuts gashed across Riza's chest. Contrary to its name, the sealant did not close the wound, it only slowed the bleeding down, just enough to stitch.

"That one time you were bleeding out on the floor of that garage wasn't particularly sexy, but don't feel bad." She nudged his knee with hers and offered him a tired version of her former cheerful smile. "We can't all look sexy constantly. That's too much work."

He grunted and held up the tube of disinfectant cream. "Suck it up," he said, and began to apply it to her collarbone.

After a moment of silence, Riza suddenly asked, "So how are you?" with an innocent tone, like they had accidentally bumped into each other at a party.

"How am I? You look like a filet, and my ear is missing. How do you think I am?"

"I don't need you to take injury inventory, Hiro. I'm asking how you are, not how you feel."

"Nothing new to say," he replied, glancing up to see if he was hurting her. She was giving him a cold stare he hadn't seen in a long time. "Stop it."

"Stop what?" she asked, her voice as frigid as her expression.

"Looking at me like that."

"Oh, do you want me to?" Her expression froze even farther. "How would you prefer I looked at you?"

He glanced at her face again before tying off the last stitch. "Not like that."

"Hiro—"

"Why did you do it?" He leaned back, studying her face. She was still lean and athletic, but thinner than the last time he'd seen her, like she'd been skipping meals again.

She widened her eyes, the irises chemically brightened to a neon shade of lime green. He'd thought the color would fade over time, but he must have been wrong. "Why did I do what?"

"Get involved with Akita and the rest. Especially the tall kid, Shotgun. He's not your usual minion type."

"He's smarter than he looks." She shrugged and glanced away, rubbing her arms. "Besides, he was kinda lonely and it was pathetic."

"You're picking up strays now?"

"What's the matter?" Her vulnerability evaporated like mist in the sun, and she leaned forward, so close he could feel her breath on his face. "Jealous of a stray?"

He gripped her jaw and narrowed his eyes at her, but her gaze refused to meet his. She looked at his lips instead as he said, "You're not married to him, why would I be jealous?"

She eased off the metal folding chair and straddled his lap. "Exactly my point," she said, resting her arms on either of his shoulders. "I told you you're the sexiest thing I've ever seen. Shotgun's cute and all, but he's not really my type. Besides, he thinks I'm his grandmother or something."

"So you're saying you married me purely for physical reasons, is that it?" asked Hiro, but he did not lean back as she came even closer, her arms draped down his back, her cheek pressed against the side of his face.

Riza tilted her head back and grinned. "Absolutely, didn't you know? It sure wasn't that gooey, soft heart you have. Sure wasn't your leadership abilities. I think it was definitely the fact you look like the human version of a lab rat."

He opened his mouth to respond, but before he could, Riza darted forward and licked the bridge of his nose like an animal. He stared, startled and yet somehow not surprised as she began to laugh, a half-hysterical, half-childish sound he hadn't heard in almost a year.

"What in the—"

She covered his mouth with a hand. "I got involved because I thought it might...because I was feeling philanthropical."

He allowed her hand to remain over his mouth, but he raised an eyebrow at her to indicate his incredulity.

She frowned. "You don't believe me?"

He arched his other eyebrow.

"Dangit, Hiro, how can we have a solid marriage if you don't believe anything I say?"

He lowered his eyelids and gave her a flat expression, to which she groaned and removed her hand. "Fine," she snapped, rubbing the buzzed back of her skull, before it rose into a long ponytail. Her voice was softer, almost inaudible when she said, deliberately, "I thought you might be proud of me."

"Proud of you?" He squinted at her newly-scarred face. "Really. That was your reason."

"I knew you wouldn't believe me," she retorted, tossing her head. A frown crossed her face, and she clenched her hands into fists and pressed them against her temples. "You shut up."

"Riz."

"I said shut up, or I'll stick a fork in a toaster and fry you to death," Riza insisted, her gaze unfocused now. She drew a hand back, ready to punch herself in the head, but Hiro caught her wrist and pulled it toward his chest.

"Riz," he repeated, gentler this time.

"What? I'm not crazy, Hiro. I am *not* crazy," she repeated, her eyes flashing with something vicious, something desperate.

He encircled her other wrist with his free hand. "Yes, you are," he said softly. "You're crazy, and I love you. Do you understand me?"

She took a deep, shuddering breath and eyed him warily for a moment before nodding slowly. "Yyyyes."

"What did I tell you?"

"You're craz—no, I'm crazy. I'm crazy, and..."

"And?"

"And I love you."

"No, I love you."

"That's what I said," she said, and kissed him hard.

# FIFTY-EIGHT

"HEY. CAN I COME IN?"

Haka glanced up as Otter shut the door. "I don't know why you bother asking."

"I'm being polite. Trying to set an example."

He rubbed his hands over his face. "What time is it?" he asked, twisting to look at the clock.

"Five-thirty." Otter hopped onto the desk, pushing papers out of the way. Her feet dangled nearly a foot above the ground, but she was taller than Haka as he sat hunched over on the cot. "So, dawn. His Imperial Excellency is prepping Takuan, Yaguchi, and Matsuda to attend the execution."

She watched him closely, waiting for a reaction. After a moment of total silence, she remarked, "Huh. Nothing. Not even a blink."

"And what reaction should I have?" He pushed himself back farther onto the cot and leaned his head against the wall, still not looking at her. "You want weeping and gnashing of teeth? Sorry. He got himself here. He didn't even resist arrest. Don't blame me."

"Heck, I'm not blaming you. Personally, I think he's being way too passive about the whole thing. It's almost stupid."

"No." Haka held up a finger. "Not *almost.*"

"Stupid or not..." She lifted a pen from his desk and spun it between two fingers. "You just gonna let him die?"

"Yep."

"Huh."

Finally, he turned to look at her. He was angry, but she knew the source of his anger, and it didn't scare her. "What does that mean?"

"Nothing," she said breezily, clicking the pen once, twice, three times in rapid succession. "Just *huh*. It's kind of a filler word."

"Leave."

"Geez, I didn't know filler words were so offensive to you."

He stood up, shoving the cot to the side and stalking toward the door. "Stay away from the courtyard. I don't want you muddying up the execution."

"Sure thing, ex-Commander." She tossed the pen at him and watched it bounce off his shoulder.

He glanced at the pen as it clattered to the ground, and then he stooped and picked it up, holding it as if it were a dagger poised to stab someone. Otter jumped a little as he stabbed the pen into the wall with enough force that the instrument stuck, half-embedded by the door.

When he spoke, his voice was too calm to match the rigid lines of his back. "Otter, take the day off. Get out."

"Sorry?" She slid off the desk, looking from the pen in the wall to the back of his head and then at the pen again. "You want me to what?"

"Get out of the precinct and don't come back until tomorrow."

"I can't just—"

He spun around and gripped her shoulders so hard she briefly envisioned the bruises appearing under his fingers. "Get the hell out of this building and go home and don't think about coming back until tomorrow morning. I'm speaking clear Japanese, tell me if you need to hear it in Korean."

Otter's mouth fell open. "Why?"

"Because I'm sick of you." His words weren't shouted or snarled or snapped, but he spat them out like bullets from a gun. "I can't focus with you around because you never shut up with your stupid questions. You goad me over and over and over, and today, if I hear one more thing out of your mouth, I'm not going to feel sorry for shoving you into the wall next."

He released her with a push, and she strode past him, opening the door and storming down the hall. Her pulse throbbed under her skin, and as she reached up to wipe angry tears away with her sleeve, she pretended it was from the pain of his grip and not a broken heart.

———

WHEN THE OFFICERS opened the cell door and began to unshackle him from the wall, Winter felt a profound sense of relief. Usually, he excelled at waiting, steeping in patience, letting the game play out. Usually, he could keep himself occupied, retreat somewhere inside himself and pass the time.

But during the last few hours, Winter had found himself shockingly and unpleasantly unable to think or pray or retreat anywhere. He was alone in a hollow, cold, empty room, and there was nothing to focus on: nothing to do but listen to his own heartbeat and count down the moments with increasing agony.

That was not how it should be, he felt. Something was wrong. He felt a strong sense of being unfinished, somehow, and he could not make the idea settle down.

As the officers chained his hands behind his back and then knelt to unshackle his ankles, Winter shut his eyes and let out a deep breath.

*Am I afraid? Am I afraid to die?*

He had never feared death before. He had faced it impassively, he had cut his way through it and moved on. No regret, no remorse. And, he had thought, no guilt.

It wasn't until now—of course, he thought wryly, not until now—that he was able to confront himself and realize how enormous his guilt was, how far he had pushed it aside and how deeply he had buried it. How it had never gone away.

As the officers escorted him down the hallway, gripping his arms like he might break free and dash off any moment, Winter found himself fighting the urge to look over his shoulder, to ask the officers where Haka was.

*For heaven's sake, man, you're about to die,* he thought; now was not the time for restraint. But still, his head never turned and his mouth never opened as he was led into the cold morning.

The weak dawn sunlight glinted brightly off Nobunaga's frame as he stood, a three-foot shin-gunto katana in his hands.

"Winter Mizushima," the cyborg greeted him, ever polite.

Winter nodded as the officers stopped walking and gestured for him to stand in front of Nobunaga, only five feet between them.

"I am sorry for the inconvenience," said Nobunaga.

"No matter," said Winter.

Nobunaga lowered his head, indicating that Winter should kneel. Winter did, settling back on his heels and taking a deep breath of the morning air. It smelled like snow—it must be cold enough, judging by the clouds his breath created in front of him.

Haka loved snow.

At least, he had once loved snow.

He had loved much, once. Winter shook his head and dropped his gaze to the stones underneath him, paving the courtyard like the floor of a temple.

"Is there anything you wish to say?" Nobunaga inquired, holding the katana with both hands, his stance indicating the blade weighed no more than a feather. Winter guessed it weighed a good fifteen pounds. Nothing to a cyborg of Nobunaga's strength.

"Where is Haka?" Winter lifted his head, the words leaving his mouth before he gave himself time to stop them.

Nobunaga turned to look at the officer behind him, who shrugged.

"Haka's whereabouts are unknown," said Nobunaga dismissively. "Please bow your head."

Winter never bowed his head.

Nobunaga never lifted his sword.

A cacophony of screaming howls filled the air, and as if the gates of the underworld had been lifted, every mutt in the dungeon barreled into the courtyard.

# FIFTY-NINE

KIRIKIZU TILTED his head to one side, watching his reflection in the mirror. The scars on his mouth startled him whenever he chanced to see them. He should be used to them by now, he knew that. He'd had them since he was three years old. But for most of his life, those scars had been covered. He rarely saw them, and when he did, they were nothing but striking reminders that he was not perfect.

No, he was worse than that. He was a freak of nature. He knew it, with no exaggeration. Who else was born with this affliction? There was no reason for it, no way it should be possible, and yet he was the only one immune to the sound of his own voice.

He shut his eyes, letting himself remember the first time the Prince-Regent had placed the muzzle across his mouth and buckled it behind his head.

*It's a gift,* the Prince-Regent had said.

A gift to whom—that had taken Kirikizu a while to figure out, but he knew now. It wasn't for Kirikizu's sake, it was for the

Prince-Regent's; so he wouldn't have to see the scars, so he knew he would be safe should Kirikizu slip and make a sound.

Kirikizu shrugged his jacket on and combed his damp hair back with his fingers. He zipped up the front of the jacket and pulled the detached sleeves up his arms, tightening the buckles so they would hold the weight of his knives.

He was incomplete without his muzzle, half-naked, exposed. And yet it was strangely liberating, strangely freeing. He brushed his scarred lips with his fingertips and smiled at his reflection. It did not strike him as a very warm smile; it was cold, unnatural. Something he did not have time to practice, even if he wanted to. It suited neither a flower nor a blade.

It did not suit him.

And neither, he thought with some slight acidity, did babysitting. *Your new charge,* the Prince-Regent had said. *New?* Was the Prince-Regent throwing him away?

That was the part Kirikizu couldn't figure out. He doubted the Prince-Regent was through with him; he was too emotionally attached. Unhealthily so, even, and people with unhealthy attachments to things were not likely to just let those things go on a whim.

But the Prince-Regent had never shared Kirikizu before, except on the nights when he brought Kiko into their bed. Kirikizu shuddered and turned away from the mirror. If the Prince-Regent wasn't throwing him away and wasn't sharing him...the only remaining explanation was that the Prince-Regent was attempting to warp Kirikizu's emotions somehow. But to what end?

Kirikizu realized the answer almost before he finished asking himself the question.

*Because you were away,* he told himself, *and he is afraid.*

An unusual, warm sensation flooded Kirikizu's senses, the

shadow of a power newly-realized. Kirikizu had never approached his relationship with the Prince-Regent from this angle before, never had a reason to do so.

But now...

He had power over the Prince-Regent, and the Prince-Regent was afraid of it.

Kirikizu finished getting ready and strode out the door. He would meet his new charge and bide his time, for now, until this information proved somehow useful.

He loathed walking through the palace without his muzzle, but he kept his focus forward and ignored the stone-faced palace guards. They would not have dared to react to his scars anyway, but they felt more like enemies than usual.

This was power, too, and Kirikizu was unsettlingly aware of it. They would be far too afraid to say anything to him when his voice was not altered by a muzzle. One phrase from him now, unfiltered, could strike any of them down without a thought.

He reached the Prince-Regent's chamber, but the Prince-Regent was already standing outside, dressed and waiting, with Kiko at his side.

"Took you long enough," she remarked. "Preening, were we?"

Kirikizu opened his mouth as if to respond and watched her flinch. He did not allow himself a smile, but he turned to the Prince-Regent and bowed.

"Good." The Prince-Regent touched Kirikizu's arm and breezed past him. "Follow me."

Kiko glared at Kirikizu and continued behind the Prince-Regent, but half a second later, the Prince-Regent said, "Come up with me, Kirikizu," and Kirikizu passed Kiko without sparing her a glance.

"This is not an ordinary charge," said the Prince-Regent. "You recall the biologist I had brought here a few weeks ago?"

Kirikizu nodded. It was difficult to forget, really.

"Well, together, he and I created a bit of an experiment. It's a beautiful creature—some ugly points, but useful and efficient. I have a special purpose for this creature, but for now, it needs to be let outdoors. Dr. Sleimann informs me it doesn't do well cooped up, and nobody but you has the skills required for taking it out for exercise."

Kirikizu lifted an eyebrow. So he was not specifically babysitting the creature, only taking it for walks.

They descended a flight of stairs and walked to the room at the end of the hall. The "guest suite," the Prince-Regent called it, although Kirikizu could not remember any residents ever leaving the palace once they entered. He wondered if Dr. Sleimann knew that.

The guard outside the door bowed to the Prince-Regent, who said, "Let us in."

The guard knocked on the door, announcing the arrival of a visitor, and immediately, the sound of something attacking the door vibrated, muffled, from the other side. Kirikizu cocked his head to one side, eyeing the door, listening to the thuds and snarls that were anything but welcoming.

"I hope that's not the doctor," said Kiko.

"WAIT A BLOODY MINUTE," crowed a harried voice from the other side of the door. There were muffled noises, and after a moment, the thumping stopped.

"ALL RIGHT," the doctor called, and the guard opened the door. "OMNES RELINQUITE SPES, O VOS INTRANTES."

Kiko frowned. "What the hell does that mean?"

"All hope abandon, ye who enter here," said the Prince-

Regent, smiling and walking through the door.

"Dramatic much," muttered Kiko, close at the Prince-Regent's heels.

"Not really," said Dr. Sleimann, and Kirikizu blinked at the scene before him. Dr. Sleimann was standing in front of a petite, crouched figure, who stared wrathfully out from behind a tangled veil of gray hair. "Please don't make any sudden moves. And please don't bleed."

"Please don't bleed?" Kiko snorted. "What is he, a shark?"

Dr. Sleimann's smile was entirely bland. "I see you're kept around for your extensive knowledge of *fauna*."

"Her," said the creature. He crept out a foot or so, his eyes intent on Kiko. His face was young—perhaps the face of someone in their late twenties at most—but his hair and hoarse, rasping voice did not fit the rest of the picture. "Her."

"I agree," said Dr. Sleimann, "but no."

The creature hissed and sat down, his legs stretched out in front of him as he leaned forward.

"Stop pouting," said Dr. Sleimann. "And to what do we owe the pleasure of your company, Your Highness?"

The Prince-Regent smiled with all the indulgence of a fond parent and gestured toward Kirikizu. "I hear the creature is in need of exercise. Kirikizu will take him outside."

Dr. Sleimann lifted both eyebrows. "Is that so? Well, he's either highly expendable or highly overconfident."

The Prince-Regent gave the English man a blank expression for a moment before saying, "I believe a demonstration may be useful for the future behavior of the creature."

The creature lifted his head and glanced up at Dr. Sleimann, who quickly said, "Alucard."

"I beg your pardon?"

"His name's Alucard."

"What kind of a name is that?" asked Kiko, wrinkling her nose.

Dr. Sleimann gave her another humorless smile. "The kind of name a brand-new creation gives itself when it sees you reading Dracula. Oh, and apparently, he reads backwards. Massive dyslexia, this one." He reached down and patted Alucard's head. "Massive."

Alucard reached up to bat Dr. Sleimann's hand away, but the gesture seemed half-hearted, his gaze once again focusing intently on Kiko. "Her," he said again, abruptly, as if the thought had just reoccurred to him.

"No," snapped Dr. Sleimann. "For heaven's sake, we talked about this."

Alucard hopped to his feet with an agility that surprised even Kirikizu. "Why not?"

"Oh, mercy." Dr. Sleimann glared at Alucard. "Because I said so."

"Why?"

"He's in a talkative mood," said the Prince-Regent, watching Alucard with attentiveness bordering on predatory. "And he reads?"

"Backwards, like I said," said the doctor. "And, yes, he speaks. He catches onto things distressingly fast."

"Excellent," said the Prince-Regent.

"Yes, well, that's a matter of opinion," said Dr. Sleimann. "What sort of demonstration are you talking about, if you don't mind my asking?"

Kirikizu was astonished at the casual, almost disrespectful way the biologist spoke to the Prince-Regent. It was as if he held no regard for his precarious position, as if the Prince-Regent was a vague acquaintance for whom he held little fondness.

The Prince-Regent seemed to tolerate it from the doctor in a way he would never tolerate from other people, and the only reason Kirikizu could see for his tolerance was Dr. Sleimann's diplomatic, political, and useful position.

Kirikizu looked calmly at Dr. Sleimann and wondered whether he realized his behavior would catch up to him once his usefulness ran out.

The Prince-Regent folded his arms, tapping a ring-encircled finger against his bicep. "Kirikizu, have a word with *Alucard*."

The doctor shook his head. "Good luck." He pointed at Alucard. "Stay."

Alucard scowled, watching Dr. Sleimann as the man moved to stand beside the Prince-Regent.

Kirikizu looked behind him and motioned for the others to back up, which they did. He could not use his ability if they were not behind him.

Kirikizu stepped forward and knelt on one knee in front of Alucard, who crouched down, his fingertips brushing the floor. He met Kirikizu's emotionless gaze with one of his own, and Kirikizu suddenly felt as if he was looking into the eyes of something that should not exist.

He did not know where Alucard had come from, why he was here, or what his purpose was, but as he looked into Alucard's pale eyes, he felt bizarrely unnerved. There was no feeling behind them, no sense of emotion or warmth. It was like looking into the eyes of a newborn, if a newborn could possibly be so chilling.

A third eye blinked once in Alucard's forehead before vanishing.

Kirikizu blinked, startled by it.

Alucard grinned. It was like watching a mask slide over

someone's face. It lacked true mirth, but there was something demonically gleeful about it. His teeth were sharper than they should have been, and Alucard ran his tongue along the upper row as he stared at Kirikizu.

Then he shot forward, but Kirikizu had expected that.

Kirikizu said, "Stop."

Alucard dropped to the ground mid-leap, three feet away from Kirikizu. The creature shook his head, as if hearing voices and attempting to dispel them. He backed away on all fours, rubbing his ear against his shoulder, his face twisted in pain.

Kirikizu rose to his feet.

"Well," said Dr. Sleimann. "Ahh...right. What the hell was that?"

"Wonderful," said the Prince-Regent.

Dr. Sleimann's expression was mystified. "Not to be pushy, but an explanation would be grand."

The Prince-Regent grinned. "Kirikizu has many talents, the most beautiful of which is the ability to injure with a word and kill with a sentence. His deadliest weapon is the art of using his own voice."

Oscar shoved his glasses up onto his forehead and stared, wide-eyed, at Kirikizu. "Bloody hell," he breathed. "What was it? Spider bite? Chemical explosion? Radiation?"

"Birth," said the Prince-Regent. "Beyond that, we know nothing."

Oscar whistled long and low before pointing at Alucard. "You might be the only person besides me who can keep an eye on the bugger."

"Bugger," Alucard repeated.

"Yes, you," said Oscar.

Alucard reached up and rubbed his palms across his ears. He lowered them, and as he saw the crimson blood streaking his palms, his eyes narrowed. His head shot up, and he curled his lip at Kirikizu, a growl emanating from deep in his throat.

"Bastard," he snarled.

Kirikizu arched an eyebrow.

"He's a handful," said Oscar. "Possibly several handfuls, but two are all I've got. Much to my distress."

Kirikizu lifted both his hands a fraction, indicating there were now four. Alucard was now his "charge," and even though he guessed the motive behind the order, it was still an order given by the Prince-Regent and he would obey it.

He would obey it.

"Yes, well," said Oscar, "no doubt your hands are stronger than mine, so here's hoping. Cheers. If it's not too much trouble, can you take him out for some exercise now, as opposed to later? If it is too much trouble, I don't really care. He still needs exercise."

"Take him out, Kirikizu," said the Prince-Regent.

"Preferably where there are no people," said Oscar.

"People," said Alucard.

"No," said Oscar.

"People," Alucard repeated, with more vehemence.

"No," Oscar repeated, matching his level of enthusiasm to the creature's.

Alucard licked his own blood from his hand. "Spoilsport."

"Kirikizu, take him outside," said the Prince-Regent. He smiled and rubbed Kirikizu's upper arm fondly. It would have been a gesture of reassurance, had he not known it was the Prince-Regent's way of telling him, *It's all right, feel free to bond with this creature.*

Maybe it *was* reassurance, just of an unusual kind.

Alucard was standing now, his head cocked to one side. "Outside?"

Oscar drew his hands over his face and knelt in front of Alucard. The creature looked down at him, his face awash in curiosity. "Outside?"

Oscar nodded and put his hands on Alucard's shoulders. "Now listen, you brat," he said, hesitatingly, "if you don't behave well out there, you'll never be allowed out again. At least not for a very, very long time. You'll like sunlight."

Alucard shook his head vehemently. "Burn," he said, not in an argumentative tone, but a pleading one. "I'll burn."

"No, you won't. You're not a—oh, for goodness' sake." Oscar stood up, a hand still on Alucard's shoulder, and looked at Kirikizu. "He's never been outside. He was transported from the lab to this room in a car. He doesn't know what it's like, and unfortunately for me, he learned to read on *Dracula*. Thus, he has some strange ideas about sunlight."

"And drinking blood," Kiko interjected, folding her arms, "or so I hear."

"That," said Oscar, "is a gross exaggeration. He rips people's throats out with his teeth and kills them in horrific, brutal ways, but he does not drink their blood afterwards. Do you, Alucard?"

"No," said Alucard obligingly, still watching Kirikizu warily from the middle of the room.

"Good. Now." Oscar strode around the short couch to the other side of the room, where he opened an engraved wooden box sitting atop the coffee table. He turned around and handed something to Kirikizu—a leash, he realized, attached to a harness.

Kirikizu frowned.

Oscar noticed the expression and patted Kirikizu soundly on the back. "A leash is the lesser of two evils, I always say," he remarked, and walked back to Alucard. "Now, Alucard, I want you to go with the man with the horrible voice. He's going to take you outside."

Alucard bared his teeth and clutched the hem of Oscar's untucked shirt. "I refuse."

Kirikizu sighed. He had never dealt with children before, but he imagined this must be similar. He snapped his fingers at Oscar, who looked over and nodded when he saw Kirikizu hold up the leash, indicating he was through playing games and it was now or never.

"If you don't go with him, then you get no more *Dracula* and you won't be able to go outside for another month," said Oscar firmly, crossing his arms and looking at the ceiling.

Alucard stared at him. "*What?*" he exploded, a mixture of rage and indignation on his face.

"You heard me," said Oscar.

Kirikizu glanced at the Prince-Regent, who was watching the exchange with intense interest. Kiko, on the other hand, was studying her talons, utterly disinterested in the current proceedings.

"Give me the leash," said Oscar, holding out his hand.

Kirikizu tossed it over, and the doctor quickly and efficiently buckled it around Alucard. The creature kept his arms horizontal to the floor, his lip curled in bafflement as he attempted to figure out what the leash was. Then Oscar handed it back to Kirikizu, and icy fury swept across Alucard's face.

"No," he said coldly.

Kirikizu motioned Oscar to the side again. The doctor moved beside the Prince-Regent and Kiko. Kirikizu watched Alucard closely, noting the creature's large, narrowed eyes watching the others move aside, remembering what had happened the last time.

Alucard shot Kirikizu a sharp glance.

Kirikizu tapped his own mouth.

Alucard hissed, and the Prince-Regent suddenly said, "I'll send someone to fetch the Dog. He can follow you."

"The Dog?" Oscar inquired.

The Prince-Regent smiled. "My pet, Doctor. An equal opponent for this beast, I would think."

"I can't exactly object," said Oscar, sticking his hands into his pockets. His voice became anything but light and casual as he continued, "But if anything happens to Alucard when he's away from me, I will wreak such havoc on the biological nature of anyone who comes through my door that soon you'll be running a menagerie, not a palace."

Kirikizu stared at Oscar, but he made no move to defend the Prince-Regent. Instead, it was Kiko. She shot her hand out, raking it across Oscar's chest in a lightning-fast gesture, leaving tears in his shirt and thin trails of blood behind.

He did not seem affected. "Deal?"

"How *dare* you speak to your Prince—" Kiko began, but Oscar cut her off.

"Look, bird, he's not my prince, right? He never has been, and I'm not sorry to say he never will be, no matter how long I'm kept around here. Alucard's like a...well, he's a science experiment gone whack, but..." He rubbed the back of his head vigorously. "Just don't hurt him."

The Prince-Regent said nothing for a long moment. He pulled his long, raven hair over his shoulder and combed it absently with his gold-dipped fingernails, his black eyes intent on the doctor.

"You are very bold with your words," said the Prince-Regent finally, his voice soft.

Kirikizu glanced back at Oscar, hoping the man said nothing further to aggravate the Prince-Regent's ego.

"I'm a very offensive person," said Oscar.

The Prince-Regent smiled. "No harm will come to Alucard today. You have my word of honor."

Oscar grimaced. "I'd rather just have your word, plain and simple."

Kirikizu wound the leash around his hand, his eyes flicking from the Prince-Regent to Oscar and back again. Oscar seemed to have given up on any hope of getting out of the palace, or even Japan. He had signed his own death warrant half a dozen times in the past ten minutes, and Kirikizu was confused.

Confused...but he couldn't help admiring Oscar's complete lack of regard for his position, or anyone else's. Kirikizu glanced at Alucard, who was half-crouched again, watching Oscar. It was almost as if he realized Oscar was placing himself in danger; he lifted one hand, his body poised to spring, like a pointer dog.

"Hurt is fine," said Alucard urgently.

"No, hurt is most definitely not fine," said Oscar, flapping a hand at Alucard. "Don't interrupt an adult conversation."

Alucard settled into a full crouch, snarling under his breath.

Kiko's lip curled. "Do you want me to cut this idiot's tongue out?"

"Not today," said the Prince-Regent. He stepped forward, placing himself in Oscar's personal space, and looked down at the shorter man. "You seem to have lost your will to live."

Oscar took a step back. "Well, I wouldn't say I lost it," he coughed. "Just misplaced it somew—oh, that's right. It fell out of my pocket when I was dragged from my hotel room to a lab."

The Prince-Regent did not smile. "You aided in the creation of a creature that is mine," he said, enunciating each word with sharp clarity. "He is not your child; he is my weapon. He is mine to do with as I wish. The only reason he is currently in your possession is because right now, your possession is also my possession, and he is not yet ready to leave the one he has imprinted on. Have you forgotten when I said I would take him away from you?"

Oscar swallowed, but his expression did not change. "As if."

"Then choose your words more carefully, and it may extend your life. Or it may not," the Prince-Regent added, turning away and crossing over to the door. To Kirikizu, he said, "I expect a report when you're through with the creature."

*His name is Alucard,* thought Kirikizu. He bowed toward the Prince-Regent, who tossed his head and exited the room.

Kiko jerked her chin at the doctor. "Be glad I didn't poison you this time," she snapped, following the Prince-Regent.

"Nice boyfriend you've got there," Oscar remarked, but the jibe sounded tired, as if all his bluster had been used up in the Prince-Regent's presence. "Just the kind you'd want to take home to mother."

Kirikizu spun around and lifted his hand in preparation to strike Oscar, but the man backed up quickly, his hands in front of him.

"Nerves," he explained quickly. "Sorry. News travels quickly. But you know, I don't judge, not me. Not really in a position to—"

Kirikizu made a hissing sound through his teeth, and Oscar stopped talking, covering his ears with his hands. Kirikizu tugged on Alucard's leash and walked to the door. Alucard gave Oscar one last look of concern before scampering out of the room after Kirikizu.

# SIXTY

"JUST KNOCK, CAPTAIN," said Shi, shaking his head. "They can't get any madder at you than they are now."

It had taken Saizou a while to regain enough equilibrium to actually walk out of the basketball court, where he realized he had been dumped earlier. He had made it to the cafeteria, where supposedly Riza and Hiro were tending to their injuries. Guilt and apprehension sat in Saizou's chest like boulders, but prolonging the apology would not help anything. He scratched the back of his head and pushed the door open, closely followed by Shi.

"Don't see 'em," was Shi's remark. "Maybe they moved."

Half a second later, Shotgun barreled through the swinging kitchen doors, his eyes wide with shock. He vaulted over the buffet counter and came to a halt when he saw Saizou and Shi.

"What's wrong?" asked Saizou, taking in the startled younger man.

Shotgun froze for several seconds before stammering, "I— uh, they're—they were—probably can't talk right now," he finished, putting his hands on his hips and nodding vehe-mently, as if affirming his own jumbled statement.

Saizou traded glances with Shi, who shrugged as if to say, *Don't look at me, the kid's crazy.*

"Why can't they?" Saizou asked.

Shotgun rubbed his face. "They're *busy*. Like, interrupt upon pain of death busy."

Shi blinked. "They're having sex?"

A laugh burst from Saizou before he realized it. "Sorry," he apologized immediately, while Shotgun's face turned as red as his hair. "I didn't realize they were...together."

"It's worse than that," said Shotgun resignedly. "They're married."

"Married?" Saizou repeated, astonished.

"Married. I thought—heck, Saizou, I thought she was an old lady!"

"She isn't?"

"No. And now I've got a mental image I really can't get rid of, so if you guys'll excuse me, I'm going to find a punching bag or something to..." His sentence trailed off in an indecipherable mutter as he pushed between them, hurrying out of the cafeteria.

Shi grinned. "The gangster is married to Shotgun's grand-mother. What a plot twist."

Saizou turned around and faced the doors, swinging from Shotgun's hurried exit. "I'll come back later."

"Good plan," said Shi.

Saizou entered the hall again, surprised at how unsurprised he was. By this point, a dinosaur could crash through the wall in front of him and it would barely feel out of place.

"Saizou!"

He turned and saw Tsuki walking toward him. Kiba was farther behind her, at the end of the hall, his arms folded.

Saizou glanced at Shi, who patted his arm. "Have fun. I'm going to find something to eat."

"Traitor," Saizou hissed.

Shi raised a hand and walked down the hall, nodding to Tsuki as he passed her. They paused briefly and exchanged a few words before continuing on their ways.

Saizou cleared his throat. "What was that about?"

"What was what about?"

"You and Shi."

"Oh, that. He told me to go easy on you."

"He did not," said Saizou.

"'You can punch him if you want to, but don't punch him too hard' were his exact words. Take that as you will."

She sounded so much like the Tsuki he remembered that for a moment Saizou only stared at her, unblinking, waiting for her to say or do something else that felt familiar.

She noticed his stare and snapped her fingers in front of his face. "Come with me."

"Where?"

"The supply room." She whistled one syllable, her tone teasing. "Heel, boy."

Saizou felt himself smile, just barely, and he followed her down the maze of hallways. She seemed to know her way around already; she must have spent the last few hours getting to know the place, out of curiosity or boredom. She always had been easily bored, but she had never had much trouble finding ways to occupy herself.

They reached the supply room, and she pushed the door open. A layer of dust coated the shelves, the boxes lining the shelves, and the floor. Saizou didn't care; he pulled out the nearest sturdy box and sat down, half-winded from the walk.

Tsuki nudged the door mostly shut, leaving a two-inch crack between the door and the doorframe. "I'd hate to get locked in a supply closet."

Saizou shifted, attempting not to stir up too much dust.

Tsuki pulled out the box across from Saizou and sat down, so close their knees were almost touching. "How's your eye?"

She sounded gentle enough, but as he opened his mouth to form the word *fine,* she said, "It's not *fine,* let's skip that word. Is it bearable?"

"Most things are bearable," he said. "It's just hard to see."

"I tried the light switch, but it doesn't seem to be working." She stood up and pushed the door open a few more inches, letting in more light. "Better?"

He nodded and looked down at his hands. He was trying not to think about his eye—about what it meant, about all the implications involved in losing half his vision. He had never banked on keeping all his limbs, but he'd never given much thought to losing his vision. He cleared his throat and leaned back, changing the subject so he could think about something else. "How are Hiro and Riza?"

She shrugged and sat back down, straddling the box and leaning forward comfortably. "They seem pretty tough. And pretty angry, but they'll get over it. But Saizou—"

"I know." He hadn't meant to snap or interrupt her, but the word flew from him before he could stop it.

Tsuki leaned back. "What do you know?"

He wanted to glare, but the gesture caused a burning sensation in his damaged eye so painful that he reached up and wiped the sudden tears away with his sleeve. He took a deep breath, attempting to regain control of himself—had he *lost* control?—and said, "I know it was my fault, that I injured them both and ruined everything, and I'm sorry."

Tsuki regarded him in silence for a moment before saying, "Well. That's all true, but that's not what I was going to say, Mr. Know-it-All."

He blinked. The fact she might have said anything else had never entered his mind. "Ah. Sorry, go ahead."

"Thank you," she said, and her tone grew serious. "Am I the same person you remember?"

The question took Saizou aback. She was far from the same person. He felt as if he barely knew her. "No," he said quietly. "You're not."

"Why do you think that is?"

He recalled Kiba's words—*She would be very unhappy if she knew I had told you*—and remained silent.

"Kiba told you," said Tsuki flatly. "Didn't he."

Saizou said nothing.

"Darn him," said Tsuki, shifting uncomfortably. "I knew it. Listen. I...people go through things, and they adapt. They have to. Adaptation and change need to happen if we're going to survive, and we've had five years to do it. I thought I hated the changes I'd made to myself, but then I saw you." Her voice softened unexpectedly. "You..." She trailed off, then shook her head. "I don't know what happened in China. I don't know what you went through. Maybe I will, eventually, but for now, I'm going to assume that you had to change drastically. I can't hold that against you."

"Maybe you can't," said Saizou. "I can."

"Come on—"

"I didn't change because of what happened to me." He stood up and kicked the box aside, no longer caring about dust, wanting to hit something, to vent his anger on something that wouldn't bleed. "I changed because of what I did. There's a difference."

For a moment, the only sound in the room was Tsuki's breathing. "What did you do?" she asked finally, angling her head up to watch him.

"I am never," said Saizou through gritted teeth, "telling you. You wouldn't..."

Pause. "I wouldn't what?"

Was it her questions increasing his headache, or was it his own anger? "You wouldn't be able to like me again," he snarled, leaning against the shelf with both hands, letting the metal edges bite into his palms.

"I haven't seen you in five years. What makes you think I stopped liking you?"

"Five years means we don't know each other anymore. We knew each other. Past tense."

"Saizou—"

"Stop." He pressed a fist against his forehead. "Please stop. I'll work it out. It won't happen again."

He heard the box scrape against the floor as Tsuki stood up, and when she spoke again, her voce was closer than before. "Hey," she said coaxingly. "Hey, Saizou. Look at me."

Slowly, he turned, knowing he couldn't face the shelf forever, and tired of this conversation and tired of existing.

He was about to ask, "What?" when Tsuki's fist collided with his stomach with just enough force that he staggered a half-step back into the shelf.

"You were a captain, for heaven's sake," said Tsuki, her eyes gleaming with a look Saizou knew very well. She was done talking and ready to see things happen. "Act like it. Your issues have issues, I get it, but in the amount of time you've been back in Japan, you've managed to get myself, Kiba, Riza, Hiro, Shotgun, and a danged *kitsune* on your side. To say nothing of Shi. Most fugitives stay on the run, alone, until they're gunned down. You have a chance. And not just a chance, you have a *good* chance at staying alive. Maybe you could even make a difference in this rotten country, and honestly, I'm tired of lecturing you already."

She shook herself like a wet dog and opened the door the rest of the way. "Sure, maybe we changed. Sure, maybe we used to know each other better than we know each other know, but guess what? You're here, and I'm here, and neither of us became a completely different person. I'd like to get to know you again. And you need to shape up."

She stepped through the door and disappeared, her footsteps fading down the hallway.

Saizou stood in the dark for several minutes. He cupped his hands over his mouth and breathed into them, once, twice, three times, four times, trying to calm down, to sort his thoughts out and put them in order.

"Hey, Saizou? SAIZOU! WHERE ARE YOU, MAN?"

Saizou strode over to the door, nearly running into Shotgun. Shotgun's eyes were wide, and his breathing was heavy as he pointed back in the direction he'd come.

Saizou reached for a sword he no longer had. He clenched his empty hand into a fist. "What is it? Are you all right?"

Shotgun nodded and straightened to his full height. He took a deep breath and said in a rush, "Some dude just showed up asking to see you."

"What dude?" asked Saizou, then blinked and said, "What guy?"

"He says his name's Matahari or something—"

"Hachi," said Saizou, his pulse quickening. "Matahachi."

He broke into a fast walk, but Shotgun called after him, "Wait, that's not all! There are two ghosts with him!"

Saizou turned abruptly on his heel. "What?"

"The Matahachi guy." Shotgun spread his hands, as if imploring Saizou to believe him. "He brought two ghosts with him. He says if he doesn't get to talk to you, they'll kill us."

# SIXTY-ONE

ALUCARD'S first reaction to sunlight made Kirikizu glad there was some semblance of cloud cover. Given the creature's high-pitched screeching, direct sunlight might have given him a stroke. Half-dragging the creature on the end of the leash, Kirikizu made it to the fountain in the west courtyard. The Dog was sprawled out in the shade of the fountain, perfectly content in the chilly weather.

The Dog lifted his head as Kirikizu approached, but his growl was directed at Alucard. Kirikizu and the Dog had known each other for fifteen years; they got along as well as anyone could in such an environment. Alucard, however, was a different matter, and as the Dog rose to a half-crouched stance, Kirikizu wondered whether the Dog posed more of a threat to the newcomer than the other way around.

Kirikizu stopped fifteen feet from the fountain and looked at Alucard, who had pulled the leash its full ten-foot length in the other direction, as if determined to snap the leather and take off.

The Dog let out one high, bizarre noise somewhere

between a loud purr and a screech. Kirikizu knew it was his version of a bark, and it caught Alucard's attention. The creature whipped around to look at the source of the noise and, upon seeing it, sprang to his full height and went rigid.

Kirikizu sighed. He needed his muzzle back.

He put his fingers to his mouth and gave a piercing whistle. It did not affect Alucard, but the Dog dropped back to all four elongated limbs and gave Kirikizu a questioning look, as if to say, *What is this thing and what am I supposed to do with it?*

Kirikizu shook his head and gestured toward his mouth. *I can't respond.*

The Dog's alien eyes took in Kirikizu's face, then his mouth. He leaned back on his haunches and began to watch Alucard, who had not moved.

Kirikizu gave the leash an experimental tug. Alucard sprang up almost three feet and landed on all fours, his eyes wide. When he realized what had happened, he turned slowly to give Kirikizu an indignant, threatening expression that made Kirikizu's lips twitch.

Alucard had attitude, at any rate.

"Don't do that," said Alucard.

Attitude and no sense of hierarchy.

"Hand!"

Kirikizu turned, relieved to see a palace servant running toward him, holding a silver box. Alucard and the Dog looked on as the servant opened the box and removed Kirikizu's muzzle.

The woman said, "It's the same as your old model, but the last one was beyond repair."

Kirikizu nodded and positioned the muzzle over his mouth and jaw, then buckled it behind his head. "Thank you."

The servant blinked and bowed hastily. "Of course," she said, backing up.

The leash tugged once, then harder as Alucard leaped forward, tackling the servant to the ground with a single bound.

Immediately, the Dog was on top of them both, his rows of teeth clamped in Alucard's neck, hauling the frenzied creature off the screaming servant.

Kirikizu grabbed her arms and hauled her out from beneath Alucard and the Dog. The servant's shoulder was bleeding, and her face already bore several deep scratches, her breathing rapid and hysterical.

"Get it away," she panted, although the Dog had Alucard pinned to the smooth stone ground with both clawed hands, his teeth still in Alucard's neck. Alucard was not moving, and for a moment, Kirikizu felt a flash of concern. If the Dog had killed the creature even accidentally—

"Go," said Kirikizu, giving the servant a firm but gentle shove in the other direction.

She needed no further instruction; she ran, leaving the box on the ground. Kirikizu looked at the Dog and said, "He'd better be alive."

The Dog narrowed his eyes and released Alucard. Immediately, Alucard threw his head back, attempting to ram it into the Dog's face, but the Dog anticipated the move and placed a knee in the small of Alucard's back, pushing him down harder.

Kirikizu picked up the leash again, winding it around his hand. "Up," he told the Dog.

The Dog obliged, but the second he was off Alucard, the creature whirled around and launched himself at the Dog, a blur of teeth and rage-filled eyes.

Kirikizu gripped the length of the leash with his other hand and yanked it back, slamming Alucard onto the ground.

The Dog bared his teeth at Alucard, who flipped over onto all fours—a position he seemed to prefer—and leveled a withering stare at Kirikizu.

"Sorry." Kirikizu shrugged. "You have to obey me. He," he pointed at the Dog, "is to make sure you don't kill anyone."

"Don't need watchers," spat Alucard.

"Your behavior indicates otherwise."

The Dog reached a long-fingered hand out on the ground toward Alucard, but it was not a friendly gesture so much as preparing to jump if necessary.

Alucard grinned suddenly, putting all his small, sharp teeth on display. "Kill him," he said simply. "Kill you. No watchers." He made a small, flitting hand gesture as if to say, *Problem solved.*

Kirikizu was beginning to feel that when Oscar had called Alucard *a handful*, he was being distressingly moderate. He decided to skip threatening the creature, as it would most likely just make him more belligerent.

"You try to kill us, we kill Oscar."

Alucard's eyes narrowed. "What?"

"If you want to keep Oscar safe, you behave. It's simple enough for even you to understand," said Kirikizu, still gripping the leash with both hands. If necessary, he could lift it up and stop Alucard, should the creature launch toward him in anger.

Slowly, Alucard's mouth fell open. For a long moment, he remained that way, his breath creating small clouds in the cold air, his gaze frozen on Kirikizu.

"Do you understand?" asked Kirikizu.

Still moving slowly, Alucard nodded.

Kirikizu rotated his neck, loosening the tight muscles. "Good," he said. "Come."

—————

RETURNING Alucard to Sleimann was much easier than taking him away, and Kirikizu had never been so relieved to return something to its owner. As soon as Oscar opened the door, Alucard barreled inside to the other side of the room and sat in the corner, his arms wrapped around his knees, watching Kirikizu with unrestrained malevolence.

"You got your apparatus back," Oscar noted.

"Yes," said Kirikizu.

"Perfect. How was he?"

That was a complicated question. Kirikizu settled on, "Manageable."

"Oh, good," said Oscar dryly, loud enough that Alucard could hear. "It's nice to know he didn't wither away in the sunlight. He didn't kill anyone, did he?"

"He did not," said Kirikizu. "But not for lack of trying."

Oscar turned to look at Alucard. "I told you not to be difficult."

"Sorry," said Alucard, without sounding sorry at all.

Oscar sighed. "Get over here, let me take that thing off."

Alucard shuffled over and allowed Oscar to unbuckle the leash before slipping out of it like an eel and hopping across the back of the couch. He settled down, reached between the cushions, and withdrew a battered paperback copy of *Dracula*.

"Don't judge," said Oscar to Kirikizu, who was eyeing Alucard with equal parts disbelief and resignation. "I had a very small selection of literature with me. I didn't plan," he added acidly, "on being here for the rest of my life."

"Life seldom goes according to plan, Doctor," said Kirikizu.

"True enough, mate. True enough. Say, how did he do with the dog?"

Kirikizu cocked his head to the side and looked at the back of Alucard's head. "The Dog had to forcibly remove him from a servant."

"Oh dear."

"He attacked her unprovoked."

"What kind of dog was it?"

The question took Kirikizu by surprise. Then he let out a one-syllable chuckle. "Humanoid."

"A humanoid dog? What kind of abomination is that?"

"The prototype for yours, I imagine," Kirikizu replied, shrugging. "No doubt you'll meet the Dog at some point."

"Describe him to me," said Oscar, hastily adding, "Please" when he saw the other man's eyes narrow.

Kirikizu sighed, but the request was not an unreasonable one, especially for a biologist. "His limbs are somewhere between a human's and..." Not an animal's. "An alien's, I suppose. Claws, fangs, sharp senses. He was one of a litter." Kirikizu frowned, remembering. "He killed the rest of his littermates. He behaves how you would expect such an experiment to behave. Better, even."

Oscar's eyes could not possibly have widened any farther. "Damn," he breathed, awestruck and disturbed. "That's... I should very much like to study him. It. Does it have a name?"

"The Dog," said Kirikizu.

"Right. Well, I'd like to examine this Dog at some point. Does he speak?"

"Not exactly."

"Does he understand English? Er—Japanese?"

"Not as well as you, but he seems to understand enough."

"How long have you known him?"

Kirikizu stretched his arms over his head. He might as well limber up and make the most of his time. "Over half my life."

"Were you raised here as well, then?"

"No. I've been here since I was twelve. That's the last question about myself I will answer." Kirikizu lowered his arms and clasped them behind his back, lifting them horizontally.

"Sorry," said Oscar, and Kirikizu heard the same unapologetic inflection there as he had heard in Alucard's *sorry*. "Does the Prince-Regent often do these experiments?"

"When the mood takes him. The Dog is his most successful."

Oscar ran a hand through his short hair. "Genius. Deranged, but genius."

"How," asked Kirikizu, genuinely wanting an answer, "is it genius?"

Oscar shrugged. "Why wouldn't it be? He has an idea and the resources and willpower to make that idea a reality. Personally, I'd love to be that morally unfettered."

Kirikizu curled his lip but said nothing. Oscar seemed to notice the sudden, tense silence because he abruptly continued. "Well, no. I suppose I really wouldn't, would I?"

Kirikizu looked pointedly at Alucard. "You brought him to life," he said, "and you think you aren't?"

The other man looked as if Kirikizu had slugged him with no warning. "That's not the same thing, mate, not the same thing at all."

Kirikizu cocked his head. "I am curious about one thing."

"You? Curious?" Oscar loosened his already loose tie. "You look like you know everything."

Kirikizu smiled grimly, the expression cramped beneath the confines of his muzzle. "Why do you show such blatant disregard for your own life?"

"I don't know where you got that idea. I happen to value my life very highly."

"Then you have a funny way of acting in your own best interests."

Oscar opened his mouth, then shut it. He leaned against the back of the couch and absently placed a hand on Alucard's head. Alucard barely seemed to notice as Oscar stroked his hair a few times; he flipped a page and held the book three inches away from his face. Then he flipped another page.

Kirikizu wondered whether he really was reading or just pretending to read as a cover for eavesdropping. He realized he could not stand around waiting for a response much longer; the Prince-Regent was waiting for a report, and he would know Alucard was returned by now.

"They're funny things, best interests," said Oscar suddenly. "We're all born with a certain survival instinct. It's why things like fear and pain are necessary."

"Of course," said Kirikizu. He stood, his arms at his sides, but did not glance at the door. The Prince-Regent could wait a few minutes before he noticed anything.

"I'm actually a very selfish person," said Oscar. He twisted his mouth in resignation. "Rotten, actually. Never done anything that wasn't for my own good, not really. But—do you mind if I get philosophical for a moment, or do you have some-where to be? I'm enjoying having another adult to talk to who isn't ordering me about, if you know what I mean."

"I have nowhere to be," Kirikizu lied. "Go on."

"Right!" Oscar rolled up his sleeves. "So I always figured, looking out for yourself's the most important thing, right? And then this bugger came along." He jabbed a finger at Alucard, who repeated the word "Bugger" before turning another page. Oscar continued, "I never figured I'd be much of a companion for anyone. Never had a girlfriend, never wanted kids. I'm a terrible son, too."

"Where is this going?" asked Kirikizu. "Condense."

"Right," said Oscar, unperturbed. "I never thought I'd be building a do-it-yourself person."

Kirikizu nodded. "Go on."

"I'm going! Whether I'd planned it or not, this little moron came out of the oven, and in less than an hour he'd killed somebody, made a mess I had to clean up after, and proved himself a general force of chaotic neutral."

"You seem to care about him," Kirikizu pointed out.

Oscar lifted a hand and pointed at him. "Yeah. I do. Don't know why, but I do. It's not because he's lovable, that's for bloody certain."

"Bloody certain," murmured Alucard, flipping the novel upside-down. "Much better."

Oscar glanced down at the book. "It's upside-down, mate."

"It's fine," said Alucard, turning another page.

Oscar blinked at Alucard for a moment before looking back at Kirikizu. "At any rate, caring about this brat's now...it's like an extension of my self-preservation. I care about him, so taking care of him is tantamount to taking care of myself. Make sense?"

"No," said Kirikizu. "You still lack regard for your personal safety."

"I don't like the Prince-Regent," said Oscar. "I think he's got a gigantic ego and a stick up his arse. But I'm the closest thing Alucard has to a parent. Besides, I stopped fantasizing about making it out of the palace alive a few days ago. Historically, people who undergo top-secret projects for tyrants don't do well." He smiled. "So now, taking care of this little guy is my life, or what's left of it. Don't care much about mine."

"Really," said Kirikizu. He found it hard to believe, although he did not say as much.

"Not really," said Oscar. "That was a lie. I don't want to die, mate." He took a deep breath and looked at the ceiling for several seconds. "I'm terrified of it, actually."

"But resigned?"

"Sure. I like to take the easy road. Being resigned is less worry." He snapped his fingers. "But if you happen to think of an escape plan and feel like telling me, don't hold back, right?"

The man was talkative, Kirikizu thought, almost as if figuring himself out as he spoke, verbalizing his thoughts as they came to him. But he now saw two things very clearly: the man used his belligerence as a shield against his own fear, and miraculously, over the course of a few days, Alucard had become more important to Oscar than Oscar himself.

Kirikizu wondered if that was Saizou's problem. But was it a problem? Was it a problem to care about someone else? Was that how the Prince-Regent felt about him?

Almost as he thought the question, Kirikizu was struck with the realization that the Prince-Regent did not care about him. Not really. Not if what Oscar said was true, not if Saizou's actions were heartfelt.

Following this train of thought, if the Prince-Regent cared about him, he would put Kirikizu above his own wants and needs—a thing he had never done. Not once.

"Hey, Kiri—whatever your name is! Are you—you all right? You don't look well. Need a drink?"

Kirikizu blinked and refocused on Oscar. "No," he said. "I have to go."

Oscar smiled and lifted a hand in a half-wave. "Better give the P-R that report. He seems like a fellow who's used to getting his own way. Probably wouldn't like it if you were late."

Kirikizu narrowed his eyes at the sudden condescension, but now his mind was at work. The condescension, when filtered through common sense, felt very much like the truth. He clenched his hand into a fist and took a deep breath through his nose. He listened to it hum out his mouth through the filter before saying, "You may want to check Alucard's neck for a Dog bite. If it looks red, ask one of the guards for an antidote from the Poisoner and do it fast."

Then he turned and left the room, closing the door quietly behind him.

# SIXTY-TWO

WHEN SAIZOU and Shotgun arrived in the foyer, Saizou noticed that Tsuki, Kiba, and Nix were nowhere to be seen. Matahachi stood in front of the cracked, dusty glass, looking very much out of place, like a piece of fine jewelry dropped in a gutter by accident.

He was not, however, as out of place as the towering figures on either side of him. They were transparent; not quite black, not quite deep blue, shifting and incorporeal. They were humanoid, but every time they flickered, like a flame blown in a sudden gust of wind, he wondered if he saw armor.

"I told you," Shotgun bellowed, gesturing widely. "Ghosts. Right there!"

Saizou put an arm out in front of Shotgun. "Stay back," he warned, walking cautiously toward Matahachi.

Matahachi entwined his fingers loosely in front of him and regarded Saizou with a narrow look before speaking. "I came to speak with Saizou. No one else is necessary."

"No way, buddy," said Shotgun. "Not with those things."

"Are those what I think they are?"

Saizou glanced at Riza, who was busy retying her hair into a long ponytail. "What are they?"

"Honestly, Tsuchigumo, I thought you'd be more read-up on folklore."

Before Saizou could respond, a throaty howl punctured the awkward tension. A form barreled down the hall toward Matahachi, and it seemed to swallow the very air around it.

The shape drew close, seeming to shift between four legs, then two, then four again, and the pulsing yellow fireflies around it swarmed like angry locusts.

Matahachi watched, seemingly unperturbed, as the figure slid to a stop not ten feet from him and rose to its full height.

"Holy crap," said Shotgun.

It was Nix, but not as Saizou had seen him before. This creature was eight feet tall and muscular, covered in shifting ink-like markings, but where a human head should have been, his broad shoulders instead shifted into the head of an enormous black fox.

Nix's eyes burned like orange embers in his face, and his teeth snapped as he spoke in a voice straight from the underworld. "You used my tail."

Five tails fanned out behind Nix and faded out like tendrils of smoke.

Matahachi looked small and fragile compared to the kitsune, but Saizou almost admired his composure. "You gave it to me."

"You *tricked me*," the creature howled, and suddenly, his hands were black and clawed and drawing back to tear Matahachi to ribbons.

He did not get the chance; the ghost on Matahachi's right dematerialized and reappeared in front of him, one arm outstretched, its fist engulfing Nix's.

Nix looked down at his hand, trapped in the ghost's grip, and then at Matahachi. "Fool," he snarled, jerking his fist away. "You summoned *oni*?"

"I knew it," said Riza, flicking the end of her ponytail at Hiro, who leaned a few inches out of the way without batting an eye.

"Oni aren't real," said Shotgun confidently.

Riza lifted her eyebrows. "And ghosts are?"

Shotgun frowned. Saizou realized Shi had left the room when he wasn't looking, and quickly, he checked to make sure both oni were still with Matahachi.

They were back in their places on either side of him, silent, looming bodyguards

Saizou stepped forward. He couldn't make sense of the situation, but now wasn't the time. He had to deal with it like it was a normal occurrence. "Nix, he's here to talk to me."

The kitsune's chest heaved with barely repressed fury as he turned to look at Saizou. "Do not make any deals with him," he snapped in that hollow, ancient voice. He shook his head, an ancient god who had somehow gotten lost in the mortal world and was not pleased with what he saw. "This fool should not be trusted."

Matahachi smiled one of his thin, insincere smiles. "Whether or not I can be trusted is hardly important at the moment. Saizou, I would very much like a word in private with you."

"You used *my tail* to summon *oni*," Nix roared, whatever semblance of self-restraint he had possessed seeming to snap. He lunged toward Matahachi again, but this time he was prepared for the oni who blocked his way. They slammed into each other, and the sound was deafening as Nix's angry, other-worldly cries meshed with a sound like a hurricane wind.

"Saizou!" cried Shotgun, "watch it!"

Saizou turned to see the remaining oni sweeping toward him—an armored, burning shadow—

Shotgun barreled into it with all the force of a raging bull.

In the midst of the chaos, Saizou saw Matahachi watching him, still waiting for a response to his request. Saizou hesitated, but he could tell the oni was not harming Shotgun. Let the kitsune do what he would; Matahachi did not seem to be here to hurt any of them.

Saizou nodded, and Matahachi strode after him as Hiro and Riza watched, making no move to stop him or engage in the fight.

Saizou pushed open the nearest door, marked OFFICE, and stepped aside to let Matahachi in. The other man stood by the dusty desk and unclasped his hands. It was only then that Saizou noticed Matahachi was trembling slightly, his lips paler than they should be. Faint shadows haunted the space under his eyes.

"You don't look well," said Saizou, with perhaps an ounce of sympathy. "But make sure your oni don't hurt my people."

"Your people are precisely the reason I came to speak with you," said Matahachi in clipped tones.

Saizou frowned. "What do you mean?"

"I don't suppose you are aware of what has been happening in your domain."

Saizou felt a cold, black hole open inside him. "What? What's been happening?"

"The Prince-Regent has been cutting out the tongue of a villager each hour you fail to turn yourself in. Your people. Or, perhaps, do you no longer view them as such?"

Saizou gripped the back of the chair in front of him, his head spinning. "Why didn't you stop it?"

"I *did* stop it. Temporarily." Matahachi sat down on the edge of the desk. "But the torture will resume at midnight if you remain absent. I convinced the Prince-Regent to give me twenty-four hours to find you."

"How did you?" asked Saizou, clutching for a question with an answer he could fully grasp.

"How did I what? Find you? I have it on good authority you are travelling with a kitsune. Oni can sense other creatures of their ilk; they were able to track you down."

*Good authority?* Saizou shook his head. His people...

"I may not like you," said Matahachi, "but as current daimyo, I have a responsibility toward my people. Their well-being depends on your return."

Saizou ran his hands back through his hair. "How do I know you're telling the truth?"

Matahachi rose to his feet. "I have no love for you, but I am not in the habit of lying." He reached into his coat and withdrew a black envelope. He held it out toward Saizou, who took it from Matahachi's trembling hand and tore it open.

In gold lettering was written, *Matahachi Shigure has been given twenty-four hours in which to find deposed daimyo and fugitive Saizou Akita.* The Prince-Regent's seal officiated the letter.

Saizou reread the letter three times. It was simple and direct, so why did his mind feel spun out in circles?

If he went, he would leave behind Shi and Tsuki and those who, as Tsuki pointed out, had risked everything for him. He would leave a million unanswered questions —why did Riza want to help? What was her endgame? Where did they fit in?

It didn't matter. Not compared to this.

He looked up. Matahachi was watching him, his lips pressed into a thin line, his gaze unblinking.

"Well?" he asked.

Saizou handed the envelope back. "I'll come. But we need to go...out...the back." He swallowed hard. "Where we won't be seen."

Matahachi nodded and moved to step forward, but something made him pause. He was looking over Saizou's shoulder, and Saizou turned to see Tsuki standing in the doorway, her hands on her hips. Shi and Kiba stood behind her. Kiba had his sword drawn.

Saizou stared at Shi, who shrugged one shoulder.

"This is why you came?" Tsuki stared at Matahachi, who nodded after a tense moment.

"It is."

"To ask him to give himself up? You know what the Prince-Regent will do to him. He won't just kill him, Matahachi, you know that! He'll—"

"I know perfectly well," said Matahachi archly, "what the Prince-Regent is capable of doing to those who displease him."

"How dare you." Tsuki's voice was low.

Matahachi's eyes narrowed. "How dare I?"

"Not you. Saizou. How dare you," Tsuki repeated. "You think you can just sneak out the back and never be seen again? Was that really your plan?"

Saizou glanced at Shi again, but the other man was not looking at him. "Yes."

"Why? Were you afraid of telling us that you were running off to die?"

"Yes," he said again, clenching his hands into fists and unclenching them again.

"You think we wouldn't back you?" The door slowly attempted to swing shut, and Tsuki kicked it back open so hard it dented the wall. "I asked you to give up the daimyo, not get yourself killed. You weren't even taking time to think of another way!"

"I..." Saizou's damaged eye began to throb.

"Leave him alone," said Shi suddenly. Everyone turned to look at him, and he lifted his head, slightly startled at the sudden attention. "He didn't want to lose his nerve."

Tsuki shifted her jaw. "Are you saying you're all right with this?"

Shi cleared his throat. "Didn't say that. In fact, I want a word with you myself, Saizou."

Saizou nodded, relieved, and stepped farther into the room.

"Everyone out," said Shi.

From the look Matahachi gave Tsuki, Saizou assumed words would be exchanged while he and Shi did the same, but if Matahachi knew "on good authority" that Nix was with them, would he also be aware Tsuki and Kiba had been with them? He tried to dispel his questions as the room emptied and Shi stepped in, shutting the door behind him.

"So," he said.

Saizou glanced down, touched the surface of the desk. "So."

"You were just going to leave, is that it?"

"For about a second and a half, that was the idea."

"Yeah, that second and a half...that was a long time, captain."

"I know."

"Did you hear the whole conversation?"

"I heard enough."

Saizou reached up and pressed a hand over the bandage across his right eye. "Should I apologize?" he asked finally.

Shi shrugged. "Should you?"

"You're angry."

"Damn right I'm angry."

"I'm sorry—" Saizou began, but Shi cut him off.

"I'm not angry at *you*, captain."

Saizou slammed his fist into the wall. "Then what is it?"

Shi laughed and pressed both fists against the back of the desk chair. He did not slam them as Saizou had; his touch was very light. All the energy he may have used to hit the chair unleashed in his voice when he growled, "Everything. I'm angry at this country, I'm angry at the so-called Prince-Regent, I'm angry at Matahachi, I'm angry at Liaoyang, and I'm angry at myself. It pisses me off that everything's conspiring to either kill you or break you, and I'm sick of not being able to do anything about it, all right? That's why I'm angry."

He yanked the chair out and sat down, out of breath after the outburst. Then he added, "No, you know what? I *am* angry at you. I'm angry at the whole damn world, you included." He released a deep breath and lifted both hands to cover his masked face. His voice was muffled when he finished, "I'm done."

Unable to stand any longer, Saizou sat down on the floor and pressed his back against the wall. He stared at the empty space in front of him, at the dust filtering through the air. "I'm angry too," he said slowly, quietly. "Because I can't do anything about it, like you said. Nobody can."

"You could stop being so self-sacrificial. That's a start."

"If there was another way, I'd take it."

"Yeah, well, why don't you just throw out another useless prayer for one?" Shi stood up and shoved the chair into the wall.

"Hey." Saizou meant to snap at Shi, but the word came out as a tired plea.

"You don't believe it would work, huh? How are you any different from me?"

Saizou closed his good eye. It was funny, not being able to tell whether his other eye closed, too. "We have a little time before making a decision. The Prince-Regent gave Matahachi twenty-four hours. So."

There was a knock on the door, and mindlessly, Saizou said, "Come in."

The door opened, revealing Nix. He ducked underneath the doorframe, swatting away one of his own fireflies, his burning eyes skipping over Shi to settle on Saizou. "Make me a deal," he demanded, his voice like wildfire.

"Matahachi claims that's a bad idea," said Shi, lowering his hands from his face.

"I am not speaking to you," said Nix, pointing a finger at him.

"What deal?" asked Saizou, the words dragging from him with reluctance.

Nix grinned, displaying two long rows of gleaming canine teeth, and suddenly, his voice changed. Saizou felt a chill sweep over him at the sound of his own voice coming from the kitsune's shifting face. "I will mimic you and turn myself in. I will die, and in return, I claim Matahachi Shigure's right hand."

# SIXTY-THREE

OTTER STOOD outside the office door, afraid to go in. She was afraid of very few things, and in truth, she was not even afraid of Nobunaga, but she was afraid of the power he held to either grant her request or dismiss it.

She took a deep breath, gave herself a shake, and knocked.

"Come in."

She stepped through the door and stared. In the span of half an hour, the interior of the office had undergone a complete transformation. Where before it had been haphazard and informal, now everything was cleaned and organized. Most items she recognized were gone: the cot in the corner, the plant she kept on the windowsill and watered because Haka always forgot but liked to look at it.

The small shelf in the corner had been replaced with a filing cabinet, and the twisted plastic blinds had been replaced with new metallic ones.

Nobunaga was bent over the desk—*a new desk!?*—and lifted his head as Otter walked in.

"Come in," Nobunaga repeated, as if he could not quite

understand why she had only half-followed his words. "Entirely."

"You've really changed the place up," said Otter, taking a few more steps into the room. "It, uh...looks nice."

Nobunaga straightened to his full height, and Otter found herself automatically leaning back to look up at him. He tilted his head to the side for a moment, the evening light filtering through the blinds casting a striped reflection across his smooth, featureless face.

Otter wondered what his face looked like behind the visor, or if he even had a face at all. "You got rid of the plant."

"The plant was unnecessary," said Nobunaga. "I have no need for sentimental items."

Otter frowned, but he gave her no time to back-talk. "What is it you want?"

"I want to be allowed into the dungeon."

"Presumably so you can see your former commander," said Nobunaga.

"Yep," said Otter.

Nobunaga shook his head, and his soft voice was tinged with a hint of regret as he said, "I am sorry, but I cannot allow that."

"Why?" Otter cried, planting both hands palm-down on the desk and tilting her head all the way back so she could glare forcibly at the cyborg's chin. "Are you torturing him? Is that why?"

"No torture is necessary; we need no information," said Nobunaga. "The facts are clear, as is his crime. He was found in the same cell belonging to one of your mutts, holding the keys. His brother was about to be executed, he concocted a slapdash and thoughtless plan to help him escape."

"So he isn't being tortured?"

"No!" said Nobunaga, the broad lines of his smooth, mechanical shoulders bracing in frustration. "As I said, he is not being tortured."

"So why can't I see him?"

"Because according to several of the officers here, your relationship with Haka Mizushima is widely regarded as quite friendly, and friends desire to help one another. I cannot risk having you hatch the second escape plan in one day."

Otter tapped her blunt fingernails on the desk before asking, "What if I promise not to try and help him escape in any way? Cross my heart, the whole works?"

"No."

She swallowed. *Dangit.* "What are you going to do to him?" She cringed, fearing the worst, but Nobunaga's response was surprisingly civil.

"He can no longer hold a position within this precinct. He will be dishonorably discharged."

"When will you release him?"

"Tomorrow morning. Now I must order you to leave this office. There is still work to be done."

Otter backed away from the desk. "It looked better with the plant," she muttered, and shut the door loudly behind her. She jumped when she saw Lieutenant Takuan standing several feet away. "You scared me."

"I thought slamming doors was my job," Takuan joked. His hair looked as if he had run his fingers through it several times too often; it stuck up on his head like grass in need of mowing.

"I can't help it if you've been slacking," said Otter, but the quippy retort lacked her usual vigor, and she felt her shoulders slump forward unbidden.

"I guess he told you about the commander getting fired."

She squinted one eye at him. "You knew?"

"I overheard him a few minutes ago. He talks to himself."

Otter leaned against the wall, underneath a framed picture of the precinct's front door, back when it was brand new. The picture had been straightened, she noticed; it was never straight. She reached up and knocked it aside.

"He's getting to you too, huh?" said Takuan in a half-whisper.

"Getting to me?" She scoffed. "He's ruining everything. What's Haka going to do? Where will he go?" She rubbed her forehead and said in a quieter voice, "What am I supposed to do here without him?"

"He won't be far," said Takuan soothingly, patting her shoulder. "I'm going to invite him to stay with us. Mayumi and the kids love him, and heaven knows he's spent enough nights on our couch anyway."

That made Otter feel marginally better. "What's his place even like?" she asked curiously. "Does he actually have one?"

"No," said Takuan. "He sleeps here or my place."

Otter's eyes widened. "Didn't he used to have a place?"

"He had an apartment in the cultural district a while back, but he never spent any time there." Takuan shrugged. "Made sense, I guess. Doesn't have to pay for a place to live."

"Is that even legal?" Otter wrinkled her nose.

Takuan grinned. "Couldn't say."

"Does he pay you rent?"

"He does the dishes," said Takuan, his eyes twinkling. "That's more than enough payment."

"Gee." Otter blinked at the mental image, not sure what to make of it. "That sounds so...domestic of him."

"You should see him in a family environment. He's great with the kids. And household chores, surprisingly. He's an excellent guest when he's not strung out," said Takuan, nodding sagely.

Otter smiled a little at the thought of Haka with two children clinging to him, attempting to vacuum the floor or do something else helpful. "You should invite me over or something then; I want to witness that. Sheesh."

"I will." Takuan grinned, but the grin faded as he said, "It's not going to be the same around here without him."

"More efficient, probably," said Otter, twisting her mouth.

"Efficiency is overrated. I'm going to miss him here at work."

Otter swallowed past the lump in her throat and managed to squeeze out a hoarse, "Yep," before tears spilled over and suddenly she was trying not to cry and failing miserably. "He's going to be dishonorably discharged," she sobbed as Takuan put his arms around her in a warm, fatherly hug. "That's not fair."

"I know," Takuan soothed, patting her back. "I know."

"They won't let me see him. That's not fair, either."

"No, it isn't."

She gripped his uniform jacket and vaguely wondered whether saltwater would stain the fabric. She hoped not, but she couldn't control the flow of tears and he was the one attempting to soothe her, so she kept crying, and she cried until she was too tired to continue.

# SIXTY-FOUR

*"I CAN'T DIE, sir! Can't we just go home? I promised!"*

The voice of Corporal Ayu died as Saizou opened his eyes. Only darkness filtered in, and for a moment, he wondered whether the blindness in his right eye had somehow spread to his left. The air smelled familiar—musty and thick and cold.

The storage room.

*Why am I here?*

He tried to call for Shi but stopped himself. He paused, listening. Nothing. No noise at all.

*Where...*

Hand. Nix wanted a hand. Matahachi's hand, in exchange for masquerading as Saizou and...dying?

Saizou recalled turning the offer down, at least without consulting Matahachi. It was not a decision he could make on his own.

He blinked. Good, he was regaining his ability to move. He took a deep breath and coughed at the dust in the air. He sat up as soon as he could, reaching back toward his head as a sharp pang hammered through it, awakening the pain in his injured eye.

He leaned his head back and groaned through his teeth, waiting for his pulse to stop hammering so the pain would die down. Nix had made his offer...Saizou had said no, and Shi—

Saizou gripped the shelf in front of him and pulled himself to his feet. He couldn't see in the dark with half his vision gone, so he felt around until his hands met the cold, flat surface of the door. He slid his hands down until they hit the doorknob. He twisted it.

Nothing.

He tried one more time before accepting the only conclusion he could draw: he had been knocked out and locked in a storage room, which meant somebody had decided to accept Nix's offer. And the only other person who had been present for the conversation was Shi.

He leaned his back against the door and took a deep breath, trying to focus. Every heartbeat mounted his anger until he could barely breathe.

*How dare they.*

It was the only thought that would replay in his mind—the only thing he could ask himself. *How dare they. How dare they. How dare they—*

He spun around and slammed both fists against the door. He did not shout for someone to come open the door; he didn't yell to be let out. He was furious, and he knew he needed to unleash his rage before he started seeing red. Again and again, his fists met the metal door; again and again, he heaved all the energy he had, until the bones in his fingers ached.

Panting, he leaned his forehead against the door, almost too tired to stand.

From the other side of the door came a small, muffled voice asking, "Um, are you okay?"

Saizou stepped away from the door and wiped his forehead with his sleeve. It had been cold in this room a minute ago. Now it felt like a sauna. "I'm fine," he managed, remembering to breathe deeply. *In and out. It's just Fumiyo.*

"I'm okay," he replied, nodding to reassure himself. *I'm fine. You're fine, Saizou. You're fine.* "Where is Shi?"

"Do you want me to go get him?"

Saizou licked his lips. "Yes."

"Um, okay. Just hang—well. I'll be right back."

Saizou looked down at his hands. He could barely see them; he lifted them directly in front of his face and smelled the copper scent of blood. He wondered how badly he'd injured them over the past few days. Right now, the ache and sting kept him focused, and he flexed his hands to increase the pain.

*You don't want to hurt anyone. You won't hurt anyone. You will be calm.* He turned in a slow circle, repeating the three phrases to himself until Shi's familiar voice came through the door.

"You wanted to see me, captain."

Saizou faced the door. "I assume seeing you is out of the question, given I'm locked in a storage room."

"I'll let you out in a couple hours. I'm sorry about this, captain. I really am."

"Don't give me that," Saizou snapped. "Did you knock me out?"

"Yep."

"Did you agree to the deal?"

A moment of silence. Then, "Look, captain, I knew you weren't going to. You would want to ask Matahachi's permission, and no man in his right mind is going to agree to give up his right hand. It doesn't matter how supposedly selfless Matahachi was in trying to find you, he wanted you dead."

"He wanted to save the domain."

"At the cost of your life!"

"Why should I want otherwise?" Saizou pressed his palms against the door, resting his forehead against it. "Those are my people! Those are people I know, people I grew up with. I would be *happy* to—"

"*I wouldn't!*"

*Breathe. Breathe.* "You wouldn't what?"

"That's the trouble with you, captain. You run around risking your neck for every damn stray you find, but you don't stop to think about how anybody else feels about it. I wouldn't be *happy* to see you throw your life away because Matahachi drags himself here and asks you to. You can't save everyone, captain. Doesn't matter how hard you try."

Saizou leaned his forehead against the door, trying to cool off. Thirty seconds of nothing became a minute, and he began to wonder if Shi had left, driven away by the silence.

Then Shi said, "The first night we spoke, do you remember that?"

"The first night we spoke?" Saizou lifted his head.

"Well, the first time we *talked*. Had an actual conversation. You remember it?"

"I remember." Saizou shut his eyes. It was the night after the...*baby, Saizou. After the baby.* Saizou recalled sitting, silent, around the campfire while the men talked.

"You noticed I wasn't with the rest of the men, and you came looking for me. What was I doing when you found me?"

"You were sitting in a tree with the only bottle of sake we still had, and you were drunk," said Saizou. He could remember it perfectly, the edges of the memory crisp and sharp. "The only time I've ever seen you drunk, come to think of it."

"Yeah, well, I like being in control of myself."

Saizou hummed softly in agreement. He, too, liked being in control of himself; it just seemed as if the universe itself had conspired to make sure he never fully had it. *Don't blame the universe,* he sighed inwardly. *Take responsibility.* "I remember you didn't offer me any."

Shi laughed. A rare sound at any given time, but rarer these days. Saizou smiled.

"Not big on sharing. Besides, you were the captain, and we weren't friends."

"True," said Saizou, then shifted his jaw, pondering.

"We weren't *born* friends, you know," said Shi.

"I know. I think it started that night, though."

"It did," said Shi. "It took a while for me to believe you weren't a complete basket case."

"That came later," Saizou agreed.

"It did. Any idea why I'm bringing this up?"

"To remind me not to strangle you whenever the door opens, I assume."

"Heh," grunted Shi. He was quiet again for a moment. "You remember what you said to me?"

"Yes," said Saizou, lying. "I pointed out you'd stolen the sake and weren't supposed to be apart from the group."

"You probably should have, but you didn't," said Shi dryly. Saizou smiled again as Shi continued. "You sat down at the base of the tree, and you started spilling your life story: how you'd never expected war to be like this, how you missed hot showers, how military gear gave you blisters. I'd never heard you talk that much before in my life."

Saizou slid to the floor, his legs stretched in front of him. He pressed a hand to his side, even the Crane's talon-wounds were hurting now. He heard Shi slide down the other side of the door, and Saizou leaned the back of his head against it.

"I got a letter that day. No return address, just *Shi Matsumoto* and my unit on the front. Pretty banged up, too; apparently they had trouble finding me. Took almost a month." Shi sighed deeply and fell silent again.

Saizou knocked softly on the door with the side of his fist. "Still there?"

"My family was dead. That's what the letter said. Farms feed armies, so the enemy blew up a bunch of farmland. Destroyed my home and everyone there."

Saizou sat still, listening with a heavy ache between his ribs.

"I was going to shoot myself," said Shi matter-of-factly. "But you talked my ear off, so I didn't. There's a point to all this," he added quickly. "I'm trying to...what I'm trying to say is that I get it. I get that you need to help people, that you feel a responsibility to them. But...you saved me first, all right? I haven't left you since. Not sure I could at this point—wouldn't want to. You're my family, captain, and if something happened to you, I wouldn't have a whole lot to live for."

Saizou drew up his knees and clasped his arms around them, staring into the darkness.

He heard Shi's elbow bump the door. "You there?"

"Shi..." Saizou faltered. Where could he go from there? What could he say that was weighty enough?

"I'm not trying to make you feel guilty or anything," said Shi, almost harshly. "I'm just trying to make you see that...ah, hell. I'm not even sure."

"Because I talked your ear off, huh?" said Saizou.

"Yeah. Don't ask me why, though. Maybe I was looking for a way out. I've wondered about it sometimes, but I still don't know."

"I guess that's the way it works sometimes."

"I guess. Hey, Saizou, I'm not..." Shi cleared his throat. "I'm not asking you to stop caring about people. I don't think you could do that if you tried. I'm just saying—the world's pretty heavy, and you don't need to carry it all, right? I've got shoulders too."

"One shoulder," said Saizou. "You need to watch the other one for a while—it's still pretty damaged."

"Shut up," said Shi, but Saizou could hear the grin in the other man's voice.

"You really think I try to do that? Is that what it looks like?"

"Carrying the weight of the world? Yep. That's what it looks like. Matahachi can lose a hand, nobody dies. Life goes on, everybody thinks you're dead for a while, your people don't get their tongues cut out. It's really not a bad trade, you know."

Saizou nodded tiredly. "I know."

"How's your eye?"

"I can't see out of it, assuming you mean the left one. When are you going to let me out?"

"You're not a prisoner, captain."

"Funny," said Saizou, tasting the bitter edge flooding back into his voice. "It feels that way."

"See?" said Shi pointedly, "I can't let you out. You might knock me out and take off to give Matahachi a hand."

Saizou blinked.

After a moment of startling silence, Shi laughed again, a loud, quick laugh that faded into, "That was unintentional."

"No, it wasn't."

"You're right. It wasn't."

Saizou was laughing before he realized it. It did not last long, but for a moment—even with the door between them—it was enough. He was surprised at the boost of energy it gave him, and he was struck with how long it had been since he had really laughed, no matter how briefly.

But...he shook his head. He thought about it a long while before he said the words, "I knew."

"Knew what?"

Saizou scratched the bridge of his nose. "I knew you were going to...I had an idea."

"You knew I was going to blow my brains out?"

"Letters go through the commanding officer first. General Isao had seen that kind of letter before. He let me know before you got it."

"Is that why you came looking for me?"

"I didn't want to lose one of my best men."

Silence fell again, and Saizou stood up. *You should have kept your mouth shut, Saizou, you should've kept your mouth shut.*

The grating of a lock being turned interrupted his stream of thoughts as Shi opened the door, his hands in fists.

Saizou lifted a hand against the sudden light, prepared to be defensive if Shi was about to take his anger out with a punch.

Instead, he was met with a solid embrace, the kind that stood in place of words.

It lasted only a moment before Shi flicked his forehead, hard, with two fingers.

"What the—"

"Don't bother trying to run out the door after me," said Shi, backing up. "There's more of us than there are of you, and you wouldn't make it to Akita Domain in time anyway. We'll release you from time-out in an hour or so."

Saizou folded his arms. "Your icy exterior cracks only so far, is that how it is?"

"That's how it is," said Shi, but Saizou caught the gleam of a half-smile as Shi left the room, shutting the door firmly behind him. He heard the lock twist again, and the sound of footsteps moving away.

# SIXTY-FIVE

*THAT YAKUZA SON of a bitch is going to pay for this.*

Virgo signed the papers in front of him, releasing Shimo from the hospital. He looked over his shoulder and saw his twin walking down the hall. He moved stiffly, and his face remained too gray to look healthy, but he smiled and spoke briefly with the middle-aged nurse who stopped to say something to him. She patted his cheek like a fond mother and continued on her way, and when Shimo reached the front desk, Virgo put a hand on his hip and said, "Nice. Get adopted again?"

"I get adopted a lot," said Shimo, giving another smile to the orderly behind the desk. "You ready to go?"

Virgo clicked his tongue. "I honestly don't know why anybody bothers adopting you. Every time they see you, you're injured somehow. Reckless. And you look horrible. Do I look that bad when I get injured?"

"Worse," Shimo affirmed.

"Don't forget."

Virgo turned to look at the orderly, who watched him with

too much sympathy in her eyes above a too-wide smile. "Yeah, thanks."

As they walked out of the hospital into the frigid evening, Shimo asked, "Don't forget what?"

"Eh, apparently they want you to have a follow-up appointment in a few weeks to see how the wound's healing."

Shimo grinned. "I'll save a follow-up appointment for a real injury."

"Atta boy." Virgo smacked Shimo's uninjured side lightly and stepped off the curb. "Come on. We need to go get your bike back, if they didn't turn it into scrap."

"Then what?" asked Shimo, following Virgo across the parking lot.

Virgo smiled and pulled up the collar of his open jacket. "Then we go hunt an albino."

———

KIRIKIZU STOOD in front of the mirror for the second time that day. His jacket, sleeves, muzzle, and knives were on the floor—all the knives except the one in his hand. It was a gutter, curved like a Raptor claw.

He had locked the washroom door, but he had to be fast. Someone might want to come in and use it, and if they found it locked, he would not have enough time to finish what he intended to do.

He blew out a deep breath. His hand, he realized, was shaking—he never shook. He stared at it for a long moment. Was it a sign? Was this the wrong idea?

It was the wrong idea.

This was wrong.

Everything told him it was, screamed at him that it was not

too late, he could hide this idea away where he hid everything else, that he never needed to look back at it.

*Don't do it. Don't do it.*

He gripped the handle of the knife harder, letting the pressure mount in his palm. His breathing was slow and even; that was good. He wasn't allowing himself to think too much. If he allowed himself to think, he would not be able to go through with it. That much he knew.

But feel...he could let himself feel. Finally, he had a reason. A risky, stupid, impulsive, dangerous reason, and he hated it, and he needed it.

He shut his eyes. He shut his mind and let the feelings flood him, washing into his soul like a black tidal wave, filling every hole, welling up in his throat, threatening to tear him apart from the inside out.

For the first time in fifteen years, he let himself feel everything.

Pain. The pain he had inflicted on others, and then pain that had been inflicted on him day after day, minute upon minute until he could hardly stand it. Pain he had endured because he had nowhere else to go.

Fear. The fear of being rejected and cut loose, of being unwanted. The fear of what might happen if he disobeyed an order, the fear of what each day might hold from the moment he awoke to the moment he fell asleep, and sometimes during that sleep. Often during that sleep.

Humiliation. He ground his teeth together, recalling every whisper in his ear, every touch from the Prince-Regent, every laugh from Kiko. Every knowing glance from strangers who knew the rumors were true, every gaze he gave his reflection in the mirror. Every time he uttered the words *my lord*, every time he had smiled or sighed for the pleasure of someone who only knew how to use him. Humiliation for wanting the acceptance of the one he hated most.

Rage. And rage, and more rage. So much rage it colored everything, ripping every seam apart, swallowing every rational thought. It was the rage that scared him—the knowledge that if he allowed himself to feel it, he would break everything and then he would break himself. He tilted his head back, his eyes still shut, and let the rage devour him, devour every inch. He let it devour every fleeting thought and misgiving, every memory. He let it devour the minutes, and rewinding, he let it devour year by year, his entire time at the palace and farther back, on the street, and farther back, to his first killing.

He was no longer human. He was something else, a surging vessel for this overwhelming feeling of memories burning in the heat of his anger, burning because he had been starved for too long, and the rage would swallow everything it could, and it would swallow it whole.

Rage was everywhere, building inside him with a power that would have frightened him—but the rage had eaten his fear, too, and when he opened his eyes in the mirror, he did not smile or laugh or cry.

He lifted the knife and cut into his flesh, and he cut, and he cut until blood dripped down him, splattered in the sink, pooled on the floor.

The Prince-Regent hated his scars.

———

TSUKI FOUND Matahachi alone in the foyer, still standing, as if the idea of sitting down would put him at a disadvantage. The oni were nowhere to be seen, but from the little she knew of oni, they were incorporeal. They would appear if he wanted them to appear.

He watched her approach, the look in his eyes unreadable. "Tsuki," he said, with guarded affability.

Tsuki almost glanced over her shoulder to see if Kiba was still behind her, but she knew he was; she smiled back at Matahachi. It was odd, smiling at him, and probably a mistake. She never smiled at him.

His expression grew shrewd. "You're in no position to ask me for a favor."

"I didn't ask anything yet."

"You are about to. There would be no reason for you to pretend amiability toward me otherwise."

He was keen. "Where are your friends?"

"They're here," he said. "They'll come if I call them."

She nodded slowly. "Then I have something to tell you."

He regarded her in silence for a moment before saying, "Go on."

"Nix has an idea."

Matahachi blinked once, the only sign he was listening. Tsuki decided to drop the pretense of being nice and just hand him the facts. It would save time, and she was unsure how much time they had.

"He has the ability to make himself look like Saizou, turn himself in, and be "executed" in his place. He's agreed to do that and buy us some time."

Matahachi nodded once, but there was no trust in his expression, only cool dispassion. "And what," he asked, "does he want in return?"

"I don't know why," she said, hesitating. "But he's going to take your right hand."

The shift in Matahachi's expression was subtle but clear.

His face seemed to tighten, his lips pressed together, and where he had been cool, he became cold. He did not move.

Tsuki heard Kiba move closer, maybe ten or twelve feet behind, but she still did not turn around. "I felt it only right to tell you."

"Then, perhaps," he said, his voice so thin and sharp it was almost a whisper, "you should have felt it only right to *ask* me."

It was not the reply Tsuki had expected. "Would you have agreed to it?"

"I suppose you will never know," he replied. "However, you might have looked at the events of the day if you wanted to provide yourself with an educated guess. I did not have to bargain the Prince-Regent at the expense of my own life, and I did not have to take the toll of using my largest wild card on two unpredictable spirit-kin. As shocking as it may seem to you, I do feel the responsibility of my position. And as such, I feel the responsibility of those in my care."

Tsuki felt her stance soften slightly as she took in the full effect of his words and realized he was not wrong. And if he was not wrong, then she was not right, and the idea was unnerving. "You accepted me as a housewarming gift," she said stiffly. "Are you telling me I've misjudged you?"

He took a step closer to her, his eyes glittering coldly in his pale face. "Anyone," he said softly, "would be a fool to reject a gift from the Prince-Regent, no matter how outrageous. You know I desire you," he continued, with frigid bluntness, "yet I have never laid a finger on you. Can you deny that?"

"No," Tsuki admitted, fighting the urge to blink and break his gaze. "Neither did you release me."

"Neither have I turned you in for your illegal activities. Do you think I was unaware, the nights you and your bodyguard went to the city and indulged in gambling? Do you think I was unaware of what you did with the money, that you gave it to the residents on my domain to ease their paltry burdens?"

"Their burdens," said Tsuki hotly, "are far from paltry."

"They are no longer starving," said Matahachi. "They are no longer unclothed. They are living in the kind of luxury they haven't known in years, and they are far better off now than they were without me. Can you deny it?"

"I cannot," Tsuki retorted, "but can you deny that you angled for the domain and stole it from Saizou Akita?"

"I have no wish to deny it," said Matahachi, but he faltered just enough. "My father was the daimyo of a prosperous domain until he was wrongfully accused of mishandling his affairs. My family was turned out onto the streets. We became nothing overnight. My mother gave all the food she found to me, insisting she was fine. Then she died of malnourishment. My father killed himself from the dishonor of it. I have lived my whole life," he hissed, "with the single goal of restoring my family's honor. Do you think I would pass by the opportunity to place a domain under the name Shigure?"

It was more than Tsuki had ever heard him say at once, and it spilled from him with such vehemence that she could think of no reply.

Unblinking, Matahachi held out his right hand and clenched his fingers into a sudden fist. He said nothing, but suddenly the oni appeared on either side of him.

Before Tsuki could comprehend what was happening, the oni on Matahachi's right had lifted its huge, transparent katana and sliced down.

Matahachi did not scream as his hand fell to the ground in a wisp of blue smoke, but he sank to his knees, clutching the bleeding stump to his chest.

"Give it to the fox," he said through his teeth, leaning

forward, curling around his damaged limb. "And do not presume to steal from me again."

Kiba moved past Tsuki and lifted the hand from the ground. He glanced at Tsuki, who said, "We can give Nix the hand when he gets back. Go get Fumiyo, we can't let him bleed to death."

Kiba nodded wordlessly and strode out of the foyer in search of Fumiyo while Tsuki shrugged her jacket off and knelt by Matahachi. He was barely conscious as she wrapped his bleeding wrist on her jacket and tied the sleeves tightly.

*Maybe I misjudged you.*

## SIXTY-SIX

THE PRINCE-REGENT HAD RETIRED EARLY. It made it more convenient, Kirikizu thought as he walked down the darkened hallway. The Prince-Regent could not sleep with bright lights, and so when he retired, all curtains in the hall leading to his room were closed to prevent light from sneaking in under his door.

The guards who recognized Kirikizu's figure knew to let him pass, and he was able to walk to the Prince-Regent's room uninterrupted. He did not knock as he opened the door and shut it softly behind him.

The curtains were drawn, casting only a thin sliver of moonlight across the bed where Mamushi lay. Kirikizu scanned the room, looking for...there it was.

He lifted the velvet sash off the back of the gilded chair by the bathroom door. Now, holding the soft, evil thing in his hands, he was free to remember every previous instant it had been used to gag him, to tie him, to restrain his movements for the Prince-Regent's pleasure.

He wound the sash around his knuckles and crossed sound-lessly over to the bed. He eased himself onto it, careful not to prematurely awaken the Prince-Regent. The man was asleep on his stomach, one arm dangling off the side of the bed, and Kirikizu took gentle hold of it before tying the free end of the sash around Mamushi's wrist.

The prince stirred but did not wake as Kirikizu straddled him, unwinding the sash from his hand and tying it around the Prince-Regent's other wrist, leaving exactly six inches of space between.

Then the Prince-Regent awoke, his eyes opening in hazy confusion for a moment. He attempted to move and realized he was restrained.

"Shhh." Kirikizu cupped the Prince-Regent's chin in his hand, his whisper eerie in his ears as it filtered through his muzzle. "It's me."

The Prince-Regent took in the sight of Kirikizu's silhouette over him and the sensation of his hands tied behind his back, and a look of mild surprise came over his face.

Kirikizu knew what he was thinking—it was the first time he had ever initiated anything, let alone woken the Prince-Regent from sleep.

"This is a pleasant surprise," Mamushi murmured sleepily, sitting up as far as his constraints would allow. "What's gotten into you, hmm?"

Kirikizu paused.

*You could still turn back. Let this be what he thinks it is.*

*Nobody will know—*

Except they would.

He had already gone through with his plan. This was only the last step. The only thing to do was continue, to see it through.

He threw the Prince-Regent from the bed and crossed over to where the Prince-Regent lay, temporarily stunned. Kirikizu had nothing to gag the other man with.

He punched him in the throat, crushing his larynx.

He did not stop to watch the Prince-Regent's reactions, to see how far he was hurting him. Kirikizu bent over the man who had twisted everything he was, and he hit him. He hit him as hard as he could, his fist smashing into the Prince-Regent's flawless face. He heard bone crunch, he felt the Prince-Regent's eyebrow split, his lips bleed.

Then he was hitting more than the Prince-Regent's face. His chest, his stomach, his sides—anywhere he saw, he struck.

The Prince-Regent was gasping for air now, each breath a desperate struggle, and it fed Kirikizu. It fed the white rage, fed the heat inside him. Each time his hand collided with the Prince-Regent's body, the Prince-Regent groaned in pain, and it felt good.

"Feel it," Kirikizu hissed, his own breathing heavy with the effort of his own anger. "Feel how I have felt every day since you dragged me into this hell. You should have left me to die. You should—have—*left me*," he said, and grabbed handfuls of the Prince-Regent's silken hair.

The Prince-Regent was barely clinging to consciousness, his face already beginning to swell, but his eyes were still open. As Kirikizu lifted his head, he saw the look of utter horror dawning through the shock as the Prince-Regent saw Kirikizu in the sliver of moonlight.

His voice was a strangled wheeze, barely intelligible as he forced the words, "What have you *done?*"

Kirikizu stood, dragging the Prince-Regent with him, and pulled the curtain aside with such force he ripped it down. The curtain fell to the floor, and Kirikizu bent over the Prince-Regent.

"Look at me," Kirikizu demanded.

The disgust on the Prince-Regent's face satisfied Kirikizu in a way he had never thought possible as Mamushi gaped, horrified, at the blood dripping from the gashes across Kirikizu's face, across his shoulders, arms, chest.

"You're ruined," the Prince-Regent rasped, tears shining in his eyes—whether from the pain or the horror, Kirikizu did not know, and he did not care.

"Yes."

"You're ruined."

"I am leaving the palace," said Kirikizu in a low voice, almost a growl as he clenched his fistful of the Prince-Regent's hair, longing to rip it from the man's head. "I am leaving you."

He dropped the Prince-Regent to the ground where the Prince-Regent remained, unmoving.

Silence followed Kirikizu as he crossed the room again.

*Kill him,* said the small voice in his mind, crying. Angry. Begging.

*I can't,* thought Kirikizu, and he left the room, shutting the door behind him.

———

NOBUNAGA HAD GIVEN Otter strict orders not to visit Haka, but Otter was not fond of orders. "I don't take them from Haka; I'm not about to start taking them from a robot," she muttered as she walked through the courtyard teeming with all eight mutts. They paused to sniff or nudge her as she passed, absently patting a thigh here, a flank there.

No guards were in the courtyard; it was too dangerous. "If you see Nobunaga, eat him," she instructed Violet.

The monster huffed in Otter's hair before lying down in the center of the courtyard, staking her claim.

Otter jogged to the dungeon door and peered through. There were no guards there, either; they were at the top of the stairs, behind a closed door.

She slipped quickly through the door before any of the mutts could try and follow her. Moving as quietly as she could, she walked until she found the cell holding Haka. He was stretched out in the straw, on his back. Maybe sleeping, she couldn't tell.

"Hey," she whispered, tapping a fingernail quietly against the bars. "Are you awake?"

He sat up with some difficulty. His breathing was labored, but his voice was clear. "If you get caught down here, it isn't my fault."

"I know that, you idiot." She crouched down, wrapping her hands around the bars and watching him through the space between them. "How do you feel?"

He crept forward and slumped against the wall, his face less than two feet from hers. "Been better," he admitted.

"Eesh." She reached through the bars and pressed a palm against the side of his face. "You look nasty, Commander. You're hot."

For once, he gave no snappy reply; he only closed his eyes just long enough to make her wonder if he had fallen asleep before he opened them again. He sighed. "Thanks."

"There's the commander I know and tolerate." She knew her hand had been on his face a tad bit long, but she was loath to remove it. She lowered it, but kept it on his side of the door, tapping the stone floor with her fingertips.

"I thought I told you not to come back until tomorrow," he said, watching her with tired reproof.

"You did," said Otter. "But I don't know why you thought I'd start listening to you today of all days. Especially after you yelled at me."

"I'm sorry for yelling at you."

"I know why you did it, Commander," she sighed. "I talked to Nobunaga a little while ago. He didn't seem to think I had a role in it, but he wouldn't let me come see you."

"Well, that was his mistake."

"Y—" Otter blinked and looked down as Haka's hand came to rest on hers. She looked up at his face, but he didn't seem to realize he'd done it. "Have you talked with anyone?"

"What?"

She licked her lips and turned her hand palm-up, wrapping her fingers around his. "Um, about your...position...?"

"I assume I'm fired," he said blandly.

Reluctantly, Otter said, "Dishonorable discharge. Tomorrow morning."

Haka's laugh was weak, and he leaned forward as if it pained him. Otter clenched her free hand into a fist and refused to obey her first instinct, which was to run and get him some more stardust. But it was too risky to go get him more right now; she would have to wait until morning. Cold turkey might be dangerous but it would certainly be less hassle.

"Winter got away."

"Of course he did."

"I knew you would help him."

He leaned the side of his head against the bars. "No, you didn't."

"I sure did. You can pretend all you want, Commander, but it's pretty easy to tell when you love somebody."

He blinked once, a new kind of tentativeness in his voice. "It is?"

"It is. You act like you hate their very existence, but you care a heck of a lot. And you do stupid things," she continued, "like give them paycheck bonuses out of your own pocket."

"What?" He lifted his head, startled by the last point.

She pointed at him, her heart jumping as she realized she was right. "Gotcha. I *knew* you were doing it! Especially when Takuan told me you don't actually have a *house*. Commander, that's just dumb. You should at least have a dumpster to go home to. And look, I know mutt-keepers don't get bonuses or paid vacation, it's okay. You don't need to—" She didn't get to finish her sentence. He reached through the bars, his hand holding the back of her head as he leaned forward and kissed her.

It was neither a long nor a comfortable kiss, but it didn't matter. Otter thought she might never remember how to breathe. Which was perfectly okay. It was a decent trade.

She gaped at him as he pulled away, his face so close she could see the faint dusting of freckles across his too-sharp cheekbones.

"Um," she stammered, flustered, "if—if that's your way of shutting me up, it works."

"Good."

"Also, for the record, I knew you were in love with me."

"I was?" he asked, but there was too much mischief in his weary smile.

"You don't fool me for a second." She reached her other arm through the bars and said, "Now come here so I can give you an awkward hug. We can make out later."

He moved closer, just slender enough to return her

embrace, and she stroked the back of his head and felt his head rest next to hers.

"*Baka,*" she said fondly.

Haka's response was faint and muffled, but she was pretty sure it sounded like, "I love you, too."

## SIXTY-SEVEN

SAIZOU WAS HALF-ASLEEP when the door opened. He had not allowed himself to drift fully away; he knew he had a concussion, and he wasn't that stupid. He got to his feet, expecting Shi, and was surprised to see Hiro instead.

"Looks like the kitsune made it," the gangster said, before turning and walking back down the hall.

Saizou followed him into the foyer, which looked like the waiting room of an entertainment agency during a casting call. Matahachi sat in the corner, his eyes half-open, cradling a bandaged arm. A handless arm, Saizou noticed with a start, but now was not the time to ask.

Fumiyo stood beside Shi, Shotgun crouched next to Riza, and Kiba and Tsuki stood several feet away. All were gathered around Riza, who was sitting cross-legged in the middle of the foyer, hunched over a laptop.

"Hail the conquering captive," she called as Saizou approached.

He glanced warily at Shi, who offered him a smile. "Nix made it?"

"He did indeed." Riza held up the laptop for all to see. Displayed on the screen was a notice in bold, red lettering, and she read it aloud. *"FUGITIVE SURRENDERS! Be it known that Saizou Akita, deposed daimyo, has turned himself in for punishment after a week evading the law. Imperial punishment will be swift."* She grinned. "Exciting, isn't it? We might even get to watch you die on live television at some point."

Shotgun wrinkled his nose. "Will it really kill him?"

"No," said Kiba. "It will use up another of his tails, I expect, but it won't kill him. Japan will believe Saizou dead until he chooses to resurface."

"What will happen to the people on your domain then?" Shotgun asked, looking at Saizou.

"He'll figure that out," said Shi, "when it comes down to it." He nodded at Saizou.

Saizou folded his arms and gave Shi a grateful look. "For now, we're safe here. We can figure things out."

Tsuki glanced at Kiba. "We need to take Matahachi back home."

Saizou watched her, interested, ready to listen. "Will you be staying there?"

"It is safer for her there," said Matahachi, his voice clear enough in spite of his faded appearance. "They are welcome to stay. I will take no part in their actions."

"Well, I'm staying," Shotgun affirmed, forming a peace sign with his fingers and thrusting it into the air. "It's fun."

Hiro rested his hands low on his hips and said, "I can't stay. I have things to do."

Riza glanced around the room. "Oh, don't look so gloomy, guys. This is me. I'm a genius. I'm always watching."

"That's comforting," said Shotgun.

She gave him a bright, entirely genuine smile. "Thanks! But

I gotta say, I'm sticking with Hiro. He's rich, and I can't resist money."

Hiro gave her a long look. It was almost tender, Saizou thought, with mild surprise. You never knew about people.

"What are you doing?" The question came from Fumiyo, who was gazing expectantly at Shi.

He snorted. "Please."

"Right," said Fumiyo. She tugged the neck of her sweater. "I guess I'm staying, too."

"Even though I'm here?" teased Shotgun.

She shot him a glare.

"I think it's in spite of you," Shi told him.

Fumiyo nodded vigorously, and Shotgun clutched his heart. "Ow. Right in the bowl of feelios."

"What?" asked Shi.

"What?" asked Shotgun.

As Saizou surveyed the gathered group, he felt a strange sense of pride growing within him; not from anything he had done, but for them, and what they were doing. For the way they were willing to risk their lives, to consort with fugitives and become fugitives themselves. They were good people.

He was too tired to smile, but as he leaned his back against the wall and watched Fumiyo stand half behind Shi, Riza poke Shotgun in the ribs, and Hiro crouch behind Riza, he smiled anyway.

*Let's see what good people can do.*

# EPILOGUE

IT WAS three minutes till closing time when the doors of the pawn shop swung open, ringing the tiny silver bell and alerting Shinya Amakuni to the presence of a customer.

It was bad timing, but a customer was a source of money, and he was in no position to say no to money. He pushed the curtain of beads aside and emerged from the back room.

The customer was a tall man in a long ivory coat, his head bowed over the cheap jewelry on display behind the glass counter.

Shinya bowed toward the customer, who did not look up. "How can I help you?"

"Weapons," said the man. "Where are they?"

Shinya eyed the man critically. "What kind of weapon?"

"Swords," said the man. "Two of them."

"You should know, man. I can't sell a blade over thirty inches. Still," he continued, not wanting to let a sale slip through his fingers, "I have a nice selection of wakizashis and tanto—"

The man looked up. "Swords," he repeated, his sapphire

eyes threatening to pierce right through Shinya to the wall behind him. "Two of them. Daito. Straight blades with fukuratsuku points. Tempered line has a hitatsura pattern. No menuki in the hilt. You forged them, you should remember them.

Now he remembered those eyes. "One moment," he said, disappearing into the back. He knew exactly where the box was —well buried beneath other supply boxes, full of harmless trinkets gathered from brief travels, yet to be put on display.

It took him a few moments to dig the box out. It was a plain wooden affair, entirely uninteresting. The swords inside were another matter.

He brought the box back out. It was light; heavy swords were no good to a swordsman. He set the box on the counter and checked the inscription he had scribbled on the tag. "Is your name Winter Mizushima?"

"It is," said the man. "Let me see them."

Shinya nodded and opened the box. "I remember you."

Winter withdrew one of the swords from the box. It was three feet long from point to tsuba. He touched the blade with a thumb, and the slight contact was enough to draw a drop of blood. "Still sharp."

Shinya smiled. "I was the best."

"Was, indeed." The look Winter gave him was not fooled. He brushed the moment aside and placed the sword back in the box, snapping the latch shut.

"Hey," Shinya called as the man strode back toward the front of the store, "I thought you said you'd never want those back."

"If you thought that," the man replied, pushing the door open, "you wouldn't have kept them."

He turned down an alley off the main street and knelt in

the light dusting of snow rapidly growing thicker. He opened the box again and shrugged off his coat, impervious to the biting November air. He had never stopped wearing his dual-sword harness, strapped around his chest and back. He removed it, put his coat back on, and buckled the harness outside it.

He was done hiding it. As he placed the swords back in their rightful places, he felt the heaviness of duty return with them.

He shut the box and propped it up against the wall.

"And they shall beat their swords into plowshares," he breathed, rubbing his hands together as he left the alley, his footsteps quickly swallowed by the snow. "Nation shall not lift up sword against nation, neither shall they learn war any more…"

## TO BE CONTINUED

# ACKNOWLEDGMENTS

I would like to thank Arielle Bailey, who is not only the best editor a creature could ask for, but has been there for my writing struggles and successes for many years [and will be there for many more; you're stuck with me].

- Lauren, even though this book is already dedicated to you, because every hypothetical conversation we gave these characters is what gave them so much life.

- Morgan, the brilliant woman who formatted and designed the beautiful book you [the reader] now hold in your hands.

- Everyone along the way who has said things like 'that's not a real name,' and 'there should be more monsters,' and 'can X please end up with Y.' I still can't promise you anything whatsoever but trust me, I do know when something shouldn't be a real name, I just have a bad habit of doing it anyway.

- Everyone reading this. Please envision this book in your mind as an anime. Thank you.

# ABOUT THE AUTHOR

Mirriam Neal is a PNW transplant living in the rural South. When she's not painting fantasy illustrations for clients, she's probably writing three different bizarre novels at the same time. She's a sucker for monsters, unlikely friendships, redemption arcs, and antiheroes; and will write passionate defenses of misunderstood characters. To learn more about her fiction and art, visit mirriamneal.com

## ALSO BY MIRRIAM NEAL

Monster

Paper Crowns

Dark is the Night